GENTLEMAN'S CLUB

GENTLEMAN'S CLUB

AVALON KNIGHT
BOOK ONE

N.T. HERRGOTT

TELOS

TELOS

This book is a work of fiction. Names, characters, places, and incidents are either the product of the author's imagination or are use factiously. Any resemblance to actual events, locales, or persons, living or dead, is coincidental.

Gentleman's Club:
Avalon Knight, Book One

Registered ® 2022 N.T. Herrgott

ISBN: 978-1-7771716-0-5 (trade paperback)

ISBN: 978-1-7771716-3-6 (digital/E-Book)

"Don't look back —
the past is exactly where it belongs."

~The Scarlet Witch

AUTHOR'S NOTE
AND CONTENT WARNING

This book contains instances of violence, descriptions of blood and injury, and allusions to sex and sexuality. Further, the ongoing series presents a nuanced depiction of socio-economic struggles and debates. It is my hope that this work adequately echoes the voices of those who have been fighting against these injustices.

The protagonist and narrator is a transmasc, he/him, high school student who is closeted (stealth) to most other characters. There is no argument being made to depict 'passing' as the objective of trans experiences, though it may be important to some individuals — as it is important to Luca.

Further examples of Queer-identifying characters in this story, as they carry themselves, are not intended to represent all Queer identities and expressions. Their role is to exist in fiction, as they exist in the world outside. However, theirs are not the only expressions of personhood and should not be taken to represent the much broader range of real-world Queer experiences.

Through this series, Luca will encounter a wider range of these experiences — and the people who witness them. My intention is neither education directed at the reader, nor representation for its own sake. But I do take this as an opportunity to showcase a small portion of identifiable diversity within the human element.

Everyone involved in the creative process of this story aims to create more constructive, inclusive content.

ACT ONE

JUST ANOTHER ORIGIN STORY

CHAPTER 1
JUST THOUGHT I'D DROP BY

Friday, October 6

Okay, so there were two ways I could spend a Friday night. Sure, I could be playing beer pong at whatever party-of-the-week. Or, and hear me out, I could be working the night job I'd started in the summer.

By 'job,' I mean a part-time gig as a crime-fighter-in-training.

So instead of tequila shots, I was about to drop down to a window sill eight feet below the roof I was hanging off. And because the element of surprise is important or whatever, I had to do it without making a sound.

"Whose idea was it to drop from the roof instead of climbing up?" I asked, catching myself on the window ledge below. The ninja mask I wore had a mic that directed an encrypted signal to a receiver two blocks away. On the other end, Tom Seong sat in his car with a coffee and barked at me for not being perfect at everything.

"I wouldn't have put you up to it if you couldn't do it," he said. He'd been a family friend for as long as I could remember, but these days he was a trainer, coach, employer, and surrogate uncle. "Get moving, the apartment you're after is two windows over—"

"I know, I'm just getting my balance."

"Wouldn't need to," he said, "if you kept your focus."

A mugging just off Central turned into a home invasion on the third floor. Two guys with a knife and a baseball bat jumped a man and woman as they were opening the door to this very building. Tom had seen them file inside and scouted the target apartment from looking in the windows before I even got there.

All I had to do was kick some ass.

"Wondering..." I asked, "is there a big difference between burgling and home invasion?"

Tom sighed. "Keep your focus on the climb, kid."

"I am focused" I heaved myself from one window to the next.

"Your weight was off on that jump," he said. "Should book a few more hours at the climbing wall."

"It's fine, I just—"

"Wasn't focusing," he said. "I agree."

Getting ready for the next jump, I took a breath. "You can just say 'neener-neener' like a normal person."

He ignored me. "I just tipped off the cops. They're gonna be on their way soon, so pick up the pace."

That was something I didn't usually hear. For a lot of reasons — *a lot* 'a lot' — Tom just didn't like cops. We avoided calling them whenever we could. When it came to small, petty stuff, Tom just had me break it up and let the 'bad guys' run off and make sure the victims were safe. He wouldn't hesitate to call an ambulance, though.

But this was a situation where somebody needed to get arrested, and I didn't have a Vigil License so I couldn't do that (yet). It was the difference between a career 'Vigil' and some teenager with discount combat gear.

"I want you in and out before the cops get here," he said. "Get a look at the apartment. Walk me through what you see." While Tom coached me, he was also piloting a stealth drone with a creeper-cam. It was probably silently hovering above my head so he could make sure I was spotting the right things.

Adjusting my grip on the windowsill, I peered into the room and sized up the mugger cramming valuables into a backpack. He looked like he lived off of protein shakes. "Not a small guy..."

"The one with the victims is bigger."

"Oof..."

"What do you notice about the apartment?" Tom asked.

I strained to get a better look while the bad guy went through a vinyl collection.

"One bedroom." I said.

"Affirmative."

"Two people live here?"

"Residents aren't relevant," he said. "Your concern is that they've got hostages."

"And they're in the next room," I said.

"Affirmative," he said. "Tell me about him, though. Any concealed weapons?"

This was the part of professional crime-fighting that I *wasn't* good at. I sized him up, trying to find what I was supposed to be looking at. "Um..."

"Watch when he bends over," he said.

Bam. Outline of a gun. "Okay... I see a pistol. Probably small caliber," I said. "Give him a codename... Trigger-Happy?"

"Works for me," said Tom. "Alright, make the jump to the bedroom window."

"Wait, shouldn't I clear this room?" I asked. "You always say to take down the weaker ones first."

"With hostages in the mix, they're the priority."

"I can take Trigger-Happy down quietly—"

"And then what?" he asked. "There's no way to control a fight with two hostages and a hostile on the other side of a closed door. Get things done quietly and quickly and you can still get the drop on him."

I groaned and made the jump to the next window.

"What's your take on this room?"

"I dunno... looks like an Ikea showroom—"

"Kid," he said, "do not make me drive over there."

"Alright, alright! Hold on..." I cleared my throat and repositioned myself.

This mugger had an aluminum baseball bat over his shoulder. Keeping an eye on the woman, he was facing away from the window. She slumped down against a door, probably a closet, going out of her way not to look at Bat-Man.

"Okay, Bat-Man is big, you called that," I said. "I see the woman, but not her friend."

"Mmhm?"

"Might be unconscious on the floor," I said. "Can you spot him?"

"Negative," said Tom.

"He could be in the closet? If that's a closet she's against."

"Not likely," said Tom. "Hostages rarely get split up. But these guys are raiding a well-lit apartment building at 9:30 PM. Nobody said they're smart. Male hostage isn't a priority. Size up Bat-Man."

"Can't be more than 6'5. Depending on how much bulk he's wearing he could be weighing in at... two-fifty?"

"Okay, good call."

"Looks like a leftie."

"Bad for you. Your southpaw needs work."

"You say 'everything' needs work!" My southpaw was actually great. There was a big, tough left-handed line-backer at school who'd given me problems ever since I broke his nose in freshman. It was self-defense, I promise. Promise. "And the cops are...?"

"On the way. You have an entry?"

The window wasn't locked but it was old. It wasn't gonna go up easy. "Jammed... Could jimmy it open but that'd scrap the low-profile approach."

"Absolutely not," said Tom. "If you can't get a jump on that guy, you're leaving this for the law."

I heard the crashing in the living room. "You know there's a gourmet donut place opened up on Fredrick Street..." I said. "Cops could be there all night."

If anything was gonna get a chuckle out of Tom, it was gonna be a cops and donuts joke. I kinda made it a side-mission to get him to break his mean-serious super-hero sensei persona. But he was back in teacher-mode in no time. "Then we'll just have to—"

I stopped listening because I made eye contact with the woman. Surprised, but not confused, she scanned Bat-Man then looked back at me and nodded.

This was the part I *was* good at.

CHAPTER 2
GUN FIGHT

Friday, October 6

Bat-Man turned to the window to see what had caught the woman's attention. Ducking down, my shin guards scraped the wall. "Careful with that..." Tom said. I could feel big, thumping footsteps getting closer. He was wearing boots? Hello, rude? I saw her rugs. Shoes off at the door, *thank you*.

Jokes aside, I was screwed unless I could get myself over to another window. By this point, I was hoping there was a way I could just pull a win out of my ass...

But then something smashed in the bedroom, and then the wall shook. I looked up and the lady had whacked him square over the head with a lamp. He dropped his bat and pushed her onto the bed. Made enough of a racket for me to slip in without being noticed.

Trigger-Happy called from the next room. "Y'all good, Ronnie?"

"Yeah, she's just getting feisty—"

I cleared my throat behind him.

"The fu—"

The instant Bat-Man turned around I hit the side of his head with his aluminum bat. His eyes rolled back and he fell forward.

"Using real names on a job. Amateur..." I mumbled. "Liked my name for you better anyway."

"Ronnie!" Trigger-Happy called again.

"You could have caught him before he went down," Tom groaned.

I whispered. "I am a third of his size, *mom!*"

"You still have an element of surprise," he said. "Use it to get that pistol out of the mix."

"Got it," I said, already wrangling Bat-Man's wrists into a pair of zip-tie cuffs. I looked at the woman. "Thanks for the assist," I whispered. "You okay?"

Wide-eyed, she nodded.

"The other guy has a gun. Keep out of sight until I take care of it."

She whispered, "Do *you* have a gun?"

"Don't worry about it," I said. "We'll be fine. It'll be great."

I did not have a gun. Even with a modest arsenal up my sleeve, most of the time I stuck to the *hanbo* strapped to my back. The traditional, leg-length wooden stick had been a part of virtually every martial art in the history of the world. Underused in movies, though.

"Ronnie!" Trigger-Happy was just on the other side of the door.

"Smooth and easy, kid..." Tom said. "You got this."

Do-or-die time.

When the door opened, the pistol came in first. Trigger-Happy got a look at his buddy on the floor and didn't notice me reach under the pistol. I flipped the safety on and kicked the door into his arm, smashing him into the frame. I threw my weight into it for an extra pop — practically felt his wrist dislocate.

Maybe I also wrecked her door? The thing splintered for like... no reason.

"Jesus—" said Tom. "Watch that collateral damage!"

"Sorry..." I said, getting a hold of Trigger-Happy's wrist and twisting the pistol out of his hand. "Sorry!" I said, a bit louder for the woman to hear.

He bashed the door open, launching me over the bed. He reached for the pistol on the floor with his good arm. Grabbing whatever I could from the bedside table, I threw a TV remote — "YEET!" — and it broke into pieces when it hit his forehead.

"Collateral!" Tom called so loud there was interference.

"Yeah sure whatever, it's not like he's gonna shoot me," I said.

I vaulted over the bed, gaining speed. Crashing into him with my knee, he fell into the TV stand. It wobbled, but I settled it before it fell over, throwing a quick thumbs-up in the direction of the drone outside.

Collateral: I was on it.

Trigger-Happy reached for the pistol again, but I kicked it under the bed and whacked his ribs with the hanbo. Leaning against the wall, he whipped out a tiny switchblade like he was from some musical about tough guys doing tough guy jazz ballet.

"Ooo-*ooh* — you proud of those three inches?"

I let him slash it around a few times. He didn't hit anything, but I'm sure it made him feel better about himself. I kicked his wrist and the knife flew out of his hand so fast it dug into the drywall. A quick whack against the side of his head and he was dazed enough for me to flip him to the ground and get his wrists zipped up.

"You're never gonna sleep again!" He squirmed, shouting when he got his wind back. "I've got all kinds of friends! One phone call and you'll be looking over your shoulder—"

I slapped the back of his head. "Well, you're only gonna get one phone-call for a while. First step to legal defense is planning ahead." I patted his cheek. "So proud of you."

Extra-judicial violence was frowned upon but I also didn't take kindly to death threats. Especially when they were as cringey as this.

"Drop your pussy-ass stick and fight me!"

"You've got a right to remain silent or something…" I ripped a strip off Bat-Man's flannel sleeve. "Here, lemme help…"

He grumbled a little as I strapped it across his mouth and tied it tight. "Wouldn't hurt so much if you'd get some chill." I tightened his zip-tie cuffs too, for good measure.

The lady cleared her throat, poking her head over the bed.

"Oh, shit— manners!" I said. "You wanna come over and kick him, too?"

CHAPTER 3

JOURNALISTIC DURABILITY

Friday, October 6

She cleared her throat. "No... I'm fine— I'm fine," she said, and left the room right away.

I looked out at the drone in the window and shrugged.

Bat-Man was starting to come to, but he seemed too dazed to be a problem. I'd hit his head pretty hard. Meanwhile, I had to zip up Trigger-Happy's legs to stop him from kicking. And then I left them where they were to check up on the lady.

It was a nice place, aside from what was pulled down or shoved into a bag, but what was left was mostly sentimental stuff. Lots of decorative things, picture frames.... most of them were empty or had newspaper clippings in them. Everything in the bag was probably gold or worth a fortune to the right online collector.

The lady was in the kitchen, on the floor behind the kitchen island where her friend was unconscious. "Found the other hostage," I said to Tom. "Out cold in the kitchen area."

"Hmm," he went. "Well... I said they weren't smart. Make sure he's okay."

I grabbed a pillow from the sofa, while she checked her friend's pulse and pulled back his eyelids. "First aid?" I asked.

"Yes," she said, a little absently, helping the pillow under the man's head.

"Husband/boyfriend/brother/cousin/other? He okay?"

She snickered, and then stopped herself. "Yes. Um... yes. He's fine. He's my brother. Hit on the head. Should be fine." She was very British. "Are they on their way? The Police. Or should we...?"

"Radio says two cars have been dispatched. Called in for an ambulance." Tom said. "Hurry up. Make sure she's okay and—"

"They're on their way with paramedics," I said to her.

"Good."

I looked back at the busted-in bedroom door. Undue damage to property was a demerit point... "Sorry about the door," I said. "And the remote — I broke a remote by the way."

"It's— It's no trouble..." She paused, thinking for a second. "You know, I don't think he was going to... do anything else."

I nodded. "He won't be doing much of anything now."

Tom cut in. "Police radio says a four-minute ETA."

"You know it's funny, a lifetime living in Birmingham, nothing. Lived in bad parts of town sometimes. Always moving. Been here for just five months..."

"Welcome to America?" I said and cleared my throat. "Well... Help should be here soon. I can stick around to keep an eye on them if you like or..."

"I'll be fine."

"You sure?" I asked. "I can make you... tea? I'm... Well, I'm assuming you have tea. Because it's California and everyone has tea. Not just because you're from... there."

You know. The tea-place.

"Just give her your card, kid," said Tom. It was common practice for Vigils to hand out 'Friendly Neighborhood' cards.

She snatched it out of my fingers, half-crumpled from resting in my pocket. "Oh! The 'new' Avalon Knight, yes?" She looked up, studying what part of my face was visible. "From the news."

"Yeah! Um... yeah! From the news!" I said. "Must have seen that story in the Herald? 'Irritatingly irresponsible hooligan?' Basically my tagline now." A local Vigil called 'The Brass Horn' was directly quoted calling me that. I had the story cut out and tucked away where Dad wouldn't find it.

"Ah," She nodded. "That's what The Brass Horn said."

"Was it The Brass?" I shrugged. "Didn't read it."

"Well, don't take it to heart," she said, her shoulders relaxed. "The Brass once called for backup on a convenience store job that was held up with a spray-painted water gun."

I blurted out a laugh. "No way!"

"Granted, that's not the official story," she sighed. "It's only what I heard, but... that's how it works with Federal Vigils, no matter what continent you're on." She flashed a bit of a smile, then looked at me different, like a switch went off. "Thank you. For tonight."

"It's what I do... since funding for extracurricular activities got cut—"

Tom aggressively cleared his throat. "Cruiser's pulling up. Get out now."

"Anyway... busy night, ma'am. Miss." I tipped an imaginary hat and lifted the living room window.

"Hold on!" She said, composed and confident. "Could I have another card? This one may get confiscated."

"Oh! Sure!" I said, whipping it out, wondering how she could have known how easy it was to stroke my girthy ego. I suddenly got the idea to start handing out two cards as a rule. For the fans.

Should I pre-autograph them?

Or wait so they can see me sign it?

"I'm Jillian Miner." She held out a hand, sounding as if I was supposed to know who she was.

"Nice to meet ya, Jill." I shook her hand, winked goodbye, and slid out the window. Catching the drainpipe, I got myself back to the roof.

"Finally out?" Tom asked. "Head south, then to Lyon and Page. Careful on the steep roofs. I'll pick you up at the intersection and take you to your social call."

"What? No! That was only the first real gig tonight."

"Double life means having an alibi," he said. "Don't want your dad to get suspicious."

"I think you're way more afraid of him than I am..." I muttered.

"What's that?"

"Nothin'."

"Get to the rendezvous," Tom said. "Smart-ass..."

Scaling, vaulting, and rolling over rooftops, I made it to the intersection first. Standing at the edge of the corner building, I did my best to look dramatic. Sucks that I didn't have a cape, but that's about the only thing capes were good for. For everything else, they were a huge liability. Tried and tested by decades of American Vigils.

They made a brief comeback for a hot minute because of Sex and the City — so said Dad. Dad always swore off capes back when he was the original Avalon Knight. That was back when he, Tom, and Tom's late brother rounded out a surprisingly famous crime-fighting trio in Seattle. But, you know... things change.

At least Tom was filling his retirement by training America's Next Top Vigil. These days, Dad was just a boring lawyer.

OH! UH... Dad *also* didn't know that Tom and I were up to this... so if you can keep a secret, I'd really appreciate it!

CHAPTER 4
DEBRIEFING AND REFRESHMENTS

Friday, October 6

"Jillian Miner is a British vigilante journalist," Tom said immediately. "She got fired from a monthly journal for writing a piece tying several A-and-B-List English Vigils to a human trafficking ring. Then she made it big in freelance after an exposé about English Federal vigils suppressing Welsh crimefighting."

I struggled to get out of the armor in the back seat. "And I thought I was a big deal…"

Tom rebounded a glare at me through the rearview. "Hopefully, she won't write a story about this, but I wouldn't put it past her."

"I know you're not a big fan of news peoples, but like… maybe give her the benefit of the doubt?"

I saw Tom's eyes in the mirror… if looks could kill.

While I changed into regular clothes, Tom went through his list of criticisms and corrections on my' performance.' He was tough to impress, but I'd gotten used to it. Instead, he encouraged what I was doing right, but never acted like I was doing better than he expected.

As for my own self-assessment? I came out alive, I saved the day, and almost did it all without a scratch. But it was the 'almost' part that Tom didn't like. "The leading cause of death and injury in this career is when you start thinking that taking one or two punches doesn't matter. You need to hold yourself up against flawlessness every time," Tom would say.

I got where he was coming from. The more you practiced, the easier it got. The easier it got, the less attention you paid to details. Tom said — basically — you had to go into every situation assuming you were gonna die. Healthy living, for sure.

"You also gotta cut back on the chatter," Tom said. "That's twice you mentioned something personal because you were trying to be charming. First time was a homeless drunk — but this is a reporter with a following."

"It's nothing that hasn't been about age," I dropped my voice an octave. "No way I would pass for more than twenty-one."

Tom snorted. "That's being generous."

"Shut up…"

Tom was just about ready to wrap it up before the Jillian Miner business anyway. There was a party and I'd already RSVP'd, so I kinda had to head over. It would be suspicious if I didn't. Not that my friends would've guessed that I was crime-fighting, but if Dad sniffed it out, I'd be grounded for years.

Forget that he was basically my age when he started Vigil-ing…

Stopped at a light, I crawled up to the passenger seat. "I can walk from here," I said when Tom turned onto Alpine Terrace. He parked a few houses away from the party spot where drunk high school students were spilling onto the sidewalk.

"Do kids from your school really live all the way out here?"

"Kelli Collins wanted to go to the same high school as Elyssa Edwards." (The house down the street belonged to Kelli Collins.) "They were best friends."

"I see."

"Kelli and Elyssa haven't been friends since Freshman, though."

"I'd say I don't miss being a teenager," Tom said, "but grown men and women don't really act any… hold on, what's that?" Tom grabbed my jaw and flicked the overhead lights on. "Damnit, Luca. How did this happen?"

"How did what?"

"You…" Tom rolled his eyes and pulled down the sunshade. In the mirror, I spotted a red mark on the side of my face. Ironically, it was probably there because of the carbon fiber mask getting bashed into my cheekbone.

"Oh, that's gonna be a good one." I kinda liked it.

"You shouldn't be getting hit at all. You're better than that."

"Yeah… but he had a door."

"How are you going to explain that to your father?" Tom asked.

I shrugged. "Got into a fight?"

"But you're not actually going to get into a fight, right?"

I shrugged harder. "Don't worry about it."

Tom sighed and, leaning over, opening the passenger door for me. "Have fun tonight. Do seventeen-year-old stuff. Drink responsibly, play safe, et cetera, et cetera."

"Text if you need me early tomorrow," I said, leaning into the window.

"Hey, we're always behind on cleaning."

"Well, no, I mean like—"

"Nope. You offered," Tom said. "You're in the schedule now, Mop Boy!"

"No! I've got like… homework to do and…"

But the Subaru was already pulling ahead.

What? Not good enough to be Mop *Man*?

CHAPTER 5
UPPER-UPPER-MIDDLE

Friday, October 6

So. San Francisco.

For starters, I wasn't born here... But who was these days, right? Until I was nine, I lived in Seattle, so I hadn't even been in The City for half my life yet. Though in the last eight years, I'd made myself comfortable.

I knew back streets, tucked-away cafes, and what you could expect to find in which thrift shop. I knew the best places to give someone the slip, and I knew which alleys to not go down. It wasn't until I realized that I could list off the streets and parks where I'd gotten every scar, broken bone, or black eye that it really started to feel like home.

But as much as I could have spent the night saving damsels in distress from half-baked burglars, I was looking forward to recharging my party-battery. This was a Homecoming wind-down get-together. The school dance was a wash — as always. This was the real party.

I had to stop and check my hair in every other car window, . It was probably important to make sure that it didn't look like I'd spent most of the night with a hood on. But lucky for me, my hair was so stubborn that there wasn't much difference between stuffing product in it for half an hour and sweating for ten minutes of crime-fighting.

As for the venue, Kelli Collins was the go-to party house and that's how she liked it. It was her claim to popularity. 'One-family homes' were rare in Potrero Hill and Lower Mission, where the bulk of Moscone High came from. Kelli was an outlier who called parties at her place 'Castro Parties.' Because living half-way up Caselli meant that you lived in the trendy, gentrified, gay part of town.

When I got to the place, I announced my arrival with a selfie in front of her victorian townhouse-mansion and threw it up on Instagram. The outside of the house said 'I respect the heritage buildings that survived the earthquake.' The inside said 'Fuck it — I own 68% of the hospitals in Dubai.'

— — —

I hadn't taken five steps in the door before I was snatched away. "So how'd it go?" Emily asked, dragging me by the wrist.

"I literally just got here—" I hissed, trying to pry myself out of her grip.

"Great time to get this over with!" she said, holding me back while a making-out couple swung into the middle of the hall. When she gauged it was safe, she tried to pull me away.

"Ugh! What's the rush?"

She looked back and smiled. "I want the deets while they're fresh." A quick look around and she slipped into a spot beside the kitchen that led to a pantry and wine stock. Everyone in Kelli's social circle knew her house almost as well as she did. Last year, apparently, Josephine MacCray gave a simultaneous BJ to two guys from an Oakland basketball team in this same corner. Other stories said that one-or-both of them got her pregnant.

But who believes that? Not her boyfriend of two years. And not the overlapping on-the-sly boyfriend of ten months.

"You know what people say about this corner, right?" I asked.

Emily rolled her eyes. "Which is why no one comes around here."

This is Emily Barnett. And she knew almost everything about me. I knew a bunch about her too, but this is about me. Stay focused.

Emily and I had been friends since we met in grade six at recess. But we weren't really close until Dad bought a house down the street from her's. Keeping secrets from her was impossible... to the point where I secretly tested her by thinking triggering thoughts about *Naruto* to see if she was literally psychic.

Turns out she did have a superpower... sussing information out of me. Specifically me.

She was one of a handful of people in San Francisco who knew I was trans (including Dad, Tom, my GP, his secretary, and my butch-lady-barber). Everyone else knew me as just your ordinary, bisexual dude-bro.

So when it came to the dilemma of the Avalon Knight secret identity, the only real solution was to keep Emily in the loop. Tom disapproved, but agreed that there wasn't really a better option. When you're that close with someone, keeping secrets is more likely to blow your cover. Emily was just thrilled to be included.

Really, what else are best friends for if they're not holding your secret double-life as a teenage superhero over your head? Perks and benefits include standing in a forbidden sex-corner talking about some loser who thought he was gonna make off with a record collection.

While she looked up Jillian Miner, Emily made me hold her drink. I was surprised there was a reporter she hadn't heard of.

"Oh, she's one of those like... hardcore investigative bloggers," she said. "Mostly British. Probably why I don't know who she is..."

"Vigil laws are different there," I said.

"Well, that's cool..." She scrolled a bit more and tucked her phone away. "I'll have to check it out later — come on, you're the literally last one here. And everyone's starting to notice that this is becoming a pattern."

Emily and I were closest, but there were six of us who were the kinds of friends who had standing invitations for dinner. First name basis with each-others parents. Stuff like that.

Branden Gilbert was the only senior among us. He was more of the quiet type… until about three beers. He was also on the football team, and nothing against football, but our team was garbage.

Then there was Joshi, but that was his last name. And it was what he went by since his folks moved to San Francisco when he was five. He was into soccer, swim team, and being a class clown in general. Bit on the anxious side, but a real people pleaser.

Kaleb MacRoye was my closest 'bro,' rival athlete, and probably the easiest person for me to hang out with. Tragically straight, but nobody's perfect. He was dating Aura Solano… sometimes.

Aura and I clicked in a class for Spanish-American literature. It counted for a language and a lit credit, so I figured I'd kill two birds. She was a big deal in volleyball, and we'd crossed paths a bit before then, but she met Kaleb through me and decided she liked our friends better than hers.

Their on-again-off-again relationship was kind of like a lunar cycle for us. We had a betting board that Joshi made a lot of money off of.

As soon as I stepped into the back yard, I got tackled from the side with the force of a drunken mac truck. In spite of being tall and broad, Branden was a cuddly drunk.

"Wexler-boyyy!" He called out, lifting my feet off the ground.

"Yep! Okay! Hey there!" I said, trying not to struggle.

He dropped me to the ground and his girlfriend tapped his shoulder and whispered in his ear before wandering off.

"Hey," Kaleb said, punching my arm. "How was work?"

Okay. Didn't realize I'd gotten a bruise on that shoulder. *Ow.* "Alright. How's the party?"

"Lame," he said with his hands in his pockets. "Football team is here, bringing down the mood because they can't win a goddamn match. Still would be nice to get this kinda turn out for Lacrosse parties..."

"Nobody cares about legends while they're alive," I said. We were the kind of bros who'd hashed out a handshake for each other: clap, snap, slick, pat. Not only were we on the school team, but we also did an out-of-school league together over the summer. Kaleb also ran track, and put big-time pressure on me to join up too.

I'd only ever did inter-murals and non-competitive teams — and even then it was hard enough to keep the trans stuff on the sly. My superhero weakness was locker rooms, I guess. I had no idea how that would work with competitive Lacrosse in March... with all the busses, and traveling, and locker rooms that might *not* have private shower stalls... But I'd decided I wasn't going to think about it until I needed to worry about it.

And that wasn't gonna bite me in the ass at all!

Also... Dad's career was a lot of 'pro-bono' work, so a lot of the money for my athletics had to come from me. Don't get me wrong he owned property in San Francisco — I'm not gonna lie to your face and tell you 'we barely got by.' But I was one of the only people I knew from school who had to work for spending money.

And these days Tom took most of my 'wages' and re-invested it into Avalon Knight upkeep.

The rest of the party was okay.

Oh shit... I forgot about homework.

CHAPTER 6
MORNING PERSON

Monday, October 9

The Wexler family (San Francisco branch) had two dogs: Lillie and Zero. Lillie was a 10-year-old Alaskan Husky and wasn't the brightest girl. But that was okay because she was still tied for being the best dog. She'd been in the family since way back in Seattle, which made her one of the only things from my old life that I kept around. Everything else got purged or buried so deep in a closet it wouldn't see the light of day again.

Zero was named after one of my favorite Vigils, and was more like 'my dog' than a 'family dog.' He'd already had his ears and tail cropped when we got him from the rescue shelter, but you wouldn't believe the flack I got on Instagram for 'abusing' him. I wouldn't have cropped anything if I got him as a puppy.

But in this house, we don't shop, we adopt.

And like... it was kind of hilarious that he was this scary *doobormon* with pricked ears who was also terrified of the sound of the shower and who also could not be any more than three feet away from me. His solution? Let's get in the shower *with* Luca!

He had his own towel. *Oy vey...*

I got home from running them, and dad leaned out of his room on my way to the bathroom. "Have you seen my teal tie?" he asked. None of the buttons were done up on his mustard dress shirt. I hoped he didn't plan on wearing a black blazer with that or else he'd look like a business bumble-bee...

"Nope. Don't think so," I said, inching closer to the bathroom.

"You're sure?"

"I keep all my ties in my room," I said.

"If you'd clean it, you could clear out the nest of gremlins that steal clothes from everywhere else."

"I don't have your tie!" I rolled my eyes. "I know where everything is. It's like how you keep your desk a mess."

Dad huffed and rushed back into his room.

I took less time in the shower and more time in front of the mirror. Sure, we can call it vanity. I flexed for a little bit to get a gauge any new muscle definition. I winked at myself in the mirror and practiced my selfie-smile. I liked the way I looked. Shoot me.

My jaw was filling out, but in spite of my eastern-European roots, my cheekbones weren't too pronounced. I had puffy cheeks when I smiled and... dimples. Which, as much as girls thought it was cute... like— I was totally over it.

Though I wasn't above loving the attention.

Didn't help that out of all my grandparents I got the hair from the one that was blonde. Which like... If I could pass for the all-American, blue-eyed, curly-blonde, boy next door, I was gonna take it. But scruffy beards and going salt-and-pepper in my 40s were both pipe dreams.

My height didn't help either... I was one-hundred-fifty-two pounds on a five-foot-six frame. Nobody really called me 'short stuff' anymore. A few detentions for hallway brawling were all it took to ditch that nickname.

It used to be a big-time button of mine. I was eight when I started training with Tom, and constantly complained about it. He would tell me: "A handicap is a perspective that others see as a weakness." I thought it was some mystical jumbo to make me feel better, but I came around.

It was about balance. Big guys were strong, sure, but you can take them down with one hit if you get the right pressure point. You just had to be that good.

And I was that good.

Tom helped.

— — —

I made myself breakfast — which usually meant a smoothie. I tried doing the whole... drinking a raw egg for a while but it was just... it was too gross. Instead, flicking frozen raspberries off the counter for Zero, I danced and sang along to Latin music from my phone. I sang louder when I turned the blender on.

"Are you sure you haven't seen it?" Dad shouted.

I turned the blender off. "What?"

"My tie!" he shouted. "Are you sure you haven't seen it?"

"Just use another tie!" I shouted back.

"What?"

I switched off the music and threw a lid on the cup. "Just use another tie!" On my way back up to my room, I dropped my smoothy off on the key table by the door.

"Needs to be *that* tie!"

"You're obsessing over color to be dramatic?" I shouted.

"No — she accents with that color! The client!" Dad rushed past my room and stomped down the stairs. Lillie in a rush behind him.

As I pulled on a sweater vest and began knotting a tie of my own, Dad came back upstairs and *heartily* knocked on my door.

"Com'on in," I said.

The second he opened the door, Lillie swarmed in and rubbed her head against my knees. Zero was sitting patiently but was very agitated that someone was stealing Luca-Time™, and he dropped from my bed to get between Lillie and me.

Dad's face kinda dropped and he sucked in his lips. "Luca..." he sighed, "that's my tie."

It was dangling from my neck while I did boops with some dog snoots. "This is teal?"

"Yes. That's the color… people mean by 'teal,'" he said.

"Dad, this is green."

"Teal is a version of green— whatever— I need it. Please?"

"Fii-iine."

My school had a strictly-enforced lax uniform policy. It was a collection of business-y guidelines we had to follow, but it left a lot of wiggle room. Unless you made some seriously tragic accessory decisions, you wouldn't get written up. Running shoes were a strict 'no' but go ahead and wear whatever else on your feet. I had like… seventy ties so, Dad commandeering this one was no big deal.

Untying the knot, I gave Dad's suit look. "Going to match this with that shirt? You sure?"

"Thank you," said Dad, and was out in the hall without another word. A few minutes later, Dad said "Love you," and was out the front door. Almost immediately, I heard it open again.

Emily shouted up from below. "Hey, slut! Let's get a move-on!"

Lillie started to get really excited and ran between me and my door a few times before deciding it was best to go see her. Emily found me rooting through a pile of shoes at the bottom of one of my closets. "Come on, fashion-*ista*, we gotta get goin'," she said, and then collapsed on my half-made bed which was mostly pillows anyway.

I managed to find the matching pair of off-brand yellow high tops I was rooting around for. ($25. Thank you, Chinatown.) The shoes didn't really go with the uniform, but that was kinda the point, right? I pulled them on my feet, sitting on the floor and ignoring Zero under my chin, begging for last-minute affection. "Late night?" I asked, lint-rolling the dog hair off me.

"Very."

"Boyfriend kept you up?"

"Ugh. Pervert." She paused. "Though really... I'd appreciate if Ian was that invested."

"Uh-oh... getting bored of him?"

"Not really. Just wish he'd be around more often..." she said. "And that he'd like. You know... be — clapemoji — more — clapemoji — invested."

I leaned over, and into her line of sight. "Sounds like you're bored."

Emily rolled her eyes. "Anyway... I was up late because Jellybean found one of Dad's secret chocolate stashes that he hides and forgets about. He was shitting like... all night."

"The dog, or...?"

Emily scrunched up her face. "Can you not make it weird for like... Ugh. I cannot deal with you morning people."

CHAPTER 7
PRIORITIES

A while ago…

Science and math weren't really my thing. Or English. Or history. Okay, I kinda sucked at school.

It wasn't surprising when I got A's in Phys-Ed. I could ace a test in Health Science without studying. But that wasn't a big deal anymore… I'd been making meal plans for me *and* Dad for years now. Even if he didn't follow them…

Athletics would give you a lot of leniency at school, for sure. But there were still more than a few times that I got pulled into Vice Principal Hulbry's office for… stuff. She was very happy to read me for filth and explain that I had to pull up my grades if I wanted to keep my spot on whatever team I was playing for.

(Cue scheduled bisexual joke.)

I could probably end up doing pretty good in Spanish if I would do homework or assignments. The same thing was true for comtech classes, too — I'd taken them since Freshman. I knew my way around a little HTML and Java, but homework on computers usually resulted in YouTube or Twitter.

"It really isn't fair," Emily once said, after we got our midterm grades back. "You're really good at what you're good at, right?"

"Right."

"See, this doesn't make a lot of sense to me," she said, "to be good at high school, you have to be good at everything. So if you're good at everything in high school, it's just assumed that you'll be good at college. But in college, your focus gets more and more specialized until you get a doctorate which is so hyper-specific that you're barely useful with anything else. And we're always so shook when high-school honor roll students drop out of college, right?"

"Sure…" I said, folding my report card into a paper airplane.

"Seems like a waste of those who can be good at everything; forcing them to specialize. Where if you're exceptional at just one thing, and not so good with other things, the gatekeepers hold you back until you can limp through with a high school diploma. By then, they've told you enough times that you're not good for anything, so you don't even try for higher education."

But I was more focused on the paper airplane soaring towards a garbage can 20 feet away. Friends and onlookers in the atrium cheered when it bounced off the rim and fell in.

CHAPTER 8
POPULARITY CONTEXT

Monday, October 9

We turned a corner off 17th onto Harrison and we were in sight of The George Moscone Secondary-Education Institute. I was on my bike like a normal person, having grown out of my oh-so-cringe middle school sk8r phase. But Emily let it fester.

She had a collection of longboards that she used to get around anywhere. But because she was a girl, the second some guy saw it under her arm he'd scream 'poser' at her. Emily could brush off almost anyone though.

"High school, and this is my firm belief," she said, swaying from one side of the bike lane to the other, "is only here to socialize children like dogs so parents can show off standardized test results to other parents."

"You thinking like... book clubs?"

Emily grimly looked back at me. "Tupperware parties."

I shuddered. "Yegch..."

The school itself was out-of-place in the industrial-commercial no-man's land between Potrero Hill and South-of-Market. It was built in the 90s, after a supervillain terrorist wrecked a bus depot. It was supposed to look 'different' from everything around. Modern, or postmodern, or something.

But honestly, by now it was hard to tell the difference between this and some of the luxury condo high-rises around Mission Bay.

Stuck between 16th street and the UCSF Mission Centre parking lot, the school had underground parking, one-and-a-half libraries, a full cafeteria, and a confectionary. And in spite of being jammed into a single city block, there were two gymnasiums (one underground, connected to the parking).

There were three 'towers' but nobody was really sure where the towers began or ended. The inside was very white, with a different color-blind-friendly accent theme in each hall. The whole thing never went taller than three stories, except for an 'observation deck' that had become where the stoners met to vape.

Most field sports teams had to play offsite for matches at Franklin Square, but hey, we had a football field that got used for… (checks notes) two months of the year. There were these really cool geometric bleachers though, built into the side of the school. It had kind of become an iconic spot.

They'd actually shot a few movies there.

Me, Emily, and the rest had a table in the Atrium. Which should give you a picture of how high we were up the popularity ladder.

See— Back in Freshmen, I happened to make a good impression on the right people.

If a little guy picks a fight with the big, burly, bullies, the super-chill Seniors kinda respect that. I wound up in the popular kids' sandbox, hanging out with bros who were three years older than me. I got invited to their parties, and I kept sitting at their table as they graduated.

You didn't sit at a table unless you were invited. Everyone memorized which table belonged to who. It was prime real estate because most people passed through the Atrium to get anywhere in the school. You were seen, acknowledged, expected, and if you weren't there, people would probably notice that, too.

So yeah. I was kind of hot stuff.

People knew how I talked, they knew how I dressed, and they expected to see me around. My Twitter got shares, my Insta got likes, my snaps got replayed.

And the best part was that my table was the one that freshmen and sophomores weren't afraid of. We were the 'not like other preps' kinda niche in the high school ecosystem. So on my way from the front door to the table, there weren't many people who didn't stop me to say hello.

Kelly Collins spoon-fed me weekend gossip, and I got a hug from Londyn Morino. Pretty sure she was just doing that to get under her ex's skin, but I was okay with that.

Mason Vaugn, her ex, was talk, dark, handsome, and a total dickwad. We gave each other a lot of heat until the end of sophomore but came to a truce. Since then, we did our best to pretend the other didn't exist.

Coming up to a crowded spot in the hall, I saw Terry Folkson and Davie Lopez moving from one cluster of people to the next. Pasty-pale redhead and a Latinx whose natural hair color hadn't been seen by a living soul since eighth grade. These were the kind of 'friends' you never saw apart, but who hadn't officially come out to anyone yet.

Maybe not even each other — know what I mean?

"Luca! Emily!" called Davie.

"Okay! Okay!" said Terry, clicking his pen on the clipboard he was holding. "Okay…"

"Okay…" said Davie making an announcement. "When you have a burger… Do you put ketchup on the meat… or the bun?"

Emily scoffed. "Oh. Meat. Definitely."

I looked over. "What?"

"Like…" Terry tapped the pen against his chin. "When you've got a hamburger. And you're going to squeee-eeeze some saucy condiment action onto it. Do you squeeze it on the burger itself… or on the top bun before you squish it together?"

I thought for a second. "Is there lettuce on it? A tomato?"

"I—"

"Can I adjust my answer?" Emily asked. "I was not aware that this scenario had variables."

I nodded. "Can you put me down for 'it depends'?"

"Another one!" Terry said, annoyed. "I told you we needed a 'both' column."

Davie rolled his eyes. "Okay! This is just like. A plain burger. Meat and bread."

"Gross…" I said.

But then, Emily decided she had enough and pulled me away. "Thanks, guys!" she called to them and then turned to me. "I hate walking with you in the hallway."

CHAPTER 9
NEW FRIEND AGENDA

Monday, October 9

First period after Home Room was Geography. Last year, I planned it out with Kaleb and Emily, and we managed to get into the same class together. We sat on the right side, one row up from the back because those desks were nasty.

I didn't mind the class. Ms. Smith was an older woman who liked to make self-aware bad jokes. She knew there was a margin of only 0.6% of students who would actually use what she was teaching, so she made her lessons fun. Maybe not fun... relaxed?

Let's be clear, just because I liked the class didn't mean I was all 'A's there. When I got a bad mark on a paper, Smith made a point of saying she liked my enthusiasm. Dad didn't like the grade, but he liked that I had a class where the teacher wasn't calling me 'disruptive.'

Most of the final grade was determined on a single project over the second half of the semester. Smith was assigning us as partners to develop an urban city plan, with highways, roadways, residential, commercial, and business lots. Stuff like that.

Lots of extra credit stuff to do for it! Develop a city history, hash out an economic base, and how trade functions. Tourism and other stuff like that. But what I liked the sound of was being able to draw or build landmark buildings. When it came to hands-on projects, I actually had a shot to do okay.

Kaleb rolled his eyes. "You get Emily for this one," he said. "You'll need her more than me."

Emily was good at things like this. Being like... the actually smart one of the three of us. Kaleb and I knew partnering up with each other meant we were guaranteed for a C or D. Emily could save at least one of us. Unfortunately, Smith announced she had already drawn up the groups.

Seriously — why did teachers do that?

It ended up that Emily and Kaleb actually got paired. Kaleb shot me a smug grin when Smith had moved on. I shook my head. "Insult to injury, bro."

I got partnered with a lanky guy who sat across the room, Rook Lang. I guess that was fine? He seemed like one of those nerdy, intellectual, protégé types. Hopefully he would help us breeze through the academic stuff while I could eat glue in a corner somewhere.

Smith was going to give us a few minutes to get acquainted and let us talk about the project a little before getting back to the lesson. Rook and me made eye contact and I waved him over. "Hey man," I said when he sat down beside me.

"Uh... hi. I'm Rook."

"I know!" I smiled, holding out a hand. "Luca."

"Heh... yeah I know. I know, too. That you're Luca..." He grabbed my hand — really firm at first but then he relaxed his arm and was a little limp.

"Rook like... the chess piece?" I asked.

"Chess piece, or the bird."

"Bird?"

"Yeah it's like a stalky crow with a big, grey beak." He nodded. "My mom chose my American name. She likes birds. Dad likes chess."

I nodded. "You know, that is so cool. I'm just Luca though so... sucks to be me."

Half a smile twitched into his cheek. "So, uhhh... what did you wanna do? I'm thinking we could do some kind of coastal mining town."

I cocked my head. "You have an idea already?"

He cleared his throat. "Just... I dunno. Off the top of my head, anyway."

"Cool. Cool." I nodded. "I thought mining towns were dead, though?"

"Well, yeah." He smiled for a second. Uncomfortable. "Uhm... It could be a west coast city that sprung up. Or something."

"Oh. Like they found gold?"

"Well... That's how San Francisco was founded, right?"

"Oh! I thought it was a navy base where a bunch of sea-men got stationed." (Kaleb snorted loudly behind us. Little did he know I specifically dropped that pun for him.)

Rook blushed. It gave me the feeling that I was a little intimidating. Poor guy. He was like a walking panic attack.

"Well, that too. Both are true," he said. "But the city administration has been pretty good at... I dunno re-inventing the city? Another town could do the same thing. Tourism push, lucrative tax cuts to attract larger business investors." He nodded. "Anything goes."

"Hey, that sounds good too." I hushed my voice, and leaned over, keeping an eye on Smith to make sure she wasn't listening. "Did we like... learn all that? Any of that kinda stuff? In class?"

"Well no..." he said. "But I flip through the textbook when I get bored — bored in class kinda thing. Heh... And some of it is there." He twitched out a friendly smile. "Really, I was just pulling all that other stuff... like... off my head."

"I can help," I said. I didn't want to look like I was just gonna let him do the whole thing. "We can meet up and plan out the city and stuff."

"Oh! That's cool." Rook fidgeted with his fingers. "And, you know, I don't mind doing the write-up."

Smith called everyone back to their seats.

"Killer," I shot him with some finger-guns. "And I can go to town on some cardboard and spray paint or whatever."

"Huh?" He made the movements, but unsure if he should stand up right away. "Oh! You mean for buildings and stuff! Yeah, that would be cool. I'm not great at that kinda stuff." Everyone started shuffling around.

"Awesome!" I held up my hand for a super-awkward high-five. Owning the awkward made it better, right? But something didn't quite feel right. Even in the way he used his hands. Seemed a little off. Then again, this guy had a meltdown-countdown clock on his forehead. So abnormal seemed like it was kind of his thing. "I'll give you my number after class," I said.

"Sure, sure! Yeah, actually, that's great, we can do that. Yeah." And then we were back at our seats and listening to Smith make a big deal about 'relief' precipitation.

I kept looking over to Rook though... I knew a little about him.

He was a theatre kid, which seemed like it shouldn't have fit because he was super shy. I rarely saw him in the hall, but just from those three minutes, I figured he'd mastered the nerd-zen art of avoiding being seen by popular people. I hoped he wasn't afraid of me like I was Mason Vaugn or someone in that douche-tier.

Jesus, I hated Mason.

Meanwhile, Emily and Kaleb were still passing notes about what gag name to give their city, and what their over-the-top major export should be.

— — —

Over the weekend, rook and me met up at the Mission Bay Library. Boy, was he awkward — and terrified of being assertive. It took a little effort to make him feel comfortable enough to relax his shoulders. We didn't make much headway on the project, but I think I made him open up a little bit.

I'll take that win.

CHAPTER 10
HOSTILE TAKEOVER

Thursday, October 12

Com-Science. I was just screwing around. Mr. Parks came around and watched me scroll on Reddit boards for five minutes before he told me to get back to work. He was a mega-laid back guy who only really kept his job to raise up one-or-two star pupils a year. Everyone else could screw around and get a B or something.

But from nowhere, someone shouted, "Search for 'Twelve-eight Manifest' — the Livestream!"

Almost all the computers projected the voice of a British man at the same time. He came over way clearer across the crappy built-in speakers than he should have. It felt so real it had ear-texture. Like velvet or suede.

The brand for his website and YouTube channel was called Humanity Against Insanity, but the media called him The Gentleman. Among anarchists and radical leftists, he was kind of an A-Lister as far as personalities go, even though nobody knew who he was.

The only face we got was a smooth, blank mask that lit up like an LED screen. It was always white, but he would flash emoticons in blocky pixels. He stood in front of a dusty blue curtain and wore a bowler hat.

By the time we started watching, the stream had been going on for three and a half minutes. "...and last night my — our — only option was to retaliate against that particular branch of oppression. I left Point Brick Reality an opportunity to relinquish their announced contract to demolish and... 'develop' Union Square Hotel.

"Now, I will reiterate for the thousandth time that I have no idea why we call the systemic removal of locally-owned business 'development.' " The Gentleman threw up quotations. A series of black letters flashed on the mask's smooth, white surface, and settled on a shape.

[ㅎ_ㅎ]

"However, despite the surplus of internal communications made public, that did not serve as very much of a deterrent. As we all know, they continued their operations with due haste. Contracting a demolition team, rolling in the machinery." He ran fingers over the sides his slicked-back hair. "Nevertheless, in light of Point Brick's *other* pending development in Union Square, I have decided to escalate the... scope of my deterrents."

[ㅁ ⌒ ㅁ]

"If you would be so kind as to make your way to my website domain, you will find, front-and-center, a link that will allow you to bypass your way into the Point Brick financial mainframe. The first ten clicks will each diminish one-fifth of the company's value."

[¬‿¬]

He leaned towards the camera. "One fifth, ten times. Please excuse the non-euclidian accounting, but I do feel that selling it all just once isn't enough of a message. Desperate times, after all."

Mr. Park stood up so fast, that he nearly knocked his chair over. "Get off that site, now!"

The room echoed with furious clicking; I just watched the video.

"I assure you the links are secure, and you will receive no penalization for following them." He folded his black-leather-gloved fingers together. "I would invite you to take my threats more seriously hereafter. I'll be in touch."

[^ㄱ^]

There was not a single moment of silence in the room. "The link's dead." Tommy Henriques said.

"Damnit," said someone else.

"Henriques!" Mr. Parks snapped his fingers at Tommy.

Emily sent me a text. It was a picture with a web browser window with a printable certificate on it that read: Congratulations! You're doing your part to end systemic oppression! And there was a very happy-looking chibi Gentleman with cat ears waving at the screen.

Today at 1:44 PM, some girl idk said:

I was numer 8! ALMOST didn't make it!

I'm gonna go get a frame for this after school. wanna come? Or are you 'working'?

...you WERE watching the stream, right?

Funny... last week The Gentleman's website was blocked by the school's security filter. He was technically a criminal hacker, even though the bulk of his website was mostly just Marxist rants about San Francisco's gentrification. So letting his domain through the firewall was a strict no. Even blogs and some news articles that mentioned him were blocked.

As far as website aesthetic went, it was the Hugo Boss of the web design world. Nothing loaded faster, it was smooth, minimalist, sleek, and bold. It had an updating roster of twitchy flash-games which you could download as apps. There were essays on economy and politics.. There was an archive of all his proclamation and rant videos, so you could find them after they got pulled off YouTube.

His YouTube account had been banned after each 'press release', and yet it was always up again by the next time he had anything to say.

Google had put out numerous statements claiming that they didn't know how the account kept getting re-activated. Well... they used to... Like, last spring. By the end of the summer, they stopped saying they were looking into it.

I didn't think anything of it. Just... normal Gentleman crap. Maybe a little bit more of a flex but it was on-brand enough.

Before, it was always just email leaks and stuff. Apparently, this time, leaking a bunch of e-mails that said the board of directors were a bunch of racist, misogynistic, cash-gobblers was so last year. Dad says some businesses thrive off of a nasty reputation. Real estate development was one of those, I guessed.

The news would be freaking out about the stock market and stuff. Like... the news shows with red and green numbers and arrows running along the bottom that Dad paid too much attention to. I went back to pretending to do work while Mr. Park hollered to get students back on track, and away from the news.

CHAPTER 11
知彼知己

Thursday, October 12

Who was the Gentleman?

The Gentleman was a dick to CEOs and investment brokers, I guess. But in my kind of radical, hashtag-woke, ultra-progressive social circle, that didn't really count against him.

There was the initial weirdness that a British guy was so invested in San Francisco's history and culture. But like... that was just the kind of weirdness that felt right at home in California. The hat and the mask and the video rants all kind of fit right in and everyone just got used to him.

Watching his YouTube videos before, they were pretty much just angry podcasts. A fancy-anon guy talking about what sucks and who made it suck. I listened to them in the background, and I listened to what Emily told me about them. Figured it was best to watch them on my own for a fresh start.

The first thing I noticed was that there was no editing. His background wasn't even a green screen. It was all just a single cut video of a talking head with an emoji mask. No editing, no... but also no 'hmms' or 'umms' — so that should tell you that they were scripted. But still... He seemed a little disorganized.

"So many people want to live in the San Francisco from movies and television," he said, talking wildly with his hands. "With all of the flowers in the hair — but they also want ten-million-dollar condos, and to live around peers of similar status. They want art and culture, mistakenly under the assumption that all artists make money like Jeff Koons.

"They want green-initiatives without the commitment, sustainability without sacrifices. They want comfort, and they want guilt-free comfort. They want hippies without squalor, and yet don't understand why San Francisco doesn't remind them of flower girls from the sixties."

[ಠ_ಠ]

"And they just... complain, complain, complain about the ugliness of homelessness." He swept his hands. "Just... get them away. Don't fix the problem, just force them out to Oakland or something. Isn't that it? They'll crowdfund a bus to take them away, but not lift a finger for affordable housing."

That video was supposed to be about how San Francisco looked in 90s TV and movies. But most of it was just stuff like this. If there was a script, he wasn't good at sticking to it.

And in another video back from July, he was talking about a whole city block near Castro that was demolished and replaced by a three-story condo complex. He was obsessing over a specific laundromat that got ripped down. It was some gay spot for local artists during the AIDS crisis and he was having *none* of it.

"Poof!" he said. "Decades of history and community. And not even a commemorative plaque. Not a 'thank you for contributing to the culture of San Francisco.' Not a thing."

[≧_≦]

"You know," he said, "*The Gays* didn't choose Castro. They grouped there because there was nowhere else for them to live. Proper, moral, heterosexual coupling shut them out of the 'good' neighborhoods. Now, Castro is one of the most yuppie-coveted streets in America. But the people living there now — who moved there because they read the first book of Tales of The City — are pricing out the low-rent culture they want to say they're part of. But in all cases, they only want the PG-13 version of—"

Knock at the door.

Frantic clicks to close the browser window.

"I'm— come in!"

Dad cracked my door open and peeked in. I made a quick glance at my computer screen to see what I'd left open, but Dad already noticed the YouTube video.

"Discussing Wages in the Workplace..." He cleared his throat. "Think I've seen that TED Talk. Exciting stuff..."

Oh! He... thought I was—

I coughed. "Yeah, just needed to... um... wind down before bed."

"Well," Dad said, as Lillie left the room with him. "Just wanted to let you know I was off to bed so I won't keep you. Night."

I waved. "Night."

Not... really the first time Dad walked in on me. But it doesn't really stop being awkward, does it? Especially when I could have told him what I was actually doing, but...

It wasn't something I wanted to explain until I actually knew why I was doing it. I chugged a Full Throttle, grabbed a handful of fruit snacks from a bulk box, and activated my super-power of not really needing more than four hours of sleep.

So... Who was the Gentleman?

He hosted regular live-streams for his subscribers. You needed to tip if you wanted him to answer a question, but all proceeds went to soup kitchens. The only questions he wouldn't answer were the ones about him and his personal life.

The guy was a library. Didn't need to look up a single thing — could quote smart people off the top of his head. He could pull facts out of his ass, and nothing he ever said was 'wrong.' In fact, *The L.A. Times* had a whole dedicated team to fact-check him. He responded by setting up a page on his website to fact-check every article they published. It was embarrassing... For *The Times*.

His brand had sparked an underground art scene. There was unlicensed merchandise, posters, lock screens, and tattoos.

Money he made from selling stuff through his website went to — you guessed it — shelters, social workers, and small, charitable nonprofits. He kept a running list of his funds — every cent was accounted for, and he took nothing for himself.

He was also pretty big in the ASMR community. A lot of his less angry videos were pretty relaxing to some people and they used them to fall asleep. Some people may have been Emily.

Rumor had it that Anonymous hated him.

Apparently, Wiki Leaks was terrified of him.

Fox News had it out for him.

So did CNN. And so did and the rest of national news.

The CIA wanted his head.

The NSA wanted to recruit him.

And the FBI was TBD.

But nobody knew who The Gentleman was. Nobody knew where to find him. And like… nobody really talked about how that was really sketchy. I thought 'transparency' was part of his M.O., but his fans and trolls overlooked that. By the time he mattered, everyone had given up trying to figure out who he was.

He was so dug-in to his bomb shelter — wherever it was — that even Vigils weren't going after him. And pros would try to take down anyone who could give them a career bump. But it wasn't like there were many A-List, Corporate-Funded Vigils left around these days.

For the last few months, America and most of Europe were in a bit of a Vigil 'problem.' Every major Vigil team and organization had taken its entire roster list and vanished. Without a trace. Governments and agencies kinda stood at press conferences and said that everything was fine, but no, we can't tell you what's going on.

So it was either a conference or a global apocalyptic threat. At least one of the two, probably.

And what it meant was that the heavy lifting was up to the B-Listers now.

Call them…

Call them B-*Lifters*!

HA! Haha!

Ha-haha!

Oh, that was a good one. Or maybe I was just tired and over-caffeinated.

Pretty soon I was going to know more about The Gentleman than almost anyone alive.

And it was going to get bonkers weird.

CHAPTER 12
STICKIN' IT TO THE MAN

Friday, October 13

I woke up to Dad rushing around the house. Nothing out of the ordinary. Maybe I'd stolen some of his cufflinks or something — I don't know.

Wearing a muscle shirt and boxers, I waited on the porch for the dogs to finish up in the back yard. Our elderly neighbors, Edith and Martin Stilt said their hellos while cordially passing an oversized, locally-sourced, artisan, blown-glass bong between them.

Edith and me made small talk — you'd never know the woman was high. Or maybe that's just because I'd never talked to her while she was sober... Martin, though, didn't say anything. Like, at all. Ever. He was either mute or took a vow of silence. He just nodded and smiled. Super chill.

It just so happened that we shared a duplex with the most wholesome home-growing weed-dealers on Potrero Hill. It was always hilarious when I'd spot teachers coming around. Oh, the grades I'd get if I set up a camera on the front porch...

By the time I got home from the dog run that followed, I heard Dad on the phone in his office. He didn't normally keep his conversations on speakerphone, so I edged up to the door.

"Yeah, I know they don't have you on speed dial anymore, but do you still have contacts there?" Dad asked, rooting around for something in his drawers at the same time.

"Of course I do, but we're talking about top-level info. I can't Karen my way in there and ask for their financial books," said the woman on the other end. She was Holly Rolland. Big deal.

As in — BIG deal.

"I'm not—" Dad sighed. "I just want to get a gauge of the playing field. Who has contingency plans? And are there others like *this*?"

She scoffed. "Oh yeah! After one of the largest cybersecurity attacks in history, they'll just openly talk about whatever plan they have—"

"Holly—"

"And if they don't have a plan, they'll broadcast that to anyone," she said. "Look, I need you to trust that I know how to talk to these people. And that doing what you're asking me to do is not how to talk to these people."

Holly was probably in L.A. She was a kind of family friend like Tom. When Dad had to make trips to L.A., He usually stayed in a guest bedroom in her apartment in West Hollywood. And, like Tom and Dad, she was a retired professional Vigil — her alias was Flechette.

She, Dad, Tom, and Tom's brother Jong-Su all worked together on taking down a cross-state tainted tobacco ring run by a biker gang. But unlike the rest of them who opted to stay 'indie.' Holly Rolland made it big when she signed a corporate contract.

She reached out to Dad shortly after we moved to San Francisco. Gap Inc. sued her because she refused to sign autographs as 'Mistress Flechette.' A bunch of white executives wanted to brand her with a 70s Blacksploitation theme, and she hated it.

Dad had been her go-to aid when she wanted to throw down with some executive-types. Seemed like she ended up doing a lot more of that than crime fighting. Guess it depends on who you say is a criminal.

By the time she was forced into retirement, she said it was almost a blessing in disguise... Didn't mean she wasn't salty about it though.

And as one of the last high-profile Vigils who took on Side-kicks, the whole Vigil community took a hit when she hung up the cape.

Dad stopped what he was doing and thought for a minute. "Yeah. You're right, Holly. I'm sorry, I'm just—"

"Stretching yourself too thin?"

"Not too thin," Dad said. "I did have my assistant call Red Rhino to cancel his costume changes suit against Virgin."

"Good!" she said. "I don't know why you wanted to work with *Benjamin* in the first place. He's basically the Mariah Cary of the Vigil world."

"Well… cases like that are what keep the lights on," Dad said. "But my time is better spent trying to find someone to lobby the state senate to have this attack classified as an Act of Super Villainy. Maybe set up a fund for affected locals."

"This is making waves out of state, too, Andy."

"Yeah, but do you want to try getting Congress' attention?" Dad asked. "So I'm just looking for whatever I can to help this case."

Holly sighed. "Well… I can tell you — and you absolutely did not hear this from me… Edward Li—"

"Ed Li From Pacific East?"

"Mmhm. He said that—"

"Ah-ah-ah!" went Dad. "Sorry Holly, but Luca's listening in around the corner."

Damnit. Every time I thought Dad was getting rusty… I crossed into Dad's office. "Hey… Holly!"

"Look at you eavesdropping!" she said. "I hope that means you're still giving dear old Andy a handful of trouble."

"Handfuls, Holly. Handfuls." Dad looked rough. Like he'd been up for a while and was already a few coffees into the day.

"I feel like I haven't seen you in years!" said Holly. "It was just in August though, when you came down?"

"I even still have my tan!" I said.

"Look at you! Making all the other white boys jealous."

"You know it!"

"Right, well, I'm actually in San Francisco right now."

Dad scoffed. "And you weren't going to tell anyone?"

"I've been working on some... ad deal with a skincare line made from ethically-sourced honey," she said. "I was waiting until that business was all done. But I would love to treat you all to dinner when this whole... Gentleman thing settles down. You know that fine dining place that opened up? Fifth season? My ex is an investor. I'll be able to get us a table no problem—"

"There it is!" Dad said, pulling a folder out of one of his drawers. "Thought I looked there..."

"What's that, Andy?"

"Dad found a perfectly-colored tie to match his outfit."

"Cute," Dad said to me and leaned over the phone on his desk. "Look, I need to get on the move, Holly. Can we talk more about this around... eleven?"

"I'm in The City if you need an extra pair of hands," she said.

"Maybe. Talk later."

"Ciao, Loves!"

Dad hit the hangup button before she did and then took off like a rocket.

"Act of super-villainy..." I said after him. "You didn't seem this concerned about it last night."

"Life lesson," he said from the kitchen, pouring coffee into the travel mug I got him for his birthday. "You don't piss off rich people without them flipping the table and walking out, leaving everyone else to pick up the check."

"What's going on?"

"Unexpected consequences that... everyone really should have seen coming."

"Huh?"

Dad sped past me on his way back to his office. "Short version: Point Brick didn't go down without kicking and screaming."

"Alright. Vague. That's okay." I warily stood where I was. "How about you though? You doin' okay?"

He grabbed a blazer from the back of his chair. "I'll fill you in tonight if I see you." Grabbing his keys, he hovered at the front door. "If I'm not home, order some food and put it on the credit card."

"You have a leftover preference?"

Dad thought, bobbing his head. "I'm feeling like... Greek?"

"Sounds good."

"Awesome. Love you—" And then he was gone.

CHAPTER 13
BUSINESS ETHICS

Friday, October 13

I'd figured out two things when I got to school.

First. Emily told me that Point Brick execs, instead of laying everybody off, drained their entire payroll account to buy back their own stock. Which is like… well it's not as illegal as it should be, apparently.

Yesterday afternoon, Point Brick played some nasty games on the stock market. Lots of people were suddenly without work, and a lot of executives were a bunch richer.

And school was buzzing. Point Brick was just one company, but they outsourced to more than a dozen agencies, businesses, and contractors.

"They always bragged about how they were 'the most connected' company in San Francisco," Emily said, while we huddled over our table in the Atrium, drowning out the shouting around us. "Their tagline was: 'Brick and Mortar, we're becoming a part of San Francisco."

Branden looked over. "How do you just… have that stuff memorized?"

"I'm the magic black lady for the modern world," she said.

"So this whole Gentleman thing was sledgehammer versus wall?" Joshi asked.

"Just a really shitty wall," Emily said. "It practically fell down on its own."

It's not like political-economic discussions were uncommon at this table. Emily usually liked to steer things in that direction and honestly, it beat talking about who was cheating on who, and which girls were or weren't friends anymore. But if there was something out of place, it was Kaleb, who hadn't said a thing all morning. And usually, he was the first to toss out clever comebacks to Emily.

"So why do you seem so eaten up about it?" I asked him.

Kaleb looked up. "Who, me?"

"You *are* a little bit of a downer right now," Aura added.

He looked around. "Dude… you know that my Dad's company works for Point Brick, right?" He cleared his throat. "Worked for."

"Oh shit…" I said, feeling myself get red. "No way…"

"Yeah, well…"

The rest of the table looked away from each other for a second.

Aura grabbed his wrist. "Oh hun… You gonna be okay?"

"Uuuuuugh!" He rubbed his hands over his face. "Aside from probably losing the house… Maybe living with my mom in a two-bedroom for a while until Dad can get on his feet again. Maybe leaving The City because mom doesn't make enough to even rent a place on her own. Maybe my parents getting divorced? Sister having to take out a student loan next year. Yeah aside from that I'll be just great."

And before long, that became a very common story around the school.

CHAPTER 14
JUST A BUNCH OF BROS

Friday, October 13

The second thing I learned at school that day was that I should have studied for a Geography test that I'd known about for over a week. But I had decided that procrastination/apathy was probably the best approach. Procrastination always seemed better at the time.

When I found myself caught up on the short answer segment about biomes and like... plateaus...? It was pretty clear I was floundering. Emily would look up at me and smile awkwardly. Even Kaleb was doing better than me. Jesus.

Then out of nowhere, Rook asks to step out to fill up his water bottle. He goes around the back, which was different for him. But as he passed me, there lands on my desk this origami-esque folded slip of paper. Carefully unfolding it under my desk, it had... well, it didn't have the answers written out, but it had some phrases. Keywords that helped jog my memory.

I didn't ace it, don't give me that much credit. But I passed. I think.

Passed 'enough.'

I flagged Rook down after class. "Hey! Thanks so much, you saved my ass."

"Yeah!" He said, over-enthusiastically at first, then he scratched the back of his head to play it cool. "I just wanted to help. You seem... like — cool I guess."

I nodded, following him. "I know how apparent it is that I have no idea what I'm talking about. Failing tests sucks, so thanks."

"If I'm being honest..." Rock scowled. "I don't think I really aced it either."

"Is that bad?"

"Well... I've never failed a test. I dunno. Could be a B for this one... Lately..." He looked away.

"Oh..." I stopped in the hall. "You... got hit by the Point Brick stuff."

Rook looked at me for a minute like he was trying to register what I was talking about. "Oh! Oh yeah. Point Brick... Um... Well... Not really hit. Dad's a... His work is really involved with this stuff. So like, he's getting called in for a lot of consultations."

"Ah! A lot like my dad," I said, getting back into the moving crowd.

"What's your dad do?"

"Lawyer. Works with Vigil laws and stuff like that."

Rook nodded. "Is the Gentleman attack a supervillain attack?"

"No, but Dad's gonna try to get it passed as one. Set up some kind of relief fund or something. I wasn't really paying attention."

"Ah... that's smart," Rook said.

In the hallway between towers A and B, I paused while he fiddled with the dial on his locker. "You know Kaleb?" I asked.

"Yeah?"

"His Dad's a mechanic. Works on heavy-duty construction vehicles—"

"Oh!" Rook looked over. "Oh so he—"

"Yeah."

"Is he going to be okay?"

"He might be somewhere else in January," I said. "Or next month."

"Well... there's a whole lot more going on than anyone realizes." Rook leaned in closer. "There's kind of a manhunt for the Point Brick execs... This whole thing is pissing off a whole lot more people than you realize. It's almost like—"

"Wexler!" I recognized that voice. I spun around and smacked right into Tegan Hale's big, stupid chest. He slammed me back into the locker. "Where ya goin', Lou?"

"Don't touch me," I said, straightening my blazer.

Seemed like I was so wrapped up with what Rook was saying I wasn't paying attention to where I was. This was right beside Tegan's locker, and Tegan was part of a bro trio that included Dan Johnson and— of course — Mason Goddamn Vaugn. As my luck had it, all three were in this hall.

"What you fellas up to?" Dan said, more towards Rook.

I scoffed, inching myself between them and Rook. "Sharing space with a couple of off-season fail-football players."

As much as I would have loved to knock Mason & Co. down a couple dozen notches, I had to be the bigger person here, right? Because like... I could definitely tell that these guys had gone far overdue without a beat-down. It was like... if I didn't smack 'em down every other week they'd get these gigantic 'I-can-do-any-thing-to-anyone' complexes.

Rook leaned over and whispered. "Just ignore them..."
Which was nerd-code for 'I'm being bullied and teachers don't believe it.'

"I got this," I whispered back

"Please—"

"Why you always so rude?" Dan asked, getting in my face, making me wrench my head back to look at him. "We're just having a chat. Right... Lou?"

"Go chat with somebody else," I said.

"...Or else what?" Tegan said.

I paused. I didn't have time to count back from ten and remember ten things I liked having in my life. So I sucked in a breath through my nose and tried to remember the *other* parts of that anger management class they made me take.

"…Else this is gonna end up like it always has…" I said.

"Come on, man," Said Dan. "Just having a talk. Been a while since I got to see my buddy, right?" He went to mess up my hair but I leaned aside and swatted his hand away.

"What did I *just* say about keeping your greasy fingers away from me?"

"Woah! Aggression!"

"Yeah, Wexler, hands off…" Dan turned to a random crowd. "You see that? This is why he's the one who needed Anger Management therapy."

I leaned over to Rook's ear. "Get your stuff while I talk 'em down."

Rook nodded.

"What's that?" Tegan said.

"Knock it off, Hale," Mason groaned. I was surprised to see that he was trying to hold his friends back. Well— 'trying.' But since when was he the voice of reason? I was so shocked I couldn't even make a clap back in time.

Dan grabbed Rook's shoulder as he tried to pass, leaned down to Rook's height, and pointed at me. "You gonna let him tell you what to do?"

My eyes were darting around, from the pack of gorillas to the crowd, to Rook. I felt like I was getting pulled in five different directions and my heart was beating so hard my fingers were tensing and I was losing a grip on my books. These asses were supposed to go away and they weren't *doing* what I was *telling* them to do and it was *pissing me off.*

"Johnson, I swear to God I will fuck you up if you don't back off." The breath coming out of my nose was hot against my lips.

The crowd: "Ooo-ooo…"

Dan got up close to me. "You wanna say something else instead, Lou?"

I lowered my voice and craned my head up. "I said: get yourself to your P.E. bukakke party, or I'm gonna give your mom the night of her life and then ghost her."

He shoved me back into the locker. "Don't talk about my mom, bro."

I shoved him back. "Then I'll fuck your dad. *Bro.*"

The rest was history.

CHAPTER 15
VICE GRIP

Friday, October 13

Nobody should really be proud of how often they wind up in the vice principal's office. But, when almost all of those times involved me picking a fight with some mush-for-brains who tried to let his arms do the talking, I thought of that as an impressive track record. A civil service, really.

Ashley Hulbry, though, was never happy to see me.

Of everyone involved in the brawl, I was the third to be interviewed. Rook waved me in on his way out. "All good?" I asked.

He nodded. "I think so. I just said what happened."

"What'd she say?"

Rook shrugged. "'Thank you?'"

Hmmm… I wondered what her play was going to be.

"Come in," she said when I knocked on the door. She was running her squared-off lilac nails through her dark hair. She saw me and took a breath. Truth be told, I actually don't think she didn't like me… But she was definitely sick of dealing with me. "I thought we had a deal, Luca?"

"You heard from Rook, right? I was trying to settle things down."

She ignored me. "For the first time in months, I searched for the letter 'A' in my contacts, and your father wasn't the first name coming up. I thought we were in the clear."

"I did my best."

She sighed. "You know, I actually believe that. But have you ever tried not punching something?"

"I didn't throw the first one."

"And you're very good at that!" She slouched back in her seat. "How are you feeling? You need new ice?"

"Should be good…" The little plastic baggie with a few ice cubes had mostly melted. The cold water was easier to hold against the red mark on my left cheek. It was from when Tegan slammed my face into a locker. "You oughta see the other guys. "I threw some extra emphasis on 'guy-s.'

I was already on thin ice about the 'martial arts' thing. There was a rumor that I had my fists registered as lethal weapons. (Not true — Tom stopped graduating me through the belt system for that reason.) Having bruises up the side of my face definitely helped my case. But then again, she hadn't given me any sympathy for being the small guy since freshman.

And unlike everyone else involved in the fight, Dad didn't have the money to make a donation and make everything go away.

"So," said Hulbry. "What are we going to do?"

"Don't want to hear my side of it?"

She waved her hand. "I can guess by now. Probably not different than Rook's version. You know… I really admire that. You don't *need* to bend the truth because you're really good at lining your ducks up… It's a talent I could admire if I didn't have six angry parents breathing down my neck."

I clasped my hands together and stood up. "Alright so. Detention? Sounds good. Only time I get homework done anyway… So how long this time?"

She bit her lip. "Sit down please?"

I did. "In-school suspension?"

"Yes, because I want you missing more time from classes."

"So…?"

"It's just…" She folded her hands together. "I need this behavior to stop, and clearly your promises aren't enough."

"It's not *me*, though," I said. "We're clear on that, right? It's really not my fault that the school has a crappy approach to bullying. If the school isn't going to have consequences, then—"

"Then it's up to you?"

"Well… no…" I huffed. "There does have to be some kind of deterrent. Rook shouldn't have to stand up for himself. Because he shouldn't be getting picked on."

"Well," she looked impressed. "You're not wrong, I guess. But it's not your responsibility, as another student to—"

"And what? You want me to go 'get a teacher' to stop the bullying? Gonna come by: 'you boys need to break it on up, now!' Or worse, one of the nerdy science teachers who thinks that since *he* got through it, that Rook can stick up for himself too. Guess what? Not everyone can stand up for themselves, and not everyone needs to make that a priority just to get through a day of school!"

I was practically shouting, and the bruise on the side of my face was heating up the bag so much the last of the ice had melted. Hulbry held out her hand, took it from me, and dropped it, suspended by two of her nails, into the garbage.

"When you were taking those anger management courses over the summer," she said, "did anyone suggest that you have a savior complex?"

"People get pushed around. Since when is wanting that to stop a complex?" I asked. Hulbry shrugged like she agreed, but that didn't mean I was out of the woods.

"Yeah figures I get singled out. My parent actually works for a living so he doesn't have time to harass you into letting me off."

She sighed. "And neither does Rook, actually."

"Rook wasn't involved."

"Sure he was," she said. I desperately scanned her face to figure out if she was even serious or not. "You wouldn't have been there except for him."

"I can go wherever I want in the halls between classes! You can't blame me *or* Rook! It was Mason... It was Tegan who started it!" I huffed. "Come on, please! You can't—"

"This may come as a shock to you, but this isn't a negotiation." She sat back. "No, I'm not putting Rook in detention. But if you get anyone else involved in any of these little... scuffles in the future, I will give them the same consequences I have to give you," she said. "I hope we're clear on that."

I slumped back. "So how long am I gonna be in detention this time?"

"Oh!" she said. "Starting next week, you're spending the rest of October in detention."

CHAPTER 16
TOUCHING NERVES

Friday, October 13

"You good from here?" I asked Rook at the corner of Folsom and 11th.

"Yeah, I usually walk home," he said. "I'll be fine."

"We can walk you the rest of the way, I don't work until—"

"Speak for yourself," Emily huffed. "No offense Rook, but I don't wanna walk all the way there and back—"

"No, it's totally cool," he said.

Emily smacked me. "See? He'll be fine." It was her idea to ambush Rook after school, and walk with him uptown. I'd told her that Rook has insider info about Point Brick and she wanted to pick his brain.

"Well," said Rook, adjusting his posh backpack. "So like... text if you have any other questions."

We said a quick goodbye before the crosswalk light up Folsom started to blink. And then we were on our way to Tom's studio. Place of employment for me, and Emily liked the vibes so it was a normal haunt for her too.

"So," she said, and then cleared her throat.

"So!" She cleared her throat again, but louder.

"What?"

"Soo-ooo..." She raised her eyebrows a few times.

"What?"

"Awfully protective of Rook, aren't ya?"

I sighed. "He's small and has 'natural victim' tattooed on his forehead. Besides, protestors are already gathering around downtown. He lives down there, I don't want him to get caught up in it."

Emily cleared her throat again.

"WHAT?" I shouted. I didn't wait half a second before sucking in a breath. "No, this isn't a gay thing."

"Okay…" Emily nodded. "It was just a joke, you know?"

"I know, I'm sorry…" I took another breath.

"You're all cranky though. Getting a headache?" she asked. "You've been saying the migraines have been coming back."

"Not right now. I'm fine." I said. "I just… Everything's getting under my skin."

Emily nodded back towards the intersection. "You tell Rook what Hulbry said?"

"No, he doesn't need to get caught up in that," I said.

"I was joking about it, but you are going very far out of your way to protect him."

I sighed. "That's me and my bleeding heart. I can't believe Hulbry's like… literally weaponizing my good nature." I sighed again, frustrated. "No like… I feel like out of everyone she actually 'gets it '… It feels personal, you know?"

"Not going to lie. She's a bit of a bitch. But like. I kind of respect her for that? Very Machiavellian."

"Very what?"

"Dead guy. His big, famous smart-white-guy quote is: 'It's better to be feared than respected, if not both.'"

I shrugged. "Well… that fits her M.O."

"I heard she gets paid more than the principal…" Emily said. "I believe it. When she shows up you know shit's about to go down. I heard she has final say on everything the school does… But yeah, I am totally down to go to detention with and/or for you. Just putting that out there."

"I'll keep that in mind, but I think Hulbry's on to us."

"Probably. She has spies everywhere." Emily sighed. "Like when everything's said and done she is totally like my mom."

I nodded. "Your mom does wear all the pants…"

In the few blocks between Eleventh street and school, she had Rook explain what he meant when he told me: "there's more going on than you think." Though really, the growing mob of angry people around the Financial district already were kind of making it abundantly clear.

Point Brick execs didn't just throw people under the bus when they got attacked… they knew it was going to happen and planned for it. But Emily wanted a second opinion from Tom, who she liked to think she could pry information from.

I let us in through the back door of the studio.

CHAPTER 17
ON THE SCHEDULE

Friday, October 13

The street-front studio on the corner of Haight and Fillmore was where Tom first taught Baby-Luca self-defense, then where I started part-time work helping out with lessons. These days, this was the Avalon Knight base of operations, so it wasn't unusual for me to spend nights on Tom's pull-out couch.

It all came together as a pretty nice situation where dad wouldn't get suspicious when Tom and I were out all night busting ass. Pretty clever right? Almost like Tom set it up that way.

Yeah, he was pretty sneaky like that.

In a perfect world, Tom would probably be fighting crime on his own, bringing me up as an actual sidekick instead of having me go solo-ish. Tom was still a master of several martial arts — but what ruined his Vigil career was the robot that killed his brother, and left him with a chronic limp.

So he left Seattle and bought this studio and apartment above it a few years before Dad and I got here.

The place was called the *West Wind Academy of Pan-Asian Martial Arts*, and between Tom and his business partner, they could teach almost a dozen of those martial arts. Most of the money came from Karate and Tai-Chi though.

Tom was saying his good-byes to his afternoon Tai-Chi class when we got there. "Ah there he is," Tom whistled. "Looks like you had some fun after all." He ducked down to get a closer look at the bruise. "Looks like an SUV hit you a few times."

"Between the three of them, they were as big and collectively as smart," Emily said. "Low-line SUV. Not one of the onboard-computer ones."

"Not even 4-Wheel drive," I added.

Emily shook her head.

Tom huffed. "Your Dad gave me the details." He waved his hand. "I don't need to hear your side of it."

I nearly choked. "Why not?"

"This used to happen often enough that I can basically picture it in my head. And…" he sighed. "It wouldn't matter either way. We're not going out tonight."

"But it's on the schedule!" I said.

"Yeah," Emily said. "It's on the schedule!"

Tom turned to Emily. "Young lady…"

"What, there's a protest! Tonight's great!"

"Yeah!" I said. "Tonight's great."

"Emily… I appreciate the enthusiasm, but this isn't how involved you're supposed to be," Tom said. "Did Luca bring you along because he thinks this is up to a vote?"

Emily cleared her throat "I just wanted to see what you knew about the Point Brick attack."

"Oh is that all?" Tom rolled his eyes.

"I'm guessing you've heard stuff through your network of sketchy underworld types," Emily said. "Alleged network."

"Surprisingly little," he said, shooting a glare at me. "I'm sure you're shocked… I'm actually a little concerned that nobody I know has heard anything… Or they're not talking. Hmmm…"

"Oooh! Conspiracy?"

"Maybe not," he said. "I haven't had my ear to the ground today at any rate. Spent most of it receiving emails from parents. Hardly anyone's bringing their kid around for tonight's lessons. I figured it was easier just to cancel altogether."

Emily scoffed. "Parents are pulling their kids out of Karate class... because of a protest?"

Tom ignored her. "And it is for that reason, that I am keeping you off the streets tonight."

"But..." I struggled for words. "The schedule!"

"I told you from the beginning that the schedule is meant to be flexible. We change it all the time."

"I've been looking forward to this so hardcore though!"

Tom gestured at my face. "Seems like you couldn't wait."

I moaned. "I had a super rough day—"

"So you're emotionally compromised?"

"No, that's not what I—"

"I'm just not sure why you're making a big deal over this!" Emily said. "It's just a protest—"

"Protests can be incredibly unpredictable," said Tom.

"What, you're worried everyone's going to start looting?" Emily mocked. "My mom knows the people organizing the demonstration! They've done this before. They're going to keep it contained. Maybe you need to worry about the protesters' safety... and not them turning into looters."

"Maybe I am?" Tom said. "Look," he said. "It's not like I'm expecting the worst, but it's best to be prepared for it. When tempers are hot, things can go any which way. I send Luca—" he turned to me. "I send you to keep the protesters safe, think about who we would be keeping them safe *from*. Because you get involved with something like this, they will politicize you.

"All and all, I couldn't be prouder to see you — in the future — out there, keeping the right people safe. But you are too early on in your career to get wrapped up in stuff like this. You need a network who can make sure your side of the story gets out there, or they will make a public enemy out of you. I've seen it before."

"Well isn't helping out the point?" I asked.

"Honestly…" Tom hesitated. "I don't think we know enough about what's going on. If you're going into a mass-demonstration situation, you need to be aware of who wants what. You need to know the lay of the land. And right now… we don't know nearly enough about the Gentleman, the money taken from the company, the stock sales, or where the CEO is—"

"Aha!" Emily snapped her fingers and pointed at Tom. "You have heard something!"

"Maybe not much more than what you'd read on Twitter," he said. "Why, what have you read, young lady?"

"A friend of ours whose dad has inside information told us," Emily explained.

"Not my Dad," I said. "New dad."

"It was a planned operation," she continued. "When the Gentleman first leaked the Point Brick email base, the directors had an emergency meeting with the shareholders and upper management. They told the shareholders to hold on to the stock no matter what so they could use the payroll accounts to buy it back for more than it was worth. They planned this!"

"People are only protesting because of shitty business practices—"

"Yeah!" said Emily. "What's going to happen when it gets out that they specifically baited the Gentleman into doing this? They didn't just plan this, they did everything they could to make it happen! Tonight is a night that people need protection and Luca could help!"

Tom nodded. "Well, you're on to something there," he said. "What *is* going to happen when people find out the truth?" He leaned forward on his cane, hovering over Emily. "What's going to happen then?"

"Well…"

"This is exactly what I mean by needing to know more about this before getting involved," Tom said. "Being a Vigil gets very political very quickly. Even for those with the best of intentions — especially for them." He gestured toward Emily. "That's more a lesson for you."

Emily sighed.

"Another day," he said. "Shouldn't need to remind you how many 'another days' you two have, so don't lose sleep about staying in for a weekend." He threw his arms up. "Go have a party. Drink irresponsibly. Smoke a mountain of pot or do whatever it is that normal teenagers do. Come on, I'll drive you both home."

"I can walk," Emily said.

"What did I just say about unpredictables?" Tom started hobbling toward the back door. "I need to get Luca home anyway. I'm sure Andy wants to have a word..."

"I'm staying here a while," I said. They both stopped and look at me. "Need to beat the crap out of Connor and Patrick."

CHAPTER 18
BENCHED

Friday, October 13

The punching bags downstairs were named Patrick and Connor. Tom named them after two brothers who used to bully him and Jong-Su when they were in elementary school.

He insisted that if he was going to teach, he wanted his students to have something real to hit. Since his students didn't end up hitting each other, he called it a win. The kids did fight over who got to punch the bags, though.

I liked Patrick better. He didn't wobble as much.

Everyone needed a steady guy named Patrick. Tall, broad-shouldered... red-headed.

Can take a hit.

And the Irish curse wasn't a dealbreaker either.

The bags were a great way to help me blow off steam, but *experts* told me that I should find more 'wholesome' ways to deal with anger.

Okay yeah. Great idea. Some meat-for-brains jock is talking shit. 'Oh, sorry bro, I need to find the nearest woodland path, and I'll be right back so we can settle this like gentlemen.'

What kind of society do we live in where you're told that wanting to punch things is a 'mis-use' of anger? That's what anger's for!

You'd put therapists out of business if we normalized punching-bag therapy. But apparently, *any* trace of aggression meant that you were unhinged and needed to medicate, medicate, medicate the rage away.

I was so busy blowing off steam, I didn't hear my phone buzzing on the table until it buzzed itself onto the floor. "Damnit..." I said, seeing a missed call from Dad. We'd been texting a little bit about... well, today.

"Hey," I said. "How's it going?"

"Not bad," he said, sounding distracted. "So. The fight."

"There was someone who needed—"

"Nope! No... that is the wrong thing to say right now. Try again."

"What am I supposed to say, then?"

"That you're sorry, for one."

"Great. But I'm not."

"Look... I wish I could be a better father and actually discipline my walking-talking-*Fight Club* of a son but I have way too much going on. So... For the rest of... Until Spring Break... you get three strikes before I need to bring the hammer down."

"Oh... Okay..."

"You have two left," he said. "Believe me when I say: you do *not* want to find out what happens if you strike out."

"Oh boy... do I need to sign a contract?"

"No. But I can add a strike for any reason I see fit, is that clear?"

"Yes *sir!*" I was getting off easy. Something was up...

"Alright, and here's the bad news," he said. "I... I'm really sorry but I'm going to be out of town. I need to be about five places at once right now."

My heart fluttered. "Oh... so a long trip?"

"I... don't know," he sighed. "Look, I know I said I'd be at home a lot more... And I know it isn't the first time I said it. We can talk more about it when I'm—"

"Hey... Dad, it's totally fine. I get it."

"I… thanks Champ," he said. "But no seriously, clean up your act. I don't mind hearing from Hulbry. I do not like hearing from Hulbry when you start fighting."

I grinned. "When *do* you like to hear from her?"

Dad cleared his throat. Single fathers were a school's most valuable resource.

"Alright, so," he coughed. "So, you can feel free to stay at home or at Tom's. Bring the dogs if you're at his place. I do want you checking in on the place if you're not there."

I heard Tom open the back door.

"And… Luca? I love you."

"Oh… yeah…"

"Come on, let's hear it."

"I'll give you one if you take away one strike from the counter."

"This is not a negotiation!" Dad said. "I love you. See you later." And then he hung up just as Tom came in. I actually was going to say it.

"That was your Dad?" Tom asked.

I nodded. "He's going to be gone."

"Oh yeah?"

"Like… he's got business for a while."

"Oh yeah."

"So… Do I get to superhero?"

"No."

"Ugh…" I threw my head back. "Why can't we just stick to the normal spots?"

Walking up to me, Tom tapped the bruise on the side of my face. "OW!"

"Sorry, Luca. The final word's 'no.'"

"Was it the fight? At school? It was the fight, wasn't it?"

Tom thought for a second and looked like he was about to say something. "It's still a no from me."

Who was Tom to insist he knew what I was capable of? Every time we'd gone out he'd get so nit-picky with details that I was surprised he hadn't come down on me for not lacing up my shoes properly.

So I just went home. I was going to make a difference and do something stupid!

…Not in that order.

CHAPTER 19
WORKING NIGHTS

Friday, October 13

11:20 PM.

Tom was right... and wrong. Yeah, things were a little bit crazy tonight. But it wasn't anything that I wasn't already used to. Just... a whole lot more of it.

The problem was that, without Tom to keep me standing around on rooftops twiddling my thumbs, I was on the move. And there was a lot more to do if you weren't locked off in the same six-block area. I got my fill, but I was only one guy and could only do so much before wearing myself out.

Someone tried to rob a twenty-four-hour pizza place with a knife. I got a free slice out of that. I had to talk a drag queen out of demanding a selfie with me after I stopped some guy from car-jacking her.

And that was on top of the normal muggings and drunken fights. Before I knew it, I found myself around Greary street and way closer to downtown than I had planned.

I'd never done crime-fighting very far from Haight. But the area around Van Ness Avenue was where I'd lived for my first few years here, so I knew my way around pretty well. Gotta say though, streets look a lot different when you're on rooftops.

I was looking over the Post and Taylor intersection and sat down to eat my packed ham sandwich, mangled from being carted around in my duffle bag of snacks and first aid. All at once, I remembered that, in a little side street around here, I got the crap beaten out of me by two other guys and a girl. I'd been in The City for less than a year.

Had a loose baby tooth knocked out of my head. Never could find it…

I put the second half of the sandwich away. Eating and crime-fighting armor was a bad mix… for bathroom reasons. But just as I was slipping the black neck wrap around my mouth, my phone started to vibrate.

My heart pounded while I tried to fish it out of a pocket.

I thought it could be Dad…

What if it was Tom…

Did I put the Vigil trunk away? Did I even lift up the ladder to the attic? If either of them found out, I'd be dead.

But then it was just Emily. All good.

"Where are you? Are you okay?" she asked.

"I'm fine—"

"Did you not think to let me know by responding to any of the 50-odd texts that I've sent?" She shouted. "I had to convince Mom to let me take the car down the street to check if you were okay or sleeping or… is that a car alarm?"

I hadn't been checking my texts; my phone was on silent. "I'm out trick-or-treating."

"It is like… a week away from Halloween." Emily paused. "Wait! Is there a secret Halloween party? Oh my God, are they doubling up on Gay Halloween? Two Halloweens in October? How'd you get invited if you're only seventeen? Is it one of those gay parties where age is don't ask don't tell — are you in international waters?"

"Trick-or-treating — on the street — in costume."

It took her a moment to think of it.

"Are you serious?" It was more of an accusation.

"I—"

"Without supervision? Does he know? You father? What if they find out—"

"Be subtle!"

"I am being subtle! You're the one running around trick-or-treating!" She said, and then I heard her put me on speakerphone. "Why didn't you at least tell me so someone could know where you were?" I heard typing. "Jesus someone just mentioned you on Twitter!"

"I didn't think I'd be out for as long as I have…"

There was a pause. "Yep. A drag queen named Lennorea Gallorea." A pause. "She gave you four and a half stars and called you cute.

"Ugh. Cute." I groaned. "And what about the other half star?"

"She said you took her… bullets away?"

I scoffed. "She was waving a pistol around without the safety on. I made her promise to take classes."

"Oh! She has a Drag Race audition tape! She's pretty, I hope she gets in," she said. "You are so lucky your 'parents' don't know how to social media. Luckily only her and two other people have mentioned you on Twitter." A pause. "Oh, Jillian Miner retweeted Lennorea! Ugh! Why do you not have a Twitter? I need to talk to—"

"You do not need to talk to him about it. I've got this covered. I'm fine," I said.

I could hear her roll her eyes over the phone. "So is it bad tonight?"

"Not so much. More quantity than quality, you know?" I cleared my throat. "Small candy. Lots of it. No full-on chocolate bars…"

"Okay I get what you mean, but this analogy is starting to hurt my soul."

"I'm coming home soon anyway."

For a second Emily's silence came across as concern. "Are you hurt?"

"A few freshly-disinfected scrapes."

"Tired?"

I scoffed. "No." I had been shotgunning energy drinks all night."

"Do you have somewhere to be tomorrow?"

"School?"

"It's Friday." She said. "You getting a migraine?"

"No."

Emily sighed. "So why are you calling it a night so soon?"

CHAPTER 20
THE FANDOM

Saturday, October 14

1:00 AM. There was a spike in the action. But there was less for me to do.

Thing is, other Vigils showed up in force to pick up the slack. Bars were shutting down early. Because... you know.

There was stuff happening.

I recognized most of the local vigils. The heroes that only San Francisco locals would be able to pick out. Like high school football heroes, you go to the next county over and nobody knows who they are.

Now the Mavericks... The Mavericks could draw national news. Sometimes international news. They were San Francisco's big-league super-hero team and the most well-armed Vigils on the West Coast.

Almost all of them were post-human. Which was the technical term for: 'born with superpowers.' And don't get excited. Nobody was throwing people across the room with their minds. The spiciest we got was telepathy, and even then, the general pattern was: the stronger you are, the more dysfunctional you get.

(For understandable reasons, nobody could prove whether invisibility existed.)

But you didn't usually get superpowers down in the little-leagues. There were so many street-level vigils that they had to fight for a shout-out on Twitter. (Most of them didn't even have Instagram.) And they were everywhere tonight. Plenty of photo ops.

So I stopped rushing to get places and texted with Emily more. I was coming up to a caffeine crash anyway.

Today at 1:11 AM, you said:

Not Silver Harrow and Heart Attack having a coffee break on a rooftop together!!!

:o

Today at 1:13 AM, some girl idk said:

I don't carew if you get arresrd — I need silver's aithograph!!!

Your such a fan

Today at 1:14 AM, some girl idk said:

LUCA

NEED THIS

nerd

Read, 1:14 AM

I was one to talk. I had a list of favorite Vigils that changed weekly. A bit of a hipster too, because most of them hadn't been operational for over ten years...

Yes, my Dad was one of them. But he lost points for not letting me go on a class trip to a nature reserve while I had the flu in fourth grade.

Today at 1:14 AM, you said;

Its just funny cuz silvers sponsored by Polished, and h/a is with inVolve. Contract Stuff.

Read, 1:14 AM

SCANDAL!!1

Today at 1:16 AM, some girl idk said:

missing your calling as a tabloid photographer.

Sometimes photographers would sit atop buildings, watching dozens of violent crimes, break-ins, and muggings, just to take a photograph that would ruin a Vigil's career. And then the photographer was the hero for exposing corruption or something.

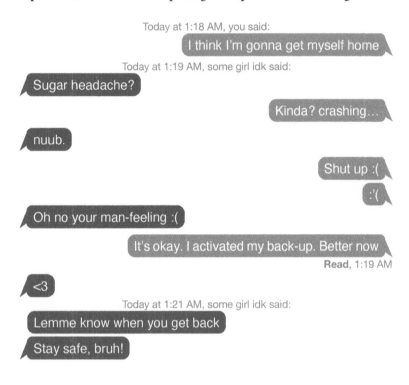

Today at 1:18 AM, you said:

I think I'm gonna get myself home

Today at 1:19 AM, some girl idk said:

Sugar headache?

Kinda? crashing...

nuub.

Shut up :(

:'(

Oh no your man-feeling :(

It's okay. I activated my back-up. Better now

Read, 1:19 AM

<3

Today at 1:21 AM, some girl idk said:

Lemme know when you get back

Stay safe, bruh!

I put my phone away and spotted a black van pulling into an alley across the street. The thing was — this van pulled in with its lights off. "That's not conspicuously inconspicuous or anything..." I mumbled.

I made my way down some scaffolding without taking my eyes off of it.

The van parked next to a delivery door in the back. Five people got out, one of them working on opening the door while the other four kept lookout. Dressed in black, co-ed — one was big. Another one had a big black duffle bag. It wasn't looking any less suspicious...

That settled it, I needed to follow them in and make sure they were up to no good—

I mean... make sure they didn't get up to no good.

CHAPTER 21
POLK A TIGER

Saturday, October 14

And from the look of the office's delivery door, they were up to no good. The lock was… melted. There were scratches on the metal that looked like they used a clamp for a… lock-melter? And the 'melted' deadbolt was cold. Metal shouldn't cool down that fast, right? I figured they were rocking some serious tech.

Didn't seem normal for an office break-in. But I hadn't dealt with one of these before, so who knew? Meanwhile, that voice in my head that usually said 'hold on Luca, this is a bad idea,' just posted that picture of Michal Jackson eating popcorn.

I followed them up the stairs, making sure they were a few floors ahead. They stopped on the eighth, and I kept hidden.

"Almost done with the door?" one of them asked.

"Didn't get to charge after the first go," replied another. "Almost done."

"Just bash it open," said a gruff one.

"Not going to bother justifying the reasons why we can't do that."

When they filed in I rushed up as quietly as I could. The door into the office had a key card sensor that was untouched. A metal sensor bar had been melted off the door and duct-taped to a magnetic sensor on the wall. The LED was still red and that meant no one knew they were here.

Going in quiet meant that they wanted to stay a while. I pushed the door open slowly, keeping away from the opening and peering through. Just dark inside, but it seemed I was being led into a hallway. I slipped through, and went for the first cover I could find…

I saw some flashlights in the main room. Echoing voices. Still no idea where I was… Tom would have thrown a fit for not knowing. Period. He researched everything he could in a few minutes before I'd break up even a convenience store robbery. Yet another reason why it's important to go into crime-fighting with a computer-buddy.

This office was modern and stuff. White floor — lime green walls. Black-and-white over-exposed photographs and ink plots. Very modern. High-rent office. No logo anywhere though. Bet they had one of those classy signs in their lobby. The kind with a little waterfall.

The central office itself was a cavern. Tall single-pane windows stretched down from the ceiling. Across the office walls, black-and-white photographs hung on exposed wire. Short-cubicles connected together in s-curves that ran in rows across the width of the room. Smokey glass dividers rose up four feet — short enough to peer over and see what your neighbor was up to.

The ceiling was bare, except for exposed cross-beams and foam-insulated piping. They'd strung rows of colorful paper lanterns. I wonder if they ever lit them or just kept the florescent lights on? I wondered if they also had a bean bag chair corner with a foosball table to complete The Look.

Most of the nighttime lighting came from a few screensavers and the downtown lights flooding in through the windows. It looked a bit misty outside. Made it look misty *inside*. The screen-savers bounced the company logo — Polk Advanced Solutions.

Only one computer was active, and two burglars crowded beside it. One leaned over the keyboard, the other leaned against the desk. Blue light shone in a cone behind them, then mixed in with the light from outside. High-res, LED shadows skittered around the room.

The one leaning against the desk was a woman, her friend was a skinny guy.

I didn't want to move on those two while the rest were unaccounted for. 'Stealth' in movies and video games was just dumb. It never worked that way. A 'silent takedown' made a heap of noise, no matter how you did it.

Unless you went lethal or expensive. Which were strict no-goes for me.

I slid behind a row of desks to eavesdrop.

"...but no, that's not going to happen this time," said the woman. Their voices were hushed in spite of the room's emptiness.

"My ex lost her condo," said the man at the computer. He was hitting the keys so fast it sounded like he was just mashing random buttons. We'll call him McTypey. Sound good?

"Word is that Feildman balked to the latest threat," said the woman. "Know much about them? Shame we wouldn't do to them what we did to PB."

"We?"

"Yeah," she said. "The whole crew."

"As far as I know, this is *his* show. We're just along for the ride."

"Whatever," she said. "We're all looped in. Implicated."

The walkie-talkie bleeped. "Your talkie is on. Over."

"Go screw yourself," she mocked. "Over."

There was a break while McTypey clicked around.

"It's not like anyone actually wants to be here, anyway," she said. "Except maybe the social justice psychos in mainframe. I heard they actually enlisted. Or whatever. Interviewed? I dunno. I get what he's doing but... man, am I screwed if this goes tits-up."

"Why?" McTypey asked. "What's he got on you?"

She didn't answer.

The talkie bleeped again. "Data flow is a trickle... What's the hold-up?"

"System's not what we expected," McTypey said. "May just have to abandon the direct uplink and let it go through the local network."

"Damnit. Hurry up," said the walkie-talkie. "It's better for everyone as long as—"

"I am going as fast as I—"

There was a loud hiss on the walkie-talkie, like a signal interruption. "I'm in the system." The new voice was so much clearer... like they slipped into the room when I didn't notice. I felt like I should know who it was. "And, Tammy... as much as you 'don't want to be here,' I do pay very well."

She cleared her throat. "You do..." I was thinking of 'Ms. Grumpypants' but I guess Tammy worked a bit better.

While they were talking I had moved to the closer row of desks. I could hear their shallow breaths. The walkie-talkie complicated things...

I'd have to take them out fast and then set up an ambush for the other guys. I ran a few visualizations of how I could take them out... but that was a risk...

Or maybe, I thought, *I could just call the cops.*

Yeah? And strike up a conversation?

Or — or maybe, I thought, I could just stay here and let them get away with the stuff. What's the worst that could happen? Point Brick all over again? What was even my plan coming in here? How did I plan on getting out?

UGH! All these things were the kind of stuff Tom would grill me over. But no, not me, Mr. 'I'm sure it'll all work out.'

But something was off. A gut-feeling. I couldn't have said what it was, but I felt like this seemed really really sinister, and that maybe I should get to the bottom of it. I looked around and spotted a fire alarm. Authority always hated when you pulled fire alarms...

"Now, you know I don't like to micromanage..." That voice — I knew that voice. "But it would seem that you have company." I'd heard it in the videos I'd been watching for the last two days.

The Gentleman.

CHAPTER 22
THE FANCY MAN

Saturday, October 14

My heart stopped. He couldn't know about me being there...
He was a hacker but could he? Shit — my cellphone? No way...

But I began to panic a little. Did they knew exactly where I was
or only that I was around?

I needed to get out ASAP.

"I can spot a few of them," said the Gentleman.

A few???

"You've done all you need to," he said. "I think it's best if you
vacate post-haste. And please remember, you mustn't forget my
flash drive..."

"Where are they coming from?" McTypey asked in a panic.

"Line's dead," Tammy replied.

"Typical," he said.

Low and quick, I shot back to the hallway and around to the
staircase door.

...

Which had been jammed shut since I made my way in.

Okay. Someone was screwing around. I was way out of my
depth and seriously regretting this. For a second I figured I'd
rather die here than have to explain this to Dad. But then... no. I
was *not* dying in an office with bean bag chairs.

So think. Where could I go? There might be another staircase,
but would I be able to get there without setting off alarms? Would
it be locked?

But then someone shone a flashlight at me.

Upside: I didn't have to think about that other stuff.

Downside: "Hey! I found one of them!"

No time to think, I had to work quick before the rest of them showed up. I took the hanbo from my back and bolted towards the beam of light. Flashlight guy tried to take a swing at me, but I was already ducking down to tackle him.

(He's Flash Gordon now, btw.)

Someone came up behind me holding a fake plant. I rolled off of Flash, and the plant dropped on him instead. In the confusion, I went for Green Thumb, and got a few hits in before I heard an electric charge ringing in my ears.

Turning around, I was too late to do anything. All I saw was a big fist with crackling static sparks. I was like...

Yeah I knew it wasn't going to go great.

There was a flash of light and a bang. I felt like I missed a good half-a-second because next thing I knew, I was flying clear over two rows of desks. Luckily, I had a hard computer to break my fall.

Nailed that landing.

(I obviously did not nail it.)

Tying to move my arm felt like I was kicking with my foot. Or maybe I was trying to move my legs and that's what got me so confused. If the room was spiraling clockwise, my stomach was doing loop-de-loops. I had to pull off the mask because it felt like I was two seconds away from blowing chunks. Even after I fell off the desk, it felt like I was still flying through the air.

"Did you *see* that?"

"You mean he gave it to you when you never used one?"

"It's not like we were supposed to get caught," Tammy said.

"Keep an eye out for the others," McTypey said. "Let's head out."

I wondered if there was a secret trick to getting over paralysis? Maybe some zen thing Tom could teach me, because trying to force myself up didn't work until about the fifth try.

Even with the room still wobbling, I grabbed my hanbo and headed to the hallway.

I clung to the wall for balance and listened while they tried the staircase door.

"Won't budge!" Tammy grunted.

"Isn't this what you're here for?"

She heaved harder and the handle popped off completely. Which made it seem like she had super-strength.

Really bad news for me.

One of the more common 'superpowers' that some people got born with... But it looked like she was one of the lucky ones who could actually make it useful and not just be a threat to everyone around her.

"There's a way out the other side," Flash said.

"What about the van?" McTypey asked.

Green Thumb threw his arms up. "Forget the van!" And he led them out of the hall, around a corner, and into the lobby. They waited while McTypey was using the door-handle-melting device on a door behind the receptionist desk. I slipped in and hid behind a large, glass sign with the company logo on it. To my other side was a window facing the street. The view was certainly not cheap.

"Hurry it up!" said the guy with the... electric vomit-glove.

"Cold melter's almost out of juice, give me a break!"

I noticed something was off about the view. It was shaky. Not earthquake shaky, but like the glass was vibrating. Around the fringe of the window, there was an orange glow to it that got brighter the more the window shook.

Tammy got pissed. "Jesus Christ, let me—"

I interrupted her by getting myself away from the window as fast as I could. Nobody could say anything before the whole thing shattered and a shockwave knocked everyone over and threw some water out of the fountain.

Including two goldfish.

Three people swung in — superhero landings for everyone. Except those of us on the floor.

One guy was a cowboy with an honest-to-God cowboy hat, the one in the middle had super-tech armor that had that same orange glow as the window did, and the other one was just a really big and tall ginger-guy in a sleeveless vest. I'd never heard of these guys, and I could spot almost every Vigil in The City!

"Okay, so here's how it's gonna go," said Cowboy. "We're gonna put you on the ground. When you get up. I know, I know, you're gonna insist on fighting but it's not gonna work out, so," he started to applaud. "Good job, team. Good hustle, all-around. You did great—"

The glowing Armor-Girl elbowed him really hard to make him shut up. "Hand over your stuff and call it a night," she said. "Get this over with quick, so we can all get out before the cops—"

Cowboy spotted me gingerly putting the goldfish back into the office pond. "Who the fuck is this?"

CHAPTER 23
MYSTERY MISFITS

Saturday, October 14

Now, I was still a little dizzy from the shock, and everyone was just kinda like: '…what.'

"You mean he's not with you?" Flash asked.

"We gotta wrap this up," Vesty Big-Arms said to his friends.

"Fine idea," said the Cowboy. He took a larger-than-normal pistol out of his hip-mounted holster and took a shot at the crowd. The thing let loose a blast of blue energy that threw McTypey back into the wall.

Team Burglar wasn't going to take that lying down, though. Tammy got on the desk and leaped clean across the room at Cowboy, but Armor-Girl got between them and put up a light barrier.

The Cowboy shot off blasts of energy that punched dents into the dry-wall. Looked like he preferred to duck and weave until he could get an open shot. And Vesty Big-Arms was doing a good job harassing the guy with the shock glove.

And then there was me with my wooden stick.

Yeah, I was fine *now*… with the other four distracted. Team Burglar clearly didn't have much of a fighting background. Green Thumb came at me and it seemed like he was trying to pull my shirt over my head like this was an after-school fight. I'm not sure he even knew what 'winning' was supposed to look like.

I blocked his punches with the hanbo specifically because it was gonna hurt him more than me. Bruise his hands to soften him up, then go in for the headshot to get him dazed then — bam! On the floor he goes.

But then I heard that electric charge-up sound. Someone said "Watch out!" and the room lit up in a flash. Next thing I knew, there was a flying ginger-hunk coming directly at me. I couldn't quite get out of the way in time, and so we both landed in a pile on the freshly-waxed floors.

Yes, I *am* counting it as a sexual experience, okay?

"Thanks," he said, rolling over. "You all good?"

No, I didn't have a concussion. Didn't mean I wasn't gonna be in a heap of pain tomorrow.

"Quit screwing around!" The Cowboy shouted. "He goes to the cops with the rest of them."

Armor Girl whipped Tammy into a wall. "Forget the cops, we're here for the drive!"

The shock-glove guy was barrelling down on us. Cowboy took a shot and the blast of energy connected with the glove. It overloaded and spat out sparks that bounced on the floor. And then Lusty Big-Arms— I meant *Vesty* Big-Arms got up and everyone was back to fighting.

As much as the fight was leaning to the Vigils' side, I don't think they really were trying to end it. There were police lights outside, flashing against the other side of the building. The 'focus' needed to be getting them on the ground, not getting good hits in. How come I was the most under-armored, out-gunned, worn-out, and superpower-less person here and still the only one in the room who knew what they were doing?

With nobody paying attention to me, I took a look around. One was missing... Where was McTypey? He was the one with this special 'flash drive' the Gentleman wanted.

And then I saw it. The door behind the receptionist's desk had its handle melted off.

CHAPTER 24
TFW WTF

Saturday, October 14

I ditched the fight to find the missing hacker. Following him through broken doors, I found a second stairwell. Echoing in the dimly lit shaft, I saw him almost at the bottom. I'd need some mad skills to make up the distance...

"Mad skills..."

I lifted myself over the edge of the rail — eight-story drop if I bungled this. "Whose idea was it to have me drop from the roof..." I said, sucking in a breath, then pushed off and twisted in the air, catching the rail the next floor down. Dismount and *twist!*

And then repeat that like — ten times.

Made it to the ground floor in no time.

Yes, my whole body was shaking and even with McTypey getting away, I had to lean against the wall for my legs to stop feeling like jelly. It wasn't a karate move, but...

Come on! That was *by far* the coolest thing I'd done since hitting a bullseye on a dartboard while blindfolded twice in a row.

But hold on... that's not all folks!

I could hear him heading to the exit and got on his tail. He kept to the hall, ignoring any other doors. When the hallway turned to the right, we were in sight of a bright orange exit sign. As he pushed open the emergency door, he looked back real quick and swung the door shut behind him.

When I crashed through the door, he swung a 2x4 at me. But I'd already ducked under and grabbed it. Twisting it out of his hands, I struck under his arm.

"Ow!" He said, reeling back and tripping backward over the two cracked steps that led down to the alley. When he tried to get up I kicked him back down and rolled him onto his back.

I raised my fist and he screamed, holding his arms up. "No! Please don't!"

I held perfectly still. I wanted to see what his next move was going to be.

We were in a deep alleyway, in the middle of a city block, with no sign of the street from here. Loading docks everywhere. Everything smelled like cigarettes and stale trash. All soggy in the nighttime urban dew.

I'd already made a quick scan of the place to make sure that we were alone. I kept my eyes fixed on him.

He looked at me from between the fingers shielding his face. "Are you going to hit me...?"

"Tell me what's up first and then I'll decide."

"Oh shit! Oh shit! Oh shit... Uhhhh..." He said, sliding his hands down his face. Mid-late twenties, 5'11, and couldn't have been more than 160 pounds. Scruffy face, gaunt, and under-slept. He *looked* like a programmer. "Oh shit! No, I can't! I'll wind up like the others— I can't! You can't do that—"

I hit him. Softly. Was more to get his attention and because he managed to avoid the brawl. He still cried a little.

"You said you wouldn't—"

I pulled him up by his collar. "And you haven't told me the 'what's up' part."

He sobbed a little. "No! You don't know what he'll do to—"

"The Gentleman?"

"Yes!"

"He's violent?" I asked.

"I don't know! No one's met the guy."

"How'd he organize you, then? And what are you afraid of?"

"I didn't want to do any of this..." His eyes darted around. I kept an ear out around us, in case he was stalling for someone to come up behind me.

"Blackmail?"

"Yes! Some of them go to him. I just got an email that told me to meet some guy—"

"You said you didn't meet him!"

"Not The Gentleman. This was a... lieutenant? Or something." He tried to squirm for more air, but I stuck on his chest. "Uhhh.... Hamen... I don't know.... Uhh... He's like... African, but a white, mercenary guy... Kyle — no... Uhhh... Kurt. Kurt Hamen." He was scared and shaking. "This other guy... British guy. I just know him as 'Temple'!"

"Is he The Gentleman?"

"I don't know!" He sobbed. "I don't want to lose my daughter..."

"So he just goes around randomly recruiting people?" I got off of him and he sat up.

He paused. "I've got a history. Getting into things that I shouldn't..."

"So he blackmails specific people." I nodded. "How'd he know about you? How'd he find you?"

"Some of those guys... They sign up. For money or some social justice stuff. Some of us, though. He's got dirt on us... The girl upstairs... The Gentleman found out she was post-human. Threatened to give her up to the CDG if she didn't do what he said." He wiped his eyes. "We're not all bad people!"

I rolled my eyes. "Like you said... you had a 'history' before you got into this?"

Sniffing, he got to his feet, slowly, in case I was going to plant him back down. "Then I had my daughter, Francine..."

"Yeah, whatever." I shook my head. "Get out of here. Probably best to avoid the cops. And if you can't, I wouldn't say much.

Seems like the Gentleman is invested in protecting his privacy. He'll probably find a way to get you off the hook."

"You're just letting me go?"

I shrugged. "We're not all bad people."

Aside from not having any snap ties, I figured it just straight up wasn't my business. He didn't seem like this was how he wanted to spend his nights off. No point in giving a victim up to the police.

"Blackmail, huh? Didn't seem very social-justice-y," I said to myself. Especially holding the CDG over a post-human's head. Tom told me what they did to folks who were even *suspected* of having superpowers.

It's not like I didn't get anything out of it. While I was distracting him with my fist, my other hand was going through his pockets, searching for the flash drive.

I thumbed the smooth, chrome drive as I watched him go. It had 'LOL' etched on it, so that was a thing I guess. I... hmm... Trying to figure out The Gentleman's sense of humor was turning into a struggle.

From a corner leading out of the back alley, I watched the guy get tackled to the ground and cuffed by cops who were waiting in ambush. While he was sobbing, I made my way up some scaffolding to the roof.

I regretted taking the flash drive.

I should have just let the cops take it with them. Now they wouldn't get it at all. This was evidence in a criminal investigation! And what was I gonna do with it? Take it to Tom and see what he could turn up?

Real top-shelf stupid move, Wexler... I was a solid B-student in Programming class, and the Gentleman was a world-class hacker. There wasn't any way I'd be able to decrypt this thing! This is why I needed Tom or Emily or someone who doesn't fudge up everything they touch...

Maybe the police had other drives? Had the cops ever busted The Gentleman's guys before? If they had... they'd kept it quiet.

And who were those Vigils? It seemed as if they knew what was going on before they even showed up. Maybe I could reach out to them?

Maybe not. They seemed a little hostile.

And the Gentleman? Well, now he seemed a whole lot sketchier than he had before. But I was involved now... might as well see where this went.

Whatever 'this' was.

ACT TWO

LIFE HACKS

CHAPTER 25
EASY STREET

Friday, October 27

Emily's Dad drove us to the Halloween party. Kind of. He dropped us off down the block because he assumed we didn't want to be seen getting dropped off in a Mazda in this neighborhood.

This neighborhood was Forest Hill. And honestly, it was one of the few places in town I don't think I'd ever been before. I felt like I should have paid a toll just to use the sidewalk. For some reason, the upperclassmen Halloween party was being hosted in someone's college boyfriend's house because his parents were out of town. Apparently there was some drama in the Secret Council of Girls because of it.

But hey, I wasn't gonna complain.

Space between houses?

Privacy hedges?

Lots of cars missing from driveways?

Seemed like the perfect place to make as much noise as we wanted.

"So I was thinking," Emily said, after her dad drove off. "After the party—"

"No."

"Hold on, let me finish," she said. "I was thinking that when we're done here we could take another look at the flash drive—"

"No. There's nothing on the flash drive. They must have never downloaded anything on it. It's a dead end—"

"Let me finish!" She looked back at me. "I actually didn't... have anything else to say."

"Ugh!" I started off in the direction of the party, Emily scurrying behind me in her glittery mini skirt.

"Hold on! Hold on!"

"It's your fault for wearing heels."

"Look. I'm just saying… we're never gonna know what's on it if we don't keep trying."

I tilted my head back to glare at her. Gold lipstick on her lips stretched into an impish smile.

"What?"

"Come on… can't I just… not think about it for a while?"

"What's eating you?" She huffed. "You're always gung-ho for super hero stuff."

"Yeah," I nodded, "doing awesome things like p'owning fights. This isn't super hero stuff… this is like… procedural cop drama stuff."

"Hey, PCD's can get *really* intense if they're good. Also if they're about cannibals instead of cops," Emily added. "But I get it. Not for everyone. Seriously though — I thought you'd be more invested seeing as how you went to the trouble to get it.

"Yeah. And it sucks that it's a dead end, but there's *nothing* on it. It's just gonna be a blank window like all the other fifty-seven times we tried to check it out." Maybe I was a little embarrassed. Because I didn't actually wait for Emily to open it for the first time, and I was worried that I'd messed something up that she wouldn't have.

Or, maybe the whole night was a sucky reminder that I wasn't playing in the Vigil leagues I wanted to. What, next to actual super strength and hi-tech armor.

And *maybe* I was also a little pissed at Tom for keeping me out of those Vigil leagues when (clearly) I could handle myself just fine. Maybe I'd been calling in sick for the last week to give Tom the cold shoulder.

Did that mean that I was missing out on Vigil training, when this whole argument was about missing out on Vigil training? Sure. But it was a matter of principle at this point.

Tom said I wasn't patient. *PFFFT.*

I'd show him 'patience.'

"You know…" Emily said, real quiet. "If it turns out that this is just an empty flash drive, I'm not really sure that would I actually believe that you fought off a post-human, and some guy with electricity-gloves, and then got rescued by a super-tech rogue Vigil team nobody's ever heard of…"

"Well first of all, they didn't *rescue* me. If anything, I—"

"Hey. As far as I know, you're just making shit up to compensate for how you wussed out and went home early."

I stopped to glare at her.

She smiled at me.

"We'll take another look. But tomorrow. I actually wanna get drunk tonight."

Emily gasped. "But think of… *the calories!*"

I put on a peak-hetero voice. "Yeah I'll dry-scoop and hit the gym twice tomorrow."

"Dry-scooping?"

"When you take protein shake powder—"

"And eat it raw? Why would anyone do that?"

"For the gains?"

"Ew! Why would someone do that? Have you?"

"Once, but only because I lost a bet with Kaleb." I shook my head. "Not something I wanna do again."

"Ugh. Boys are gross."

"Thanks!"

"Hey, question though," Emily said when we turned a corner and could see the party spilling out onto the street. We could already hear some of the bass — luckily it seemed like most of the neighbor's driveways were empty. "Do you think that like... Halloween is gonna be a pale imitation?"

"Imitation?"

"Of the real thing," she said. "Now that going out in costume is a regular hobby of yours."

"Find me someone who's spent more money on their get up and then you can call my armor a 'costume.'"

"Hmmm." Emily raised her eyebrows. "Yvette — you know, Yvette Gerden — apparently, she flew to Milan last Saturday to pick up a $7,000 Versace mini-purse that was only-in-store." Emily put on the pretty blonde girl's voice. "'I just like... had to have it, you know? Literally, like— actually, literally nothing else was going to work.'"

"What's she going as?"

"Sexy Medusa," she said, and then dropped her eyes to the side. "It's actually like... a really nice purse."

"Oh... Huh..." I brought up a mental image in my head like a slide projector. "Yeah, Yvette could pull it off... Medusa's the one with—"

"The snake-hair."

"Yeah..." I nodded. "Yeah, I can see that.

Emily smacked my arm. "Can you *stop* thinking with your dick and hate on rich bitches with me?"

"Psssh. I can do both."

CHAPTER 26
(UN)DRESS-UP

Friday, October 27

As soon as I showed up, I was pulled in twenty different directions. Girls screaming when they saw each other, guys shaking the walls from cheering and chanting. And all of them wanting a selfie with me.

It was a weird kind of combo when you were irresponsible enough to host underage drinking, but conscientious enough to throw plastic mats on the hardwood floors and covers on the furniture. Speakers were set up in the corner where Ronnie Wilks was the go-to DJ. It was a point of pride for him, even though I was pretty sure a shuffled playlist would work just as well.

Really, he just liked to show off how expensive his set-up was.

And on top of it all, you had half the crowd dressed as the sexy version of something that was never meant to be sexy. Halloween was pretty much the one party of the year where you could show up in fetish gear and no one would question it.

Wait. That's a lie.

Folsom.

I'd only actually seen my friends for a split second when I showed up. Kaleb had badgered me into two tequila shots, giving me a buzz because I'm a crazy lightweight. But then I got yoinked away by Londyn Morino, who came as a plague doctor, with thigh-high lace garters and the signature bird mask hanging around her neck.

She told me she wanted to go as a nurse, but Alexis Carrington said she wanted to be a 'victorian nurse' in April. And showing up in the same costume was how you start a girl-war, apparently.

"I decided to do the mature thing," said Londyn. "I ordered some custom shit, drove to a costume shop in San Jose, and blew her out of the water when I showed up."

"I'd say…" I said, eyes fixed on her thighs

She grabbed my hand. "Come dance!"

It was a bit early in the night for balls-to-the-wall drunken dancing. Instead, I found myself in a tasteful 3-way soft grind with Londyn and Danielle Faulk. The whole thing got me… bothered enough that I put my drink down.

But then Londyn got a text from Olivia Cole and had to go find her. "What are you doing after this?" she asked me.

I shrugged. "Non-committal."

"Ooh! Well… what would you say to heading out to get some milkshakes later tonight?"

"Milkshakes?"

"Sure!" she said. "Not a fan of dairy?"

"No, no… That's just really… 50s kinda Rockwell."

"Oh… *shit*. Rockabilly girl would have been a better costume." She adjusted her corset. "Coulda worn something… I can actually breathe in."

"I'm not complaining."

She giggled and pushed me back. "Pig."

"All I'm saying is that I… really — I'm just a huge fan of plague-era European history."

"Mmmm…" She said, pulling me in for another selfie. "Well, I expect a full dissertation on medical advancements leading into the European renaissance."

"Mmhm!" I nodded, getting my selfie-smile back on. "Over milkshakes!"

Before she snapped the pic, she leaned in to kiss my cheek. And then she was off and I was bothered and Danielle decided we needed something else to do.

We made our way to one of the rooms where someone was ruining a perfectly good party with an acoustic guitar. As far as chill vibes go, it was either this or head downstairs where the whole basement was hotboxed.

Somewhere along the way, we met up with Kaleb, Aura, and Emily. Kaleb, since he'd bleached his hair, made a convincing Gordon Ramsey (though shirtless because: sexy costume). Aura had this cyborg thing going on with LEDs and everything. It wasn't deliberately 'sexy,' but there wasn't much that didn't end up being sexy when Aura put it on.

Emily, though, was bitter for two reasons. First, her boyfriend, Ian, had ditched her. They had a two-part costume, and Emily had to explain to everyone that Isis was an Egyptian goddess and, yes, Egyptians were black.

Emily pulled me over by the collar. "I swear to God, I am going to dump Ian if he keeps pulling this shit."

"I've heard that before," I said.

Emily threw her head back. "Ugh! Fuck it. Maybe I'll just dump him over text right now."

I grabbed her phone out of her hands. "Do not drink and text. Bad choices!"

She rolled her eyes. "I've got other prospects!"

I handed her phone back and was about to ask her what she meant, but then she yanked me into the dance pit again.

Bit more crowded and a bit more drunk than before.

Kaleb ended up teasing me a little bit, practically humping my leg. I kissed his cheek to psych him out, instead he locked his lips on mine. Aura caught it on video and threw it up on Snapchat. And not a second later, she and Kaleb were a swaying disaster of tangled arms.

Bisexual privilege is dreaming about getting in-between your friends who are already dating.

...

I'm kidding. That part was actually the worst.

And just like that — the mood ended and my fake-ish-drunk was over. I was kinda standing there, wondering how I'd convinced myself that this was fun in the first place.

On my way out, Emily tried to grab my shoulder, and I just shouted back that I needed another drink. And maybe I wasn't lying this time.

CHAPTER 27
LIFE OF THE PARTY

Friday, October 27

Oooh, sorry. You wanna do a sex, Luca?

Well that involves everyone getting real interested in what's *actually* in your pants. And then suddenly, your social mobility goes out the window! You'll have to start dodging weird questions and reading into literally everything that literally everyone says.

And then when I try to tell anyone how exhausting that is, people'll tell me I'm getting worked up over nothing.

I knew how people at Moscone High talked. I'd been talking to them all night. I'd been talking to them for the last three years. And I was not going to waste my life obsessing over how people treated me before and after I un-stealthed myself.

Dad was constantly on my case but he actually had a good point. If I was going to go into varsity Lacrosse — and I'd pretty much been told point-blank by Coach Milton that there was an empty seat for me — I would probably have to disclose the amount of testosterone I was taking. That's assuming that Milton wouldn't randomly change his mind—

FUCK.

There weren't any tiny umbrellas left, and I was hyped up for one of those glitter-flamingo-at-Folsom drinks. What's the point without one of those cheap little parasols? I dumped the punch back in the bowl, tossed the cup, and reached for a vodka cooler.

Then I figured... why not speed up the process? Shots of... something the label had peeled off of in the ice bucket, but it looked like hard liquor. Smelled like pine needles.

I started dumping a generous 'ounce' of whatever this stuff was into the tiny disposable cup. I hadn't screwed the cap back on before a hand swooped in and stole it.

"Nope!" Emily said and shot it back herself. Her face twisted. "Nasty. I had no idea there was a first-forty-pages Neil Gaiman protagonist here." Emily took another shot. "Gross,"

I reached for it but she got to it first.

"Sorry, I lost my buzz, and you don't drink."

"I do—"

She gestured at me. "What's even going on with you right now?"

"I'm literally just vibin'."

"Total downer vibes, though, bro." Emily put her hand on my back and pushed me further into the patio where strings of over-sized lightbulbs hung between the trees. And with them were strings of glowing bats and spiders with smiley faces.

"So what're the drinks about?" she asked when we were far enough away from the thumping music that we could lower our voices. "Like by all means, if you wanna get wasted, please do. But like. As a responsible friend, I'm not going to let you get sad drunk."

I waited for a second or two and then huffed. "I dunno, you're all in there like—"

"It's the sex thing?"

I threw my head back and groaned. "Yes, it's the sex thing."

Emily sucked her lips in.

"Don't say it…" I said.

"You know there's a way to change that…"

"'You know there's a way to change that!'" I mocked. "You know coming out'd change *everything*, you know."

"I think you're being a tiny bit dramatic."

"I don't know."

"Well like. Alternately, it's not like absolutely everyone's getting laid."

"Seems like it… Joshi was making out with two girls. At once. Our little Joshi! Meanwhile, I'm in this dead zone—"

Emily groaned. "Oh shut up! You'd have to fight to keep people off of you— Oh wait. You already do! I see you distancing yourself from everyone trying to get down your pants."

"They might unclip my dick trying to get at it…" I said. "And then it'll fall on the floor, so I'll have to go rinse it off, and by then the mood's probably gone… so."

"I'm not saying you have to broadcast it… I'm just saying you know. Maybe start with — you know — the people who matter. To you." She cleared her throat.

I squinted and looked at her with my head tilted back. "What did you do…?"

"I…" Emily bobbed her head. "I may have been testing the waters with the others."

I dug my fingers into my hair and *lsdkfjalsdkfjlkjdshfa—*

"Hey, hey! It's not like I went to them like 'herp-dee-derp Luca's…'" Emily looked around, we weren't really in private. "Yeah. But like— They're cool with all gender stuff. Well, Branden doesn't really get non-binary but we're making progress on him!"

"Emily!" I got close. "This is *my* closet, okay?"

"Yes. Yes, you'r right. But. Don't you think you'd feel better if you…" She gestured. "…Opened up just a little?"

"Fuckin' maybe? I'm fine where I am."

"Oh yeah!" She rolled her eyes. "Seems like it."

"Ugh."

"Look. Everyone's here. Kaleb's on cuddle-probation because Aura's on her period—"

"Gross—"

"I'm SORRY, but we're living in an era of holographic dead celebrities, and we can't openly talk about mensuration?"

"Okay, frig. Sorry."

"So like." Emily got hr phone out. "Everyone's here. Everyone's having a great time. Let's do it now."

"Let's?"

"Everyone involved. We're part of your life, bro! Just come out. Get it over with. We can even just keep it in the circle, right? Safe space rules apply!" Emily smiled. She... honestly thought that it would be fine. I could tell that *she* knew it would be fine. But that was 'fine' by her standards. "And then we can all leave and get ice cream, and you can finally cry in front of other people."

"Emily!" I said, pushing her arm down. "Stop..."

For a second, Emily looked worried. Then she rolled her eyes and put her phone down. "Okay. I may be a little drunk. Sorry for..."

"It's fine. I just—"

"But please-please-please-please, Luca..." She sighed. "Don't come out to some pretty, popular Japanese girl who wants to shag you to climb a social ladder before you come out to your actual friends.

"I'll think about it," I said, letting my eyes wander. "But like... Can I ask... why does it matter to you so much?"

"Because I really really want you to get laid, so you'll stop complaining about it."

But I didn't hear her and kept staring off into nowhere. Over the privacy fences, it looked like someone was shining a flashlight in the dark second floor next door. What time was it? Why were there no cars in that driveway?

"Because like... maybe I wanna get laid too. But I can't because I have to follow you around massaging your man-feelings." She said. "That... was a joke. You okay?"

"Huh? Yeah. I just need to take a leak."

CHAPTER 28
DOING IT ALL

Friday, October 27

But no, seriously, I did have to pee.

I had to go upstairs because it sounded like someone was puking in the downstairs bathroom. The second-story bathroom had a great view of the house next door . I turned off the lights to get a clear view into the neighboring darkness. Someone was going around, room to room, with a flashlight. Oh no…

What did I just say about goddamn home invasions?

I pulled off bits and pieces of my costume as I made my way to the coat closet. My heart was beating in my throat… Nothing like crime-fighting to turn a bummer night around!

I bumped into a very drunk Branden. "Oh! Hey man," I said.

"Hey…" He punched my shoulder. "Hey bro."

"Hey… Bro!"

He put his weight on the wall and slid towards me. I caught him before he fell over. "Hey bro…" He giggled. "Where ya goin'?"

"Oh, just… just out for a minute."

He looked at me with a raised eyebrow. "Where ya been all night anyway? You got somewhere better to be?"

"Nah just need some—"

"I know!" He poked at my chest. "You're going to go make out with Londyn again."

"He-heh… No."

"Then who ya gonna go make out with?"

"No one… I just gotta go—"

He leaned in and pressed his mouth on mine. Eyes closed. Open mouth. Lips mashing. Tongue- wrestling. He tasted like craft beer and orgasm.

So... I kinda went with it. He put his hands on my arms, got in real close-like. He was a little sweaty. I had to crane my head up because he was really big... Real top-shelf gentle giant big. I felt him push closer.

Like... this wasn't just a drunken bro-kiss... (Which happened more than you'd think while away for sporting events.) He was dating Meghan and all. But like... I didn't expect him to be like... into dudes.

Not that I was complaining.

And then it ended and we were both kinda there and my hands were on his body and he was burning up and he was breathing really hard and I was breathing really hard and he had these shoulders and an arm that was leaning against the wall and he was way tall and he had his other hand cupping my ass and—

Holy shit.

I pulled away. "Alright," I said, finally. He had his eyes half-open, goofy-grinned. "Uh yeah. So, we're gonna put a pin in that for now. But I do kinda have to step out."

"'Cus like... you're really hot, right? Like really hot..." He stood up, biting on his bottom lip.

"Heh-heh... Yeah..." I cleared my throat.

"Oh! Yeah, for sure," he said, running his knuckle along my jaw. "You uh... you gonna be long?"

CHAPTER 29
HERE FOR A GOOD TIME

Friday, October 27

I seriously considered skipping the whole robbery thing to see what would happen with Branden... but I guess we could pick up where we left off when the cops took over.

Ooh...

Ooh!

I'd always thought of Branden as being a little bit in his shell. Wound up tight like a clam. Though like... flashback to all the obvious displays of affection that I kinda brushed off as just being a bro, and always hugging, and touching, and yeah...

This had been going on for a while.

I got to my senses long enough to text Emily. Told her to call the cops, just in case.

How could I not have seen it?

My head was swimming... was he into dudes, or did he only like me? Specifically me? Kind of like I was an exception to straightness?

I forgot to tap send. I tapped the send button.

(Flashback to Brandon's tongue. I never knew that tongues could be so... forceful like that.)

Maybe he just liked kissing? Straight girls kissed other straight girls when they were drunk. Maybe Branden was that kind of guy? Which like... I'd love to live in that kind of world. We already had bro cuddling — was this the future liberals wanted?

Suddenly, I found myself in the shadows of the neighbors' house. What was the name on the mailbox? Stutton?

The Stuttons. Yep.

This was the Stutton's house. The Stuttons were being robbed. A burglar in the Stutton residence. Just saying... You could have chiseled marble with Branden's nipples—

Tom: *'Damnit, Luca, FOCUS!'*

Right. The Stuttons.

One of the basement windows was open with the screen punched out and a little magnet over the alarm sensor. This was how he got in... now I just had to cover the exit to make sure he didn't leave before the cops got here.

But I realized he'd been in there for a while. And I felt like I needed to resolve the whole Branden thing ASAP... So I snuck in behind him, through the basement, just to keep an eye on him.

I made my way up to the main floor quietly and could hear someone rummaging around upstairs. He wasn't exactly making an effort to be quiet, not with the homeowners away, and bass from next-door cut through the walls.

As I looked up the stairway, there was a thundering knock at the door. "SFPD!"

I sighed. Goddamn, they got here fast. There must have been a cruiser in the neighborhood. My first step was leaving through the basement and then pretending like nothing had ever happened. Not 100% legal or ethical but... you know... mistakes get made?

That would have been a great idea, but then I heard a window open upstairs. Trying to escape out the back?

Now, because I was great at making decisions, I decided that he wasn't going to get away that easy. I bolted back downstairs, not giving much care to the racket I was making. He had a leg up on me, so I had to close the gap. I jumped through the basement window and lifted myself up to the patio.

This guy was already hopping the fence, into the trees and down a slope leading to the street below. I headed for the fence when—

"Hold it!" the officer shouted. "Hands behind your head! Now!"

—*record scratch*—

So this was a strange situation.

Let me explain.

On the one hand, I could peacefully comply. I would be arrested and Dad would spend the next few weeks of his life convincing the police that I'm innocent. Can't imagine they would actually believe me and go after the actual burglar.

But if I could get the actual burglar... I'd be free and clear! Maybe even get a medal. I... think.

So. There I was, running from a cop with a pistol pointed at me—

"Stop—"

Just as I swept myself over the fence, she fired two rounds that splintered the wood. *Jesus...* Trigger happy, a little? Everyone started screaming next door. Open fire! In a residential zone!

I hit the ground running. Bit of a slope but nothing I couldn't handle. It was dark though so I had to watch my step. I was a better athlete than Mr. Burglar so I gained a lot of ground on him before we ran across the next street over.

He was slipping between two houses.

Sirens were approaching.

I hopped on an upturned garbage can and launched myself clean over a fence, cutting the distance between us in half.

I caught up and grabbed his backpack, tossing us both down to the ground.

Hopefully, nothing was breakable.

Please let nothing be breakable...

He lunged for the backpack, but I lurched forward and stuck my leg between his feet. While he stumbled, I pushed myself up and tackled him down again. Straddling his chest, I decked his face before he pushed me off.

He tried to make a run for it, but I grabbed his pant leg. Before he even got up, the street lit up with red and blue lights.

"Hands on your head!" Officer Trigger Happy demanded and then repeated it when I didn't immediately do what they said. But louder and with profanity. They seemed to be more focused on me than the other guy...

I looked down at myself, at my meticulously detailed Halloween costume. An unlicensed vigil I had a man-crush on.

"Goddamnit" I mumbled.

"On the ground!" The angry one called back.

And then, before you know it, I was spread across the hood of a police cruiser. My cheek uncomfortably pushed into the hood, I couldn't help wonder if the other guy was getting a kick out of this. They twisted my arms and double-cuffed me.

When it came to unknown, Rogue Vigils, cops always treated them like they were post-human until proven otherwise. But for those of us without super-powers, it was just very uncomfortable. I should have probably just felt lucky that they didn't shoot me on sight.

Oh wait. They already tried that.

CHAPTER 30
WAITING GAME

Friday, October 27

Let's be honest.

This probably would have gone worse if I wasn't white.

I smirked for my headshot (good picture). The officers got a bit... funny with me after they put my name into the system. I'm not gonna say why but... you know why.

I'm sure some of you might be wondering why my name is even in the system. Me? Problems with authority? I have no idea what you're talking about!

No really, my first three years in San Francisco were spent in and out of the back seats of police cruisers. But then I cleaned up my act and legalized my name. Funny how both those things happened at about the same time...

If we're being real, then I think getting stuck in the men's lockup would have been the most gender-affirming thing of the night. But I was underage and initially suspected of having super-strength or being telepathic or something, so I got dropped off in an empty interrogation room.

And they left me there to cook... spending the whole time regretting my decision to not smash with Brandon... before I even got the chance to call Tom who... Well it wasn't the first time I'd called him from a police station.

"Hey Tom..."

"...What happened."

"I maybe got in a bit of trouble—"

I heard him suck in a deep breath, and I briefly explained the situation to him.

"Oh," he said.

"Yeah."

"You okay, though?"

"Yep."

"Well. Your dad landed as of five minutes ago."

"Oh. Good timing."

"Oh!" he said. "He'll absolutely agree. Totally."

Tom had always been my go-to contact when I had police run-ins. He was easier to get a hold of and was always better at getting in touch with Dad than I was. And like... He always seemed much less disappointed in me for getting picked up. He didn't like the cops anyway. It was a great buffer!

But... I was still gonna have this out with Dad.

He was my lawyer, after all.

Ugh. I could be having sex in a guest bedroom right now.

CHAPTER 31
WHO'S A GOOD COP?

Friday, October 27

Eventually, they did send someone to 'check in' on me.

The officer seemed 'nice' enough, but I kept tight-lipped. He even promised he wasn't going to try and make me say something incriminating. I'm paraphrasing. Cops would never admit that they're just trying to get you to say self-incriminating stuff.

Haven't you heard? They're actually trying to get to the bottom of helping the community and definitely not out to make any arrest for any reason they could possibly find. Because pressing charges on a minor, apparently, was great for a career bump.

I couldn't get the possibility out of my head that I would be spending the night here. I was horny, and angsty, and... horny...

And this officer wouldn't get off my case.

"You hungry?" Was the first thing Officer Twink said to me when he sat down at the table. "Need anything?"

Like... I would have loved a painkiller to nip this headache in the bud... It was gonna be a migraine night. But taking a prescription pain killer in front of the cops would probably get me off on the wrong foot.

"So..." he said, "Your name's Luca?"

I shrugged. "Is that what my Lawyer said? You'd have to ask him."

He didn't acknowledge that. "Sounds very European. I've always liked names like that."

"Thanks, I chose it myself," I said. He wasn't sure how to respond.

"Well, I think... you did a good job. Good choice."

I shrugged.

He pushed my folder aside and leaned forward with his right shoulder over the table. "I wasn't much into parties when I was your age. You're probably a lot cooler than I was." He smiled. "So... cool kids at costume parties. Man... Halloween never looked *that* fun when I was your age."

I sighed, made it look like I was going to say something meaningful to get his hopes up. "Can't really remember. I think my Lawyer could jog my memory, you know?"

He nearly rolled his eyes. Not the best poker face.

Here's some advice, kids. If you're ever being questioned by a police officer, you don't have to say a damn thing. In fact, you probably shouldn't. It's one of your literal rights as an American citizen.

You know when they say you have the right to remain silent? And that everything you say can and will be used against you? They say it like it's a threat, but it's actually a warning.

Legally, they can't force you to say anything. In the criminal justice system, they are permitted to take anything you say out of context. (It can be used against you.) It doesn't matter what you say, they'll spin it. (It will be used against you.)

The only thing you should say is 'I want my lawyer.' Even if it's a public defender. This is all in theory... There are a whole lot of 'ifs' when it comes to how this works in practice.

— — —

The worst part was being phoneless. But that might have been for the best because I'm sure I was the talk of the school at this point. Like... the central character in one of those high school myths that would hang around for years after I graduated.

Officer Twink decided I was a dead end and left me alone to cook some more. Dad was taking a while to get here... but I wasn't about to hold it against him. I didn't even want to begin to think about all the ways this was interrupting his evening plans.

By the time I saw shadows in the door's window, I figured I was going to get the 'bad cop' routine next. But Officer Twink opened the door and held it open for Dad. Sorry. Not Dad. Super Attorney.

Super Attorney wore a tailored charcoal suit — he liked Italian cuts because they made his shoulders look intimidating. He kept his hair feathered to the side, and wore narrow, silver glasses. Funny how you'd never see Super Attorney and Andrew Wexler in the same room together...

And trying to get a read on Dad while he was like this was way outside my pool of skills and talents.

Officer Twink (okay his name was Morgans) had given Dad the run-down on what they knew. Apparently, the police had taken my headshot around the whole party to try and suss out a story. Which... was totally aces that everyone in every high school from Moscone to George Washington knew I was in police custody.

The idea was that I'd been sent over on some kind of drunken dare, and the rest was a coincidence.

"I need a moment with my client," said Dad.

Officer Twink nodded. "Alright. Take your time." And he left.

I looked at Dad in the mirror window. "So... How was your trip?"

"Oh boy..." he said with a sigh. "How on Earth did you find yourself here?"

I thought for a minute and decided it would be best to tell it like it happened. Instead of one of the couple other stories I'd thought up since I got here.

Dad sat silently and nodded when I finished. "Alright. Bad news: that does fit the vigilantism bill better. May have been best to go with a dare from a drunken friend who may not remember giving it to you."

"Kaleb would take the fall," I said.

Dad sucked in a breath through his nose.

"What? We have a pact!"

He paused. "That said, you did the right thing: by calling the cops. You should have gotten confirmation that it was supposed to be empty." He sighed. "Why'd you go in, Champ?"

I shrugged. "We could tell them I was being a concerned citizen?"

"Already have. But what I'm asking is: why did Luca..." he poked my chest, "go in the house?"

I shrugged. "Same answer?"

Dad dragged his hands down his face. "I need you to repeat after me... 'I have nothing to live up to.' Can you say that, please?"

I sighed. "I have nothing to live up to."

"Now do you mean it?"

I couldn't say anything.

"You've got... *so* much going for you," he said. "You've got sports and some really great friends. And... sports. And somehow you managed to learn half a dozen languages — which. You really don't give yourself enough credit for that."

"Oh, believe me I do."

Dad snorted, then got serious again. "But..."

"But...?"

"I know what's on your mind." Dad looked at the two-way mirror. "And I know Tom enough to know what he wants to do. And... your body, your choice. Only... No, that's... That's a very hard choice, Luca. It's a very dangerous choice Luca, and I would like you to make... almost literally any other choice. But... It's not my choice." Dad put both hands on my shoulders. "Just... please be a kid for a while longer. Just focus on being young? I didn't... and... and it messed me up real bad."

"We've talked about it—"

"No," Dad said. "No we haven't actually."

"So…" I said after a pause. "You gonna tell me about it? Or. Wait. Not until I'm older, right?"

"No," Dad said, getting his unreadable wall back up. "Not until *I'm* older."

CHAPTER 32
ANGRY > 'DISAPPOINTED'

Friday, October 27

Tom was at our place by the time we got home, and by then I was having a full-on migraine party. He and Dad exchanged helloes, and I went to the kitchen to heat up a leftover piece of pie. Dad slipped into the kitchen so quiet I wouldn't have heard him if it wasn't for Lillie on his heels.

"Did you take any codeine? Imitrex?"

"No yellows. And I'm not taking the... Those other ones."

Dad reached into his pocket and took out a small bottle of round, yellow pills. I didn't let on that I saw.

He paused. "Hey! Look at me."

I whined and scowled.

He held out the bottle. "Take one, please."

"I'll ride it out, it's fine."

"Luca…"

"Yeah, I don't want to spend the next two days backed up. These are constipation pills with pain-blockers as a side-effect."

"Great that you don't have anything athletic going on until March, then."

Dad and I held our ground for a second. I groaned and held my hand out. I choked one back and chased it with a glass of water. Got my slice of pie and made my way upstairs with Zero.

"Night Dad. Night other Dad."

"Night, Champ," said Dad.

"Night, Kid," said Tom.

I could only imagine what Dad and Tom would have to talk

about. Hopefully, Tom would steer the conversation clear of talking about me and my 'problems.' Dad seemed like he wanted to avoid the conversation anyway.

This whole thing seemed to bring out something strange in Dad... at least something I hadn't seen before. It wasn't just the normal, typical parental concern. His hand was shaking when he handed me the bottle. The whole time I'd been reading him like he was mega pissed. But that wasn't it, after all.

CHAPTER 33
HANGOVER

Saturday, October 28

I barely slept that night. Even less than normal. I'd wake up now and then, and then fall asleep for another twenty minutes. Hard to fall asleep with a migraine, and this one wasn't going away.

My doctor had said that it was a side-effect from the testosterone, but I *swear* I was getting them long before I was on T.

But it might not have been just the headache keeping me up — I kept waking up from dreams.

I saw the police officers who'd been in the station. I saw their families; what their nightly routines were like. I saw things from their eyes. I thought like they did… but I couldn't remember much about it.

But I kept seeing someone… the same person in all of the dreams. She blended in like she belonged there. It wasn't even something I noticed until I was awake and thinking about it. And when I thought back, I couldn't remember what she looked like. Only that she was there.

Must have been nerves.

I knew part of it was the wall of… everything I saw on my phone when I finally got around to checking it. Over 200 notifications, including text messages, tweets, mentions, snaps, Instagram photos of the crime scene, and live streams of panicking classmates wondering what was going on. My mugshot was plastered everywhere.

At least with the dirt on my face, the grass stains, the scuff on my lip, and my hair full of twigs, I got that gruff, masculine look I wanted. Text messages from Emily, Kaleb, Aura... a lot from Branden. Londyn. And like... everyone.

Before I went to bed I'd sent Emily a text saying that everything was good, and then ignored anything incoming. I didn't need that while my brain was trying to Xenomorph itself out through my eyes.

Hulbry had posted on the school's Twitter feed, asking students to refrain from gossiping about students involved in criminal investigations. While she didn't officially run the school's social media, I always read the tweets in her voice anyway.

I'd probably hear from her come Monday. Ugh. Still though... I liked the mug shot... It'd probably be my profile picture for a while.

— — —

6:30 AM.

I laid in bed for a little bit. Played with myself a little to see if that would get me snoozing — but it didn't. Yeah that was always a crapshoot. The way my cis-boys talked, it zonked them right out. Instead, I got up and made myself a smoothie. I felt exhausted and full of energy at the same time. Like there wasn't enough room in my brain. Like it was one of those rooms filled with balloons.

Since my Geography meet-up with Rook wasn't until 10 AM, I decided to take the dogs for a longer-than-normal run. Lillie hadn't been taken out for a marathon in ages, and I needed to clear my head. They got biscuits, I changed into workout clothes, and then we started running. About forty minutes later, we found ourselves at Mission Creek Park.

The three of us huffing and puffing, a break was best. After filling up a portable water bowl with a bottle of water I got from a vending machine, I sat down on the grass beside a cluster of trees, facing the water. I bent the rules a little and let Zero off leash so he could sniff around.

I know, I know. This was a leash-only city.

But Zero had never ever run off before. Even on hikes in the forest, he stuck to a solid ten-foot rule. Come squirrel or pigeon, he wouldn't budge. It took over a year before he would run for a frisbee without begging for permission. I wanted to find whoever broke him and punch them.

Lillie, though — you couldn't trust her. Ever. Even when she was being good. *Especially* when she was being good. I wrapped the leash around my ankle so I could stretch my hands out.

"Who's good bo-ooy?" I sang while I rubbed Zero's snout in my hands and then gave some love to Lillie. Which made Zero jealous so I had to give simultaneous snoot-rubs to both of them before I got bored and laid back. Lillie tugged at the leash and Zero just laid down with his head on my chest.

With my head in the grass, I looked up at the clouds. Still a little pink from the morning sun. Was this our own light? Or was it just second-hand light that had already washed across the rest of America?

Did we thrift our sunlight? Or did we just get everyone else's cast-offs?

— — —

And then I bolted up — damn near throwing Zero off me. I was panting. Lillie bounced, excited and yowling, pushing her head against my knees. I held my chest, almost like I was stuck in sleep paralysis.

I had some kind of dream, but I couldn't... It was about...

I... There was an explosion. I saw myself in a reflection? Water? Hands in water.

Ugh. It was gone.

I slammed back down into the grass. Zero nudged his face against mine for a little bit before he started to lick my cheek. Listening to my pulse pound in my ears, I wondered what I could have dreamt that spooked me so much.

Getting a hold of myself, I looked around. The sun was basically in the same place.

My phone said it was only 8:15 AM.

This was going to be a long day...

CHAPTER 34
SHUT UP AND FLASH DRIVE

Saturday, October 28

The dogs started tugging before my house was in view. Surprise-surprise, Emily was waiting on the front steps on her phone.

"Don't you hate mornings? Shouldn't you be hung over?" I asked, letting the dogs go.

"Hello babies!" Emily said, letting them lick her face. "Ooh! Who doesn't get enough love? Who doesn't get enough *love* from their mean, old daddies?"

"Hi?" I said.

"And I'm sorry that I'm *bothering* you," she said. "However... as you may have forgotten, you were literally arrested last night — which is not a doubt in anyone's mind because your headshot is now your profile picture."

"Looks good, right?"

"You totally killed it — that's absolutely not the question though," she said. "Because some of us are worried about you and want to make sure you're okay."

I sighed. "You want to check the flash drive."

"You know... I woke up and saw you posted on instagram and I started thinking about it and I couldn't get back to sleep." She stood up. "Took your sweet time getting here. Come on, I've got some ideas."

I let Emily in and took the dogs around the back for any last-minute bathroom breaks, and then came in through the sliding door into the kitchen. "You want anything to eat?" I asked, fully aware that Emily had already helped herself to a bowl of cereal.

"This is kinda stale," she said. "It's like there's fitness freak teenager living here who keeps everyone on a fascist diet plan."

"Huh."

"You should be glad I'm around." *Crunch.* "Eat up all this junk food before it goes bad."

"Come on, let's get this done."

"Jesus. Don't sound so enthused."

"I wanna get to it before dad wakes up," I said. "No way there's an easy way to explain this."

"Oh! Your Dad left when I was on the steps."

"What?"

"Yeah he left with Tom."

"Ugh. They're probably going to meet Holly for breakfast or something."

"Wait what?"

"Didn't even invite me," I said.

"Holly Rolland?" Emily sighed loudly. "Why didn't he invite *me*? Holly Rolland: AK-fucking-A Flechette? Icon? Aspiration? Legend? And like. Just doesn't even ask if *maybe* I wanna meet her. He knows I'm a fan right?"

"You've met her before! Like... every other time she's down here."

"And yet, you still haven't gotten me an autograph."

"Ask her yourself!"

"Uh... I know she doesn't 'do' autographs, dummy. I'm just some rando fan, but you could actually get one for me." She shook her head. "None of my extended family actually believes I'm proxy-friends with Flechette... No big deal, real casual-like."

Emily was cool to chill out on her phone while I took a quick shower and brushed my teeth. I was still drying my hair with a towel when I got back to my room. "Did you see Tom?" I asked.

"Yeah. Said hi," she took a seat in my computer chair. "Still not talking?"

"I called him from the police station," I said. "Other than that, not really. Probably best I wasn't here. He'd only say I was throwing a fit and avoiding him."

She looked confused. "But… you *are* throwing a fit and avoiding him."

"No, I'm not."

Emily scoffed. "Maybe not anymore, but it was kind of a fit."

"Was not…" I shook my head to force the water out of my ear.

"It… he said 'no' to you and you didn't take it great." Emily hung her head off the side of the bed.

"You were totally encouraging me to stay out!"

"Yeah, but the whole reason you were out in the first place is 'cause your delicate masculinity couldn't handle rejection. Or authority figures."

I tossed the towel at her. "I've gone through hell for this fragile masculinity. Don't you take it away from me."

"I wasn't judging." She pushed herself up and grabbed my junker laptop from under my nightstand. Plugging it in, she flipped it open to the boot-up screen. "We've got some fun toys to play with because of it."

"I don't know what you expect to find that wouldn't have been there before," I said. "But sure, help yourself."

"I wasn't asking for your permission. I co-built this!"

This machine was a combination of Dad's old computer and some spare parts I 'bought.' (Stole from a bin of discarded parts at a computer store). Emily, Joshi, and me spent a week in the summer working on it so we could go on the dark web without being tracked.

Everyone thought that deep web access meant super-hacker. But really, all you had to do was download TOR and watch where you go. There was a piece of red duct tape over the webcam, and we ripped out the microphone. Aside from that, it was basically just where I stuffed all my porn.

"A fresh perspective can make all the difference," Emily said... just before the background lit up of two muscle-hunky men making out with their faces pressed in a set of massive tits. Her fingers reeled from the keyboard. "Do I need to disinfect this?" Before I could answer, she'd already grabbed some hand sanitizer from her bag.

"It was fine..."

"I don't trust your qualification of 'fine,'" she said. "Gross..."

When she plugged in the USB stick, I stopped paying attention. I took selfies with my dogs and put them on Instagram.

"When's your Dad coming home anyway?" she asked, clicking around on the trackpad.

"Friday," I said. "Tentative." Dad's itinerary had changed at least twice a day.

"I thought he was back?"

"Nope."

She laid back. "Does that bother you? Being alone. It would drive me crazy."

"Well, you're always with me," I said with a dry sigh, "so I'm not bored."

"I suppose you can't do much better than me, as far as friends go. I don't think I'd live without my Dad around though."

"Not your mom?"

"Don't get me wrong I admire my mother. But she's more like... a distant, commanding admiral in stilettos. Dad's the teddy bear."

"So how's that investigation going?" I asked, coming under the urgent need to switch the topic. "Solve the whole thing?"

Emily shot me a glare and looked back at the screen.

"What's your deal with the Gentleman?" I asked. "You used to be a fan."

"Bitch, I still might be..."

"No really, what's your angle?"

"He's getting people to pay attention to him. White people are *talking* about gentrification. Renter's rights are trendy all of the sudden because he's making it a pageant."

"Right... I feel as if there's a 'but' after that..."

Emily sighed. "I guess a little bit of corporate espionage is alright. But... What you saw... coercing people into it? And blackmailing post-humans to work for him? Someone who actually does stuff like that can't have the best of intentions."

"Well, what's it matter?" I asked. "I don't know why you're so conflicted..."

"You can't make an omelet without breaking eggs, no." Emily paused. "But like... you want to enter into a discussion about how many eggs is too many?" She paused again. "Some people don't really have the time for that debate... But it's probably best to figure out how many eggs the Gentleman is actually cracking open before we figure out if it's worth it."

"It's... really hot..." I said.

"And that's another thing! Social justice is really hot right now. We've gotta make sure the Gentleman isn't just some corporatist who's slapping a pro-cause brand on himself so he can... do something nefarious."

"Sure. But no, the *computer's* hot."

"Oh..." said Emily. "Wait, what were you running?"

"Nothing..."

She put my hand under it. "Ow... Why isn't the fan on?"

I made a few attempts to remember how to bring up the console commands to turn on the fan. "Well the fan works—" The fan turned off. "Or whatever."

Emily brought up the CPU usage monitor. "1617.0719-18-percent CPU capacity... That's not normal, right?"

"Doesn't seem normal, no."

CHAPTER 35
FEELING THE HEAT

Saturday, October 28

"How did we not notice it turning into a hot plate the other times?" I asked.

"Because we had it on a table."

"Well was it like that when we plugged the stick in before?"

"No…" I twisted my mouth. "I don't think? I didn't grope it."

Pushing my desk-clutter to the side, I set the computer on an ice pack I got from the freezer. It helped… but didn't really explain why the fan wasn't going. Or why the fan stopped when I did get it going.

"Weird…"

For some reason, the CPU was a solid block of red — over-capacity and confusing. But stock programs opened fine. Minesweeper, Internet Explorer, notepad. But when we tried opening TOR, it took five minutes, and a window hadn't even opened.

We took turns suggesting ideas, trying to figure out why it was doing this. "It's… trying to search for an internet connection" Emily showed me the terminal line.

"What? That's it?"

"Yeah," she said, "It's trying really hard to sign on to a network."

"Joshi took out the Wifi card, remember?"

She huffed. "Why is it even trying to sign on to the internet? Even if this was a modern operating system, it wouldn't be killing itself trying to connect, would it?"

I was out of my depth, but after she gave it a second, Emily populated the terminal window with a list of running commands.

Suddenly, there was a wall of thousands of attempts to log into a network. Each attempt was also trying to decode a password. And that was happening once every few seconds. The commands just kept coming.

Scrolling up to the top, I saw that this started the second we plugged in the flash drive. And then everything on the computer got copied and packaged up into zipped files.

…There weren't exactly any corporate secrets on here anyway. If the Gentleman wanted all my porns, he could ask me himself like a normal human being.

Emily searched for these zip files, and found them in a folder titled 'Ask the Local Gentry'… hidden in a maze of over sixty sub-folders… in a hidden directory on the D: drive, named 'Last Stand for Chivalry.'

Each one had a proper name: 'The Pestilence; The Soothsayer,' 'Sylvan Trees go Marching,' 'Lark Eggs in the Brush We Cut Down', 'Five Black Eyes of the Fates,' and other weird-ass things like that. Sounded like a bunch of 80's heavy metal albums.

Most of them had folder-chains that always lead to nowhere.

When we unplugged the flash drive, the commands stopped, erased themselves, and the folders and zipped files disappeared.

"Freaky…" I said.

"Isn't this why Tom hates computers?"

"It's more about… like. Robots in general."

"So…" she said. "It's packing up all that data… and it's trying to get online so it can send that data somewhere… And by coincidence, The Gentleman mysteriously manages to get his hands on copious amounts of corporate data."

"So he uses this Trojan horse thingy…?"

"Right." She leaned back. "But if it's sending the information out there somewhere, isn't there a way to track where it's being sent to? A link has to be made."

I thought for a minute. "Mr. Parks put up a tutorial for how to track IP addresses…"

"And you think the Gentleman would just be online without bouncing his address around the world a few times?" Emily said. "Then again, he seems to be moving a massive amount of information… Could be worth a shot… but you realize if you connect this here, the Gentleman is gonna know where you live?"

"Could do it at a public spot," I said, and held down the power button to turn it off.

"Okay great! I know *just* the place we could test that out—"

"Oh! No, I can't right now."

"What? Why not?"

"I've got a homework meet-up with Rook in a bit and I should head out to find the place."

"Ugh!" Emily leaned back. "I don't get to meet Holly Rolland and you're not letting me hunt down a social justice warrior who brings 'hacktivism' to a whole new level. You *never* take me anywhere nice."

CHAPTER 36
COMMAND

Saturday, October 28

Rook and I were planning to meet in a coffee shop just off New Montgomery. I was going to be pretty early, but I could use the time to clear my head and eat.

When I went to grab my wallet from my computer bag, my fingers slipped along the chrome surface of the flash drive.

And well... I did have my junker with me. Oops. Must not have been thinking when I deliberately slid this twenty-pound dinosaur-computer into my bag, completely aware that I was going to be on a public Wi-Fi network. And I just *happened* to pack my wifi stick. Silly me, right?

Would Emily be pissed that I was doing this without her? Sure but... honestly I just wanted to take a quick look to see if there was anything worth getting my hopes up for. I set the computer on the glassy tabletop. Hopefully, there wouldn't be any overheating problems if it actually could connect to the internet... With my back to the wall, I fired it up.

I had the CPU tracker open, and a text command window. "Here goes..."

It took four tries to get the flash drive in the right way (don't judge me). The second it snapped in the CPU had a huge spike, and then down to nothing. I opened the drive in a window and it was suddenly full of those strange folders.

Text commands started appearing in the terminal. Something about sorting folders? Randomizing intake storage. But then it all erased itself. I got my phone out and started recording.

```
uploading…

PROGRESS: 8%

New Entry: unexpected file contents

New Entry: initial scan indicates
         unlikelihood of file significance.

New Entry: PLATFORM scan required.

Preliminary Scan: PLATFORM… drive: D:

Progression: … drive: C:

Observation: PLATFORM storage and processor
         capacity does not indicate any
         further tactical significance.


consulting Terminal…

…

accessing complex_command_matrix…

Downloading Execution List…
```

Why was code in plain English like this? That was the wrong language…

I kept recording.

```
New Entry: unknown PLATFORM

New Entry: unknown AFFILIATION

New Entry: scanning network

New Entry: public network access via local
         Wi-Fi

Network Ownership: Lazy Goat Café.

…

Operation: on-board analysis
```

There was a huge spike in the CPU for a few seconds while the fan kicked up like a rocket taking off. I guessed it wasn't trying to be subtle anymore.

```
Addendum: PLATFORM of insufficient computing
         power. Accessing off-site server.


pending...


New Entry: Private business. Owned and
         operated by Wendy Danielle
         Westworth.
New Line: Resident of San Francisco.
New Entry: PLATFORM unrelated to any known
         targets
New Entry: PLATFORM of no tactical
         significance


deduction_matrix Conclusion: UNIT suffered
         rogue acquisition.
levity_engine Interjection: To put it
         politely...
```

"It's telling jokes?" I whispered. What was it downloading? What was the 'Terminal'? None of this was how we'd learned normal computers worked in com-tech classes… Then again — normal memory sticks didn't just decide to log your computer online and gather your files. Probably not something you'd cover in a 100-level course.

And I'd never gotten a memory stick from stealing it off a corporate espionage squad.

Sucked that I wouldn't get extra credit for this…

```
Logging…
New Entry: analysis of rogue anomaly may
         yield counter-insurgency data
New Entry: approval of data analysis pending
         terminal command
```

I was sweating under my collar. The computer… or whatever—whoever— was thinking fast. Each command… Each line was entered in clusters. Terminal… the information was being uploaded somewhere off-site.

```
New Entry: data transfer approv#>g@#m$
New Entry:
New Entry: upload complete
Consulting deduction_matrix: …
…
```

Was the flash drive some kind of Trojan Horse? Did that mean there was someone on the other end? If I had to guess… The Gentleman? Definitely someone who worked with him, for sure. Or was it just a really… snarky program?

```
Conclusion: user commands on PLATFORM attempt
         to interfere with operations
New Entry: accessing resources to determine
         interloper identity…
```

I scanned the room again. Whoever was using the flash drive on the other end had no idea I was watching the command terminal. They were scanning my computer; they were downloading their files.

By then I figured it was time to see if Mr. Park's ten-minute reverse DNS tracking lesson could out-smart a super hacker.

Reverse DNS tracking is basically watching someone whose watching your computer without them knowing. The FBI hate it.

I opened a second window and started typing in a line of code when…

The other terminal window went black. I entered line after line of commands anyway. My mouth was open, my tongue was dry. My eyes darted around—

Rook just walked in. Damnit. My computer was so slow… So much of the network bandwidth was occupied with the flash drive's uplink that my commands were only trickling through. I smiled at Rook when he spotted me.

"No, no, not yet…" I whispered to myself.

Rook twisted his way around the line in front of the counter, seeming a little out of place. My face went cold.

The text window reset again.

```
New Entry: DIRECTOR-2 Commandeering
           Operations
Pending…
```

Shit. My own command window stopped taking my commands. "Pending…" appeared there too.

I hoped that it was thinking and not just frozen. But then just as Rook sat down, another few lines populated in the original window. Before I slammed my laptop shut, all I saw was that there were a bunch of numbers. I yanked out the wifi stick. "Hey!" I said, a little breathy. Too quickly. I think my cheeks were a bit numb.

Rook looked concerned. "Are… you okay?"

"Yeah? Fine!" I smiled. Feeling the hairs on my neck settle down, my collar was suddenly cold with dry sweat. My hands were shaking.

"What were you up to?" He said, suspiciously.

"Just... ah... Trying to fix my computer." He looked at my phone, propped up and still recording. "I'm... recording this for the... computer place. So they can see. I'll delete you out of it, don't worry."

"Okay... that's fine."

"It was a pornado," I said.

"A what?"

"A pornado. When you're on the internet and then just... seventy porn windows show up?"

He looked blankly. "Ah... well now I can... put a name to the phenomenon."

"My fault for not having this thing virus protected. But it's a junker computer so I don't really care. I'll wipe the hard drive tonight."

"Did you like... build it yourself?" Rook got his own, pristine laptop out. Latest model.

"I did with Emily and Joshi," I said.

Rook nodded. "Joshi seems cool. Wouldn't peg him as much of a computer guy though."

"He's not, really," I said. "We just wanted to check out the dark web, and between the three of us, we had enough spare parts lying around to make this."

"Emily invited me to the party last night..." Rook said.

"Why didn't you show up?"

"Not big into costumes," He said. "Not very crafty."

I snorted. "Most people just buy a pre-made one, that's not an excuse!"

"And like… I didn't get like… an invitation-invitation."

"Huh?"

"I didn't even know who was hosting…"

I looked at him sideways. "You think half the people on Instagram were invited by name?"

"I…" Rook shrugged. "I assumed?"

"No man. You just show up. Nobody's gonna check you at the door," I said. "If parties just aren't your thing…"

"I guess…?" Rook sighed. "Emily was super angry with her boyfriend though. She was saying."

"Yeah, Liam's a flake," I said. "I kinda turned off my phone after… Oh crap. You heard, right?"

Rook's eyes opened wide. "Heard… what?"

I rolled my eyes.

"Like. The police thing?" he said.

I nodded. "The police thing."

"I… wasn't gonna say anything. I assumed it's private…"

I put my elbows on the table and leaned towards Rook, my chin in my hands. "Ask away. I'm an open book."

Rook laughed. A little embarrassed, so he wasn't gonna ask about it. "No, it's… Alright, well." He took a breath. "I'm gonna like… Assume it's not true. I'm assuming, that is, anyway…" He cleared his throat. "That your dad didn't blackmail the DA to cover up a break-in assault?"

I whistled. "Is that what people are saying?"

He nodded, nervous about it. "That is what people are saying."

"Not a bad story."

"Not true?"

I shrugged.

Truth be told, I was still kind of shaky from the computer stuff, and I wasn't sure if I was coming off as smooth as I wanted to. I probably would have thought of something better to say.

I hoped that the lid being shut meant the whole thing had gone inactive. A few times I reached down to feel the bottom of the laptop, and it seemed to be cooling off.

Also, I hoped that all the data had stayed up on the screen. Or that my phone wasn't too blurry to make out details.

After giving Rook an overview of what had happened with the police last night, we got to work. He had brought a small folder of blank papers, crayons, and a large history book of about fifty years of urban sprawl in America: 1945 to 1995.

We ate. We drank coffee. (Okay, he drank tea.) And we worked on our geography project until noon. All the while, a malicious computer program was trying to destroy my computer.

Good times.

CHAPTER 37
HOMEWORK PARTY

Saturday, October 28

Papers sprawled out over the table, many of them blank computer pages where we (Rook) had drawn concept cities. The plan was to use a real landmark in Oregon, and while I didn't like to boss Rook around, I had to put my foot down and pick one. He might've never decided otherwise.

He made rough outlines of the southern bank of the Columbia River. After that, we sketched out a rough historic district.

Alright, mostly him. But I was determined to make it look like I had something to bring to the table except for dashing good looks.

"Upon incurring tax breaks for computer hardware companies in the 80s, a new business district would be set up here." He pointed to the page we had worn down with mechanical pencils and eraser marks.

"I thought a residential district was going to go there. You know, a kind of East Egg waterfront thing," I said.

"You know the Eggs don't really exist right?"

"What? Great Gatsby says so."

He twisted his mouth and pushed up his glasses. "It's fictionalized."

"No way!"

"Yeah…" He smiled a little. "Kind of. Real place, fake names. Fitzgerald needed to cover his legal bases… but it ended up having some pretty cool symbolism."

"I am… severe shock! I've been to New York like… twice."

"Well, we can still have our 'Egg'. It's okay. We could even call it 'The Egg'. It would be a cool reference... if that's okay with you."

"I'd be down with that."

He twitched a smile. "I think we'd get bonus marks for incorporating a social history into the geographic layout. And we can move that over... here? Oh but that would cut into the commercial district... would have to move the stadium."

"Rich people don't like living *in* the city, you know."

"Guess not..." He thought for a second. "Oh! You're saying they can live out of the city, Like Malibu."

I finished off my second coffee. "Gotta say, I'm really into this... building a city as it evolved over time."

"Huh?"

"Like, you're even drafting multiple versions where roads got demolished and stuff," I said. "This is intense."

"I..." Rook's eyebrows dropped. "I didn't realize there was another way to do it..."

"Just... build the city as it is?"

"Oh..." Rook said. "Well then you just don't get the weird quirks that every city has. Like How Madison Square Gardens totally messed up traffic in Manhattan when it was specifically designed not to have traffic problems."

"Well... I watched Emily draw out her whole city in front of me."

Rook blushed. "Yeah... Emily's already told me her city's whole history. She's one of those super creative types and just has her entire city history memorized." Rook leaned closer. "She's working on bus routes and rival taxi companies!"

"Oooh..." I said. "Do I hear the sound of nerd-envy?"

Rook cleared his throat and sat back. "...Maybe."

After working for a few solid hours, keeping me interested on pencil lines was getting difficult. Rook, though, was a little bugged out from the lunchtime rush.

"You're a performer. I thought you'd be comfortable around people," I said.

"That's as a character though."

I nodded, pretending to get what he meant.

"We can keep working at my place though," he said.

"I'm easily distracted. Which means that I usually become the distraction."

He smiled. "I'm sure we'll manage some progress. I'd like to get the core layout done today. At least drafted. Can't start on the suburbs until then…"

CHAPTER 38
EGGHEADS

Saturday, October 28

You know those Bond Villain lairs? I'd just stepped into one.

Rook's apartment was almost like a loft, but way long and with rooms on the wings. The ceiling must have been at least fifteen feet high, with rafters running the width. Half the room was deco-style, the other half was more modern. A few walls jutted out to give a sense of division at weird angles and at varying heights.

The noir side had long, velvet curtains running the length of the windows. Mossy green with brass fixtures. There was an antique dining room set. Most of the table was covered in clutter. Against the windows, there was a display of about a dozen instruments.

The whole other side was just a glass wall. Everything was squared off, colored graphite and chrome.

"Shoes?" I said, my eyes gazing around.

"Just uhm… drop them wherever. By the door."

The excess of the apartment kind of overshadowed the clues that human beings actually lived there. Shoes were just a messy pile by the door. Jackets and sweaters hung over chairs all over the place.

Taking a quick glance into an office, I spotted Rook's dad. It was a mess of tables and sheets and laptops. Two giant TVs were mounted to the wall, and both of them had the screen split four ways, all global stock market charts.

He had smooth jazz playing from large speakers that covered up his mumbling and the squeaking of his dry-erase markers. Everything he wrote had a dollar sign in front of it and lots of zeroes after it.

Rook pulled the door shut. "Sorry, Dad's working. Can't break his train of thought. He'd wanted to meet you though."

"You talk about me?" I followed him to the kitchen.

"Well… yeah?" He got red. "I tell dad about how my day actually goes—"

"Does he want to know about the police stuff?"

Rook almost choked. "No… Um… probably don't mention it."

"Sounds like a plan.

"See… I don't usually talk about friends often. He already met Emily though so that's new."

I looked over. "She was over here?"

"Yeah, I missed a day last week. She dropped off some stuff."

"I was probably in detention then…"

"I think she mentioned that." Rook's eyes darted around. "I couldn't sleep for the whole night. I think I accidentally forgot to order decaf that afternoon—"

"Hey. We all skip school. It's no biggie."

"Right. Sorry." Rook rubbed the back of his head. "You and Emily are…?"

"Bros."

"What I mean to say—"

I snorted and leaned against the kitchen counter. "We're not a *thing*. Liam is still in the picture for some reason."

"Right."

"Not to make it sound like… I'm salty or anything. Full disclosure, we tried that." At the time, I figured someone who already knew I was trans was a shoe-in for dating. "Lasted about a week. Kissing was…" I scrunched up my face.

"So you're gay?"

"I'm whatever."

"Bi? Pan?"

I shrugged. "Non-committal."

"That's... kind of how it is with the theatre crowd..."

"Or the music crowd?" I gestured at a 'modest' collection of instruments arranged just beside the kitchen by the windows. There was a piano, and a cello, two violins, a guitar, an electric guitar, a bass signed by Paul McCartney, a keyboard, a trombone, a dented trumpet that was on a pedestal. There was a Celtic harp by the window, and a... was that a lute? In a glass display case. "Musical family?"

"Dad likes music. He can't play for sh... he can't play well." Rook said, tossing his stuff on a coffee-colored sofa.

I nodded. "I'm not exactly musical myself. Not really anymore." I took a step and looked over at Rook. "See, I had one of those... mega-structured childhoods."

"Structured?"

I plucked away at the cello. "Oh. Did gymnastics." (Mom wanted me to go into dance, I wanted to do boxing... Dad brokered a compromise.) "Piano, violin. I did Scouts for a little bit. Kept getting shipped off to summer camp." I paused and added under my breath, "Where I was someone else's problem."

"Sports camps?"

I took a moment. "Uh... yeah. Soccer. I guess."

"You guess?"

I chuckled and faced away. "Different city, a different life, you know?"

"Yeah." Rook nodded. "I uhh... I hate going to see my mom."

"Why's that?"

"Oh! Nothing against her! She's fantastic. But it's just..." He sighed heavily. "Beijing."

"Oh!"

Rook laughed. "I was born there."

"Oh, that's... far!"

"It's not comfortable there. Lived here since I was five and it's a bit of a culture shock going back... One time I went home and a cousin replaced the contents of my suitcase with bananas. My luggage got confiscated at the airport because there was a nest of spiders in one. I had a delay in Hawaii for two days in the same outfit," he said. "Still haven't gotten that stuff back yet. I was twelve. As far as divorce cases go, I'm a legal contract."

"I'm glad my folks' split ended up being a clean break." I huffed, with a bit more pride than I should have. Seemed like every child of a divorced set of parents was terrified of being the reason for the split. I enjoyed it.

"Don't see your dad anymore?"

I plopped down on the piano stool. "I live with my Dad."

"Right... you said that. Sorry."

"It's what everyone thinks. You have any idea how hard it was for him to get sole custody?"

Rook thought. "You don't see your mom at all?"

Oh shit oh shit oh shit. I'd never really got that deep into talking about *her* with anyone so I'd never thought of a non-pink-blanket-related reason for the divorce. "Uhh..."

There was a wave of upbeat jazz as the office burst open. "Hello boys!" Rook's father drifted into the room, his dress-shirt sleeves rolled up. Hair that had once been styled was now disheveled, going slightly grey on the sides. His glasses were propped up on his forehead. "How's the city coming along?"

"Great!" Rook said.

"You decided which landmark you're going to name after me?"

"Dad!"

"Mr. Wexler, I hope you don't mind but Rook has told me quite a bit about you!" He had a dusting of an accent. And honestly, it made him sound smarter.

I was surprised to see he was only a little taller than me. He was stacked with confidence and charisma. Next to Rook, who was both taller and squirrelier than him — I wouldn't have assumed they were related.

"You can call me Don. Don Lang," he said. "Donnie, also. Actually go with Donnie, when people call me Don it makes me sound like I'm the villain of an Italian Opera. Though if you're feeling ambitious you can call me Donghou. It's a family name, apparently, for generations. But that is a bit of a mouthful in these parts."

Handshake time! Loved this. And he had helluva shake. Like. I had a grip but he had that business-world practice going I guess. I had to flex my hand behind my back to stretch it out. "I'm usually told I'm too ambitious." I puffed up my chest a little.

"Too ambitious? No such thing in my experience." He warmly smiled. "Well... make yourself at home, make sure Rook plays a good host—"

"Yes, Father," Rook rolled his eyes, "I'm being nice to the guest."

"And respect your parents." Mr. Lang comically squinted and waved his finger. "Have fun, boys. And get some work done."

Over the next few hours, we did manage to get some work done, despite my best efforts.

— — —

While Rook was out of the room, I opened the laptop. Everything was frozen... I'd need to reformat it again.

But the IP address I was after was still stuck on the screen. I took another picture and closed it before Rook got back.

Not long after, Rook's dad came in. He looked a little nervous. "Alright, I'm sorry Luca, but something's come up and... I've got to head out for a bit. And Rook has some music lessons he needs to get to," he said.

"What?" Rook said. "But I wasn't supposed to—"

Don said something in Mandarin. He said it with a smile but I was picking up sinister vibes.

"Oh right!" Rook nodded after a second, then looked to me. "Yeah, sorry, I totally forgot. Uhh… can we pick this up during the week?"

I said "Sure" and Rook helped me pack up my things. He was nervous. Well, more nervous than normal. But I figured it was a good time to head out anyway. I had an IP address… now I needed to figure out what to do with it.

CHAPTER 39
CROSSOVER

Saturday, October 28

Emily's phone rang a few times before she picked up. "Where are you?"

"Street car."

"How pedestrian! No bike?"

"Tire's losing air again." I kept my voice hushed. "Long story, but I got an IP address off the flash drive."

"Jesus! Ask me to go to my room first before you drop stuff like that..." she said and closed a door. "Okay... What?"

"While I was out I... maybe plugged the flash drive in and tested it out."

"And you did get an IP address? I heard that right?"

"I got a video of the whole thing." I shuffled in my seat. "But I need you to look up the IP address."

"You wanna go in-vest-i-gate?" Emily asked. "What? Isn't your Dad home?"

"He drove to San Jose," I said. "He said not to expect him back tonight—"

"Yeah but what if he *does* come back?"

"I'll say we went to a movie or something," I said. "If you don't mind covering for me."

"You're acting like I'm not going to be helping you."

"Helping?"

"As in like. While you break, enter, and kick some ass?"

I sighed. "I don't want to make a scene... I just wanna look around. See what's up."

Emily gagged. "Where's your sense of adventure?"

"Hey look, I'm getting a weird feeling that whatever's going on is going to start getting... bad..."

"Bad?"

"Aside from the super-strong girl and the magical technology glove that thew me across a room?" I asked. "It's like— There's more to this. Something's going on... I can't explain."

Emily hummed. "Give me an hour. We'll meet at your place."

"An hour?" I whined. "You live down the street!"

"We wouldn't be headed out until after dark anyway!"

I sighed. "We?"

— — —

I'd already looked into the IP address by the time she let herself in. Lillie borked and went to her, Zero followed but came back when Emily got herself up the stairs. "Okay so— Oh..."

At the time I was shirtless and going through stretches in the middle of my room. "What's up?" I asked, folded at the waist and looking up at her from between my calves.

"Oh... That's..."

"Stretching."

"You know, you always brag about how flexible you are but I never really realized you were this..." she poked my butt cheek, "...limber— that is *taught*..."

"I don't skip leg day."

"Right. So um... lemme know when you're... done?"

"Done?" I stood up straight. "Why? Why do I need to be done?"

"Because that's making me uncomfortable," she said. "Seriously I did not need to know the human body was that flexible."

"I'm sure it'll come in handy," I said. "For sex reasons."

"Ew. Sex. Don't you know? Cool kids get *freaky* for Jesus."

"You're just mad you're probably not gonna find a man who can do that."

"Jee-eze. You don't gotta rub it in." She grinned devilishly and emptied the contents of her backpack on my bed. "But when you're done with your wine mom workout, it's time to get down to business!"

"To defeat... The Huns?"

"Stop it."

I took a look. "Cameras?"

"GoPros!" She said. "One for the front, one for the back. Dad's had these for ages. I figure we can cut holes in that sweater and then affix them to some of your dad's old armor? You think he'll notice if you get them too scuffed up?"

"It's hard to imagine them getting anymore scuffed up than they already are."

"Awesome. Figure we can get the off-brand night vision one on the back. Then link it up through a phone's Bluetooth. I've got an earpiece... here. That can be hardwired. We can live-stream it."

"We're not using my phone," I said, "That's one reason why this is a bad idea."

"Well—"

"On the off-chance that I'm being monitored, it will incriminate you. As an accomplice. You know."

"I thought of that!" She handed me an old phone with a cracked screen. "We'll use this. It's my almost-off-the-grid aunt's old phone. Pay-as-you go plan through this awkward Russian telecommunications company. I put some money on it — we've got about five hours worth of streaming data, with video quality at the lowest settings."

I looked over the stuff. Some wires and fixtures. We could definitely make it work. I looked to her. "We doin' this?"

"Oh son," she said, "we are."

CHAPTER 40
COMPLEX

Saturday, October 28

"Oh," I said.

"Oh…" Emily said. "This is—"

"Really close to home."

"Insanely."

"Check the address again?"

"Yep, this is it."

I cleared my throat. Emily took a breath.

350 Rhode Island Street. Even when we plugged it into Google Maps, it seemed like it would be a lot farther away than it was. When really, it was stuck between Potrero Hill and South Market. Like… literally a few blocks east of Moscone High.

"So like… we still doin' this?"

Emily thought for a second. "Not if you're getting cold feet."

"I don't get cold feet."

"You're just all… 'Rah, there's more going on!' 'Rah, this is close!' So I'm just like—"

"You agreed!" I said. "You also said it was—"

"I know, but you—"

"I'm fine! I was asking if you were fine."

"Doesn't sound like you're fine."

"I'm fine!"

We stopped to stare at the office building. Silence.

Emily looked at the map on her phone and the office building in the rearview. "I mean it is really close…"

"Which is why I was asking…"

Emily sighed and drummed the steering wheel. "Well... When it comes to cyber-security, does it matter how far away we are?"

"I guess not... But it would really suck to go through the trouble of being careful only to get followed home."

"So... we'll take the long way home?" Emily suggested. "Stop down in Daly for that Thai place?"

"I'm sure I'll be able to spot someone following us if we take that much of a detour," I said.

"So... what's your take? Is this a spy movie or a superhero movie?" Emily asked.

"These days, there isn't much difference."

As far as anyone's parents knew, Emily and I were out to see a movie. So as long as Emily was home before midnight, we were all good.

Took a little bit of troubleshooting, but we managed to figure out how to make the camera rig work. I was surprised it worked so smoothly. The cameras were hooked up to the burner phone by an adaptor. The earpiece was hardwired to the audio port. And the whole thing was hooked up to an external battery.

I had so many wires running under my sweater, I was gonna turn into a cyborg.

"Now..." I said. "Wondering how to get up to the roof... Hopefully, there's an unlocked maintenance door up there."

Emily scoffed. "Building's closed but the custodial staff is still around Just check the doors. Duh."

"That works, I guess—"

"Come on!" She swung herself out of the car, and scurried across the street before I'd even gotten out. Darting from cover to cover, she ducked and scampered while I passed some people on the street with my head down and hands in my pockets.

"You're gonna get us noticed," I said, passing her while she peered around a corner.

"Me?" she asked, taking off ahead of me and waiting in the shadow from a pillar. "I'm doing stealth!"

Emily was about to swing herself out but I grabbed her and put my arm around her, keeping my pace without skipping a step.

"What— hey!"

"I'm acting casual and keeping my face from cameras," I said. "Like the one you were about to step into."

I let her go after we were out of the security camera's view.

"Fine. I guess this is allowed to be your wheelhouse. I'll permit that! But... I do wanna pick the lock on the door," she said, with a utility door in view.

"You don't know how to pick locks, do you?"

"Well you can do it..." Emily said.

"Ouch."

"Come on! Learning by doing! Gimme your kit and watch my back." But just as she knelt in front of a utility door and chose a set of picks, I noticed a block of wood between the door and the frame. I pushed it open.

Emily looked up at me slowly. "Taking the credit for that." She got up and dusted her pants off. "I suppose I'll get back to the car and watch your back. But you are *absolutely* teaching me how to pick locks."

"That depends on who's locks you want to break into..."

She groaned and pushed the lock pick pouch into my chest. "Mind your own business!"

I kept the block in the door as I slid inside. Half-lights were on and I could hear the hum of cleaning equipment echoing around corners. "We probably should have gotten some kind of building layout..." I said into the earpiece.

"Can you do that on the internet?" she said to herself. "I'll check..."

"Just focus on the camera feed—"

"Oh...?"

"What?"

"Their rental agency has a floor map posted on their website."

"That...was quick."

Emily whistled. "This place is a maze..."

"Can you just let me know when anyone's coming up behind me? You can see, right?"

"Shut up and read the signs," she said. "You just passed the hallway to the stairs."

Down into the basement, and then to the second basement. Checking online, there were insanely cheap rates for office spaces without windows. Who would have thought?

And then I was at the door to the office that the IP address was linked to. Office B2-6. Drop ceilings and unpolished tile floors. The walls were painted something like sea foam. Teal? Was this Teal? I'd bet Dad would know.

"Locked?" Emily asked.

"Yeah, but not a keycard," I said, getting my lock picks again.

Grimy hallway or no, I wouldn't have expected this kind of low-security from an evil lair. Then again, I was getting the feeling that The Gentleman's main line of defense was not getting found in the first place.

I didn't have a plan on how to deal with whatever was on the other side. Getting ready to make it up as I went, I pushed my weight into the door.

CHAPTER 41
OFFICE SPACE

Saturday, October 28

Probably less exciting than you were expecting. Empty office. Clean, but empty. I flicked the lights but it seemed to be stuck on emergency lighting. It was very cold.

"I can't see much," said Emily.

"Honestly, I wasn't expecting armed guards."

"You were checking for cameras on your way in, right?"

"Yeah. Didn't seem to be any downstairs," I said.

I saw mounts for security cameras on the ceiling, but no actual cameras.

"Haven't even thought about what I'll tell Dad if I get caught..."

"What's that?" Emily asked.

"Never-mind. Nothing."

I was in some kind of reception area. Small, wrap-around counter-desk to the side. Like my doctor's office. There'd be cheap plastic chairs in the corner, and a wall of pamphlets right beside them.

That reminded me... It'd been longer than normal since I'd gotten the chance to complain about my testosterone levels.

I took a look in the main room. No windows and the few lights that were on gave everything the same haze. No shadows. Carpets were plain, with an ugly geometric pattern. Looked like a room that would have fit a dozen cubicles? The point brick office room was smaller, but also had private offices to the side.

Instead of cubicles, there was only one thing in the office: just a single computer.

Looked like it was built custom, but that didn't mean it was pretty. Exposed wires and the monitor didn't have any casing — just an LED screen fastened to some welded metal stand. The tower casing looked liquid-cooled.

Lots of LED lights going on inside. Multicolor, they cast twinkling patterns on the wall behind it. I tapped it with the hanbo and there was a bit of a rattle. Not very solid.

Now, the funny thing was that it was set on a kind of antique-style table. Very gothic. Lots of curves. And the chair in front of the monitor was some old, riveted blue-velvet thing that probably looked a whole lot more comfortable than it was.

The chair was heavy and dug deep into the pile of the crappy carpet. Thinking about the word 'carpet' pulled up a bunch of mental images of hairy chests. And then made me think of Branden's chest.

And... no he wasn't hairy but it bought it back to my mind and I couldn't believe that it had been almost 24 hours since I stuck my tongue in my friend's candy-liqueur flavored mouth and I'd barely thought about it at all.

I started to panic a little bit and went for my phone. Branden was a little needy, and I hadn't responded to any of his messages since last night. Branden went into depressive withdrawal spirals if he didn't get a text back from one of his guys within five minutes—

"Homygosh Branden's gay!" I said, a bit louder than I meant to. I cleared my throat. "Yeah just ignore that." I said to Em, getting my phone out because I *still* hadn't responded to literally any messages.

All my social outreach was being handled by Emily. Branden might have been getting anxious that I wasn't texting him back.

Shit. Did he think I was ghosting him?

"Yo?" I said, thinking that outing one of our friends would have gotten a bigger reaction from Emily. "You probably could already tell. Nobody clock's 'em like you."

Nothing.

I sighed. My phone had no signal bars... which meant Emily probably couldn't hear me either. And at the same time, I was in an evil lair and I was obsessing over horny texts. Read the room, Wexler. Time and a place.

Time and a place...

Put.

The phone.

Away.

I grumbled. "Really should switch to using gel. Injection day hangover is getting out of control..." I sighed and turned to the computer. "Alright. Let's see what you've got."

I moved the chair to the side and spammed the mechanical keyboard until the whole thing lit up. If it wasn't Mac or Windows, I would have expected some kinda DOS entry system. But no. It faded from black to white. A flat-black hat appeared, and a faint outline of a mask. And then a black silhouette of a gloved hand holding up a finger.

A couple of usernames faded into the bottom right corner. I clicked on 'DIRECTOR' and a password field appeared. "Okay... what's the worst that could happen?"

I typed in 'c-a-p-i-t-a-l-i-s-t-p-i-g' and an emoticon appeared on the mask.

[ಠ_ಠ]

I typed in 'c-a-p-i-t-a-l-i-s-t-p-i-g-o-i-n-k-o-i-n-k' and the emoticon shook and switched to another.

[╱_·]

I took out Emily's phone and held it up. I heard a little bit of something getting through. "You there?" I asked.

I seemed to get a bit of a response but it fizzled out.

I sighed. "You feel like looking up 'top ten supervillain lair passwords?'"

Speakers around the room crackled to life. A pleasant tone played over them.

"My good man, any truly maniacal individual worth his salt knows to use inspirational quotes from water bottles. The kind made by retailers that exploit yoga as a trend marketed towards middle-class married women." He sounded almost happy to see me. "Aged twenty-five to fifty. Coveted market to break into, that one."

As for me, my heart had reached up into my throat. "Holy shit," I whispered into my phone. "He's here."

CHAPTER 42
FACE TO FACES

Saturday, October 28

"I'm sorry about this place," the Gentleman said. "I had meant to leave you some coffee, given our encounter earlier, I'll assume that you like coffee. But meeting online is always a risk. You never know who you're going to get. And quite frankly, you're a bit shorter than your profile..."

The mask on the computer changed.

[^ ▽ ^]

"I'm only kidding. I've just never 'dated' online but I've always wanted to say that. Ha-ha!" It sounded like he was in the room, but coming from everywhere. It was creepy as fuck. Figures that an over-dramatic techie like him would optimize a speaker system to intimidate someone who *maybe* found their way to his lair.

"Would probably do you better to stick with tea though... Proper drink, should you ask me." He sighed, then cleared his throat. "I left our encounter in the cafe under the impression that you had... hmm... chickened out before you could extract any information." His voice was as smooth as silk.

[⊙_◎]

"But you've been such a pain in the lower back until now... Thus — quite frankly — I'm pleased to see that you haven't given up! Gives me the pleasure of underestimating you. Oh I *do* love re-adjusting outcome projection tables!" He appeared on the monitor screen, in front of his blue velvet backdrop, and gave me a golf clap.

Meanwhile, I was there, frozen and not knowing what to do. I was thinking how much Tom was absolutely right that I wasn't ready for this stuff because I couldn't think on my own two feet. Still needed the umbilical cord.

…Or did I? I looked back to the computer. I had an idea. Or like. A developing idea.

"I have to say though. Going rogue? Your rag-tag crew of misfits isn't prone to solo-ops… are they waiting in the wings? Probably should have sent one of the more tech-savvy friends, yes?"

I turned the monitor so I could see the door and took the keyboard. "Crew?" I said, absently focusing on the screen.

"You're not with them?"

"I guess not," I said, typing random passwords.

[¯\(©¿©)/¯]

"What are you doing? Also how old are you?" He sighed. "Well if you're not with them, that throws quite a wrench into my projection models. That means *two* free-radicals caught onto my trail. Oh my, I must be getting sloppy."

"You did kick a hornet's nest."

"Ah yes. Never such wasps as capitalists." He shook his head. "Though now that I mention it… how long has it been since I needed to update my protocols? Suffice, I daresay you've made more progress than them. Granted, it's a dead-end from here. And can I ask again what you think you're doing, Mr…?"

"Avalon Knight." I tried 'p-r-o-l-e-t-r-a-i-t,' 'm-a-r-x,' 'm-a-r-x-i-s-m,' 'r-e-v-o-l-u-t-i-o-n,' 'g-u-e-s-t,' 'x-x-m-a-r-x-6-9-x-x.'

[O‿O]

"As in — the Avalon Knight? The new one, I should say! I read about you in such and such blog. I've been withholding making an opinion of you. Not the one who died a few years back, but the original-original was quite a favorite of mine. Real… Man of the People, you know?"

Dad's ego really liked 'Original' Avalon Knight compliments.

The Gentleman chuckled. "You found me, though... well, maybe you're not a total write off after all. Suppose you think you're up to that 'man of the people' brand, then? I assure you that, by standing against me, you are woefully misguided." He cleared his throat. It sounded weird.

"Do you not read the news?"

"I read people, my dear man." He cleared his throat. "Also I'll let you into the system if you can spell proletariat correctly..."

I ignored him. Jesus I thought my mom liked to play games... "Plenty of people don't seem to be a fan."

He whistled. "Depends on the people."

"Working people. Real people."

"Ha! Ah yes. These 'real' people I hear so much about... yet am bereft of a descriptor of who they are."

Without an idea of where he kept his cameras, I kept one hand typing out passwords and slipped the flash drive into the USB port. I'd just need a minute or two to see if this would work.

He continued, "You see, I'd consider real people to be the ones being priced out of the city they've lived in for their whole lives and for generations. The City has so few... 'real' people remaining, I'm afraid."

"What about the people here now? They're not rich." I was getting distracted, but the computer fan was working harder now.

"Wealth is not the problem. It's the problem of real estate being so coveted and so scarce that there is nobody of authority preventing real estate from becoming too expensive to sustain lower-incomes."

"Well, it wasn't lower-income people that got a golden parachute. To a lot of people, you helped those executives out. They're doing fine, right?"

[✖ ︵ ✖]

He looked offended. "While I'll admit that was a miscalculation on my part, comments like those are hurtful and quite unnecessary. Excuse me for assuming there was still some shred of decency in business practices."

"Yeah. Literally, anyone could have told you businesses are like that," I said, thinking of something snotty to say. "You should have asked one of those 'real peoples' you seem crazy about."

In case he was watching, I kept my eyes focused on punching in fake passwords, and not the computer tower. But — ho boy those LEDs were firing a lot faster and turning a lot redder. I could feel the hot air venting out even from where I was standing.

[ب_ب]

"Oh, my word— See, this is..." he waved his hand as if trying to think. "This is what really upsets me about you... *Yanks*. Yanks? Am I using that right? I digress... See. You berate me for assuming human empathy exists... As if I should just know better than to expect more than the status-quo of selfishness.

"Not only do you tolerate it, but you also act as if this is just the way things are supposed to be... and poo-hoo whomever questions this. It's impossible to get through to you because you're all so indoctrinated. Any time some kind of social-ethics does catch a following, it's all about... communes and buying food with interpretive dances or such nonsense."

"There was probably a better way to get your message across," I said.

"By all means, I'm open to suggestions!" he said. "However, you will sit in the bonfire and sip fair-trade coffee and tell yourselves you're doing all you can. Perhaps someone ought to fan the fire a little bit... lest you complain about how hot it is, and actually do something about it instead."

"People are blaming you, though."

"Some of them. The news certainly is. Any time they want to avoid talking about how much their own CEOs make off of exploiting America itself, they talk about me instead. Yes, I've lost followers among the injured parties here, but my base is swelling across the nation and the world."

I scoffed. "So you're going to tell me you're breaking eggs to make omelettes?"

[ಠ‿ಠ]

"No, my good lad. I'm making *brioche*." He leaned in. "But have you given any thought about what *you're* doing?"

I pulled the flash drive out and kicked the desk over.

The Gentleman choked. "What... are you doing???"

"Figured if you were stalling me, I may as well stall you right back." I got the staff from my back and hammered it into the side of the toppled computer tower.

I heard him scoff. "Honestly, I wondered why you were just daft and sitting there for me to send my people along to, but I'm still not entirely sure what... you're doing...?"

The tower was really hot, hotter than I'd expect. The inside of this thing was a BEAST. Thick, blue coolant spilled out and onto the carpet. Except for the row of solid state drives, I didn't even recognize what any of it was.

"Running diagnostic..." the Gentleman mumbled. "Reading network feedback and..." He choked. "You put the uplink in... Well, I guess I'm as surprised as you that it worked. And there you go ripping out an SSD. I didn't see that coming... Becoming a pattern. Hmmm..."

My hand burned even through the glove. I juggled the SSD from one to the other, lacking anything to sit it in. I slipped my hoodie off and yanked out another two drives, folding them inside the fabric and tying it around my waist.

I knew he had people coming for me. I'd assumed that from the beginning. Actually, I was surprised that it had taken this long — figured he'd have someone on standby. Or... people on standby.

I'd need to find a back exit. There must have been another way out except for the front. I didn't think it was legal to have only one exit in an underground office.

"Well, regardless, I have my doubts about you making it out of here," he said. "But you have a knack for surprising me... The charm of being surprised does wear off before long, though, so watch your step."

Going past the reception desk, I scanned through the back offices for some kind of exit. And then, hidden beside a giant shelf, there was a green staircase symbol with an arrow. I followed it.

"Silent treatment..." The Gentleman sighed. "Oh well. We'll be speaking before long..."

CHAPTER 43
TRAIL BY (LIVE) FIRE

Saturday, October 28

Maybe I should have clued in that something was wrong when I opened the door: *it wasn't locked.* But I rushed out in a hurry — only to find myself face-to-face with some scruffy looking guy in full combat gear and a lowered pistol. He seemed surprised to see me, and I was sure as hell surprised to see him.

I immediately turned around and went back into the office, two gunshots ringing in my ears before the door slammed shut.

"For the record, he wasn't using lethal force…" said the Gentleman. And then it sounded as if he spoke to someone beside him. "Those were rubber bullets he's using, right?" … "You mean you can't just use them in regular pistols?" … "Well, that's on me for not being clear, I suppose. I did say I wanted him alive, didn't I? Best make sure I clarify myself… Wait— is this thing on—?"

I was already booking it to the front entrance.

I swung the door inward, immediately spotting a giant shadow to my side. Someone was waiting for me. I threw myself out, keeping low. The look on the guy's face was priceless when he realized he couldn't just grab me. I whacked his knee with my staff as soon as I had a clear swing. His knee gave out and he yelped before collapsing to the ground.

I pushed myself back and ended up rolling into a goon. She toppled over me but I managed to get to my feet while she was righting herself.

The big guy had already recovered though, grabbing my chest piece and throwing me backward.

I fell to the floor in a heap, my head banging on the wall behind me. Big Guy was approaching fast. Jesus, he must have been seven feet tall.

I rammed the end of my staff into his nose. Blood gushed down his face and he stumbled backward, giving me just enough time to get to my feet and run.

I heard the goon talking into a mouthpiece as I slid around a corner. I couldn't remember how I'd even gotten here. Should have left breadcrumbs.

I needed an exit plan... I slid into some cranny and got Emily's phone out. It was swarmed with messages and missed calls.

"Holy shit!" she said when she picked up my call. "Wait. AK?"

"It's me."

"Holy shit!" She'd been hyperventilating. "Look! Some sketch-as-fuck guys showed up just before the call cut—"

"I know. Ran into them."

"Like... there were a good dozen."

I leaned my head back against the wall. "I saw three. One was post-human. Or just really big."

"What? Okay. Shit. Okay. Shit. Where are you now?"

"Underground," I said. I looked around and saw a sign on the wall. "D-Wing."

Emily cleared her throat. "I'm near the—"

"Nope. You stay where you are. We'll meet up when I'm out."

"Okay... I got a building layout map..."

"Okay, listen," I said, trying to be as soothing as possible.

"What?"

"I'm fine, okay? Okay?"

She cleared her throat again. "Okay."

"I've been in worse places." (I hadn't.) "This'll be fine. I need you to stay calm okay?"

"Right." Emily took a breath. "Okay. Right."

"They're going nonlethal. They want me alive. If that happens... Well, then go see sensei and let him know, okay?"

"Right."

"So... Any ideas?"

Emily took another breath. "What's the closest office?"

I peered out from behind the pillar. "Closest door reads... B2-11." Didn't have time for secrecy. If the GM was listening in, I'd have to move faster than he could respond.

"Okay..." Emily said. "I see you."

"I can't use the main entries and exits."

"Right..." She hummed. "What about the roof."

"Might not be able to open it from inside without a key card."

"Right..." She paused. "So... Loading dock?"

"How do we know it's open?"

"Because I'm looking right at it."

"Alright. Where to?"

"Shipping elevator," she said. "Should be a T shaped hallway intersection near you."

"I see it."

"Go the other way."

"Got it."

I retraced my steps. Generally a bad move but I didn't have a lot of options. I heard some scurrying around a corner just as I slipped into the freight room, but I closed the elevator door before I could see if they were on my tail.

"So," I said, catching my breath. "How's your night?"

"Oh you know," she said. "Chillin' with the homies. You?"

"I... have a migraine coming on."

CHAPTER 44
MYSTERY MISFITS: THE REMIX

Saturday, October 28

Right out of the elevator, someone took a pass at me with a crowbar.

I managed to duck, but someone *else* kicked me in the stomach. Someone grabbed my hanbo and yanked it away from me as I fell. Getting kicked on the ground wasn't something I was used to, but my armor took the brunt of it.

"Holy shit!" Emily screamed. "GET UP AND KICK HIS ASS! GET UP!"

Okay. Fetal position. Works great in a situation like this. Not saying that it didn't hurt, but it gave me a second or two to figure out my next move while I tried to ignore Emily screaming in my ear.

I pulled off a spinning kick on my back, knocking the three assholes away from me long enough to get to my feet. "Kay," I whispered into the mouthpiece. "I need you to stay calm when I'm getting my ass handed to me like that—"

"FUCKIN' WRECK HIM!"

The bitch-ass who stole my staff swung it at me like a baseball bat. I grabbed his arm mid-swing, twisting his wrist and tossing the hanbo away. Crowbar-dude (sorry, but it wasn't the best time for nicknames) came at me from the side. I wrenched the other guy in front of me and the crowbar hit his ribs with a thud and a crack. He fell with a gasp.

And then I kicked Crowbar-dude in the balls.

…Sorry. This was a do-or-die kinda deal.

"Ummm," Emily said. "Watch out—"

Looking over just in time, someone decked me so hard I couldn't help but fall over. Someone else picked me up and pushed me against a concrete pillar. Even though I landed two guys on the ground, more of them were flooding into the bay.

I huffed. "Weren't gonna say anything?"

"You said 'be cool.'"

"We're gonna have to talk about this..."

Even though these guys weren't on my level... there were a lot of them. I tried to keep them at a distance, ducking and weaving instead of sticking to the offense.

I just needed to wait for an opening to—

There was a tell-tale electrical charge-up behind me, and at the last second, I ducked under the shock gauntlet. I grabbed his arm and threw him judo-style over my shoulder into the crowd.

But then the gauntlet went off in a blast of blue light. I felt my stomach turn upside down and I almost dropped to my knees.

Luckily... it seemed like a bunch of the other goons also had the same reaction. That left me an opening to get out.

But that very second, a white van pulled into the loading bay. "Of course it's a white fucking van," Emily scoffed.

A quick glance to the street — we had onlookers. Would only be a matter of time before cops came around. Still no sign of the guy with the gun.

"Hey! Hey! Heads up!" Emily called.

I thought she was talking about the guy with shock gauntlets coming at me... but no...

The same group of mystery misfit Vigils stormed the garage. The cowboy was taking potshots at the group, Armor-girl was throwing up a barrier to cover him. The Big Guy was rushing in. And there was a fourth... a mask-less blond girl dressed like a super spy with an Ariana Grande ponytail.

"Holy crap! Is that them? The ones you were talking about! They look so cool!" Emily called. "Why don't you look that cool?"

It was a blur of people attacking other people. And with the super-powered misty-barriers and the tech gun launching bolts of energy in every-which direction, the scene turned into a shit show.

Just the kind of shit show I needed.

Between the two Gentleman thugs still focused on me, I grabbed one and swung her into the other, making for the street.

I was almost to the sidewalk when someone said: "Get him!"

But then there was a flash of light, and I got kicked off my feet.

"Ooooooh!" Emily said. "Ooooh, that looked like it hurt."

I coughed until I got my breath back. Looking down the street, I spotted Emily's car. "Having a great time, aren't you?"

I couldn't tell exactly where it hit, but it must have been on the armor somewhere. My whole body had gone numb from the blast. I tried to push myself up but the cowboy showed up, pointing his pistol at me. The brawl behind him was kept in the loading bay. Just him and me on the street.

"Look, I really don't want to shoot you point blank... Not that it isn't fun... Nothing personal. Thing is — you have something we need." He held his boot on my ankle and pointed the high-tech pistol at my chest. "Blast from this close is gonna hurt a lot worse. Come on, make this easy."

"Light that motherfucker up!" Emily howled, clapping her hands with every syllable.

I cleared my throat and got a few breaths in. "Look... Look man..." I sighed. "Real sorry about this."

Let's talk about that arsenal I mentioned way back.

Tom didn't want me using guns — for a whole bunch of reasons. But sending a minor into battle with a wooden stick sounds a little irresponsible, right?

Right. So that meant I had to keep a few other tricks up my sleeve.

While he was looking at my left hand untying my hoodie, he wasn't looking at my right hand going for the Taser I had on my belt. It wasn't powerful enough to just go around zapping people unconscious, but that didn't mean that cowboy didn't feel it when the two darts dug into his leg.

His eyes shot open wide and his body went stiff while he tried to stay on his feet. I ejected the cartridge as he went down, and was on my merry way.

There was a building across the street from the loading dock. Yeah, Emily was right there, but I wasn't going to lead two different flavors of bad guys to her. I wasn't even sure if anyone had seen where I'd gone, but by the time I'd gotten to the third-floor roof, there were sirens not too far away. I wasn't gonna stick around to see how anything was going to go down.

CHAPTER 45
MERCENARY

Saturday, October 28

I was sucking in deep, wet breaths.

"You okay? Where'd you go?"

"I slipped away," I said, taking the lay of the land. "Okay, meet me over on Carolina."

"Beside the baseball diamond?"

"Sounds good." I slipped down to the sidewalk as cop cars drove past. It was dark enough now that I could stick to shadows without being seen. It was chaos all over the place. Shouting. Guns firing.

I wondered if anyone was shooting back... if those stupid fake Vigils would be crazy enough to return fire.

Whatever. Not my problem.

I took a breath, still a bit woozy from the pistol blast.

And the shock gauntlet.

And the migraine. Which... it hadn't quite set in yet, but it was a-comin'.

Carolina street. Okay. One block to the east. I could make it as long as I kept to the dark and kept off the street as much as I could. "You on your way?"

"On 17th," said Emily.

"Okay. Park somewhere."

"Don't take long."

"I'm in combat armor during an inner-city shooting... I need to take it slow and stay out of sight or one of these passing cop cars is gonna pick me up."

I checked my phone — nothing from Dad. He might have been too distracted to check the news. But I did have a text from Tom. I got a lump in my throat... had someone taken a video of the fight? He would have recognized Dad's old armor. He probably would have even recognized me just from how I fought...

Today at 9:08 PM, TOMINATRIX said:

Important: where are you?

Okay. That seemed harmless enough.

Today at 9:14 PM, you said:

Just leaving the theatre with emilt

There's a shooting. Between your place and downtown.

Take the highway and stay out of town until I let you know.

Calling your dad.

omg WHAT???

is anyone hurt?

What's going on?

Read, 1:14 AM

Today at 9:16 PM, TOMINATRIX said:

Police in pursuit. No reported injuries.

Don't worry about it. Just keep safe.

"Doing my best..." I sighed. "I think."

My skin shivered. Checking my blind spots as I crossed the street, something seemed off... but I couldn't spot anything that would be giving me the creeps like this.

"Good to go," said Emily.

"Get ready to gun it…" I said.

"Why?"

"Call it a weird feeling…"

There was a parking lot running the width of the block. SUVs, company trucks, vans. Lots of containers and shipping slats. And on the other side was the baseball diamond. All quiet now… except for a bar playing very loud, live music.

About halfway across, my feet stopped. I didn't mean to but… I saw someone. Out of the corner of my eye, in plain sight, standing in the floodlight. But when I turned to look, no one was there. And then a burning pain in the back of my head.

"Oh shit… There it is"

"What?"

"Headache. Showed up faster than I expected…"

Something was wrong. I turned toward the street I came from. A gunshot.

My chest plate slammed against my body, and I stumbled to the ground.

"Luca!" Emily screamed.

"Fine. Fine. Fine…!" I said, even though I wasn't sure if I was.

Panicking, I grasped my stomach and chest. My whole body felt numb. There were so many dings and scratches on this thing, I couldn't tell you where I'd just been hit.

No sign of a breach though. "Okay… I'm fine. Stay right there…"

"You see him right?" Emily asked.

I craned my head up. There he was! The mercenary-looking guy from the stairwell. "Yes… I see him…" There was more screaming nearby while I got to my feet. Th music continued next door.

"Non-lethal. I clocked your armor in the office," said the mercenary. He was British — but not fancy like the Gentleman. "But your kneecaps? Awfully under-guarded... professional advice." He aimed the pistol down. "Ever been shot there?"

My neck throbbed with my heartbeat. "Still a virgin..."

He flicked the safety on. "Another day then. Best to pop that cherry sooner rather than later... but I have very clear instructions." He holstered his pistol and took a bush knife from the back of his belt. Scratched and worn. "You have something that doesn't belong to you."

He was gruff, grizzled, and had a nasty burn scar on his cheek under his right eye. Maybe mid-fifties? Though more likely it was probably a very rough early-forties. Shaved bald under a skull cap, and roughly shaven jaw.

I stood my ground. Just like I did with all tall guys. "I'm not sure it belongs to you either."

He launched forward. I could tell right away that he wasn't going for kill strikes. The blade was a distraction, his focus was incapacitation. But unlike Tom swinging a newspaper at me, this guy meant business.

I was already exhausted, sore all over, and struggling to keep my eyes focused while my head pounded. If I could just get the knife out of his hand...

I lunged when I saw an opening to strike his wrist, but he dropped the knife instead, grabbing the hanbo, and punching me in the gut so hard I fell over.

As if I didn't already wanna puke.

While I coughed on the loose gravel, he kicked my hanbo away and slid his knife back into his belt. "Give yourself some credit, kid," he said, "you've had a busy night."

Emily cleared her throat. "So... are we calling sensei or not?"

"I'll... be fine," I whispered between heaves.

"Absolutely not what I asked," she said. "Just gonna get his number..."

Just as the mercenary took a pair of cuffs from his pocket, there was a blur in the shadows.

"Incoming!" Emily shouted.

The Vigil with the Ariana Grande hair rolled in from a blind spot. By the time the mercenary heard her, she'd swept his legs out from under him and tossed his knife away. She grabbed his arm and flipped him over her shoulder, landing him face-up on the ground.

In a flourish, she reached for my arm and pulled me in. Her cold grey eyes didn't show a speck of feeling. "We can help. Reach out to Jillian Miner." And then she pushed me away, going back at the mercenary. On his knees, he went for his pistol, but she stomped his hand to the ground before he'd lifted it.

I made eye contact with Emily before I'd made it to the road. "Back window—" I said.

She was already on the move by the time I hoisted myself in. I stared back at the mercenary and Vigil in the lot, still exchanging blows. Without me there though, it looked like the mercenary was trying to back off.

And then I laid down in the back seat of Emily's car, and let my eyes lose focus.

CHAPTER 46
TRICK OR TREAT

Saturday, October 28

Emily ran two red lights before she slowed down. I was hyperventilating in the back seat while I dug through the first aid pack that I'd stuffed back here. Had to swallow a few pills dry.

Ugh. Gross.

"You're not going to bleed out on my back seat, are you?"

I didn't say anything. The vibrations from the engine felt nice.

I'd seen someone. I know I'd seen someone. Someone else in the parking lot. Not the vigilante girl. Or maybe... I felt weird like my brain shattered, and the sharp pieces were stabbing my other brain.

A wall fell. And crashed on my head. But the wall was my head. And the bricks were my eyes. And the cracks were my fingers. And my fingers were someone else's fingers—

"Luca!"

I shook and bolted upright. "What? What is it? What?"

The car was stopped, and Emily was leaning back between the seats. "Jesus... that was scary."

"What?" I looked around. Well, squinted...

Actually, the headache seemed to be going away. Weird.

Emily let out a breath and relaxed. "You were asleep for like... I dunno. A few minutes."

"Where are we?"

Emily took a second. "Buena Vista." She was breathing hard. I guess I freaked her out.

"Well... I'm fine," I said. "I'm... so sore."

"I had no idea you were so intense."

I coughed up a lump in my throat. "Oh yeah. That's like…" I yawned. "Just a Tuesday for me. Getting shot and… getting shot with laser guns."

"How much shit are we in if anyone figures out that was you out there?"

"Well, I'll try to keep you out of it."

Emily glared at me. "I don't need a white boy to keep me out of trouble, kay."

I snorted. "Well… trouble depends on what's on these drives. At least I assume they're drives."

"That'd suck if you just grabbed some graphics cards."

Then, despite my pounding head, we started giggling uncontrollably. Everything that we'd pulled off that night was stuff that we shouldn't have been able to do. And that was hilarious, apparently.

Or we were just coming down from an adrenaline spike.

"So…" Emily said, wiping each of her eyes with a finger. "What's the haul?"

Untying the hoodie around my waist, I handed her one of the SSDs. "I've got three."

"What do we do with them?" she asked. "I've never seen ports like these…"

"No idea," I said. "That super spy-lady—"

"Ariana Grande rip-off?"

"Yeah her. She said her friends want to help me, all of a sudden."

"Oh yeah?" Emily scoffed. "John Wayne wants to shoot you in the head, but she wants to play nice?"

"Seems like it…" I said. "She told me to get in touch with Jillian Miner."

"Oooh! How cloak-and-dagger. Did she give you a secret passcode? Will you be taking a red umbrella to the wharf and lighting a cigar with two matches?"

"That would have been more instruction than she gave. She just said: 'reach out.' Like… just pop in for a house call?"

"So …?"

"I… have no idea." I stretched. "OH! I got to talk to the Gentleman!"

Emily jammed her keys into the ignition. "We are so getting some homeless guy to buy us vodka, and I am totally staying the night, and we are totally going to go over everything. And then we are totally binging that gritty Netflix remake of *Murder, She Wrote*."

You know the one. With Judy Dench? Kinda like *Sex in The City* meets *American Horror Story*.

CHAPTER 47
MY ADORING FANS

Monday, October 30

The downtown shooting was all over TV. But honestly, when it came to mass shootings, everyone was kind of over it. Maybe a bit out of place in San Francisco, but since nobody actually died and no arrests were made, it was kind of stale news by Monday morning.

After everything... I actually kinda forgot that this was the same weekend that I got arrested. Time flies when you're having fun, am I right? The problem being, while I was going after sketchy wannabe supervillains, I was also dead center of the school's rumor mill.

The school hallway, 8:48 AM.

"You didn't actually sexually assault a forty-year-old milf?"

"No, he stopped a forty-year-old from getting raped."

"Can I see your gunshot wound?"

"Did you really run the cops on a city-wide chase?"

"I heard you fought off four guys!"

"All that's bullshit, right? The actual charges were for a DUI, right?"

"You mean Drunk and Disorderly?"

"That's what DUI means, right?"

"No, Driving Under the Influence. DUI..."

"Ah!"

Emily pulled my arm as I tried to clear up any misconceptions, while also plugging how awesome I was. I may have used the Halloween party chase as an excuse for how I somehow had some new bruises. I was wearing t-shirts out of the shower... but Dad was so distracted I didn't think he even noticed.

I had a *nasty* purple mark where I got shot.

When we passed by her locker, Londyn leaned over into me. "We still on for lunch?" she asked.

"Think so."

"Awesome. See you then." And then she booped my nose before Emily dragged me away and around a corner. Trophy case hall, where there weren't a lot of lockers so traffic was light.

"'Still on?'" Emily asked.

"Londyn insists that she owes me milkshakes." I couldn't help but grin.

Emily sighed. "Is it wrong I'm kinda jealous? She's the type who kinda makes me wish I was a lesbian. How flirty did you get at the party?"

"Like." I held my fingers apart. "This close to heavy petting."

"Just... don't mention it to mom. You know the only reason you get to stay the night is that she thinks you're full-on gay-gay," she said.

"That is literally bisexual erasure."

Emily thought for a second. "Does this mean you guys are gonna be official?"

I shrugged. "Pretty sure this is just a for-friendsies thing."

"Ugh. Coward."

"What?"

"You know what."

I scoffed. "You don't know that. Maybe I'm taking what you said to heart."

"About letting people in your pants?"

"Pfft," I rolled my eyes. "Maybe I'm looking into my options. You know. Playing the field." The field may have been Branden's treasure trail.

"Shopping around?" Emily gave me a side-eye. "As much as I'd be thrilled to hear that you're putting your hypothetical slut days behind you, I'll see it when I believe it."

"Maybe I'm just not comfortable dating someone while you're single," I said. "You've never *not* been in a relationship."

Emily scoffed. "Maybe I'm just giving you a chance to catch up…"

"How sportsmanlike."

"I dunno… I might not be single either."

"Ugh!" I threw my head back. "I thought you broke up with Liam! You need to cut him loose, bro!"

Emily shrugged like she was baiting me to ask about it.

"Don't tell me you're dating someone *else* now—"

"I didn't say that…" she said. "I said I might be…"

I was just about to dive into her stupid 20 questions game… but with the atrium in view, Ms. Hulbry appeared from a doorway like a vampire. Emily and I both stopped because we knew it was for me.

"Figures she's got my route around the school memorized," I whispered.

"Maybe she injected you with a tracking device," Emily whispered. "Get Tom to check on that."

"He'd be in on it, too."

Hulbry leaned on her left leg, orange velvet heels, and waited a second. Power play. "A word, Mr. Wexler?" She gestured into the room she came from.

I gestured for Emily to go ahead. Hulbry didn't actually bring me into the room, just kept me at the door.

"Now, I realize there are no ongoing altercations with law enforcement regarding your… events on Friday."

"That's right — there hasn't."

"I have been tracking your activities on social media, however… And I would ask you to keep any discussions and posting regarding this run-in relatively scarce," she said.

"Sorry. Why?"

"I've gotten some… concerned calls—"

"P.T.A. had an emergency meeting?" I said. "Dad told me."

Her train of thought interrupted, her eyes rolled back in her head and she took a breath. "It would help some parents feel a little bit more comfortable if this business with police washed over relatively quickly. So any part you can take to avoid fanning any fires would be beneficial."

"For who?" I shrugged. "You're not the boss of my Insta."

"No, I am not. But it would be in your interests."

I shrugged. "I'll think about it."

"Please do," she said, and then walked away, squawking at some guys down the hall for throwing a football.

CHAPTER 48
ROUTINE

Thursday, November 2

Getting out with Tom was like picking up where we'd left off. Both of us were the kind of guys who didn't bring up arguments after they sizzled off. "I'm surprised you haven't atrophied without the practice," he said, collecting me at a rendezvous.

"I keep myself busy," I said.

"I'll say." He smiled. "It's good to be out again." The smile faded. "Though you need to focus on your takedowns for now. You're pretty good for legwork. We need to work on ending the fight before it begins."

He turned back to me after looking away. "Andy's made it very clear we're not to talk about the…" He cleared his throat. "But did you manage to avoid punching a police officer?"

I sighed and rolled my eyes. "I managed to restrain myself."

Tom hummed. "That's a shame."

CHAPTER 49
THE LUCA-SIGNAL

Tuesday, November 14

Emily asked to go to the bathroom in Geo and didn't come back for the rest of class. I leaned over to Rook (he'd started to sit beside us). "Where's she gone?"

"She said something about..." Rook shrugged. "She said something... I didn't hear."

And she didn't respond to my texts either. After class, she pulled me aside and away into the empty all-purpose room. Nerds made out and played D&D over lunch here, so everyone else generally gave it space.

"What's going on?"

"Someone has to check your publicity for you," she said.

"Someone's been mentioning me?"

"Not you..." She handed me her battered iPad. It was open to Jillian Miner's website. "I've been keeping an eye on her since Saturday night when Ariana-Fake-Blonde-Bitch-Grande told you to get in touch."

"And...?"

Emily winced. "You can read, right?" She snatched back the tablet. "She wrote an article about the history of the Avalon Knight on Sunday."

"Okay? So? She's a fan."

"She's written six more since then," Emily said. "Granted, they all kinda say the same thing and are super rushed..."

"What are they about?"

"You don't get it?"

I shrugged.

"They're about nothing," Emily said. "Some random speculation about who San Francisco's AK could be. Gossip. And like... A breakdown of Avalon Knight merchandising before your dad gave up the mantle—"

"Okay? So she's obsessed with me." I cleared my throat. "Don't blame her."

Emily swatted me. "Dummy! She's trying to get your attention!"

"Right. But we already decided it was a trap," I said.

The warning bell went off, and everyone in the hall immediately started to move in the direction of their classes. Emily scanned to make sure nobody was looking. "Okay honestly... what was our plan for the hard drive? Keep an eye on Amazon to see if we can find some cable that can read them? What then? What if it's encrypted?"

I shrugged. "Maybe we could... Explain it to Tom? He's got resources."

"Alright. So then it's out of our hands. And maybe it never gets solved? Or worse, Tom puts you on superhero probation? And I get in shit? Look..." Emily moved with her back to the crowd. "Maybe we can do that? You got three of them. We've got a chance to play the field."

"You think I can trust the sketchy-af spy-chick?"

"Maybe not trust but... Like you said, they're as illegal as you are." Emily sighed. "Maybe you can help each other. It's not like they're gonna tie you up and hand you to the police or The Gentleman." Emily looked at the entries on the blog page. "Better you go sooner than later. She seems to be overworking herself."

I couldn't really see any other way to push the investigation forward. Emily was right — we were kidding ourselves if we thought we could do it on our own. This was the only way to get help without getting busted by Tom or the police — or worse, Dad.

"Fine," I said. "But I'm skipping class and doing it today."

Emily didn't see a problem with that.

CHAPTER 50
GOOD FAITH

Tuesday, November 14

I had a hoodie and a scarf for my face if things got screwed. Luckily it was raining, and I wasn't boiling up inside all the layers. Unluckily it was raining, which meant I had a tough time getting up to Miner's window. I looked inside for a few minutes before inviting myself in. She was on her couch, dressed in PJs, and drinking tea.

"You really ought to lock your windows," I said. "All kinds of hooligans get in that way these days."

"I'll keep that in mind," she said, only slightly shocked to see me. "Tea?"

"Water or coffee," I said, and then realized I'd already slammed back two energy drinks this morning. "Or... just water." She handed me a glass.

"So... welcome back," she said. "Need a towel?"

"I'm fine. No one's given you trouble since then?"

"No," she said. "And my brother's fine."

"Still in the city?"

"Flew back last week."

I nodded. "So, against my better judgment, I've decided to listen to a little bird who pointed me toward you."

She sat back down on the couch in front of her laptop. "I was worried you wouldn't take the hint, and I'd have to keep those dreadful blogs up."

"Why? What's your personal stake in this?"

"Personal stake?"

"I'm just noticing how many British people are wrapped up in this. Is this some kind of espionage thing?"

"Well… there's The Gentleman?"

"He's got some mercenary working for him. Or something."

"Ah," she said. "I've also heard about his thugs. He recruits from disgruntled laid-off programmers and post-humans he blackmails into working for him. You're saying he's hiring professionals?"

"At least one," I said, wondering what she meant about blackmailing post-humans…

"Something to look into…" she typed out a note and then looked up. "This really ought to be a matter professional Vigils should be looking into."

I plopped myself down in the armchair beside the couch. "It's not my fault they decided to go on a sabbatical. You're a reporter. You must have connections."

She looked at me, eyebrows raised. "…Wish you would have taken a towel before you sat down."

"You wanted my help." I shrugged.

She cleared her throat. "Would be nice to get some kind of exclusive when all is said and done."

"Exclusive?"

"A piece," she said. "The Vigil community and the CDG might be brushing off this Gentleman business as something for the FBI to take care of, but I know how to sniff out something big."

"You mean like… an interview with me?"

"Sure. Or your 'new friends.' But you seem a little bit more forthcoming… Assuming you get to the bottom of this, that is."

"Well I don't have a problem with that…" It would be a hard 'no' from Tom, but I did need her help, for now. "I can't exactly make promises, though."

"Maybe not," she said. "But think about it. It's a fact of the industry that every up-and-coming Vigil needs at least one reporter on their side. Especially the illegal ones. You and your friends are stepping into very illegal territory."

"Those punks who tried to jump me? Stop calling us friends."

She shrugged. "They seem to think you can help each other."

"What's your connection to them?"

"They know that you've been here, that we've met, and that you know who I am."

"And how did they know that I'm the Avalon Knight?" I asked. "I wasn't wearing my normal colors."

"Apparently, they managed to listen to some of a discussion between you and The Gentleman..."

"How'd they get in touch with you?"

"Aren't you nosey..."

"Says a reporter."

"Touché." She chortled. "I've been in touch with them for some time. They formed specifically to take down The Gentleman. They were my main source about him and whatever his long-term goals are. Before you, that is. You can trust them."

"Assuming I can trust you."

"What's the worst that could happen?"

"I have an active imagination."

"I have something for you," she said, going around to the kitchen counter. While she was rooting through a drawer, I realized my phone was buzzing in my pocket. Incoming call — it was from Dad, and I'd just missed it.

He'd already left multiple text messages:

Today at 10:45 AM, super-DAD said:

Skipping class counts as a strike. You are running out of chances, champ

you do NOT want to run out

>:[

Yeah, I should have seen that coming.

"Shit," Jillian said, and then went to her room. "It's around here somewhere!"

Today at 10:47 AM, super-DAD said:

At least tell me where you are and we'll call it strke 1.5

Okay. Dad backtracking was a pretty good indication that a joke would buy me some time.

smoking weeds

illegaly

Read, 10:47 AM

Today at 10:48 AM, super-DAD said:

Edith will be heartbroken if u didn't buy from her...

No rlly. Where are you?

Making a joke made Dad respond by being cute. It gave me a few extra seconds to build an alibi with a Google search.

The brunch truck is at the food park

So like

sorry

but yeah...

Read, 10:49 AM

Today at 10:50 AM, super-DAD said:

UGH

Makes me wanna blow off this client for a waffle.

Get your ass back to school when you're done.

"They left this in my mailbox on Saturday with instructions," Jillian said when she brought out a ziplock bag with an old flip-phone. The removable battery was in a separate bag. "Check it once a day. Keep the battery out of it when you're not using it. Only turn it on when you're in a different public park — never the same one twice in a row. The number the group will contact you from is engraved in the top here." She pointed at some etched squiggles over the screen. "Factory reset the phone if you get a text message from any other number."

"I thought you said I could trust them," I said.

"This is more about taking precautions about the Gentleman." She gestured at my iPhone. "If you're not paranoid by now, then I'm a little concerned."

CHAPTER 51
METHODS

Two days later and still no message from my new Vigil friends. And having that phone around was putting me on edge — like maybe I should keep it hidden under a shingle on a rooftop two blocks away. I was actually going to toss it into the bay if it wasn't for Emily convincing me not to. She even offered to take the phone and keep it, if I was being so paranoid about it.

But I wasn't about to let her become a target if there was some kind of hidden tracking device inside. I was torn between feeling like this was a terrible idea and feeling like I was on the edge of a breakthrough. One known-unknown had opened the door to a whole room full of unknown-unknowns.

After school, Emily was in the living room helping me with my homework. Zero had decided he was a lap dog, apparently, and that his normal people weren't giving him enough attention, refusing to listen to me when I told him to get down. Emily liked it but, I hated when he pretended like I hadn't trained him properly.

At 4:51, Twitter blew up on both our phones. Didn't take much scrolling to tell that The Gentleman had once again done something to piss off the news gods. Emily and I looked at each other and rushed downstairs.

"Dad what happened—"

He sighed. "It's nothing important—"

Emily didn't care. "Has there been any official statement?"

Neither did I. "Is the CDG going to get involved?"

"… they're going to do to protect their stock?"

"Are we going to have to import Vigils from Canada?"

Emily looked at me. "Wouldn't we just borrow Mexican Vigils? Closer."

I cleared my throat. "The Ferguson Act from the 70s makes it really difficult for Vigils to move between here and Mexico. They basically have to un-register in Mexico, apply for a visa, apply for the American registry, and then undo the process to go back."

Dad waved his hand. "More or less," he said.

Emily squinted. "How did you flunk the history test last week?"

"...You said you got a 60%." Dad squinted, leaning forward.

"Well," I cleared my throat. "I said I got a 62%."

Dad clicked his tongue a few times. "You lied."

"Yeah."

"You're grounded."

"What!"

"You're grounded," said Emily. "Apparently."

Dad pointed. "I will ground you, too, Barnett."

Emily gasped. "Woah! Don't kill the messenger."

"You ratted me out!" I punched her shoulder.

"How can you ground me?" Emily demanded, ignoring me.

"I'll call your Mom and tell her you snitched."

Emily's jaw dropped. "I totally did not—"

"You can't seriously ground me!"

"Sure I can."

I whined. "No, you can't. I'm only at one-and-a-half strikes!"

"Well you're at two now," he said. "*And* you're grounded. It's really cute that you think the Grand Consequence will be 'just' a grounding."

"I didn't even know I was snitching so it shouldn't really count," Emily said. "Isn't what you're doing snitching on *me* though?

He scoffed. "No, this is blackmail."

"Dad, what about my birthday!"

Dad shrugged. "So? What *did* you have planned?"

"I dunno," I said, and pointed at Emily. "They're planning something."

Emily shrugged dramatically. "Are we? I dunno! Are we? I guess you'll have to wait and find out!"

Dad rolled his eyes. "I'll think about it."

There was a bit of a pause while we stood there.

"So..." Emily said.

"Right, the..." Dad looked to the TV mounted on the wall where a news anchor was left on mute, The Gentleman displayed in the corner beside her. "The 'that guy' problem."

I grabbed the remote and took the TV off mute when they started to play the Gentleman's video.

This was about Engles and Welsh, he explained: an architecture firm that had designed and constructed any number of luxury condos across the city. The Gentleman claimed that they were 'influencing' the city's administration to grant more and more building permits to construct luxury housing, instead of affordable housing.

"In the last decade," he said, "this city has built nearly two-hundred percent of the needed luxury housing — I'm rounding down... But we have only about twenty percent of the needed middle-income housing and far less for lower-incomes. Even as far as what passes for low-income in this city. (I'll source all this over Twitter, fret not.) From where I'm standing... it seems as if Briggs and Welsh is, in no small part, contributing to this cycle of rent hikes and eviction that has become so commonplace in The City."

As a solution, The Gentleman had managed to 'acquire' the office space that Briggs and Welsh 'owned' downtown... and sold it to the Tall Trees Habitat Conservation Group for three pennies. Specifically the ones, he said, that had been sitting behind a houseplant on a table in the lobby of their current offices.

Creepy? Creepy.

And then the program went to commercial, where Captain Hurricane, in his colorful costume from the late 90s, fought against bad odor with cans of air freshener.

Emily explained that Tall Trees was a non-profit that organized protests and lobbied to protect the redwood forests on the West Coast. The Gentleman said it was deliberately symbolic... because he was trying to conserve the San Fransisco social habitat.

The TTHC group had yet to comment on if they would accept the offer, though the Gentleman said he'd do worse if they just 'gave' it back to E&W. "Well... at least he's helping an eco-justice group at the same time," Emily she.

"What happens if they accept the offer?" I asked. "Wouldn't that make them accomplice... To theft? Cyber terrorism?"

Dad snapped his fingers. "Maybe! Actually. I doubt they even have the staff to fill the E&W office... He's just... put them in a really weird situation."

"Well..." Emily grinned. "They're gonna need a lawyer, right?"

Dad pretended he didn't hear her.

"Do you think this will make it easier for you to peg him as a supervillain?" I asked.

"Assuming that this doesn't light another ten thousand fires I have to put out?" Dad mused. "Well maybe? Who knows. This is just a loss of office space, so nobody's going to get laid off."

"No layoffs?" Emily looked at him.

"Well... who knows. But this cuts into the equity of the company without draining payroll accounts." Dad snorted. "Actually the funny thing is, seeing as how he's targeted the owners and shareholders a little better this time... yeah... He'll probably be on the supervillain list in no time."

CHAPTER 52
IT'S MY PARTY

Friday, November 17

Another day and there wasn't anything on the burner phone. Maybe I should just drop it off the Bay Bridge. Maybe do the same with the SSDs. Pretend like all of this never happened.

Hello, sir? Yes, I'd like to cancel my subscription to stalking this sketchy masked hacker/terrorist philosophical weirdo with people on-staff who have literally shot me.

I was still kinda like: *Holy crap — I literally got shot. With a gun.* And I was kind of over it?

Even the whole personal vendetta was going away.

I was back out with Tom; he was back to snapping at me over my footwork. Emily kept teasing me about her mystery boyfriend. I was gonna get an A on the geo project thanks to Rook — and I was actually pulling my weight too!

But that said… things between Dad and me—

Well… they weren't really *bad*… but they could be better. For a second there, I almost thought he was actually gonna cancel my birthday but no…

"Surprise!"

"Ahh! Nice!" I said, catching my breath. "Ya got me." Dad had sent me to get more dog food. He was always bad at coming up with decent ploys.

"Come here!" Aura launched herself at me, wrapping her arms around my neck.

I looked at Dad. "You know the tip-off was telling me that we absolutely needed more dog food and I needed to go get it."

"We always need more."

"We have three bags of it in the closet because you kept forgetting if we had any…"

Dad shrugged but Tom snickered. "Your father's always had problems with making excuses—"

Dad swatted him.

Full house, with all the usual suspects. But this time it also included Rook who was pretty much part of the team at this point.

Gift-giving was kept on the cheap side with a $15 limit. Showing-off your gift-giving skills was less about out-spending and more about who could get the best reaction.

For example, Kaleb made my birthday cake. Some… multi-level thing that looked like experimental European architecture that honestly none of us knew how to start eating.

"Come on guys, pshhh," Kaleb said. "It's like no one's ever eaten a cake that took eleven hours to make."

"You only made it so you could throw it up on Insta," Joshi said.

Kaleb slowly put his phone away. "Not the only reason."

The cake wasn't the featured gift of the afternoon though.

At the end of it, the best thing was just being around my people. I'd been under so much pressure and I'd been so grounded that I hadn't really had much of a chance to just hang out. This is how things had been before all the weirdness in the last few months. I was glad that we could all get together like nothing was really that different.

The best part was seeing Kaleb here and acting like himself. I don't think he'd relaxed his shoulders in weeks. It's not like we had regular updates, but it seemed as if his parents were sorting things out. They'd found an apartment that was actually pretty close to Tom's. His mother was looking into starting a business to fill the vacuum of laid-off contractors. Still, a lot of uncertainty… but everything wasn't an 'if' anymore.

Which… was more of a load off of my shoulders than I'd have thought. My friend's life was getting back together and I was *maybe* being the angel on the Gentleman's shoulder calling him out for his bullshit. I guess when you're a cyber-hermit content-creator who doesn't read the comments, you don't get a whole lot of valuable feedback.

I liked to think that our talk sent the right message to him.

He was willing to hear me out… surely that meant the Gentleman wasn't such a bad guy… right?

Right?

But no. There he was hanging over my head for the entire birthday party. A 'good guy' wouldn't wreck my damn party with shitty vibes! I couldn't stop thinking about the phone, the drives, and when I'd get my next news notification saying he'd ruined someone else's life.

That was why I hadn't ditched the phone. That was why I kept hoping I'd get a text message. And that was why I kept needing to slip away from the group to get a few breaths to myself.

And on top of that, Dad was taking every chance he could to needle me. "This… get-together is a gift itself, understood?" he said quietly, while we were alone in the kitchen together.

"Awww… You shouldn't have," I said.

"Drop the attitude. Please."

I sighed. "Fine. Sorry."

"I am *letting* you go out with your friends tonight. Because I believe that these things are important and not the kind of privileges that I feel should be taken away," Dad said. "I'm not asking for anything unreasonable." He ruffled my hair. "Go have fun."

Sounded like that was a threat. Like he had to stop himself from saying 'or else.' Maybe, I thought, I should have stopped being such a dipshit about it… after all I was serving him some pretty thermo-nuclear lies about what I was doing while I was skipping class. On top of the already radioactive lies about what I was doing with Tom.

ANYWAY.

We actually did have somewhere to be, now that all the birthday stuff was out of the way. Apparently, they'd been planning on heading over to a screening of *The Stupendous Man of the Southern Mountains*. It was kind of like the penultimate Superhero B-Movie. It got screenings around this time of year in tiny indie theatres. There were callbacks and shouting. It was more of a social experience than a movie you'd like… watch.

That said, Rook had to bail before we went to the theatre. He felt really bad, but he had a doctor's appointment opening pop up at the last minute. "And it won't be another five months before the office has another free space," he said when he took me aside. He was almost hyperventilating.

"Hey, it's totally okay," I said.

"I really do want to go to the movie."

"Hey! It's okay! Shit happens," I said.

"Aura convinced me that this is something I needed to see…"

"It totally is!" I smiled. "But no one says we can't do it again in like… Joshi's living room."

Rook nodded. He was way more shaken up than he should have been. But. That was Rook and that was okay. He'd be fine.

Meanwhile…

I kept getting looks from Branden.

Okay. I didn't know what was going on with Branden and me. Sometimes I could swear that we were flirting, but then when I'd try to follow up, he'd clam up. I kept trying to take him aside but he was like:

¯_(ツ)_/¯

And then, there we were in the theatre. He was sitting beside me and doing his absolute best to brush up against my arm or nudge my leg. But when I started to return the favor, he backed off. Which… I guess he wanted to keep it subtle around the rest of the crew. He was, after all, already dating someone, and wasn't openly into dudes.

But it did leave me kinda… agitated? Bothered. Definitely bothered. I went to the bathroom to splash some water on my face to try and… reset I guess? Go back to acting super excited with everyone else.

Branden was leaning against the wall outside the bathroom when I got out.

"Hey," he said. "You okay?"

"Yeah," I nodded.

"Sorry about the…" he waved his hand. "Don't know what I was thinking… I was just…"

"Yeah."

"Yeah." He nodded. "You uh… You want me to drive you home when this is done?"

Which really spiked my heart rate. I knew what he meant. Or did I? "I… Dad needs me back home ASAP," I said.

Alone with Branden in a car? I knew exactly where I'd want that to go. My muscles were getting weak thinking about how much I wanted that. And how much… I didn't want that. Couldn't we just stick to flirting over text until…

Until what, Wexler?

Branden scrunched up his face. "Lame."

"Yeah."

"When you grounded to?"

"When Dad figures that out, I'll let you know." I snickered.

"Damn… you didn't even do anything that bad," he said.

"Dad thinks so."

"All you really did was get in a fight… get a bunch of detentions… lied about grades… And then skipped class…" Branden shrugged. "Actually, yeah I'd be in way worse shit if I did that."

I wanted to lift up his shirt and bite him. And I... wasn't really sure where that idea came from. Get his pants down in the middle of the hallway. And—

"You okay?"

I took a breath. "Yeah. I'm... Just got a lot going on."

He punched my shoulder. "Well... you got my number. We can talk."

I still wasn't even sure if he was into me. Since Halloween, I couldn't tell if he'd been trying to get a little closer... or if he was just always like that. I'd tried not to stare, trying to gauge how he acted with other guys to see if he treated me any different or if that was just how he bro'd around.

So far — I couldn't tell.

But here he was. Following me around and offering to drive me home.

If I'd asked, would he have followed me into the bathroom with the lockable door? Or was he just trying to be a good friend because he saw that I was kind of losing my mind? I really needed to start thinking of ways to get things off my plate...

I wished there was a way I could tell Dad about the superhero stuff.

Was it too soon for that?

Yeah, it was too soon for that.

CHAPTER 53
VIOLENCE
(THE GIFT THAT KEEPS GIVING)

Friday, November 17

I got home an hour and a half later than I was supposed to. Not surprisingly, Dad was still up with Tom — I could definitely tell they were talking about something else before I got inside. Dad and Tom both saw different sides of the Vigil world and they passed information between each-other that would either be confidential or dangerous.

Dad was pretty… *liberal* about keeping client confidentiality around me. From his tone of voice, I could tell which secrets I was supposed to keep and what was something I was supposed to pretend I'd never heard.

On the other hand, Tom was airtight about almost literally everything. (Do NOT play cards with him.) So I didn't know how he was even involved with any kind of Vigilantism outside what we did. I always got the feeling that I wasn't the only 'student' he brought up (not that he ever talked about others).

I waved. "Hey! I'm just headed to—"

"Nope!" Dad said. "Come here."

My brain was sending me signals that it was a trap. And like I said about Tom — he has a helluva poker face. He shrugged when I looked to him to see if it was safe.

"Sit down, please," said Dad.

"Daaaaa-aaad."

"Sit."

I took the armchair across from Tom.

"We are going to work on your school attendance…" he said.

"Right." I nodded.

"And those scrapes and marks that keep popping up on your chest... Face. Arms." He shrugged. "If you're trying to hide that you're still getting into fights, you could always wear a shirt once and a while."

"Dad, it's fine—"

"No..." He shook his head. "It's not fine. I thought we were done with this—"

"Really, Dad?" I huffed. "You want to bring this up at almost midnight?"

Tom looked like he was about to say something, then got a look from Dad.

"You were the one who stayed out well past curfew," said Dad. "Which... I figure a birthday gets a bit of leniency."

"Okay... well... I'm sorry." I cleared my throat. "I'll cut back."

"Cut back?"

I lowered my eyes. "It'll get better."

"As in?"

"It'll stop."

Dad clapped his hands. "Good. I am proud of you for owning up to it! But you're definitely at two strikes now."

I let out a breath. "Okay."

"It's his birthday!" said Tom, very suddenly. "Take a strike off or something."

Dad sighed. "One-point-five again, then." he looked up. "That's what Tom got you, I guess."

"And not all!" Tom said and went into his pocket. Gifts of any kind from Tom were usually small and meaningful.

Dad threw his head back. "Oh please don't let it be something violent—"

"I saw these on the internet. Thought they were neat. Wanted to see if they lived up to the hype." He pulled out a small, finger-length cylinder. "You just..." He flicked a switch at the end and it extended so forcefully that it burst through a paper lamp shade beside him. "Oh shit... Sorry Andy. I'll uh... Next time I'm at Ikea..."

"Right. But you're giving Luca a weapon? In this house?"

"It's not a weapon, really," Tom said. "It's just a... like a fidget spinner. But for... you know. Kids who like meatier toys."

Dad looked at Tom like he was summoning a demon.

(I was the demon.)

I grabbed it when Tom held it out to me and swung it around a little. It was a lot heavier than I would have expected it to be, being as *shrinkable* as it was.

"Watch it!" Dad ducked.

"He's fine!" Tom said, and nodded at me. "You're fine."

"Does it actually work?" I said, making a pose. "Like. In a fight?"

"You wouldn't need to know that," Dad said. "Because you're not getting into fights and certainly none that include assault with a weapon." And then he gave the brushed-metal staff another look-over. "Actually, can I see that?"

Dad flexed it a little bit. "It's sturdy... but it's got just enough give..." and then he looked to Tom. "*Does* it actually work? I remember when we were cruising around, they tried to make collapsible weapons like this... but—"

"They were shit," Tom said.

Dad laughed. "Yeah, and you started me carrying around that... damn sword..."

"...Which you let the CDG confiscate when you sold the brand rights..." said Tom.

Dad cleared his throat. "Yeah, something like this would have been useful."

"Not as iconic—" I grabbed the staff back from Dad when he wasn't looking.

I tried to get it to collapse, but it was a hassle. And then I flicked the switch and it sprung out of my hands across the room. Going to fetch it, I spotted a bit of a dint in the paint... but I didn't tell Dad. I made a quick glance over at the two of them talking before nudging a house plant in front of it.

"Well," Tom said. "They work *enough*. Cheaper, hobbyist ones are good for a bit of sparring — I did some stress testing with a few brands. That's one of the more mid-range ones. Pretty sturdy but they'll collapse when they come under pressure. So we probably won't see a whole lot of use for now... Especially as high-lethality Vigilantism is getting popular again..."

Dad grumbled very disapprovingly.

Tom looked back at me. "But... if you want to get creative, they've got use. To be practical, you would need to carry about five or six of them as backups. Take them out when needed, and then discard them as they break. Vigils always drop their weapons on chases and stuff. Still... a good idea... Bad guy thinks you're disarmed and then — bam! Backup."

"You're usually a whole lot more pro-sustainability than that, Tom," Dad said.

"I'm also pro-against-getting-married-to-one-weapon. Because then you could drop it or, I don't know... surrender a priceless artifact to an authoritarian governmental department."

Dad grumbled.

"Don't worry. My sister bought it back at the Avalon Knight II death auction," he said. "Ask me how much the bill was."

CHAPTER 54
THE MODERN VIGILANTE

Saturday, November 18

Turns out I'd read the room right, and Tom wanted to start putting these puppies to field use. "They won't throw your weight off as much when you're free-running." He said. "But if you're carrying six of them, it's gonna be a little bit more strain. Also want to get the motions down of drawing them and collapsing them."

"I thought we were just gonna ditch them when they broke."

"Well, they're not single-use. And they are expensive. We're gonna try these ones out, and if it jives, I'll invest in a few sturdier ones."

"Like… different sizes?"

"You'd have to memorize belt placements, weights…" Tom sighed and weighed his head. "But I'm not opposed if you're up to it."

"Nice—"

"But we stick to the classic wood until I decide. You understand? *I* decide when you're good for it."

"Right—"

"And you're gonna have to stop getting into fights," Tom said, getting progressively louder. He snatched the pole away from me because I was spinning it instead of listening. "Seriously, are you trying to blow the lid on this whole operation?"

I nodded. "Sorry…"

Tom hesitated. "You're kicking ass though, right?"

CHAPTER 55
EXTRACURRICULAR ACTIVITIES

Monday, November 20

This was the day. I checked the paranoia phone on the dog run, and there were unread texts waiting.

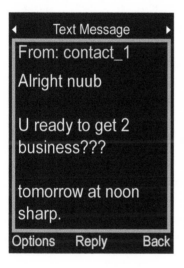

"You're going right?" Emily said on our way to school.

I fumbled for an answer.

"You really thinking of turning this down?"

"I'm considering it," I said. "Look, I never really wanted to be ace investigator. I just wanted to do that friendly neighborhood stuff. Take selfies. Maybe license a comic book line and make a movie series that would feature the world's first trans action star — you know. Little things."

"Wow…" She sighed.

"What?"

"I have literally never known you to back down from a fight."

"This isn't a fight..." I said. "This is taking what Tom normally has me doing and making it illegal times ten."

Emily veered her longboard in front of me and stopped dead. She grabbed the sides of my head and shook a little. "Luca Wexler! What is wrong with you? You sound ZERO percent like you."

I thought for a minute and brushed her hands away. "I don't know... ever since... I don't even know. Something seems... Strange. I'm having messed up dreams, and I'm not sleeping very much—"

"Less than normal?"

"I woke up three times last night. I'm having weird dreams."

Emily blinked. "Weirder than your fetish dreams?"

"If I was having those again, I wouldn't be complaining." I sighed. "Most of the time I can't even remember them, but last night I remember standing on the side of a really... deep pit. And there wasn't anything around. It was like a dessert. And this pit was *really* deep — But something was inside."

Emily whistled. "Creepy."

We got walking again. "And then I try to see what's inside. And then I looked around, and I was in the hole, but it was a tunnel. When I woke up, I had vertigo for half an hour."

"And for this reason, you don't want to get involved in an up-and-coming Vigil team which could help you take down America's first real Super-Villain to pop up in years?"

I shook my head. "Something's wrong about this. I'm telling you."

Emily punched my arm. "Well... if you stay away — then you'll never know if you were just paranoid or if there actually were black helicopters overhead."

She was usually right about things anyway.

CHAPTER 56
MUTUAL PARANOIA

Monday, November 20

I could piece together who 'Glow' was. I assumed I was meeting the girl with the armor that could make neon barriers. I hoped she wasn't gay... that would be way too typical and... branded. It'd be like me draping myself in a trans-flag cape. Even though it was kind of in-style for professional vigils to slap a Pride Flag patch on their shoulder. Right under the American Flag and their state flag.

Apparently, Tornado Force VI (the sixth Vigil to be registered as Tornado Force) spent more than $85,000 on designing and testing an entirely new costume just so she could use the Pride flag with the brown and black stripes. Apparently, you couldn't really make out the extra two stripes on her old one.

So.

There I was only a dozen blocks south of where I literally lived, meeting with someone who might have wanted to arrest me, or worse. Someone who I would only be able to notice because of a vague fashion choice and a coffee addiction. (No judgment.)

Inside, there was only one person in the cafe with a purple hat — because there was only one person in the café.

"Not much point in cloak and dagger," she said. Two of the mugs were empty. She was a strong-jawed, early twenty-something girl with frizzy hair tied tight against her head and bunched into a ponytail. I wasn't sure who I'd been expecting, but she wasn't it.

"I know I'm early but..." I sat down. "You been waiting long?"

She shrugged. "Yeah. Hazard of the craft." She sent off a text message. "One of us is keeping a lookout," she said, pointing out the window and across the street. Someone was hanging out on the roof, peering inside. Cowboy.

He darted away when we looked at him.

She huffed. "Can't be too careful. Sorry."

I snorted. "I'm the one walking into what might be a trap."

"You could have led the ambush to us."

"So we're both paranoid."

"Yeah."

"The difference is you have a sniper trained on me. I don't have shit like that."

"Good time to make friends?" she sighed. "Our HQ isn't far from here."

"Never follow a stranger to a second location," I said. She just looked at me. "But do I have a choice at this point? Or do I get a bullet if I get wet feet?"

"I'm sure you've got some tricks up your sleeve," she said.

I might have, but I wasn't confident. Honestly, I think I was less worried about them and more worried about where this rabbit hole was going. I grabbed a coffee of my own on the way out.

She led us to a self-storage facility on the corner of 25th and Indiana. Very plain, but imposing — red brick, with multi-panel windows. Industrial Stalinist. The entrance was cut out of the corner.

We kept to the ground floor, but it seemed we were headed for the back. "I'm Afterglow," she said, stopping at unit door 1-D14. She knocked in a specific pattern. "Don't use your real name."

"We're dealing with super-hackers and cyber terrorists. You really think that Aliases are going to hold up?"

"I don't make the rules—"

The door swung open so quick it spooked both of us.

"She does," said Afterglow.

And on the other side of the door was a tall black woman who wore bright purple glasses she didn't need. A flared blazer and jeans, and multiple stone-beaded leather-braided necklaces.

The retired American Vigil known as Flechette. Also known as Holly Roland.

CHAPTER 57
DEGREES OF SEPARATION

Monday, November 20

She... wasn't someone who was ever at a loss for words. Except now, apparently.

A few seconds passed where she blinked a few times, trying to reset her vision to see if it was me or someone who just looked like me. And... you know. I was kind of in the same camp. I didn't really trust myself at that moment to keep my cool about this.

"One exception," said Afterglow. "And... I can see on your face that you're a little star-struck. This is Holly Rolland — Flechette—"

"Oh! Yeah. *Mistress* Flechette. How could... Oh my god, it's really you!" I held my hands up to my face. "Oh my god... I'm such a huge fan. You know I heard that you were in the city — this is so... Could I get an autograph? For a friend?"

She held an innocent expression as best as she could — grinding her teeth and pinching the corners of her eyes. I shook her hand with two of mine; she yanked hers away. "We should get inside," she said, and shut the door behind Afterglow and me.

This was a storage room with a docking bay, so it was a bit bigger than what I expected. Also — a little more lived-in. There were cots along the walls, folding tables in the middle, a coffee station, a TV, and takeout boxes scattered around. Definitely had more 'clubhouse' vibes than headquarters of semiprofessional vigils.

The part that *did* scream 'I mean business' was the computer set up beside the tables. Multiple monitors and computer towers, cords and wires bundled together with velcro, one of those glowing rainbow keyboards, and a big green trackerball mouse.

My... survey of the room was cut a little short when my eyes crossed the baby-faced, barrel-chested, freckled ginger leaning on the table. Tall, broad, and too cute to be intimidating. And he could fill a pair of jeans... from the back and the front.

And the thighs.

Woof.

"Time for introductions!" said Afterglow. I hadn't even realized I was staring — I'd even forgotten all about Holly. Afterglow pointed around the room. "Silhouette."

The spy-girl who told me to get in touch with Jillian. She looked my way but didn't say anything.

Afterglow pointed to the baby-faced big guy. "Tank—"

"Hi," the big guy said. I was still having a hard time not staring at him.

"Hi." I didn't even mean to say anything. I just kinda. Yeah. Kinda came out.

I said W O O F.

Afterglow carried on. "Six-Shot."

Wowie... *Cowboy's* actual alias was somehow dumber than the nickname I gave him. A lot lankier without his overcoat, he gave me a quick, cold salute. His blast pistol was in its holster on the table.

"And now, the new Avalon Knight..." said Holly. "A lot shorter than the original... You've got some very big shoes to fill."

"Could have at least made your own name," said the cowboy.

"Because Six-Shot is peak creativity," I said.

He held out his arm. "Why is he even here?"

"You know exactly why," said Afterglow.

Someone poked her head out from behind the computer. She had an undercut, a sternum ring, a flannel shirt, and tattoos climbing up her neck and down one of her arms. "Yeah, about that," she said. "New guy — I've been literally wet-dreaming about getting my hands on one of those drives for weeks."

"How did you find it?" asked Six-Shot, stepping between Hanna and me.

Holly guided me around him. "Not important right now."

"Yes, important!" He followed her. "What if he was planted here?"

Holly ignored him. "A.K., this is Wench. She runs our tech. Also goes by Hanna Tellerson."

"How come she gets a name?" I said, then got another look. Serious androgyny vibes... "They... Get a name?"

She/they shrugged. "I mean whatever works. But no really — you've never heard of me?"

"Not everyone reads FBI reports," said the burly one — Tank.

"*You* were raised on a literal island," said Hanna.

"I'd never heard of you either." Afterglow admitted.

"Should I have?" I asked.

Hanna threw up her arms. "Seven separate intelligence networks have specific teams to track me! And two are international!"

"I... Wouldn't think that's worth bragging rights." I said.

"Actually," said Silhouette, stepping out of the corner. "That's kind of an accomplishment. To the right crowds."

Hanna drummed on the plastic folding tables. "SSD SVP! That is an SSD and not a normal hard drive, right? Gimme!"

I had a small duffel bag with some gear in it — and *one* of the SSDs. The other two I had stashed in a safe place down the street from my house. Nobody needed to know I had more than this — Hannah certainly didn't question it, and immediately went to work trying to reverse-engineer a cable to read it.

"So, New Guy," said Holly. "While they're working on that, I'd like to get to know you a little bit."

CHAPTER 58
CONNECTING TISSUE

Monday, November 20

The second we were out in the hallway, Holly slapped me. "And what exactly do you think you're doing?"

"Ow… child abuse…"

She slapped my other cheek.

"Ow!"

"This whole operation is barely legal as it is—"

I snorted. "Barely legal…"

"But taking an actual minor into urban war zones is something my lawyer might not be able to argue. *Lawyers*." She threw her head back. "Plus, your father may literally murder me." She looked my way. "I'm under the assumption he doesn't know."

"No."

"How are you managing to get around the city as much as you are without him noticing?"

"He's out of the city a lot…" I said. "And I have an alibi—"

"Tom!" Holly threw her head back and moaned. "You know, I am kicking myself for not seeing this coming. 'Scrappy young kid who doesn't take 'no' for an answer living a stone's throw from him.' Don't know how I didn't expect it… I supposed I thought he'd wait until you were older but… No, I know Tom better than that. No idea how you're keeping your father in the dark." She sighed. "How long have you been doing this?"

"I started lessons with him when I was eight…" I said, and she gave me a look. "And then the Vigil stuff when I was twelve…" I said, and she gave me a look. "Got in on blindfold training, firearms, free-running, and gear training a few years ago," I said, and she gave me a look. "And then he started putting me on the streets in the summer."

"So he's been planning this for a while. Isn't that just like him?" She sighed. "Suppose it's best if you get 'em young. Get it working like second nature." She popped her tongue and sized me up. "Shouldn't you be in school?"

"It's lunch break."

"It's lunch break..." She nodded. "You go to Moscone, right?"

"Yeah."

"I'll forge you a note or something." She sighed. "Lord above..."

"Because those guys are peak maturity..."

She flicked my shoulder.

"And I'm guessing Dad doesn't know about your island of misfit superheroes?"

"Andy has a lot on his plate. He likes to stay out of less-than-legal tangles. We exchange information, and we don't talk about where we get it."

"That sounds like Dad..." I said. "What about Tom?"

"Tom has his own... 'hobbies.' The less anyone knows, the better. For now." She sighed. "Though with you here, there're enough points of contact to implicate Andy, specifically. Might as well give 'em the whole gritty affair. Hand over my social insurance number. Lord..."

"Yeah, what exactly are you doing?"

"Right now? Asking myself what I'm doing." She shook her head and paced a few steps. "But... there's a Vigil problem. "She sized me up. "I've had half a mind to get Tom into this."

I nodded toward the door. "They could use the help."

"They're talented but... unpolished." She looked at me. "Stop smiling. The whole point of this group is to have a new generation of vigils who actually give two shits. Which brings me to you."

"I thought this already was about me..."

"Right, but now we need to figure out what to do with you."

"What? Just going to kick me out?"

"Six-Shot has trust issues."

"Trust issues. Attitude issues. Style issues."

"A little bit of skepticism is perfectly normal," she said. "But sending you away would look suspicious, given that you already know where we are and what we look like. Which is ironic because you're the only one I know with complete certainty is not a Gentleman plant so... you get to stick around."

"Gentleman plant?"

Holly sighed and rapped on the door. The same pattern as before. "That's a group discussion."

CHAPTER 59
MEET N' GREET

Monday, November 20

"New Kid wants to know why we're after the Gentleman."

Everyone looked at me, and for a second I felt like I was gonna get stabbed... How many times did Ceasar get stabbed? I should know that I literally just had an English test on that.

I shrugged. "You just all seem like the... radical Communist type of rogue crimefighters." I looked at Hanna. "Especially you, cool-girl."

She nodded and gave me some thumbs up before turning back to the screen. Six-Shot rolled his eyes and went back to gaming on a classic Gameboy. Afterglow stuck with Hanna while she hacked her way into the drive.

"Come on, we'll give you the rundown," said Holly, and led me to the corner where Tank and Silhouette were sitting.

"Believe me," said Silhouette. "The hardest part was convincing the group that the Gentleman was bad news."

I looked over to her. "Started with you?"

"I was running the beat in Warsaw four years ago," she said. "Not sure if you can tell, but I'm not from around here..." It was a joke, I think, but didn't get any laughs. "Well. Thugs were raiding a house for a secret room in the basement. Owners had only lived there for a few years. No idea it was there. It was full of old Soviet stuff. I handed it over to authorities. I got the feeling that there was something deeper and started to dig into it.

"Followed some leads from a document in that house and ended up finding similar raids on old soviet house bunkers. I learned they were hired by a British guy. So…" She shrugged. "Tracked down his whole Eastern European operation over the next few months. One day he goes silent — it was like he dropped off the map. A while later, my contact at Deutsche Bank said some accounts I linked to him were transferring funds overseas. Not long after…" she waved her hand. "Gentleman launches his first YouTube videos."

"Then you know who he actually is?"

She shook her head. "I followed money and soviet documents, not a name."

"A while back," said Tank, "when the Gentleman showed up, we didn't think much of it. We were running around doing small investigations. Human trafficking, drug running. Corruption on the police force—"

"Pet project of mine," said Holly. "With a vengeance."

"Then the Mavericks disappeared," Tank said leaning against the table and crossing his arms. Jesus his forearms were as thick as his head. I was doing my best to get my focus on but…

But… that fur trail down from his belly button?

"So did everyone else," said Holly, a little louder.

She knew me way too well…

It brought me out of my #HornyBrain so hard I choked a little. I needed to find something else in the room to focus on… Like to coffee machine! Good old coffee machine… not erotic in any way. See? Coffee was always there for you when you needed it.

Six-Shot scoffed. "Rude of your old friends, not letting you know where they were off to."

"It's amazing how many parties you stop getting invited to when your sponsors drop you," Holly said.

"Were they ever really friends?" Six-Shot asked.

Tank rolled his eyes. "It's not like that, Six. It's just business."

"No, no. It really was like that." Holly said with a hair flip.

"Long story short," Afterglow said, forcing her voice to get us back on track. "The Gentleman has a weird collection of high-tech weapons, possibly mass-destruction devices — this is what he was looting in Europe. Since then, he's amassed an absurd number of connections to arms dealers, drug lords, kingpins... bad people."

I squinted. "How'd you gather that?"

Holly took a breath. "Silhouette came to me with some files she'd collected."

"Why these losers?" I said to her, making eye contact with Six-Shot.

"I needed to be sure that who I was working with couldn't be leveraged," Silhouette said. "These people didn't seem corporate and they were under the radar. I was more worried that they'd be working for the Gentleman—"

"I actually got an offer from him," Hanna shouted over. "I used the invitation to plug a spike into his network. For a whole two and a half minutes I had access to terabytes of data. Not that I managed to see a whole lot of it."

I squinted. "What did you see?"

"More or less the same thing that *Silhouette* brought to Holly. Plans, weapons, schematics. And a heap of sensitive corporate information. Wikileaks kinda shit."

I crossed my arms. "Still doesn't explain why he's so obsessed with San Francisco."

"I think it's because he's autistic," said Afterglow. Everyone looked at her kind of weird. "What? My brother has a weird, inexplicable obsession with commercial shipping lines." Everyone kept staring. "Like anyone else has a better explanation."

"Right," said Holly. "I figure we can discuss the why after we figure out the who, how, and where."

Hanna called out. "WAIT HOLD ON! Hold on. Right there..."

CHAPTER 60
THE IMPORTANCE OF W

Monday, November 20

We looked at each other while the pace of her typing hit a fever. Nobody moved. Holly had her hand reached behind her orange leather jacket, and her eyes darted around to the exits. I assume she had her hand on a pistol strapped to her back. Six-Shot also inched toward his gun. Afterglow didn't really know what to do, and Silhouette didn't seem to react at all.

"What's... are we okay?" Tank asked, just loud enough to break the silence.

Hanna waved. "SHUSH!"

Afterglow took a look on Hanna's screen and gave the rest of us a reassuring thumbs-up. "All good," she moved her lips. Everyone relaxed a little bit.

After another minute, Hanna clapped her hands. "Okay! So. We were saying 'figure out who, whatever, and *where*'... well—" She cleared her throat. "Well, as it happens... I can help you with *where.*"

That only made the rest of us more confused.

"UGH! You guys are *stooopid.*" Hanna sighed. "Okay, so I wanted to know what was on the drive. Figured it'd be something exciting. Turns out... Maybe. Kind of. Ish. See, this thing," she waved her hands at the SSD connected by yellow and blue cables to the computer. "This thing isn't for storage. Well, kind of—"

"Hann," Afterglow rolled her eyes.

"Okay! So. The station we raided—"

"I raided," I said, and winked at Six-Shot.

"Whatever. That wasn't for storage. This thing has a complex algorithm that seems to be designed for sifting through a metric tonne of data. There isn't that much information on these guys because most of the storage space is occupied by the processing algorithm. Seriously..." She looked to me. "How many of these things were there inside the tower?"

I twisted my face. "About... six?"

"Yeah, okay. So that's probably dangerously close to being an artificial intelligence setup."

"Which is illegal," Tank said.

"Of course, it's illegal," said Six-Shot.

"Actually, it isn't illegal in California," said Holly. "But most tech firms won't touch them because the state has also passed an extensive bill of AI rights. Any company working on them can come under a massive amount of scrutiny. So unless contracted by the government, schools and companies won't use them—"

Hanna snapped her fingers. "I don't think Gentleman actually built a full AI, though. If I had to hazard a guess, he was going for an asymptote of non-completion—"

"A what?" asked Six-Shot.

"Yeah, what?" I said.

"When tech firms want to play with illegal code or regulated territory, they'll go for 'almost but not quite,'" said Afterglow. "There's no law against conspiracy to create an AI or possessing an unfinished one. So, if you want a program that has AI-like properties without Government intervention, you work with an unfinished version. You stick a bunch of non-complete AIs together, and they can basically do the same things a regular one can—"

"Only without the backtalk," Hanna added.

"Which applies to literally every other corporation trying to get around a regulation," Cowboy scoffed. "But why am I not surprised that this self-proclaimed anti-corporatist peacock does exactly what his 'competition' does."

"That's the thing," said Hanna. "He's a criminal. He has absolutely no reason to dance around laws. Why doesn't he just use an actual AI?"

Holly made a series of faces while she thought about that. "Actually... you might be on to something..."

"Am I? I mean, Right???" Hanna smiled. "So why isn't he just flat-out breaking the law, since he's now on a terrorist watchlist?" Hanna cleared her throat. "Right, I forgot to mention. I hacked into an FBI email account, and they're officially sticking him on a watchlist next week."

While this conversation moved in a direction that would drive Tom further and further up a wall, I was watching Silhouette in the reflection of the chrome air-exchange tubes running up the wall beside her.

She tensed up when I looked in her direction, but when she didn't think anyone was watching, I could read her body language a bit better. Seemed to me like she knew all of this already... And I'd wager she knew a whole lot more and would get more and more uncomfortable as her friends got closer to finding out, too.

"So," I interrupted, "what's this gotta do with *where*?"

"With what?" said Hanna, pushing her thick-framed glasses up her nose. "Oh! Where! Right. Well, the point of the station we — you/we — raided wasn't to store information. It was to store this AI, which would receive data from the trojan virus his goons planted in corporate servers. It would sort through that data, find the juicy stuff, and then send that data to another, remote server." She held out her arms like it was a punchline. "As in... I found out where..."

Holly flexed her fingers. "You hooked that thing up to the damn internet?"

"I bounced the signal out of four local proxy addresses, and then I bounced those signals out across twenty different spots in Brussels," Hanna added. "Seriously, I'm better than him, or who-ever he hired... he just has the defender's advantage."

Holly sucked in a deep breath. I literally felt everyone else in the room back away like she was about to blow up.

Hanna stood up. "I mean— I was careful, you know that, but... thing is, I don't think he had any idea that we were going to run a trace. His back door was wiiii-iiiide open. The office we raided was supposed to be the firewall — I just walked right in and grabbed an IP address in the city."

Holly nodded. "I trust you," she said. "But are you confident enough, or will we have to relocate?"

Hanna smiled awkwardly. "But like... all things considered...? Wouldn't hurt."

Holly rolled her eyes.

"Okay, but point being..." Hanna said. "Did he expect it? No. But he will sure as shit knows we found him. So we should prob-ably go get it... Like, now."

CHAPTER 61
MAGIC BICEPS

Monday, November 20

At the end of Van Dyke Avenue, there were three small warehouses on the left side of the road. Silhouette was poised on the lookout on a rooftop across the street. Afterglow and Six-Shot planned on storming the front, while Tank and me would slip in through the back. If it were my decision, I would have gone around the back door with Silhouette because she seemed stealthy and looked to be the only one aside from Holly who knew what they were doing.

Tom would've had an aneurysm if he found out about any of this. I'd never gone in anywhere without the element of surprise, and I'd never worked on a team. I also didn't like that the best we could do was hope that the Gentleman didn't have enough time to get his goons together. I brought it up with Holly, but she shrugged and said: "Welcome to the Vigil life."

On top of that, I was dancing dangerously close to Dad finding out that I was skipping class again, and my only alibi was a celebrity breaking the law.

But on the other hand… eye candy.

I sat beside Tank in the van on the way over here. His outfit was a bare-armed, sleeveless look. Popular in movies, but Tom would have ripped him apart for being exposed. But I thought that this was a very sensible exception to the rule.

Every time the van hit a bump I pressed up against those arms.

Him's muscles was F I R M.

So there we were: me, Tank, and the sweat beading on his arm. We'd gotten to the back door, stuck against a dingy, barely-paved backstreet, and signaled over the com that we were in place. It wasn't long before Afterglow gave her signal.

"Teams ready?" Holly took a breath. "Alright Hannah, get the door."

There was a short flicker of power, lights blinked and air conditioners roared to life for half a second. And then an explosion went off inside the warehouse and shooting started.

"What's going on?" Silhouette asked.

"Smoke grenade," Afterglow replied.

"They're returning fire!" Six-Shot said as gunfire popped off inside the warehouse.

"Alright, crew," Holly continued. "Keep your head down, we kicked the nest. Team 2, head in."

"Our cue," Tank said, and lifted me up to the utility window above the door, pushing it open just enough for me to slide in and land on the other side. The back room was an office. The place looked like it'd been abandoned for months.

"Problem," I said, getting back to the door.

"What?"

"No lock latch. Double-keyhole," I said. "I can pick it open but—"

"No time, stand back," he said.

"What?"

"Stand back."

I had *just* enough time to get back before a fist-sized mound appeared in the metal. It was almost as loud as the gunfire. And then another one bulged, close enough to the handle that it warped the door. Tank kicked it open, with a golden glow under his skin where his arms were bare.

"Woof…" I said. "I thought you were just pretty and basic."

"Woof what? I—" He cleared his throat. "We should get on. Stay behind me, I'm mostly bullet-proof."

"Mostly?" I said, as he cracked open the office door and looked into the outside warehouse where World War Three-and-a-Half was at a fever pitch. "That isn't like any kind of post-human strength I've seen."

He looked back at me. "You know we're like... doin' a *thing* right now, right?"

I zipped my mouth and gave a thumbs up. But no seriously, that was cool as shit.

He went first. I wasn't even out of the office before he got jumped by a guy with a shock gauntlet. Tank obviously hadn't been taught to check his blind spots. I rushed to help him but ducked back just as a shock gauntlet swung at my face. (Apparently, I didn't check mine either.) It discharged in the air and threw us both away.

As I lifted myself out of a pile of shredded cardboard and packing foam, I was getting the distinct impression that accidental explosions were a bug and not a feature. Luckily, I was starting to get over the whole nausea thing.

The guy who decked Tank came at me next. I rolled to my feet and grabbed the closest thing I could get to — a hand truck. Definitely not a weapon, but I pulled it around so that he punched his glove through it. Twisting it, I swept my leg under his feet and rolled to the side before it went off. The blast threw him into the office wall.

I went to help Tank to his feet... he was still a little dizzy. "I'm not electricity-proof."

Another thug ran at us. I pushed Tank back and ducked under a swing. He hadn't charged the gauntlet, so I guess he was just throwing his weight around. Something that heavy would hurt if it hit either way.

I cracked his jaw and kneed him in the ribs. Pushing him into a shelf and then onto the ground, I yanked the gauntlet off his arm and zipped his hands together.

"Those are handy," Tank said, "How come we don't use them?"

"Quit screwing around, we need a flank!" Six-Shot shouted.

"We're dealing with shock gauntlets!" Tank said.

Six-Shot scoffed. "Ooo-oooh!"

I heard a ricochet over the com. "Silhouette, you're up," Afterglow said.

"Affirmative."

We pushed toward the front of the warehouse. Another shocker tried to ambush us, but Tank was ready and batted him ten feet away through a wooden divider. Then a flash of light ripped through the room. The box next to me exploded, and I got that nauseous feeling again.

"Get down!" Tank tackled me onto the ground just as another white arc of electricity hit the metal shelves behind us.

"I can't believe I'm saying this," I said, "but I need you to get off me."

"Huh?"

"Off," I pushed him off and rolled over, barely slipping the mask off before I emptied my stomach onto the concrete floor.

"You could have told us they had laser guns now!" Tank shouted.

"More like pre-localized electric discharges, but... good try," Six-Shot said.

"It's sucking the juice out of my shields," Afterglow said. "I need it gone!"

"I'm on it," Silhouette said. "Coming down from above. See if you can grab the gunner's attention."

I spat blood onto the pavement and wiped my mouth with the back of my hand. Tank tried to stop me when I got up but I shrugged him off. "You go that way," I said.

"Be careful…"

"Don't tell me how to do my job!"

Ducking out into the main opening, I got a look at the gunner with the electric cannon — she shot at me but the arc went way over my head. Then she saw Tank, who threw a whole slat at her like a frisbee, and she dove for cover.

Silhouette dropped down into the electric gunner's cubby and took her out real quick.

But I was out in the open, and one of the other gunners stepped out of his cover to line up a shot at me. Without blinking, Silhouette took up the electricity-rifle and blasted him.

The other two gunners gave up, and everyone looked at her. She shrugged. "This one's non-lethal, he's fine. He'll be fine."

CHAPTER 62
PEOPLE PERSON

Monday, November 20

The last guy threw down his gun and surrendered. Silhouette dragged the girl who had the electric rifle to the main room while Tank went back to get the other three that we'd missed, then came back and stood by my side. Woof.

"Probably won't be long before the cops show up," said Holly. "Everyone in one piece?"

"Glad you finally got around to helping," Six-Shot spat at us. "We almost ran out of juice. I was barely packing a punch, and Glow's barriers got so spent, a bullet overloaded one of her plates."

"I'm fine," she said, but all the armor on her left leg was blown out, and there was a bit of blood dripping down her ankle.

"And *you*—" Six-Shot pointed at Tank. "You weren't supposed to let New Guy know about the light show."

Tank batted the finger out of his face. "It was either that or let you two bite it."

"Gonna ignore the bleeder?" I sighed. "Silhouette, I'm gonna assume you've got first aid? Get Glow to the van and get some pressure on that. Six, look for wherever the server room might be. The office was empty. Tank and me are gonna watch—"

Six-Shot laughed. "Nu-uh, New Guy, you don't boss anyone around."

Holly cut in over the com. "Six, shut up and take a look around. Silhouette, get Glow to the van. Bring the tech weapons with you. AK and Tank, watch the crowd."

Six-Shot threw his arms up and left.

"I'm fine, I can stick around and look—"

Silhouette tapped Afterglow's shoulder. "Come on. Let's get you looked at."

And then it was just me, Tank, and the cluster of seven Gentleman thugs. Tank flared up his skin-lights to be intimidating.

One of them looked up at us. "So…" she said.

Tank flared up brighter and she backed down.

"Easy," I tapped his shoulder. "I'm a people person. I got this." I stepped closer to the group. "So… How many of you don't want to be here? Who's only here because Gentleman's got leverage on you?"

Of the five who were still conscious, four raised their hands. "Sheep," said the one holdout girl.

"Okay, don't pay attention to her," I said. "Maybe you can help us along so we can be on our way—"

"Please!" said the one that I beat up with the hand truck. He crawled forward. Tank tried to get between him and me, but I waved him down. "Please, you have to let us go — he said he has ways to shut us up… even if the police have us!"

"Alright," I said. "What's your name?"

"That's rich, coming from a guy in a mask," said the holdout. "Who owns you? Google?"

"Shut up!" said one of the other captives.

"We're independent… Island of Misfit Vigils, you know? Ooh!" I hit the com's talk button. "Okay! Team name. How'd you guys feel about *The Mystery Misfits*?"

"Not really important right now," said Tank.

"I like it," said Silhouette.

"You don't get to name the team you just got here!" Six-Shot bitched.

"But is it a bad name, Six?" said Holly. He just grumbled.

"Okay, we're the Mystery Misfits," I said to the crowd. "Just took a vote." I hit the talk button on the radio pack. "I'm also the team leader and a founding member: The Avalon Knight III. Going official soon. And unlike everyone else, I can actually get the Alias rights. So. Mark the calendar."

"Somebody mute him!" Six-Shot cried. Could hear him from the other side of the warehouse.

"Right, but who are *you*?" asked the holdout. "What's your name?"

"Come on! We just need to get out of here!" said another.

"Exactly, you know what's up," I pointed to him. "Gold star for... You." I tapped my chest. "I'm Ben."

"Fake name," said holdout.

Finger guns. "Yes. But you know why I can't tell you. So are we gonna get friendly or...?"

Hand-truck guy cleared his throat. "Shaun."

"Georgina," said the girl who tried to shoot me with the Electricity rifle.

"Will."

"Chet."

The last girl crossed her arms. And when I say 'girl'... yeah, she wasn't much older than me. "Alicia." I hated her already.

Six-Shot lit up the com. "This place is fucking deserted. Hanna, you better be sure this is the spot."

"If it wasn't the place, then why would there be people shooting you?" Hanna spat back.

I squatted down to be roughly eye level with everyone. They were all young. College-age or young professionals. Squirmy types. Definitely looked like they wanted to be anywhere else, and not because they just got their asses handed to them.

"So. What's got you so spooked about the Gentleman? Outside of the... blackmail thing. He seems like he'd be kinda reasonable."

"No! Not him!" said Will. "His recruiters."

I nodded. "Recruiter... About six-two? Healed-over third-degree burn on his face? British accent?"

They looked around. Chet broke the silence. "That's Kurt. Kurt Hamen. He's one of the guys the Gentleman hired to... He's like a right-hand man."

"I know of him," Holly said in my ear. "I'll have info on him when you get back."

"Our point of contact is a guy named Temple. Put us through drills."

I recognized that name.

"I don't know of him, but I will," Holly continued.

"Temple says that if we talk, the Gentleman doesn't want to know details about how he deals with us."

I hummed. Well... they really weren't great at the 'no talking' part. "Well we're not the police," I said. "And we don't need to know much about meetings or anything. We just want to know where the Gentleman keeps his data cache. We'll find it either way, but the sooner we find it... the sooner we can be on our way. That means the more time you have to scram before the cops show up..."

The four helpful ones jumped up, ready to show the way. I took Will because he seemed the most innocent. I told Tank to keep an eye on *Alicia*, who kept sulking with herself and her unconscious coworkers on the floor.

Tank grabbed my arm. "What do I do?" he whispered. "They're waking up."

I picked up one of the rifles from the floor. Looking over my shoulder to make sure none of them saw, I ejected the clip and cleared the barrel. I pushed the rifle at him. "Just wave it around a little bit." I doubled back to him. "Remember to keep your finger off the trigger... yeah like that, and don't point it *at* anyone, got it. Keep the safety on just to be sure, right?"

"Safety?"

I reached over and flipped the switch on and off again. Six-Shot must have been listening because he joined me, and we followed Will to a corner where there was a shelf on wheels. It rolled out of the way to show a staircase downward.

Will went back, and Tank got him and the others out before the police arrived. Six-Shot and I cautiously descended. This was the only part of the warehouse that wasn't covered in dust. It was clean, cool, and dark.

Downstairs there was only a small desk. On it, there was a laptop hooked up to a couple more SSDs. We were both expecting more, but Hannah was over the moon.

CHAPTER 63
CLUBHOUSE

The new clubhouse was on McKinnon Avenue, even closer to home than the storage facility. Great.

The inside was an oven, dirty and humid. Posters were laid out on the table, but the rugs were on the floor. And the floor was filthy so they were definitely needed.

Hanna's computer set-up was still being unpacked when I got there. Looked like most of the tables had to get left behind. What we had instead was a large, round antique table. It was nice, but falling apart. The coffee machine was good to go, though.

Priorities.

"I've got ID's on the two names you folks pulled," said Holly. "First up, Kurt Hamen. British Ex-Special Forces, dishonorable discharge eight years ago. Unpleasant doesn't begin to describe him. He's been working with a Private Security Contractor called 'Rex' ever since."

"And Temple?" I asked. "The other one. Is he also Rex?"

"Temple, South African, made a name for himself training up militia cells in Africa and South America," said Holly. "He doesn't work for Rex, but he has connections inside the organization."

"Don't forget about the third one," Afterglow said. "Could they also be working for Rex? Could narrow down the list."

"There isn't any guarantee that the third would specifically be a mercenary," said Holly. "Hannah's convinced that he's a computer specialist. She's gonna work on cracking the cache. Shouldn't take long so sit tight for a while."

"Do we really need to be here though?" I asked, antsy to get on my way to school and think of an excuse on the way there.

"Not sure why you wouldn't want to know what's inside that thing," Six-Shot said, hoisting the tech rifle from the duffle-bag of seized equipment. "You know, because you worked so hard to get it."

Holly sent a glance my way like she wasn't going to talk him down.

Hanna hooked up the stolen laptop to about fifteen different cables. Everyone else got comfortable except Six-Shot and After-glow, who got to work on disassembling the tech-rifle. Putting screws into small plastic cups and making notes on a clipboard.

I cautiously approached. "You aren't worried it's gonna be radioactive or something?"

"No," he said. "Probably not."

"Reassuring," I said, sitting down at the table not far from him.

"Hey. We've got the schematics for a plasma rifle—"

"Oh is that it?" Afterglow asked.

"Looks like it.

She whistled. "He actually got it running?"

"If you have the blueprints for his stuff, why don't you use it against him?" I asked.

Six-Shot pulled his pistol from its holster and waved it in the air. "Well... I had the base-model built myself. Kinda was a... blunderbuss shockwave thing. Between the Gentleman's schematics and getting a look at Afterglow's armor, I've been improving it where I can."

"And by all means," said Afterglow. "We've tried to build some of the stuff, but a lot of it is based on theoretical technology that never existed. Kind of like... if this technology exists, we can build doomsday device No. X. Gentleman's pretty good at making the 'if' happen though."

Six-Shot wrenched off a metal hatch on the rifle. "Honestly with this... I'm hoping I can salvage some bits I can use to upgrade Kitten."

Silhouette cleared her throat. "Kitten is his pistol."

"Is your armor based on Gentleman tech?" I said to Afterglow.

"No. Brother's in MIT. He cracked portable light-mass field generation. He passed his designs to me so I could test it. At least... without selling out to a military contract."

"Military can't seize tech that's for-use in the vigil-sector," I said. "That's clever."

"Yeah but the becoming-a-vigil thing is easier said than done. Need to be registered before I can own the patent the tech," she said.

"You send your genius brother the Gentleman schematics?" I asked.

"We keep our family and friends away from business," said Holly, glaring at me. "That's one the rules."

"I'm not a tech person," Afterglow said. "But between Six and Hannah, we managed to build a working prototype."

Six-Shot looked over. "Yeah and we've been talking about how smart Glow's brother is and Hanna hasn't even gotten salty. You doing okay over there?"

But Hanna wasn't even typing. Her eyes were fixed on the screen while we sat in silence, watching her scan the screen while she scrolled. After a minute, she sat up. "Sorry what? What was that? Someone called?"

"What did you find?" Holly asked, leaning over the screen.

"Well... More than we hoped but not what we expected."

"Shit..." Holly said.

"What?" Everyone else said at the same time.

"It's a big pile of blackmail," Holly explained, and pushed Hanna's arm. "Scoot. I need to take a look."

Six-Shot cross his arms. "We were expecting that. What's he break into the offices for?

"Like… yeah, there is a 'Corporate Acquisitions' folder… And that's like most of the storage space because there are like.. pictures and videos and stuff. But a good chunk of what's finished decrypting is just a bunch of dossiers on people and—"

"He's using algorithms to automate his recruitment process…" Holly said.

Silhouette sighed. "Oh no…"

"Oh no?" Six-Shot looked over to the rest of the group. He'd ignored everyone else and taken to disassembling the plasma rifle we took from the warehouse. "What's so scary about that?"

"I… yeah," Hanna cleared her throat. "So, Google logs your searches onto your account. Same with Facebook. Amazon too, probably, because they own a dump load of server space. Even when you don't have Facebook open, it can read the cookies that your browser logs while you visit sites.

"This information is now owned by these companies, and they can sell it to advertising agencies. The whole process is automated in most cases, which is how you search for something or watch a video on YouTube, suddenly you start seeing ads for it everywhere."

Six-Shot scoffed. "And the Gentleman is interested in what I buy online because…?"

"It's bigger than that," Afterglow said.

"Damn right," said Holly, eyes glued to the screen.

"Like, yeah what she said," Hanna added. "These algorithms get intense. They can track your web history and automatically develop a psych profile on you. More or less. They track what dispositions you have toward companies, political leanings, and trends.

"Every change.org petition you sign or visit and *don't* sign helps a program develop a model of who you are. And this model is used to target you with political ads, suggested sites, even the order of sites and images listed in a search engine."

"Kind of old news as far as evil internet corporations go," Six-Shot said. "What's it got to do with how he gets his information?"

"This isn't about how he gets his information," I said, "this is how he finds his people. Can he *seriously* flag a post-human from a couple of google searches?"

Tank nearly choked. "Wait *what*?"

Six-Shot eyed him up. "We always thought he just rooted people out... Did *you* ever get contacted by him?"

"Stand down," Afterglow said. "We screened him, remember?"

"Yeah I—"

"Relax. I'm not accusing the big guy of holding out on us." Six-Shot finally set down the tiny screwdriver he was using. "We already knew he was keeping his post-humans in line by holding the CDG over their heads. I'm just—"

"If I got an email from him, don't you think I would have told you?" Tank said.

"I'm just wondering why not," Six-Shot said.

"Honestly, I think that's more because he doesn't really know how to use the internet in the first place," said Hanna.

Tank scowled. "What's that have to do with anything?"

"You asked me why I didn't have Internet Explorer on my computer," she said.

I snorted. "So if you're too tech illiterate to look up online post-human tests—" (they existed) "—he doesn't reach out."

"I don't go around blabbing about how post-human I am!" Tank said. "I know what I can do, and I can control it. I'm not looking for a chatroom because I 'want to know that there are other people like me' or something."

Hanna scoffed. "A chatroom, he says..."

"Besides," Tank said, "I've been told that I shouldn't go on places like that because that's how the CDG finds you."

"Been told by who?" I asked

Tank cleared his throat. "People…"

"Even without the internet though, you're not great at keeping it under wraps," I said. "And those are the kind of powers that the CDG would love to sink their claws into—"

"Hey!" he said. "I know that."

"I'm just saying…"

"Don't worry," said Holly. "I've set Tank up with a specialist who can help him get legal protection if it comes to that."

I snorted. "Specialist?"

But she shot me a glare from over the monitors.

Oh.

She meant Dad. Oh shit…

CHAPTER 64
VIRAL

Monday, November 20

Jesus, this whole thing was getting too tangled. I didn't even want to think about the kind of leverage it would take to keep the CDG away from a new toy like Tank. And he was a helluva toy.

…I wondered how I could coax Dad to give me his number without letting on…

"So," Holly broke a silence, "this is worse than I would have thought. Specifically the CDG angle." She pointed at the computer. "This is a time-bomb. One: there are seven kinds of dirt on everyone in upper management from here to Wall Street."

"And that's not even the whole thing," said Hanna.

"And Two," Holly continued, "The algorithms. It goes from maniacal to outright irresponsible. With the FBI and NSA, not to mention a growing army of private hackers hired by corporations, trying to sniff out the Gentleman, it's only a matter of time before they find these hidden algorithms. And then it'll be like…" She shook her head. "No, you're all too young to know what *Minority Report* is."

"It's a movie based on a short story," said Hanna. "The Government has the ability to see crimes before they happen and arrest people before they commit them."

Holly nodded. "That's the gist of it."

"But then someone learns that it's all bullshit and like… Commentary on the growing police state and—"

"Hanna…" Holly smiled.

"Right," the techno-enby cleared her throat. "Sorry. Go ahead."

Not that I couldn't see where this was going. "So if the CDG ever gets their hands on these programs," I said, "they could start snatching up anyone who goes on the wrong website."

"That probably wouldn't be the worst of it." Holly sat down.

"No?" Tank said, chest starting to heave. "Federal laws say the Military has the right to apprehend any weapons they want, and those laws are extended to the CDG and post-humans now and—"

Six-Shot put his hand on Tank's shoulder, and gave him a second to breathe and calm down.

"A valid concern," said Holly. "But right now we need to figure out what to do with this."

"Dump it," Six-Shot spat out.

"We're not dumping the data," Hanna shot back.

"Are the algorithms *on* the drives we have?" Holly asked.

"That's a complicated question," Hanna whistled. "See, technically some code that's snuck into corporate servers which grant the Gentleman the ability to manipulate existing—"

Holly snapped her fingers. "Hanna!"

Hanna sighed. "No... You can't access the programs or even reverse-engineer them with these drives. The Gentleman probably keeps that close at hand. If not outright memorized. This is just a collection of profiles."

"Even then," Tank said, "it's a list of people who are being blackmailed. Most of them are dirtbags with secrets, sure, but some of them are post-humans. Innocent people. Because we have this information, that second group is now in danger. Well I mean they were in danger before but what if someone hacks *us*?"

Hanna's jaw dropped. "How dare you! My network is secure—"

"What else is on there?" Six-Shot asked. "What can't we see?"

"Blackmail is dangerous..." Silhouette said. "Especially if he has more than just San Francisco secrets on there."

Blackmail is dangerous...

Something clicked in my brain. "Wait," I said. "We got this stuff really easy."

Everyone looked at me.

"When I stole the hard drive and... you shot me," I gestured to Six-Shot and he tipped an invisible hat again. "There were what? A dozen guys? More? But at that warehouse, there were like... six guys? And that Hamen guy wasn't even there."

"Right," said Six-Shot. "You'd think that if he wanted to take care of business, he'd send the professional."

Tank looked confused. "They had *guns* this time. We got shot at."

"No," I said, and then pointed at Afterglow. "They got shot at... you and me just got non-lethal shock weapons."

Silhouette lowered her head. "Shit..."

"What?" Tank asked.

She pointed at the computer. "He's smart. What does he think we're gonna do with this?"

Six-Shot crossed his arms and looked at me. "I don't want to give you the credit, but you might be on to something."

"That's ridiculous," said Afterglow. "We took the drives apart in the van to look for tracking devices. They're clean."

"The Gentleman likes to stick viruses in things that he can use to track something," I said.

"Hanna, your new network is secure?" Holly said.

"All internet connections are disconnected."

"Check and see if there are any background programs looking for a connection," I said.

A few tense moments passed before Hanna turned around. "Not that I can see. No." She nodded. "No. Nothing."

"So it's fine," said Afterglow.

"But that doesn't mean they aren't there," said Six-Shot. "Those are complicated algorithms, right? Maybe they can detect shit. Maybe they can *tell* when you're looking for them?"

"If that's the case, then we're fine because this computer is network-dead. No connections. Not even remote," said Hannah. "You're making me wanna wipe it and re-program it though…"

Six-Shot continued. "The reason the new kid found the other place was because he found a program! Gentleman's learning from his security gaps, and we're walking into it! We shouldn't have even done this! We should have thought this through, Holly!" he said.

"Better with us than The Gentleman though," Silhouette added. "This was basically his backup server. He might not have this information now.

"Then let's just wipe it!" Tank shouted, his lights flaring up a little bit under his cheeks.

Silhouette nodded. "Then again, there's no guarantee this is the only info-dump the Gentleman has…"

"This is our only lead on the GM!" Hanna protested.

I drifted over to the computer while they argued and elbowed in beside Holly to get a look.

Holly grabbed my arm. "I'm not here to parent anyone, but knowing more can get very dangerous." She let me go. "Be careful."

I didn't know about that… In my opinion, if the information could be used to hurt people, we should just get rid of it. But the GM may have hard copies so that wouldn't matter.

As I scanned through the information I recognized a few names. "This guy is on City council…" I said to Holly. She came behind me to have a look. She let out a whistle as my heart stopped.

Lang, Donghòu, — post-human asset.txt

"Are you kidding…" Rook's dad?

"Hmmm?" Holly leaned in.

I scrolled down.

"Oh, just more city council," I said, I found myself suddenly jittery like I was overly caffeinated. There could have been like... multiple Donghou Langs in San Francisco, right? Maybe it was a Donghou Lang from another city?

But in the next thirty seconds, it was like every last piece fell into place. The iron-grip handshake, and how he was always calling Rook away for whatever appointment.

It *was* Rook's Dad... I'd *met* him. I shook his hand and he nearly broke my wrist! He had natural-born super strength and he knew where I lived, too!

Shit-shit-shit!

My head turned into a beehive, buzzing with information. I knew from the beginning Donghou Lang seemed a bit different... but this...

"I need to head out," I said to Holly.

She scanned the room and subtly nodded toward the door. The rest of the group settled on waiting to decode the rest before taking any course of action. I slipped away while they were speculating about what to do after that. The more I had to do with this group, the less I wanted to do with this group.

CHAPTER 65
LIKED, SHARED, SUBSCRIBED

Monday, November 20

I met Emily as she was leaving school. We'd agreed to meet on the bleachers, where it'd be easy to spot anyone trying to listen in. Also, it would be a great spot to film my Lifetime movie in thirty years.

"You know, for a second," she said, "I thought that you got kidnapped."

"They kept me around to do some superheroing."

"Oh. Behind my back," she rolled her eyes.

"Look… they had a no-phone rule and they were *constantly* on me. I would have sent a text if I could have but… I get why they're so paranoid now." I didn't know where to start. "So…" I said, "Turns out that they got put together by Holly."

"Holly… Rolland?" Emily sighed.

"Yeah, this is getting real close to home, right?"

"No. Well… yeah. But also like… Big respect for Holly. I didn't think she had it in her." She kissed her fingers and held them in the air. "Respect."

"It gets better…"

— — —

"So yeah, blackmail is bad," she said. "And yeah the Gentleman is trash who's putting on a fresh coat of Social Justice Warrior brand paint to conceal his horse shit. Holy crap I've never felt so vindicated."

"About?"

"Turns out he's just a fake-ass social media shitposter after all. Go us!" She shook my shoulder. "But you look like someone killed your puppy... Can you like... Enjoy anything?"

"That's... There's a new thing."

She squinted. "A thing?"

"Rook's Dad—"

"Yeah?"

"He's... He's one of those Gentleman Thugs."

She paused for a second. "Wait, what?"

"He's..." I leaned back against the seat. "He's post-human—"

She literally almost choked. "No way—"

"And the Gentleman's been using him on operations."

Emily's Jaw dropped. "But... he's an accountant!"

"He's also a post-human, and because he's a Chinese citizen, the CDG wouldn't have access to any information that he's a post-human."

"If the CDG took him... and he's Chinese... That'd be an international incident!"

I shook my head. "I don't know."

"Granted... he's a 'freelance accountant,' so I guess there's more than one way to leverage him into illegal stuff." Emily sighed. "Like... using him as muscle seems like a waste when you can have him cook the books."

"Money doesn't seem like a problem for the Gentleman."

"Well, maybe this is why..." Emily tilted her head back and screamed a little. "Jesus Christ, this is fucked up! This is probably why Rook is such a flake." Emily's wheels were turning. She wanted to know what she could do about it and honestly, so did I.

CHAPTER 66
PARENTING INTENSIFIES

Wednesday, November 22

So. It seemed like Holly never got around to excusing me from school. Sure, I got that she was a little bit occupied at the time, but like... I was grounded. Really grounded — to the point where the only time I could socialize was at school. Which was ironic because I got in trouble for missing school.

That was how you used *ironic*, right?

That also included time spent with Tom, though. Avalon Knight training was on complete hiatus because Dad wasn't even going to let me bum around with Tom after my shifts.

"Quite frankly," Tom said, "I think this is a perfect consequence of cutting class."

So Tom was on Dad's side, and nobody was on Luca's side.

Dad was so peeved he couldn't remember what strike he was on. "You know what? I'm not even surprised." That was the line that really hit me in the feels. The whole thing was a test where the expectations were so low all I had to do was show up. Figures, with all the third-chances I'd gotten.

The thing I hated was that it wasn't even my fault.

Well... it was, but you know. It was a bunch of do-or-die situations. Dad was giving me such a hardcore cold shoulder I thought about letting him in on the Vigil stuff just to get some kind of response out of him.

Punishments were *stiff*. My dog walks were the only real times that I got to leave the house unsupervised. I'd lose my phone/computer/whatever for an hour per every minute that I was over what Google said the route would be. And Dad *also* connected my phone to a family tracker app and said that I wouldn't want to know what he'd do if I deleted it.

And this time, the way he said it told me he already had something in mind.

But being stuck in the house alone got me cranky, and I avoided doing homework even more than normal. This pissed Dad off even more. And there he was hoping I would use the chance to refocus on school work. It's not like any other time this happened I suddenly swung around. Getting stuck inside alone just made me want to sleep.

I avoided talking to Dad because all he had to talk about was how I was throwing my education away. "It just kills me to see you wasting opportunities."

"Oh that's great, I'll just pool all my energy in something I hate, and something that virtually everyone is better at than me, instead of focusing on my natural talents." I poked at the spaghetti. Not much point in loading up on carbs if your only permitted physical exercise was a forty-minute run.

"It's not like all the other things you like would disappear," Dad said.

"Right but…" I stabbed a meatball and split it apart. "What's the point of wasting all the effort and getting half as far when they can go the whole way without breaking a sweat."

"And what are your natural talents, then?" Dad said. "How would they help you pay the bills?"

I rolled my eyes. "I'll get an *OnlyFans*, Dad. Or *just4fans*. I'll play the field."

Dad rolled his eyes so hard I think he passed out for half a second. "Well… Athletics isn't a secure career. If you want to go pro, great. But you need a backup."

I poked some more.

"Luca, you can choose to succeed at—"

I dropped my fork against the ceramic plate. "No, I can't, *Andrew*. It's not a muscle, you're just born that way and you don't get it because it's easy for *you*. And you think that the work you put in is all that anyone else needs to do."

Dad sighed. "Luca, I push you because I know you're better than this."

"No, you only 'know' because you're smart and mom was smart. Smart people have this idea that people choose to be stupid!"

"But you choose to not succeed, Luca."

"No! Fuck that!" I shouted. Dad bit his tongue to stop himself. "I do succeed! I succeed at what I'm good at!"

He leaned back in his chair. "There's a difference between not being great at school and just not trying. You're not stupid."

"Yeah, and you need to tell yourself that because if I come by stupid honestly that means you're responsible. And the idea that anything stupid came from you is *unreprehensable*."

Dad rolled his eyes. "First, you mean 'unfathomable.'"

"Well…" I scoffed. "That's my point, right?"

"If you put half as much effort into studying as your little mind games…"

I snorted. "I'm sorry that yours and mom's perfect genes shat the bed, and that nobody's happy with what came out." Dad's face went blank. "You gave me the wrong chromosomes. I gave you the wrong *legacy*. I'd say we're even."

I could see that Dad wasn't sure whether to be angry, sad, or disappointed or whatever he should be feeling. I never liked using the pink blanket as a guilt trip, but if Dad was gonna fuck around, he was gonna find out.

Sometimes… I don't know.

Sometimes I just didn't have a whole lot of say over what I said.

I pushed myself out from the table. "Don't worry. I'll go."

"Luca, don't— Come back," Dad said, still lost in a confusion of what-to-do parenting questions, but I was already on my way out of the kitchen.

I didn't answer.

Dad met me at the bottom of the stairs. "Where do you think you're going?"

"Taking the dogs for—"

"Do *not* say it—"

I looked Dad in the eye for half a second.

"For a walk."

And suddenly the dogs sprung to life as if they weren't hiding under the table because their people were fighting. There was no stopping this. Dad had to let it happen or else deal with Lillie on his own.

I was out the door before Dad could say anything.

CHAPTER 67
HANDS-ON

Saturday, November 25

I had already arranged to work on the geo project with Rook on Friday. The presentation was in the first week of December and we were pretty much done, but we were putting together a model of the city. He wanted to 3D print it, and that would have been cool but... neither of us wanted to spend a weekend teaching ourselves how to use a 3D printer for a geography project.

Instead, we met as his place to build a city out of foam and glue. His apartment had more open space and much less dog hair. The model itself was a rectangle block. Two-point-five-by-three-and-a-bit feet.

Most of our model foam was used in trial-and-error for carving out the landscape. It took us a few tries before we got something we could work with. It was all white but covered in pencil marks for how the buildings and roads would be placed. The painting would be next week.

Definitely would be worth extra credit, and given that this was mostly my baby, I could say that I made a meaningful contribution. Can I tell you how stoked I got whenever I got a project where I got to build something? And where someone else did all the thinking?

The only real condition was that Dad wanted to reach out to Rook's Dad to let him know the terms of my grounding.

Donghòu Lang, post-human asset.

And 'Donnie' would be making sure we kept focused and on track, and that we wouldn't leave the apartment, as per my Father's instructions. Now... I don't have to go over the reasons why being around him made my hair stand up. Nothing against him — he likely didn't want to have anything to do with The Gentleman.

But it meant that The Gentleman was watching him... which meant he may recognize me. So not only was he reporting to Dad, but he was reporting to my *nemesis*. It made staying focused a little difficult.

But Rook... Rook was more stressed out than normal. It looked like he hadn't slept last night. When we were trying to glue sky-scrapers to the molded landscape, he accidentally snapped one in half. He jerked his hand away and ended up crushing half the downtown region.

"Woah there, Godzilla." I was trying to break the tension, but for a second it looked like he was about to cry. "Hey, hey, hey. It's all cool." I patted his shoulder.

"Yeah. You're right. But... it just took us so long—"

"It's fine... We'll build more. It just means I get to stay away from my place for even longer," I said. "Plus, this could totally be part of our city story."

"I don't think we could get away with that. There hasn't been a significant sea monster attack in like... forty years."

"Not in America," said *Donghòu Lang, post-human asset*, while he scribbled math in dry-erase marker. "Be glad you guys weren't in Singapore for that. Scary stuff. My plane had just left for Melbourne six hours before it started."

While he was writing on the living room window instead of the white boards in his office, I realized I hadn't seen him on his computer... or in his office. Actually, aside from a phone connected to a bluetooth speaker for Rook and me, there weren't any electronics on in the apartment. I could guess why.

CHAPTER 68
THE MORE WE GET TOGETHER

Thursday, November 30

When I walked the dogs, I did my daily check-in with the Misfit Micromanagers. Though I wanted nothing more than for them to forget who I was. I felt like I was getting in way too deep.

I got a message at about 3:30 that read:

I was about to drop the phone and step on it, but then I got another text that said basically the same thing but with more swear words and a threat to find me if I didn't show up, signed by Six-Shot.

Figured I should see Emily for a second opinion.

Dad didn't even try to stop me. All I said was "I need to talk to Emily" which definitely wasn't a lie. He looked like he was gonna stop me for a minute, but seeing what we'd been butting heads over lately, I figured he wanted me to have an outlet. Better that I vent some steam off to Emily than stay at home and let it stew.

When I got to her place, Emily took a look at the text message. "Well, I'd think if you were being lured into a trap, they would have been less conspicuous?" She shrugged.

"That's what I thought."

She handed me the earpiece. "Keep yourself connected this time. I'll record the whole thing — I'm finally getting a chance to use that note recorder from Christmas!" Her excitement dropped. "You're having doubts?"

"There's so much that can go wrong," I said, "It's easy for you... you're an accomplice. Underage also. So charges won't stick. Underage or no... me being involved in this is a big risk."

Emily, for the first time, looked concerned. "Do you want to stop?"

"I'm in this now. No way to get un-implicated." I sighed. "If the feds have caught up with us, it'll probably be easiest on everyone else if they catch me red-handed... instead of getting all of you tangled in this."

Emily shook her head. "You're going in with a wire. I'm going to listen and record the whole thing. Very least it could help your defense."

Right. Sure. Maybe. But getting caught by the police wasn't my worst-case scenario.

CHAPTER 69

nice

Thursday, November 30

I kept turning street corners expecting to 'bump into' Rook's dad. He'd be the only one on the GM's payroll who could ID me. Who knew?

Part of me thought it was possible that the FBI had been following me for weeks, and that the whole gig was about to get blown up. But I felt a... like a flash. Of excitement! Like holding a barbecue lighter trigger and filling up your cupped hand with butane. And then hitting the ignition and — BAM — you just threw a fake fireball in shop class and got suspended.

I did decide that today was a great day to put Tom's birthday gift to use. The retractible staff was weighing down my pants real bad. I'd need some kind of belt holster for it or something. I also had my taser. And a syringe of bullet-hole foam. I was going into a big mystery situation and I was nervous that I didn't have time to sneak more stuff away.

But I only had so many pockets.

Civilian clothes, right?

There wasn't any sign of anything afoot until Silhouette let me in. She leaned over to whisper in my ear. "Be careful..."

"Oh there he is!" Six-Shot exclaimed. "Surprised you came! Thought you'd have vanished into—"

"Enough!" Afterglow said. "Get your head out of your ass."

"Come on! Everything is going smooth. Slow-progress — but smooth until this dickhead shows up with a magical lead—"

"Cool it!" Afterglow spat.

"Yeah, great leader-ing." Six-Shot shook his head. "Just shutting down your teammates' concerns."

Tank rolled his eyes. "We don't need to shut it down because we've already discussed—"

I marched up to him and shoved Six-Shot. "What's your damn problem with me?" I held out my arms. "Huh?"

"Oh you want it like that?" He came back at me.

"I want to know what your deal is!" I said.

Hanna snickered. "Any popcorn left?"

Afterglow firmly pointed a finger at her. "Do not start."

Six-Shot shoved me back. "Not one thing I've seen you do is something we can trust you for."

"Trust me? What about you? All of you!" I said. "I put myself at a huge risk to get this stuff, that I gave to you, and I haven't gotten anything out of it."

"Yeah? And what did you expect to do with what you got? You didn't even know what you were doing? You're a phoney."

And then he was trying to pull my shirt over my head while I punched him in the gut.

Afterglow started shouting. Nobody else really knew what to do. Not your average high school hallway fight, the two of us were on even footing and going for blood. He didn't stop until Tank grabbed him. I wasn't gonna stop there, but Silhouette's foot appeared in front of my face and knocked me off my feet.

She reached down to help me up. "Sorry, we need cool heads right now."

I swatted her hand away and got up on my own, bleeding from the corner of my mouth.

Tank swung Six-Shot into a rolling chair that he nearly fell off of "Look, just calm down. Nobody's accusing you of anything, but we need to get to the bottom—"

"What would I be accused of? What's going on?" I called.

I saw red. My neck was thumping.

Tank got closer, reached out for my arm. "Okay calm—" I jerked my arm away, but he reached for it again. "Calm down!"

"I swear if you tell me to take a seat—"

"Jesus Christ, take a pill instead," Hanna huffed.

I took a breath. Mostly to humor Tank. "Alright, what's up," I said.

Everyone looked at each other.

Afterglow sighed. "Now nobody's saying you did it," (Six-Shot rolled his eyes), "but the data cache has gone missing."

What? "Like... it disappeared from the warehouse? The GM's a little late... or maybe we missed something and he—"

Afterglow bit her lip. "All the information we got. It's... gone..."

"So you can understand why there isn't a whole lot of trust here," Silhouette added.

I processed for a moment. "Like... from the computers? It's not just in a folder you forgot the name for?"

"Christ." Six-Shot shook his head.

Hanna's face slumped. "Do I honestly seem like that kind of noob? It's gone! Poof! It is ex-data! It is deceased! It is no more—"

I paused. "So you think I took it?"

Afterglow shook her head. "No, we've—"

"Think about it," Six-Shot said, "he wants that information for whoever hired him, or maybe he's going to sell it. He can't get it, so he needs us to help him—"

"That theory means nothing now that he's here," Silhouette said stoically. "For the amount of information there, he could sell that to any number of people and be richer than most countries."

"I'm gonna go out on a limb and say you have some of those people saved on your phone?" Hanna said.

Silhouette ignored her. "He would have disappeared half a second after he lifted it if he knew who to sell it to."

Six-Shot huffed.

"So what now? This a whodunit standoff?" I asked. "Let's just play Clue and use that to decide—"

"No," Hanna said, "if you could hack into my computer and get the information, then no one would have needed my help in the first place."

"Does anyone have your passwords?" Tank asked.

"Getting into my stuff isn't just a matter of typing in 'guest' to some text window! It takes me half an hour to get through startup because I have to hack into my own OS with a proxy computer." She cleared her throat. "As a matter of fact, if you think about it rationally, the person best set up to take the information and run is me."

Everyone took a collective moment to... not say anything.

Afterglow's eyes darted around. "I liked it better when we were accusing New Guy..."

"There was enough information there that if the information was taken, we'd be in a few different scenarios," Silhouette said. "One, whoever took it would be gone. Two, whoever took it would be gone, and the rest of us would be dead. Or three, it would be found out that we have the information — we'd be dead, arrested, or missing."

"Ray of sunshine." I nodded.

She flipped her hair back. "You want optimism? Go to Holland and sniff a tulip."

"Out of season," said Afterglow.

"So what now?" Tank asked.

I would have thought if anyone took it, it would have been him. If he needed protection from the CDG, he had the most to gain. And the Mavericks had the resources to arrange a sale. Or buy it themselves.

"Has anyone told Holly?" he asked.

Afterglow nodded. "Yeah, she's on a flight back from L.A. We can't get into details over the phone. Obvious reasons."

"She called this a disaster..." Hanna huffed. "She's so pissed..."

"She didn't sound like it," Afterglow said.

"Would she even know where to start looking?" Six-Shot asked.

Nobody knew what to say.

"What if we don't need her?" I said.

Afterglow crossed her arms. "You have an idea?"

"My idea from the other day... about the GM letting us get the cache... Hanna, you said that he might have snuck in a malware program to send out a signal if it got connected—"

She immediately sprung to life, popping open one of the spare laptops. "Even if there isn't any malware like that, there's a good chance that there's a program in the cache data that will draw in any information sent out from the proxy drives. Like the one you stole." Her whole body was focused on the laptop.

"Wait, won't that compromise our position?" Silhouette stepped closer.

Hanna looked sheepish. "Well, it took hours to set up the precautions when we went after the cache before..."

"The van," said Afterglow. "Get whatever you can on the road. See if you can do it remotely so you don't lead them back here. We can't risk this information being found out by the wrong people."

Tank looked over to her. "And what if the right people have it?"

"Who are the right people these days?" Silhouette raised her eyebrows.

Tank went quiet and then drifted over to the coffee machine. Something... seemed off. I followed him, figuring I could use a coffee of my own.

"So," I said, watching him make an espresso shot. "You know who these 'right people' are?"

He looked at me and then back to the coffee. He didn't seem good at keeping a secret. Also just as bad at making coffee. I snatched the portafilter from him, dumped his grinds, and started over. "Look," he leaned in closer. "I've got an in with the Mavericks."

"...Do you? Aren't you a bit young for that?"

"Aren't you a bit young to be here at all?" he asked. "You look like you're a twelve-year-old."

Okay. Wow. Rude. "I'm sorry not everyone can look like they've been on steroids for their whole life."

"Whatever, look..." he said, looking around. "Silhouette's keeping an eye on us."

"Don't trust her?"

"I don't know if I can or should. Look. I'm from... long story. But you were right, the CDG is on my trail, and they would have got me by now if it wasn't for Oscar."

"Riot Rider?"

"Yeah. The philanthropist billionaire, and the superhero who have never been seen in the same room together. He signed me onto a Mavericks fast-track, training, reserve-list thingie..." He sighed. "He's protecting me from the CDG."

"But he's not here right now."

"Before they left, Oscar set me up with Holly. Thing is... I don't think Holly or Oscar expected this Misfits thing to blow up like this, and now I think I'm kinda fucked and—"

"Maybe you should go for decaf..." I said.

"Look, I know these guys are kind of anti-establishment. But we can trust Oscar."

"You have a keycard to the Mavericks Penthouse?"

He shuffled from one foot to the other. "More like my eyeball is in the system."

"Retina?"

"Yeah that," He said. "And my fingerprints. And pulse. And some… face-heat scan."

"Okay I get it, you're in the club…" I didn't even notice the shot was overflowing. I poured it into a cup with hot water from a kettle with some sugar. "Question though."

"Hm?"

"Why are you telling me?"

Tank looked around. "Holly seems to trust you a heck of a lot more than anyone else here and I don't know why, but that's good enough for me."

"But do *you* trust me?" I asked.

"I think I have to… I think sometimes you can't not trust people. I think sometimes you can't help it," he said, looking down. "I'm Jonah," he whispered.

"Luca," I said, without much hesitation. I padded his big… firm shoulder… "I have some contacts of my own. If you put in a good word for me with Oscar-Fucking-Colton, I'll do what I can."

— — —

Hanna got a buzz on the data. Turned out that the blackmail cache was bugged after all. But I didn't gloat. Not a single 'I told you so' from me. Nothing.

"Whoever has it isn't very bright… They're wide open," Hanna said, all of us crammed into the back of the van.

At the same time, Afterglow had popped open a laptop to check the status of the GM's minions. Apparently, they were mobilizing. Maybe all of them. "Well whoever took it, they kicked the hornet's nest."

CHAPTER 70
THE HAPPIER WE'LL BE

Thursday, November 30

Downtown. 9:45 PM.

Down a well-lit alley off of Howard Street, 'O'Morgan's Pub' had an atmospheric neon sign. Out front, there was a carpet, a velvet rope, and a female bouncer who flashed some tattoos by shaving the sides of her head. You didn't want to mansplain the wage gap to her, but you *might* want her to step on you.

This was the kind of safe-ish place where hipsters and students would flock to get all the edge of city living, and none of the heroin. The pictures online showed poorly lit tables, secluded privacy booths, and extensive dressing rooms. Lots of velveteen.

You'd likely find any combination of three things inside: a hand-off, an ambush, or hip, cabaret acts. Aura and I snuck into a place like this for an Amanda Palmer show. Didn't get caught until after we snuck into the afterparty. Got sent away with free merch because we had some balls.

All jokes aside, the place did have a liquor license, and Ms. Gunshow was in the business of taking IDs and slamming back fitness shakes. And she was all out of protein powder.

Woof.

"Okay, you three go on in," I said. "Tank and me will stick together and find another entry point."

"You're giving orders now?" Six-Shot said.

"We were the flanking team last time," I said. No way was I going to let on that I was under the legal drinking age. Not that I think I fooled anyone…

"You and Tank, sure, but don't enter." Afterglow had to push Six-Shot aside. "Wait around the back in case we flush them out."

"And keep an eye out for the GM. No telling if he's got his crew here already," Silhouette added.

Jonah and me didn't wait for them to get in, we went up and down the alley again looking for a second entry point. But it didn't seem like there was another entrance from this side. Jonah wanted to split up to look around, but I thought that was doing things the hard way. "Hold on," I said, and walked up to the burly bouncer.

"Yeah, hey," I said, sounding casual.

"Can I help you?"

"Yeah," I said. "I've got a subwoofer and half a drum kit in a van on the street. 'Supposed to drop it off like...' at the back' they said..."

She smiled. "Oh! Yeah, it's a bit confusing." You've got to keep going down the street. Next left past the building — follow that, take another left, and you'll be at the back."

I slouched like I didn't give a crap about this conversation. "So, is anybody going to be there? I'm a bit early and don't know if anyone's gonna be around to let us in."

She shrugged. "Sorry, bro. I don't deal with the back crew. Everyone goes on break back there so you should find someone."

Finger guns. "Thanks, bro."

She smiled. "No problem, bro." If I wasn't sitting on an atomic bomb of information, it would have been flirting.

When we were out of earshot, Jonah yanked me close to him. "See, I have no idea how to figure you out," he hissed.

"Don't worry. I'm all cool, *Jonah*." I tried to yank myself away.

"No really, who are you?"

"I'm the kid the other parents told their kids not to play with," I said. "Don't worry, I use my powers for the forces of Good."

He thought for a minute while we walked. "What's that mean? Other parents told their kids not to play with you?"

"Bad seed," I said. "I apparently corrupted the neighborhood."

"Like what... you... started smoking?"

I stopped. "You think smoking is the worst thing I've done?"

"Like... as a kid." He shrugged. "May...be...?"

I hit the button on the mic. "Hey Hanna. You seem like you'd get me. What's the worst thing you think I've ever done?"

Jonah sighed. "We really ought to..."

No answer.

Jonah hit a button on his power pack. "Hey, Hanna?"

No answer.

"Did you guys not check the mics before we went in?" I said.

"Afterglow always checks the mics," he said, then hit a different button. "Glow, you there? Six? Silhouette?"

"Nothing on mine." My chest tightened up.

"Not mine..." Jonah looked over his shoulder.

I cued in, hit the open call button on my power pack. "This is an old gag, you limey bastard," I groaned.

Audio cut in halfway through casual laughter. Again, the cold, reserved voice of a distinguished gentleman. "You know," he said, "what's her name, Wench — oh wait — she's telling me she prefers Hanna. As you wish. When she opened up her data flow, I did get a look at what she's packing...

"Not a whole lot, granted. Just a peak. She's the real deal, you see, as far as script kiddies go... oh, she takes offense to that, also. She means... serious business! What is it you young lot say? 'Triggered'? But I digress. I was able to get a look at some of your com information and well... Here I am."

Ahead of us, two smooth, featureless black vans barrelled down the street toward us, before taking a sharp right into the alley that we were supposed to be heading down. Jonah and I exchanged a glance and took off after them.

"I think I'm most surprised to gather that you're not responsible for this..." he said. "I thought that you lot were passing the information off to legitimate channels in the FBI. Though... I didn't have to look very hard to discern that Special Agent Patrick Goodline isn't a very 'legitimate' channel, per se. Funny.

"But you seem to be here, at least attempting to clean up this ordeal. I have to admit, I'm relieved to learn that you young pains-in-the-backside aren't just out to sell my hard-earned labors to the highest bidder. Not that I would imagine the FBI would be the highest bidder."

Jonah and I turned the corner, tire screeches and van doors slamming echoed through the chasm. I took a hard left, watching shadows up ahead, figures rushing around.

"Letting the data leak like this is quite an embarrassing mistake. I don't know who has it, but they're keeping it on a Samsung tablet. Really? Android? It lit up like a lighthouse.

"But here you are! My faith in your generation was temporarily reaffirmed, but then I realized that meant that you let the data slip out of your fingers in the first place..." He sighed. "The important thing is that you're learning..."

As I turned the last corner, Jonah went all glowey and shielded me from the first gunshots and then pulled me back behind cover.

"That still hurts, right?" I asked.

"Not until about ten minutes after," he peered around the corner.

Someone down the alley was shouting, telling others to get inside.

"What is that *marvelous* ability you have? If I would have known that you could do that I would have sought you out..." said the Gentleman. "Funny, those abilities seem to match the description of a certain Maverick-in-training. Funny indeed..."

God, I hated him.

"I still have to admit," The Gentleman went on in our ears, "That having the data stolen from you isn't nearly as bad as making the howling errors that whoever took it is making. No, Ms. Afterglow, please sit back down, I can see you from security footage. It'll be best if you just wait out the rest—"

I yanked the earpiece cord out of the power supply. Jonah did the same. It sounded like there was a commotion breaking out in the club.

"There must be what? A dozen of them?" I asked. "We need to get in there!"

"You're not bullet-proof!" he said. "Stick around here and wait for me to clear it!"

"Right, so go make them distracted and I'll follow up," I said.

"You need to stay right here," he commanded, his whole body lighting up and turning the corner to a new slew of gunshots.

I took the earpiece cord and plugged it into my phone. "Still there?"

"Yeah," Emily said, calm and collected. "You're gonna fuck 'em up anyway, right?"

I flicked my hanbo out. "Wouldn't miss it."

CHAPTER 71
WE'LL LAUGH ABOUT THIS SOMEDAY

Thursday, November 30

As soon as Jonah got the gunman's attention, I lifted myself on top of a dumpster. A gunman was aiming at him, but I was inches from him before he even noticed me. There was a burn scar on his face.

This bitch.

I set myself up like I was going to strike from above. With the staff over my head, I hit the pavement and swept my leg under him. He fell backward but recovered fast. I went for a quick jab, but he just took the hit and jabbed his rifle stock into my shoulder.

Felt like I got hit by a truck.

He aimed straight for my face, but I punched his ribs and circled around him. Not fast enough, though. He hooked his rifle around my hanbo and yanked it from my grip. I dashed to the side, trying to keep out of his sights — as soon as he had a clear shot at me, he pulled the trigger. I heard a bang and then ringing, but at least he missed.

"HOLY CRAP!" Emily called.

I didn't think he was going for killshots — he paused for a second after pulling the trigger. I think he expected the gunshot to spook me. But I kneed his thigh and shoved him back into the van. Without letting up, I closed the gap to punch his head against the siding, but he rolled off by the time I got there.

He aimed at me, but I knocked the rifle up before he fired and it shot into the sky. Grip on the rifle, I threw my shoulder into him to wrench the rifle out of his hands. He pushed back, and the rifle flew away from both of us, bouncing on the pavement.

My eyes trailed it while his didn't. Instead, he went for the knife on his thigh. Figuring the rifle was the bigger threat, I didn't expect him to shove me back and pin me against the van. He held the side of my face firmly, his shoulder digging into my ribs. The flat of the knife pressed firmly against my neck as he looked into my eyes.

"Okay…" I gagged out, trying not to move a muscle. "I'll give you that…" With my head pushed against the metal siding, I scanned for anything that could help me get out of this pinch. Accidentally, I made eye contact with the one Gentleman thug who wasn't getting his ass kicked by Jonah.

It was Rook.

CHAPTER 72
SO YOU COME HERE OFTEN?

Thursday, November 30

Rook Lang. The squirrelly, lanky kid that had to take deep breaths before talking to cashiers. Who froze when he was within ten feet of a girl.

And here he was with this crowd!

Attacking a nightclub!

I was shook.

Maybe a little impressed…

And he looked just as surprised to see me. And not entirely sure what to do with himself.

And then, without warning, Rook, in the headlights of the van, tossed one of the person-sized plastic recycling buckets.

With one hand.

It flew along the side of the van, into Hamen ploughing past me before either of us had a chance to react. The bucket collapsed on the pavement, with the asshole under it.

But Jonah saw Rook and took him as a hostile.

"No— Wait!" I called, but he'd already thrown Rook at a dumpster. "Stop! Jesus cool it, dipshit!"

Jonah looked at me. "Dip-*what*?"

"He's not…" I sighed, checking Rook's pulse. He was unconscious, but groaning softly. "I know him."

Emily chimed in. "Wait, what?"

Jonah looked between me and Rook.

"I didn't expect him to be here! He's a friend of mine from school— erm… college."

Emily protested. "AK. Come on! What's… Fuck!"

I hit the mute button on the earpiece.

Jonah squinted at me. Puffy cheeks flaring. "Guys from 'college' just say 'school'." He used his height to his advantage, getting close and making me look up at him.

But I was immune to height intimidation. "And you know a lot about college boys, do you?"

He went red. "Uhm. Yeah. Uhm… That guy—"

"He's an arts kind of guy. Wouldn't hurt a fly on a bad day. I have no idea what he's doing here."

There was suddenly a flare-up through the cabaret doors. It caught our attention, but Jonah was quick to look back at me. He stared for a second before heading toward the commotion.

"And this time you stay here, or I will arrest you so hard." He turned the corner.

I took Emily off mute. "I can't tell. Are you following?" she asked. "Is he even deputized yet? You're trying to get in his pants right? Totally picked that up. Bad time? Also, that's the beefy ginger, right? Bad time. That *is* Rook you found though, right?"

I sighed and went back to Rook against the dumpster. "Yes, it's Rook."

"Oh my God! How? The post-human asset was his Dad!"

"Rook's only his middle name," I said. "His father said Donghou was an inherited name in the family."

Emily coughed. "You knew?!"

"I'm sorry!" I shouted. "I fucked this up. I should have seen it. I could have *helped!*"

"Take it easy. I wouldn't have picked up on it. Don't think it's common…" Emily said. "So like… Super-strength right?"

"He threw a plastic dumpster at the guy who was trying to shoot me," I said. "So yes. Obviously."

Emily whistled. "Kay. So. What do we do now?"

"Well we get him home and pretend like this never..."

But the recycling bin beside the car shuffled, and Hamen shoved himself to his feet. Too quickly though; he was dizzy and had to hold his hand out to the van for support.

"Yeah, I hear you," he said, holding his earpiece. "Ran into a bit of trouble. One of the kids that you recruited..." As he looked around he caught sight of me. I was still in place, unmoving. My eyes darted, scanning for whatever could help me.

He spotted it at the same time I did — his rifle — but it was closer to me. He went down to grab his knife, but I rolled and took up the firearm and landed on my knee, the sights fixed on him. He stopped, with the knife loosely in his grip, half-bent down still. He didn't move.

Jesus. I hoped I didn't look scared. I always hated those scenes in movies. The Villain approaches our innocent hero and says: 'you don't have the guts, kid.' Those scenes bothered me because I always figured that when people were scared, they'd pull the trigger on reaction, rather than decision. Fight or flight.

My hands weren't shaking. Shouldn't they have been shaking?

I'd shot at targets... but safety off, finger on the trigger... at a living thing. Somehow it seemed like it would be worse to shoot an animal than a person...

He spoke slowly. "I'm going to set it down, okay?"

"Just drop it instead," I said.

He smiled, let the blade fall to the ground, and stood up straight.

"What's... on?" Emily said, breaking up a little bit.

I mumbled into the mic. "Shut up a second."

"I'm just going to leave..." Hamen said. "I'm going to back up, alright?"

I wasn't sure what I should do. Tell him to stay? Kneecap him? I was a crack shot, but he was wearing knee pads. I just readjusted my grip on the rifle and didn't say anything.

He nodded. "Alright..." He backed away, slowly at first. All the while there was still fighting in the club.

"Knight— you..." Emily called out. "Can't hear... Oh come on..." I kept the rifle trained on Hamen as Emily lost contact, fading into static. I could fix that later. At a safe distance, Hamen turned heel and quickly walked around the corner.

I let out a breath. "You there?" I said, flipping on the safety, and yanking out the clip. "Hello?" We'd never had connection problems before. I was partially worried that The Gentleman had managed to hack into the phone. That could compromise Emily. I could get to a payphone, or use my own phone to send her a text letting her know.

But first, I had to check on Rook, who was coming to. "Hey!" I tapped his cheek. "Hey, come on."

His eyes were unfocused, pupils clearly dilated in the light cast from industrial light bulbs. "Luca!" he said, in a flurry of trying to stand up but stumbling.

"Hey, man! We need to get out of here, alright?" I said. "No time to explain now, the cops are on their way."

"Wait—"

I braced him on my shoulder and hoisted him to his feet. He was a little wobbly. "Come on, hurry."

"I'm fine... but—"

"No, no! We've got to get going. Quick, come on."

He took a breath. "Yeah."

"We'll talk as soon as we can—"

The static stopped, going into the faint hiss of someone being on the other line. I was expecting The Gentleman. I was surprised...

"Avalon Knight, right?" said Hanna. "This is Avalon Knight, right? Anyone there? Hellooo-ooo?"

CHAPTER 73
NIGHT ON THE TOWN

Thursday, November 30

"Yes, Hanna, it's me!" I said.

"Oh thank Buddha!" she sighed. "You seemed like the type who would keep a wire on. No judgment. Silhouette did too but she didn't know that I knew. Well, she probably assumed—"

"What do you want? You interrupted a bit of a conversation."

Rook looked at me. Very confused, but I didn't blame him.

"Right! Sorry. Look, I can't get through to the others, so I need your help."

"I'm not interested in helping right now." I pushed Rook along, he was still a little unsteady.

"The data package!" she said. "I found it again! It isn't in the club anymore — it's moving. You need to go get it!"

If Hanna could see it, then the GM could see it. And that meant that was exactly where Hamen was going... I looked back to Rook.

"What?" he asked.

I looked back in the direction of the club.

"What's going—"

I put Hanna on mute. "I need you to keep going on your own. Something I need to take care of. Go home, unplug everything, and stick close to your dad. Alright? I need to get this sorted out."

"Um..."

"Come on, you got this," I tapped his shoulder. "I think I can make this all right."

Rook took a breath and nodded. "Okay."

"Alright, hurry. Keep away from the cops. Act casual as you can."

He nodded and set off on his own. I fired off a text letting Emily know I was going after the package.

I took Hanna off mute. "Give me a direction."

"What happened? What's going on?"

"Just tell me where I need to be."

She said a babble of words and phrases that ended up meaning 'westward.' Which meant I could cut off Hamen by going through the club. Jonah wouldn't like that, but he wasn't the boss of me.

I passed through the club as quickly as I could. Through the kitchen and then the main room. There was so much going on, I doubt anyone even noticed me. It was a mess.

Sorry I missed it, but I had a job to do.

"Where'm I going?" I asked, when I got to the alley.

"Uhhh... Downward! On main!" she said. I guessed 'down' meant south. Crossing the street, I lifted myself over a cab's roof. A gunshot echoed over the cars behind me.

"Shit!" I instinctively ducked.

"Shit!" Hanna called, also sounding like she ducked.

Everyone started screaming. I didn't have a good line of sight, but I could guess it was Hamen, and probably a warning shot. I kept going anyway, through crowds of people.

It's following the road! Sansome!" Hanna said. "Hurry!"

Then Pine. Hamen was following, but I was putting ground between us. Then onto Leidsendroff. I could keep this up, but I was worried about being so worn down if Hamen did catch up with me...

Hanna growled and I heard banging on a keyboard. "Hold on — it's gone."

"What?" I stopped at the mouth of a thin street.

"It's gone! They may have disconnected the data... but no, the bug would reactivate it... they must have turned it off. It was halfway down the street last I saw."

I sighed and looked for somewhere to lay low. So of course I went high. Up onto the roof of a two-story building with giant windows. No lights on so my dark clothes helped me blend into the shadows. And thank god for the darkness because I could feel a migraine coming on.

My head was filled with like... fuzz and glitter. Like it was pushing on the back of my skull, pushing on the backs of my eyes and making them bulge.

A long shadow slowly trotted into view. I froze. The man casting it held a pistol in one hand. This was the first time I'd ever felt like I was going to die. My heart felt like it was trying to leap out through my throat. It's something you had to get used to.

It's not for everyone.

"What are you doing?" Hanna asked. "What's going on?"

I tapped the microphone hard, fast. My hands were shaking so hard from my heart thumping. This time, I thought, he wasn't gonna go for kneecaps. And I didn't have any armor.

"Oh! Okay!" She said. "I guess that means 'shut up'?"

I tapped it again.

"Gotchya."

Like I thought, the shadow was Hamen. He stopped and looked around. The GM must have also lost the signal. But he noticed something. Maybe something I missed? He went to a security gate up ahead, pushed open the squeaky door. It hit the wall, making a clang that echoed through the street; I heard his footsteps pass through and out of earshot.

As I relaxed, I spied a security ladder hanging down from the building next door. I took a deep breath and wasted no time swinging up to the top.

CHAPTER 74
ET TU?

Thursday, November 30

"I think I'm on to something," I said to Hanna, walking forward, though cautiously. There was some light shining up from skylights sticking out of the rooftop layer of gravel. Lots of things to hide behind, lots of shadows. I was getting closer. I just had to keep an ear out—

And then... I was on the ground. Gravel in my face.

Getting tasered wasn't a great experience. Especially the projectile taser that nails itself into your skin. Not my first experience — I'd had that cherry popped in a department jewelry store.

Breathing kind of doesn't happen. You can't move. And for the duration, there's this seemingly justifiable fear that your heart is going to erupt.

"Stop it," called a woman. Familiar. "Christ! That's one of mine."

The sensation stopped and my breath huffed back into my chest. No. Way... I spat out a mouthful of dust.

"That—" I could feel Hanna have the same reaction. "That sounds... like..."

Holly Rolland helped me up. She had her shoes in hand, the heels she would have worn to the club. I sat beside her and caught my breath. She her tablet, the screen was cracked. I felt every part of my skin tighten, and I pushed myself up.

"You sold us out!" Pulling away from her.

She tried to grab my arm again. "Hold on—"

"No! You — you took it!"

"How did you find us?" The FBI guy asked.

Holly looked back at him. "Because you insisted on turning the tablet on so you could verify. Verify my ass… I told you it was bugged."

"Holly?" Hanna said. "You're sure? I'll text her, give me a second!"

"I wouldn't have expected to get tracked down so fast. Especially by your… people…" He grimaced. "Your young people."

"The Gentleman also picked it up," I said.

Holly's phone lit up in her pocket.

"Text sent!" Hanna said. "Did she get it?"

Holly tried to ease me, moving her hand to my shoulder, but I backed up again, snuck between two triangle skylights. "Why would you do this? The FBI? You're selling it? I didn't realize the FBI would just buy information!"

"This isn't one-hundred-percent legal…" he grumbled.

"Shut up, Goodline," Holly spat. "Look, this information is dangerous. We discussed that. It needed to get out of our hands. Goodline's a jackass," she looked at him, "but he's the kind of jackass who keeps his skeletons out of the closet. There's not much The Gentleman can blackmail him with." Holly sighed. "So this is, really, the best way to handle this."

I was burning hot. I didn't want her to look at me. I was sick. She knew who I was. She knew who Dad was. She sold the information we took. Information that I took.

We wouldn't have found it if not for me, and she took away our — my ability to choose what to do about it. And if there was anything I couldn't stand, it was *'mother knows best'* and making decisions for me.

"This is stupid!" I said.

"Well, it needs to be." She heaved her chest. "It's not ideal. I know that."

"Then dump the information! Why sell it to some…" I gestured to the agent. "You look like a greasy Vegas lounge singer!"

He scoffed.

Holly sighed. "Because running the operation — you and your friends — it can get expensive, and I—"

"You're loaded!" I hissed. "United paid you out twice your contract's worth!" The agent looked at me, a little impressed.

She sighed. "I don't have the money to keep it sustained forever. Especially because of how successful it is here… I need to focus on ways to keep this up, set up other organizations in other cities. That takes a lot of capital."

"Success?" The agent rolled his eyes. I reached down, grabbed a handful of rocks, and catapulted them at him. "Ow — hey!"

"…Lu— AK, please, I'm trying to keep our operation going for as long as I can — the world needs more young heroes to pass the torch to, and if doing my part means—"

For half a second she jerked out of the way. And then… I don't know… the way I remember it, I stood there playing it over a few times like a skipping record. I couldn't quite see where it was coming from, but it was like paint.

Thick, and globbed together — like black paint spraying out from her. I remember only hearing the gunshot crack after I noticed she was falling… but I can't actually remember what happened in what sequence.

I felt like I blinked a lot. Everything got brighter, like details I wouldn't have spotted lit up. I guess I ducked. Instinctively? But I kept staring at Holly, suspended in the air, falling over and over again. But the record flashed forward, to when the FBI Agent pushed me face down onto the ground.

"Stay down kid!" he said, crouching behind the skylight.

I knew he wasn't going to get Hamen…

I started to panic. I couldn't see Holly. Was she dead?

Bullets hit, sparked, broke the glass, shattering into smaller pieces in the room below. I could feel bullets hitting the gravel around me.

"Move!" the agent shouted.

I did what he said, rushed behind an exhaust fan. I felt myself come back to me. *Get up and hero-up.* I peered around with just enough time to see the agent take a shot to his shoulder. He kept firing.

Get up—

Holly. I saw her. She was crawling away. To cover, dragging herself over gravel. She looked at me and showed me the tablet. Yes. I got it. She wanted me to hero-up too. Not dead. She'd be fine. They were fine all the time in movies. I darted over to her. I think Hamen took a shot at me. It missed. Did it? I checked.

It missed.

Get up—

I couldn't.

Holly grabbed me. Blood came out of her mouth. Half her white shirt had turned black. It... it looked unreal. Or it looked too real. Like a B-movie that blew its whole budget on gore effects. But it wasn't like a movie because I was right there in it.

She clutched my hand and shoved the bloody tablet into my chest. Her voice croaked for a second, and it seemed she couldn't move her head to look at me. She didn't say anything. No... she couldn't. It was like a hammer suddenly drove a spike into my head.

"Alright kid," Hamen said, from behind me. "Get up."

CHAPTER 75
STANDING WHERE I AM

Thursday, November 30

I didn't get up. I stayed with Holly. I couldn't just abandon her. The earpiece had fallen out. But I didn't move. I... I didn't know what to do.

Something hit the ground beside me. It rattled like a can—

Then my ears were ringing, I was on my back, and everything was very bright. Laying in the middle of the gravel, in the open where Hamen could see me. I tried to get up, stumbling, writhing, off-balance. Ears ringing. My whole body felt muggy.

The mercenary named Kurt Hamen let me get my balance but kept his revolver trained on me. "Come on. Give it up. See? I'm not going to shoot you if you don't move." His accent was rough, distinct. Like someone in a movie who owned a pub on the wrong side of London.

I looked at the tablet. Cracked, scratched, bloody. And it was full of poison. Tom would tell me to give it up.

"You're too young for this," Hamen said.

"Dying?"

"No. The Lifestyle." He nodded. "You handle a trigger like a pro."

"Didn't even take a shot."

"Mm trust me, that's only twenty-percent of the work."

I shook my head. "I wasn't going to shoot you—"

He laughed "No, because I wasn't going to give you a reason to."

"I wasn't going to..."

"Ehhh..." He lifted his shoulders up high and pouted. "Professional opinion, mate. Starting at your age... by the time you're my age, you'll end up exactly where my boots are, looking at someone else like you." He pulled the hammer back. "Nobody starts out wanting to be the bad guy."

I took a breath and tossed the tablet toward Hamen's boot.

"Hey, I know that wasn't easy. Live to fight another day, though, right?" He reached down and with a free hand, slid the tablet into a backpack. "Sorry about your... lady—"

"She was Flechette."

Was. Jesus.

Hamen stopped for a second, mouth ajar, head cocked. "Aw, shit..." He sighed. "Liked her. Was the right type of Vigil, you know?" His posture slouched. "Business is business though." He cooly saluted with two fingers. "Take it easy. Nothing against you just... don't let me see you again."

Then he slid down the ladder.

Walking over to the edge felt like walking through quicksand. Hamen was nowhere to be seen. Sirens were in the distance. I looked back to Holly, the agent. There wasn't anything I could do for them now — and the actual murderer was gone.

Compared to the rest of the illegal stuff I was involved in, fleeing the scene of a—

Fleeing a crime scene wasn't anything compared to the rest of it.

But I thought... Maybe I should go back and check — just to be sure. But the sirens were getting closer and the next thing I knew, I was already sliding down the ladder.

From a distance, I saw the police putting up a checkpoint at the intersection far to my right. I went left. Someone was honking. I casually flipped my head over to make sure it wasn't at me. No. they were honking at the cops.

'*Someone like you...*'

What did that mean?

Burner phone off. No way I wanted to talk it out with Hanna. I crossed the street in a haze. Away from the sirens. What time was it? I checked my phone. Luca's phone. I needed to get off the streets. Get home, start to nurse this killer migraine—

Rook. Rook! He was there. Jesus, that disaster waiting to happen. Another honk, this one longer. Oh no... a Corolla pulled up beside me...

"Goddamnit" I sighed.

"Come on, get in," Tom said, a bit of a grin on his face, "let's have ourselves a talk."

Emily was in the passenger seat, trying to look as sorry as possible. Not that it lasted.

I think they noticed the blood because they both kind of lost the color in their faces at the same time. I got in and Tom made a u-turn away from the growing wall of cop cars.

CHAPTER 76
CHEWED UP

Thursday, November 30

Tom took us to a quiet place where he could park and yell at me for a while. He got out of the car so he could pace. Emily was out the door before I even had my seatbelt off.

"I'm gonna give you two a minute," Emily said.

"No!" Tom snapped his fingers. "You are going to stay right here. I don't for a second believe that this was all Luca's idea."

"Oh, *you're* such a judge of character," I said as I got out of the car.

"I'd like to reiterate once again that I have half a mind to take you in for an MRI to see if you're missing a part of your brain." He took a deep breath. "But one more time — do you know what the worst-case scenario of this was?"

"Yes, I do!"

"Then let's hear it?"

"Well, that would implicate you and—"

"No, you don't know. It's not implicating anyone. You could be dead!"

"I wasn't stupid about it! I have armor on under my clothes. I was prepared."

Tom ignored me.

"All the damn time the real fight isn't even protecting myself or saving people," I said, "It's trying to meet your goddamn standards! You never trust me. I was trying to help people. Can I get a little credit?"

"You should have stayed home!"

"You weren't taking me out!" I called back. "What? Do I need a chaperone?"

"Yes! You're seventeen!"

"Dad was seventeen too when he went out on his own! With no training except for some shit Papop taught him because he was getting beaten up at school!"

"Your father was a hot mess until my brother and I got a hold of him—"

"And you, The East Wind Dragon, was eighteen when you went out on your own!"

"I had been trained since birth—"

"You've been at me since I was eight!"

Emily choked. "Holy shit!" We both glared at her. "I just... didn't realize... been going on a while..."

Tom snapped back to me. "I certainly didn't train you in these brazen acts of stupidity!"

I kicked some gravel at Tom. "I am not stupid!" I yelled.

"Then stop acting stupid," he said with a quick flick of his cane at my shin, "you got lucky and you know it."

"Bullshit. I didn't get lucky. I took opportunities!"

Tom shook his head. "Luca, you're not clever enough to use my own rhetoric against me."

"Come on—"

"You got 'lucky' when you got arrested before. If there hadn't been a Halloween party, forget good-cop-bad-cop — do you have any idea how much the police despise licensed vigilantes? Forget illegal ones! But you didn't think about any of that, did you?"

"Guys..." Emily said.

"Oh look at you suddenly on cops' side."

"Do *not* pull that shit with me, Wexler—"

"Guys!"

"WHAT?" Tom and I shouted.

But then looking over to her we saw a pair of headlights that had crossed through the gap in the chainlink fence and onto the gravel stretch between warehouses. "Get back," Tom said, keeping a hand behind his back where he had a derringer tucked in a concealed holster.

Not that it was hard to hide a derringer.

The white van looked like a yacht. Sleek, aerodynamic. Nothing like anything you'd usually see driving around. It drove past us, and Tom hobbled to stay between it and Emily and me.

The side door opened and a rough-looking guy dropped out. "Evening Gentleman," he said. "Ma'am," he said, nodding at Emily, who got behind me. Sounded British. Maybe South African? I didn't know how this was going to go until he rapped on the back of the van.

Immediately the back doors swung open and—

Oh.

Out he stepped. A tall, thin man dressed in finery. A top hat, gloves, a cane of his own. And a white, eggshell mask.

[˙‿˙]

CHAPTER 77
MASK FOR MASK

Thursday, November 30

Tom dropped his cane, yanked the four-barrel magnum derringer from under his jacket, and aimed right at the Gentleman's head. The mercenary drew his pistol and pointed it at Tom.

"Don't—" Tom said.

"Drop it," the Mercenary said.

The Gentleman, unlike everyone else, was calm. He stood in place and gently tapped his cane on the top of Temple's hands. "Mr. Temple if you would?" His voice... it was so strange. It sounded more real when he was talking on a microphone or over speakers. In-person, it was fuzzy and grainy. Maybe his mask filtered his voice to keep people off his trail?

"If I would...?"

"Put that thing away," said the Gentleman, pushing the pistol down. "If you would."

"Boss..."

"This is the East Wind Dragon, my good man," he said. "As much as I enjoy a good wager, I'm rather not keen to play those odds. So please, do let it to the ground."

[∪ ‿ ∪]

Temple hesitated.

"You can pick it up before we leave if you like," he said.

Temple flipped the safety on and returned it to its holster.

"Or that! Excellent!" The Gentleman leaned to the side to peer around Tom. "Luca, Ms. Barnett. Evening."

I waved. "Hey."

"You sound a little shaken," he said. "I heard you had some issues with Mr. Hamen. I hope he didn't give you too much trouble—"

Holly was falling down in front of me—

"He's quite effective, but I'm afraid his bedside manner isn't as sophisticated as Mr. Temple's." He spun his cane around onto his shoulder and leaned down to sweep the dust off his pants. "But you're all in one piece."

"You're talking to me, not them," Tom said.

[^—^]

"I came here to talk to everyone involved."

"Where are the others?" I asked, stepping out in front of Tom.

"Friends of Miss Roland?" He tilted his head. "Well, I ordered my subordinates to back off when I saw the data package was on the move. I'm assuming they're all fine."

"How did you find out who Luca was?" Tom asked.

"Find out? Young Mr. Wexler?" The Gentleman snorted. "My good man, I never *didn't* know who he was! What was that charming little cafe where you..." he gestured his hand. "Where we ostensively met? I pulled security footage of everyone who ordered a drink and then cross-referenced faces with social media profiles. Following that, I narrowed it down based on a combination of profile likelihood and then read some exchanged text messages to confirm... and now here we are."

The three of us stood in disbelief.

[⊕ ‿ ⊕]

"Make no mistake, Mr. Seong. Young Wexler took every precaution necessary. Nearly, that is. Ones that any cautious, yet inquisitive, individual would deem appropriate. However,, there simply is no such thing as 'being safe' these days. Anonymity?" He shrugged. "Idle comforts."

I coughed. "You've known the whole time?"

"Luca, shut up—"

"If I was a problem, why not come after me?" I demanded.

[ಸ_ಸ]

"What am I? A barbarian? A cartel drug dealer? Shall I 'whack' any problem that stands in my way?" he asked. "Annoying or not, you were a problem I could navigate — exploit, even! As I did with sneaking a bug into the cache I let you steal. Even though you surprised me, again, it seems the 'grown-ups' acted a bit more predictably.

"And though it may come as a surprise to you, I do place a great amount of value on the potential you have as a Vigil. Not to mention all the good work your father does. I'd bought a few of the collectibles he put on eBay to help him along. Has he ever considered Patreon? No that's more for artists... GoFundMe? I would have loved to contribute.

"Suffice, both of you are good men who, if authorities had been alerted to Wexler Jr.'s illicit activities, would have been hindered from bringing their good work into the world. By far, it would be a petty waste of both of you for whatever minor relief it would have brought me. Also would have run in complete contradiction with the vision of San Francisco I have."

Emily scoffed behind us. "I'm sorry... What was that?"

Tom shuffled a little to get between the two of them.

"Ms. Barnett... don't tell me you don't believe me!" said the Gentleman. "Even past the point where you convinced Luca to go after me, past the point of discovering my use of post-human assistance, you remain a subscriber to my social media."

Emily had her arms crossed and her leg out to the side. "I'm just... what's your angle? Why are you here now, and not earlier? Why not just kill us when you had the drop?"

"Let's not give him ideas," said Tom. "He's probably got a sniper on us."

[￢\' o'/￢]

"Precisely why you haven't taken the shot, I assume," said the Gentleman. "Your leg must be getting sore... I assure you, I do not have any 'snipers' on us. My people are stretched thin enough as it is, and I certainly wouldn't want to ruin a delightful conversation. But you won't believe me either way — good on you. Yet it occurs to me that pointing that thing at me isn't going to get you anywhere. Is it really necessary?"

Tom slouched. "What do you want?" he said.

The Gentleman held out his arms. "An understanding... You see... things have been getting a little out of hand lately. Mr. Hamen, as I alluded, has been forgoing some terms of his contract, and has been going around willy nilly. He's very much of the 'whatever it takes' mindset which... I suppose works when hired by Sudanese warlords, but this is a different kind of warfare, no?

"Long and short of it, I would like to apologize for you getting so deeply caught up in this. The intention was for Luca to have never been in any real danger, Mr. Seong.

"Thus, I decided to seek you out in the flesh to offer my apologies... To all of you. I'm sure this hasn't been and is not easy..." Then he gestured to Tom. "I would also... like to advise you not to ride Mr. Wexler too hard... You, after all, wrote the book on parental defiance, Mr. Seong, regardless that you claim to have 'learned better.'"

Tom scoffed and shook his head.

"I dunno," Emily said, after a silence. "That sounds like a threat. And not an apology."

[ð . O]

"I'm sorry, my dear?" said the Gentleman.

"What about Rook?" Emily asked. "Don Lang Jr.?"

He nodded. "Ah yes... The eggs we crack."

"Doesn't seem like an accident that I ran into him..." I said.

"Maybe it wasn't," he said. "Maybe you don't know someone until you put them in uncomfortable circumstances."

"So why does Luca get a 'respected member of society' card when Rook doesn't?" Emily asked. "You seem to like 'profiles' a lot… What do your notes say about how well he does under pressure? He's super-strong, I guess. But I can't really see him being reliable with illegal stuff."

[˚∠˚]

"I'm not the CDG," the Gentleman said. "I have to do the best with what I have."

"See," Emily said. "That's why I'm still a subscriber. I'm kind of confused about what it is you're trying to do."

"I feel as if that's a question…" The Gentleman sighed. "I am trying to restore a sense of identity and culture to San Francisco."

"No, no-no," said Emily. "You gotta get outta here with that pussy-ass vagary. What do you want? Specifically? Because your whole operation is a fucking mess."

[ʊ_ʊ]

"Excuse me?"

"You've hurt a lot of people. Some of them are even the people you claim you want to help—"

[◑△◑]

"I'm not fond of that implication."

"But you haven't helped anyone in the city. You've thrown money at shelters and kitchens. But you — yourself — haven't put any chips on the table. And San Francisco is not a day closer to the late great sixties."

"I came to apologize," he said. "And yes, to infer that I would like you out of my hair. However, do not believe that this is a negotiation—"

"No, but you are gonna listen," she stormed right up to him.

"Wait—" said Tom, but she was off to the races.

"Because I get it. These losers don't," Emily pointed at me and Tom. "They haven't lived here their whole lives. I have. My family has been here for three generations. Grampop bought the house in the sixties—"

"Nineteen sixty-four," he said. "And it burned down in nineteen eighty-two. Police investigation indicates a faulty outlet."

[ˆ ('–') ˆ]

Emily cleared her throat. "Okay. Well. Yeah. I'm pissed off too. I've wanted what you say since way before you came here to do it. I don't know *why* you want it, but sure. A lot of the 'workers' that felt the hit from Point Brick were gentrifiers themselves. I'm not going to tell you that making privileged people a little uncomfortable is the 'wrong way' to do things.

"Things are messed up," she continued, "and to fix messed up things, you might need to do messed up things also. But the thing is, the way you're doing things isn't working. And the more time—"

[(-＿-)ﾉ]

"If my intervention continues: in the next 10 years, average rent in the city will decrease by 45% at a minimum!" The Gentleman said. "But I must assure that the city keeps its soul in the interim. That requires more drastic measures."

"Nobody owes a gentrifier's feelings a damn thing," she said. "But those 'drastic measures' are making them dig their heels in deeper. The people you're targeting are the people who have the privilege of demanding protection. Not the communities who are getting gentrified out of existence."

[⊙ω⊙]

"So you see the vast complexity of dismantling this machine!" The Gentleman said. "De-gentrification is unprecedented in modern economies! There simply isn't a rulebook — I'm sorry that trial and error is messy—"

Emily snapped her fingers in his face. "You're running your

whole operation like the sketchy-ass corporations you say you oppose! You say you're better than them but you sure don't act like it."

[˙ O ˙]

"You have this implicit fixation that I'm somehow out for personal gain in this!" he said.

"Like… You do seem really self-conscious about it…" I scratched the back of my head.

"Shut up, Luca," Tom said.

"Give it time…" Emily shrugged. "Putting on that get-up and scaring the competition away is a classic Scooby-Doo move. You could be a long-lost Walmart heir behind that mask."

The Gentleman reeled back. "How dare you!"

"Blackmailing civilians into doing gruntwork? Collecting an army of unwilling post-humans? Hiring literal mercenaries who start shootouts in the streets? That's not the kind of stuff that benevolent saviors do."

"I'm sure the daughter of a four-star chef's heard the analogy—"

"About breaking eggs? Yeah. But you actually have to make the omelet, and all you have to show for yourself is a stack of attempts. A-for-effort! Is a pat on the back gonna get you to the part where you actually get something done?"

[ʊ~ʊ]

"You want me to bankrupt a few billionaires then? Hack into some Swiss bank accounts? By all means, I'd do it on a whim if you dared me. But that would change nothing. The problem is not a few bad apples. It's systemic. I'm trying to pull problems out by their roots!"

"Why don't you buy a politician, then?" I asked.

Tom swatted at me.

[~(⊕ _ ⊕)~]

"I own several." The Gentleman said like it should have been obvious. Then he turned back to Emily. "But my political focus is directed at supporting political campaigns that will lead to a greater amount of protection for heritage sites and the people who live there."

"You can't really say the Robin Hood gig doesn't pay well when you can suck money out of a multi-billion dollar corporation," Emily said.

"My budget is torn between long-term goals and causes that require immediate relief. For instance, were it not for my abrupt and chaotic Point Brick intervention, they would have arranged to purchase and develop a number of historic structures around Union Square.

"I am usually much better at handling those things behind the scenes, but Point Brick decided to 'call my bluff' — as it were. Had I not acted rashly, the permits would have been granted by now." The Gentleman paused and then cleared his throat. "Also, I offer danger pay to my underlings, on top of contract salary."

Emily sighed. "Okay, so you're a slightly-better-than-average corporate overlord—"

"What I'm saying is that I am but one person, against an army of greed. The more we become entangled in a debate of 'how far is too far,' or that we should go high when they go low, the longer we divide our efforts and give easy wins to those we all oppose. So yes, when they go for low blows, I will fight back, and fight dirty—"

"Fight as dirty as you like, fine," Emily said. "But you're making something very clear. And this has been in all your videos— you aren't thinking about the human part of gentrification."

She relaxed her posture. "Sure, buildings are great. And lower rent in ten years sounds great. But that doesn't change the fact that this used to be a place for poor black people to have a community. And even though it isn't anymore, black people are getting priced out of their neighborhoods over in Oakland. And Berkley. And it's happening right now. By the time your ten-year plan hits — they will have already been forced out!"

[¬_¬]

The Gentleman started to say something, then rolled his head on his neck. "I'm doing all I can, within the boundaries of what is at least somewhat civil. What do you want me to do? Fly drones overhead that play obnoxiously niche music to lower property values? I could dip into some of Mr. Wexler's rather obscure tastes for that." The Gentleman thought for a minute. "Actually, that gives me an idea—"

"You're a smart guy, I'm sure you'll figure it out either way," Emily said. "And I'm sure you'll find out how to do it without your underlings."

The Gentleman chuckled. Like, with his hand up to his chest. "Ah! There it is… you want to campaign on Mr. Lang's behalf."

"You're blackmailing people into working for you. You're even threatening to give them up to the CDG if they're post-human—"

"Sorry what? You didn't mention that" Tom looked from Emily to the Gentleman. "Are you serious?"

"They're getting paid regardless—"

"Do you have the slightest idea what the CDG will do to them if you give them up? Have you given anyone up?" Tom demanded.

[ʊ_ʊ]

"Idle threats, Mr. Seong. Nobody is—"

"Have you?"

The Gentleman paused. "No, I have not. Nor would I."

"Because I can guarantee you, all those people you're black-mailing know what will happen to them if you do."

"I'm aware—"

"You can hack into every server they have but you will never know what it feels like to have that over your head!" Tom shouted. "Getting snatched off your feet. Tested for any kind of post-human capability you could have. They break your bones to see how strong you are. Hours of psychological torture to get an ESP spike!

"And if they're wrong and you're normal, or not post-human enough to get dropped into Afghanistan in some black helicopter, you get left outside the nearest hospital. Do you have any idea what it's like to live with that threat?"

[...]

The Gentleman nodded. "More than you'd know... but leave it at that."

"If you have the slightest idea what that feels like, then you wouldn't want to do that to someone else!" he said. "Goddamnit, I used to think you had the right idea. Now I'm just sick and dis-appointed..."

The Gentleman looked at me. "Is he always this razor-sharp with the guilt trips?"

"Hey, compared to what I usually get, he's letting you off easy..."

[ಠ_ಠ]

"You can't possibly think that you're building a better future when you're leaving people behind who are living in fear," Emily said. "Maybe Rook's the only child prodigy, but if you want San Francisco to have a soul again, you've got to start thinking about the people. You want Luca out in the streets because he's better there than on your squad? Then you can't keep Rook there and think he's doing more for San Francisco than like... part of a Jazz band or something."

The Gentleman rapped his fingers across the handle of his simple, smooth cane.

"Yeah!" I said. "That's like... using child soldiers. That's literally a war crime, right?"

The Gentleman threw his hands up. "Oh, that's it! Mr. Wexler you just... wow, you convinced me. The error of my ways, right there."

I scowled. "You don't have to be mean about it."

Tom whacked the back of my legs with his cane. "Luca, shut up."

[∩_∩]

"You've got gumption, heart, and an unexpectedly devilish left hook, I'm told. Best you default to those of expertise when it comes to heavy thinking," The Gentleman said. "Ms. Barnett... you've given me something to consider going forward. Perhaps I am best suited to less... invasive measures in the future.

"My current trajectory seems to be rounding up more shootouts than I would have deemed acceptable." He paused. "But I can't do it alone. To take these beasts on, I'll need more active support than the Change Dot Org activists that I seem to accumulate."

"People liked you more before you started doing the intense stuff. I think you could snowball an active following if you'd just stick it out a little bit longer," Emily said.

"And what about in the meantime?" he asked. "Berkley and Oakland?"

"Believe it or not, people really like being included in the fight for their homes," she said. "Instead of throwing fits at billionaires, help people in their own communities. Use your resources to help them organize, take time off work, and find affordable childcare. They will lead the charge if they can get a leg up." From behind, I could see Emily's knees were shaking a little.

But come on. Pretty sure she'd never been within arm's reach of someone with a loaded gun.

['_']

The Gentleman nodded. "Rest assured... I will use a lighter

hand in my influences, come the future..."

"That would be fantastic," Emily said.

"Now, it's been a pleasure, all of you," he sighed. "Don't take this the wrong way, but I hope we do not have to meet again." He gently bowed and then retreated back into his van with all his monitors and blinking lights.

We all stood where we were until the van was back on the street and away.

Tom kicked at the ground a little. "Anybody hungry? Nothing like negotiating with terrorists to make you crave a burrito."

CHAPTER 78
TREMORS

Thursday, November 30

What Tom had already told Dad was that I'd bummed around with Emily for a while. And when I didn't want to go home after that, I went to go blow off some steam at Tom's where we had an angsty heart-to-heart about... teenager things?

Which... you know, *technically* that wasn't a lie.

Honestly I was surprised Dad took it as well as he did. "Still grounded, but good to see that you're actually talking about it, instead of getting angry and doing stupid things. Granted... I'd wish you'd have talked about it with me, but I'm just glad you're okay."

"Well, you didn't have to be worried—"

"I know you well enough to know that I should have been."

I stayed the night at Tom's, getting grilled. I kept quiet through most of it. My head was looking for any reason not to get stuck on... Yeah, the rest of that night. The Holly thing had finally started to sink in.

When Tom said that we were going to put the Avalon Knight program on the shelf for another few years, I didn't even kick up a stink.

— — —

Then the next morning it was all over the news. Holly Rolland was found late last night.

But they found her alive.

"Shit!" I gasped and dropped a plate full of hash browns. "Shit..." I was hyperventilating.

The whole thing flashed in front of me again.

"What? What?" Tom looked like he didn't know what was more upsetting. His comatose friend in critical condition, or me hyperventilating in his kitchen. "Okay, stop pacing, there's broken glass."

I had my head in my hands. "I..."

"Luca..." Tom grabbed my shoulders, and he started to take deep, rhythmic breaths. That got me into the pattern of matching him and I leveled out.

He sat me down on the couch, and I let loose. Told him everything. The confrontation with Hamen, giving up the information. The FBI agent. Leaving Holly to bleed out on that roof—

"You didn't do a damn thing wrong," Tom said. "Except... for all the other stuff you did wrong."

— — —

I didn't get any more texts from the Misfits. I assumed I was toxic now. "Good riddance," I said.

"Glad you agree," Tom nodded. "They won't last long without Roland."

"She was in it for the right reasons," I said. Defending her, I think. "I'm worried about Jonah though. Post-human. Working with Dad and The Mavericks to avoid the CDG."

"He still has your Dad," Tom said. "But if what I've heard about him is true, he better stick himself underground until Colton comes back around. He'll be fine."

I nodded.

"But I may not be if I don't get you to school on time."

CHAPTER 79
GROSS MISUSE OF SUPERPOWERS

Friday, December 1

When I got to school I nearly fell over when I saw Rook, who was in much higher spirits than he had been for a while.

The Gentleman live-streamed an apology statement on YouTube and Twitch that played across the vast majority of news channels and radio shows. The stock market evened out. Point Brick hired back nearly all their formerly laid-off employees. Briggs and Welsh got their offices back.

I expected him to find a new way to seize the means of production, but I could hope that he'd find more productive methods.

We were let out of Geography class almost as soon as attendance was taken. Well, we weren't 'let out' — we could work with our partners in the school, as long as we kept the noise down and stayed on campus. Having missed so much time already, rook and me opted to actually do work instead of heading off school grounds to take bong hits like everyone else.

"So yeah... he called. Like. Phone call. And told my Dad that he wouldn't be reaching out to us again." He told me.

"Maybe we can all start getting back to normal," I said.

"I'd been... working with him since before you and I started talking," Rook told me. "I don't think my old normal works anymore."

I'd given him the TL/DR version of what'd been going on. He said he never would have guessed that I was up to superhero stuff. But then he thought about it and he said that he might have.

Meanwhile, Emily was over with Kaleb actually doing work. She shot a snide look in our direction now and then because we got to talk about Vigil stuff, and she had to be a student.

Rook kept his voice hushed. "I knew you knew Karate... but you were like... fighting Mr. Hamen... He's scary..."

"I lost..." I sighed. I kinda wished there'd been a rematch. Take away his lame guns, and I would have kicked his ass. Also his knives. I get to keep my staff, right?

"So like... what kind is it?" I asked.

"Huh?"

"The super strength? Always-on kind? You rip doors off by accident?"

"No, no," he blushed. "I need to focus and then everything gets." He held his hands beside his face. "Woosh!"

"Like you came?"

His face turned solid red. "What? Shut up."

"No really. I've read testimonials. They say that's what it's like."

Rook ignored me. "I have selective muscular hyper-efficiency. I burn through like two thousand calories in about ten minutes and then I feel like I'm gonna pass out."

"So... like you just came."

His face was about to pop.

"Hey, it's perfectly natural for a man your age."

"Stop it."

"You don't want me in your health class, then," I said. "So what can you do with it?"

"Um... With my—"

"Superpowers." I winked. "I meant superpowers."

Rook cleared his throat. "I dunno... I'm towards the lower end of the spectrum—"

"Which means it's manageable," I said.

Rook nodded. "It was always just a thing between me and Dad. Nobody else was gonna know... The Gentleman found me because dad was talking to extended family about who else has it. I have a great aunt on my mom's side that has it, but that's it. I don't know why he'd thought I'd be any use."

"Yeah..." I said. "He's got a few wires crossed."

"I was on three assignments. I bungled two of them..." Rook sighed.

I thought for a minute. "You know... my trainer — he knows some martial arts for super-strength."

"They exist?"

"Yeah. Most martial arts are to help people fight *against* super-strength. But he could help you out. Probably put you through exercises to help you use the 'woosh' better."

Rook nodded. "I always assumed that people who have that kind of strength wouldn't need any kind of discipline."

"Yeah. Like a handicap," I said.

"Meaning?"

"I'm talking about like... a handicap in sports."

His eyes widened. "Oh..."

"A handicap is a unique perspective that others will dismiss as a disability," I said, "quoting said martial arts teacher."

"Huh," Rook said. "He sounds Asian."

"Pfff. Racist."

"Dude, I'm from Beijing!"

"He's Korean, actually." I rolled my eyes. "Racist."

Rook smirked. "I *will* throw you through a wall if you don't cut the shit with me, Wexler."

I slapped Rook's back so hard his glasses almost fell off. "Where's that big dick energy been hiding this whole time?"

CHAPTER 80
THREAD-PULLER

Saturday, December 2

Dreams. I had a lot of dreams.

I was at a lake. And it was all grass around me. There was something in the reflection of the lake. Someone was watching me under the water, but it was mirrored so I couldn't really see.

Lillie woke me up. I let her out and she didn't even have to go. I got back in bed and got to sleep. There was a big section I don't remember. I woke myself up. Then I rolled over and got back to sleep. Something happened in my dream. Then I was in a city. Gridlocked — nothing but skyscrapers. Then I was at an outdoor cafe with Silhouette. Her name was Adelia, Katerina, and/or Nadya.

The Gentleman was there too. We were all having a great time.

Lillie woke me up again, whining and trying to cuddle against me harder. "Okay, okay," I said. "I'm right here, everything's fine." It was like there were fireworks going off. Zero was fine though... which was a total script-flip.

While I was trying to get to sleep, a piece of the dream crystallized in my head.

"But what I mean is that," said Silhouette, "you understand how... people change..."

"Oh, now that you're in America you're putting a copyright on these things?" asked the Gentleman.

I'd said: "I don't think that's how copyright works..." And I said it while I laid in bed as it happened.

"Maybe not, but you don't understand change, dear, not completely, so don't incorporate it into your ideas," said The Gentleman.

I remembered Silhouette rolled her eyes. "And what do you know about change that I don't?"

The Gentleman sipped tea. But I couldn't remember if he had his mask. "People try to... moralize change."

"You're one to speak, Mr. Make San Francisco Great Again!" We'd all thought that was hilarious.

"No, no, no, listen to me. This will make sense, I promise." The Gentleman said. "People think that when things change it's either good or bad. But they're missing the point..."

I remember it was my turn. Like it was a script and it was my turn to say something. "Change is for survival," was my line. There was more after that, but I couldn't remember it.

I got up to get something quick to eat. It was 4:40 AM, and I debated just staying up, maybe going for an early run. But decided to play with myself back in bed. Instead, I fell asleep.

Well... I don't think I was quite asleep... It was one of those half-awake/half-asleep naps. Like I felt aware of my room, and I also was somewhere else.

Walking down into a metro station. All the lights were out. Someone was in there with me, but I didn't need to be afraid of them. I felt like I should have known who it was, but I couldn't see anyone.

Someone else said: "You know what I like about you—" like it was a fuzzy recording that got cut off. I followed the sound, it kept repeating every few seconds. It was getting louder.

Right on the other side of the cross-guard, in the oblong spotlight... was The Gentleman's mask.

[L O L]

But it flickered with every syllable it spoke. "You know what I like about you—"

There was an image on the screen between the flickers... like subliminal messaging. I thought I could almost make it out... it looked so familiar...

"You know what I like about you—"

CHAPTER 81
RISE AND SHINE

Saturday, December 2

"Luca!" Emily said, shaking me awake. "Hey, you need to get up!"

I had not slept enough for this. I felt like I hadn't slept at all. "Why'd Dad let you in?"

"Your Dad's not here, get up!" The dogs didn't even bark this time.

"I'm naked, go away." I buried myself deeper in the blankets. "I'm naked."

Emily slapped my shoulder.

"Ow!"

"A building collapsed in an earthquake," she said. "It was downtown. A 17-story building."

I sat up, squinting in the light. "Is anyone hurt? How did I sleep through that?"

She sighed. "The thing is... the earthquake was localized to only one city block. Everywhere else just got micro-tremors..."

"What?"

She bit her lip. "The Gentleman's taking credit..."

ACT 3

FAULT

CHAPTER 82

FOUNDATION

Saturday, December 2

I got dressed, grabbed an energy drink from the fridge, and sat down with Emily at the kitchen table. Dad was... out? He sent me a text message telling me to stay at home, and that was it. The dogs were all over me.

On my laptop, Emily pulled up The Gentleman's latest YouTube video... which had since been deleted when his account was banned. But Emily had it saved so she could show me.

He was silent on the screen for a few moments; his mask was dim, inactive. He took in a long breath and exhaled it slowly. His mask flickered to life.

[oops...]

"You know... I didn't even really like the building." He shrugged. "It was ugly. It clashed with the... the essence of The Golden City. Especially taking into consideration what it had replaced..."

He sighed. "Well, the important thing is that no one got hurt, right? But such a strange event — for an earthquake to only happen in one building. I originally thought to use... I don't know — demolition charges on all of the buildings I don't like. But... explosives are so done, and done, and just so... 'supervillain,' you know? How does one stand out? And nobody really takes bomb threats seriously nowadays...

"And The City — The City has such a... well such a calling for Earthquakes, doesn't it? I'd say we're about due for another *big* one... Think of it as a cleansing. We'll make it a centennial thing, no? The City always bounces back best after a big shake... Just make sure to vacate the premises when you feel the floor start to tremble."

[ᵕ_◕]

"I'll be in touch," he said. And the broadcast ended.

— — —

Emily and I got downtown by 10:00 AM. Getting anywhere near Third and Mission was tricky. The cops had blocked up Third Street past the Yebra Buena Gardens... But it was clear that the sleek concrete skyscraper was missing from the skyline. Just... gone.

The dust had stuck in the air, making the humid overcast sticky-gross. But the ground was still blanketed with soggy debris that was once the building.

Emily and I kept to our phones for the news, but she wanted a closer look... Past the tall dividers to keep people from seeing the wreckage, but news helicopters swarmed overhead anyway.

So, cutting through the Marriott parking garage, we skipped around the roadblock and got through to Jesse Square. Without the cops seeing us, we kept low and snuck up to the remains. Only a few hardened supports stood upward, and none taller than the first story. The rest was a heap of rubble and dust. It was hard to just think of it as all gone...

It was all in a neat little pile that barely spilled out into the road. In fact... there was almost no damage done to the surrounding buildings. The only large structure directly beside the now dead-building was the Park Central Hotel... and there were only a handful of broken windows on the lower levels.

"It's like it just... came apart," I said, "like Legos—"

"Lego is its own plural," Emily said.

"What?"

"It's not 'Pokémons.' It's just 'Pokémon.' Same deal."

"Okay...?"

"Sorry. Just bugs me."

I sighed. "We're standing beside an ex-tower and you're obsessing over Legos."

"No," Emily stuck out her hand, "I'm thinking and you're distracting me."

Just then, I got a call from Dad. "One second," I said to Emily, moving a little bit away.

"Where the fuck are you?" Dad shouted.

"I'm—"

"I swear to shit if you're out near ground zero..."

A police officer noticed us. "Hey! You kids!"

"Shit..." Emily hissed.

I swallowed. "I'll be right home."

"You'd better be," Dad said, and hung up.

CHAPTER 83
QUAKE ENGINE

Saturday, December 2

I got re-grounded. Conditionally. "Treat it like you're grounded while I'm out," Dad said, he pointed at Emily. "And don't you decide to go out either. Your parents trust me, I'd like to keep it that way."

"Why aren't you at your place anyway?" I asked.

"Mom and Dad are with the twins in Oakville since last night. The bridges are closed, so I'd just be home alone."

I sighed. "Well, Dad, I doubt that we'd have to worry about any buildings collapsing around here. In all honesty, the safest place to be is at a park or something—"

Dad grabbed some toast from the toaster and started to spread peanut butter on it. "Nobody knows how the building collapsed, or even if it was an earthquake. But if he has some kind of tectonic agitator that can generate seismic events in such a localized area... that means The Gentleman is part of a league of supervillains we haven't seen since—"

Emily cleared her throat. "He wouldn't need that kind of technology to bring a building down like that. He probably just managed to build a functional Tesla oscillator."

Dad and I looked at Emily. "A what?" he asked.

"Nicola Tesla... Russian philanthropist inventor who's pretty much responsible for the 20th century — not that you'd know that — because of how Edison gets the credit for virtually all of Tesla's breakthroughs—"

Dad huffed. "Yeah, I know who he is, but what—"

"I don't know who he is," I said; Emily and Dad looked at me with tired eyes.

Dad shook his head. "What's an oscillator?"

"An earthquake machine... It's a small device that Tesla built," Emily explained. "He strapped it onto a support beam in the basement of his New York apartment building. It used steam to move a piston back and forth. Through trial and error, he experimented with speeds to find the resonant frequency of the building—"

"What frequency?" I asked.

"Resonant frequency means..." Dad started. "Everything made of matter can be shaken with a frequency. When you vibrate one part of the object at that frequency, the vibrations will carry through the whole object."

"Or it will only vibrate certain parts of the object. Like some back massagers," Emily said, "you put them on your foot and you can feel it in your jaw."

Dad interrupted. "So you think a device on the building's foundation would have found the resonant frequency of the building's frame and shook the building down?"

"Yeah," Emily said, "it would give people time to... you know... evacuate while it was shaking... And explain why there was like... no damage to anything around the building..."

Dad gave the two of us a look.

"Which we know..." I said, "from pictures. On the internet—"

"Yeah shut up," Dad said, chewing on toast. "How big would the device need to be?"

"Tesla's was about the size of a microwave. But phallic."

"And it used gas?"

"Tesla's used steam," Emily said. "The whole point is moving a weight back and forth so the steam isn't necessary..."

"So explosive or volatile materials wouldn't be needed. Bomb-dogs wouldn't pick it up... Did he ever get it to work?"

"Who?"

"Tesla?"

Emily snickered. "According to legend, Tesla's test caused an earthquake in and around his apartment building for several minutes. He didn't expect it to work... he had to take a hammer to it to get it to stop... Which—" She scratched the back of her neck. "Some detective on the police force must have suggested it..."

Dad swallowed and tossed the rest of his toast to Lillie. Zero was still under the table. "Well, I'm going to suggest that anyway. Maybe someone hasn't thought of it."

"That might not be it."

"No bad ideas in a situation like this." Dad grabbed his blazer from the back of a kitchen chair. "Last I heard, the only people working on analysis was the bomb squad."

"Since when are you involved in this?" I asked. "Collapsing buildings isn't exactly your... field?"

"I'm on a case where I'm trying to prove The Gentleman is a bona fide supervillain." Dad nodded. "An earthquake machine made by a literal mad scientist kind of puts him in that camp. Even to Congress."

He made his way to the door and we followed him. "Stay here. Stay safe. I'll call Tom and get him to stay here with you, too. Emily, text your parents and ask if that's okay."

"It'll be okay," she said.

"Ask anyway, please." Dad sighed on his way out.

CHAPTER 84
HOUSING MARKET CRASH

Saturday, December 2

Around 1:10 PM, a second building came down a little bit after Tom came by. A high-rent condo complex off of Oak Street. Not long after, reports coming out of Pacific Heights said that a luxury commercial office building was starting to shake.

Reportedly, three firemen were caught inside the Oak Street property while searching for stragglers. The Third and Mission collapse took about fifty minutes of shaking, the Oak Street condos came down after only half an hour. The total estimated dead or missing was up to eighteen.

Tom was over at our place, keeping an eye on things. He took a little while to get over here because he was busy checking on the other residents in his building — making sure they have somewhere suburban to go. And he was playing Dad's game. Sit down and watch the kids, even if Emily and I wanted to do something about all of it.

"The Mavericks are in Iceland or something," I said, "and I get the feeling that no one else really—"

He shook his head. "Are you saying that you want to get back in touch with your Misfits?"

"No, but—"

"Then this is a no. We're out of our league…" Tom said.

"Well…" Emily said. "What if this is all our fault. Kind of. My fault?"

"How so?" Tom asked. He and I turned to her.

"We were the ones who talked to The Gentleman. We got him to change his mind. If we... Well, I guess it was me. If I hadn't, maybe this wouldn't be happening."

Tom sighed. "Jeeze. I haven't had the talk with you yet..."

The Talk.

"The Gentleman is a terrorist," he said. "We can prove this by using Tesla... what? Tesla Oscillators to rip down buildings because he doesn't like looking at them. You can't be held responsible for the actions of terrorists. Because they're unpredictable — it's part of what makes them terrorists.

"The only other option is doing nothing. And that's almost always worse because it's letting them win; it's giving them their way. It's saying: 'hey, you go ahead and run the show because we don't want a tantrum.' And what that does is it encourages worse behavior whenever there's any pushback. Before you know it, you have narcissistic, delusional man-babies running the country.

"But if you start beating yourself up for all the people you don't save... or all the people that terrorist hurts because you were trying to stop him from hurting people... you're going to go crazy," Tom said.

We sat in front of the TV for a few minutes. "That said... we do have a lead that nobody else has..." He sighed. "And it's a lead we can't just turn over to the police... because that may destroy an innocent person's life..."

I knew who he was talking about. I didn't like it.

— — —

"So Dad's off doing..." Rook waved his hand, "who knows what — trying to do whatever he can to protect my PH status in case The Gentleman takes that information to the CDG!"

"The Gentleman said he wasn't going to hold that over you—"

"He also said he wasn't going to do the Point Brick thing again!" He was in a panic, too manic to be in tears. I hadn't seen many people freak out like him. He couldn't stay still, he probably hadn't managed to straighten out his elbows or drop his shoulders since long before we got there.

"I'm... screwed! I'm going to get pulled out of schools in hand-cuffs and nobody's going to see me again." He made some whiney noises. "I don't... I don't want to hurt anyone... and they're going to make me hurt people."

I wanted to tell him it wouldn't be that way... but that was kind of how it went with post-humans...

Emily stood up and gently tried to force him into a hug. "It's okay... I'm sure it won't be that bad..." she said. "You're talented in other ways—"

"No, that's not — nobody's going to care about that."

"Well then, your dad will probably work out something anyway," she said. "And that will be fine."

"No, no..."

Emily sighed. "Look... we — Luca and me — we want to stop The Gentleman for good. If what you say is true, that may be your best shot at getting out, free and clear."

Rook's chest swelled. "Well if the police get him... then they'll know everything. About me! And there are others working for The Gentleman. Like me. And they don't want to be there either."

I stood up to stop him from pacing. "The Gentleman is a lunatic. Even if the police find everything he has — he's done so much international espionage, they may not even get around to you. They may not be able to use it as evidence. As long as you can fake your way through strength tests, you'll be fine..."

He nodded in Emily's arms.

"You hear?" I grabbed his shoulder. "You'll be alright, got it?"

He nodded more. Blank expression across his face.

"But we need to find him to stop him from hurting anyone else. And we need your help for that."

We gave him a little time to think. He sat down on the couch and leaned back. "I'm not sure what I can do…"

I sat beside Rook. "Is there any way you can get in touch with him?"

He thought about it. "Not him… but I can send a message to Temple."

— — —

Emily, Tom and me waited in the car — phones off except for mine. Rook turned his phone on long enough to text me something about the geography presentation, an idea how to get extra marks. That was a signal code that he was half an hour out from heading out to wherever The Gentleman told him to meet.

CHAPTER 85
ROTARY PHONES

Saturday, December 2

"Did people really have to function like this?" Emily said, after trailing Rook without any assistance from mobile devices. Every other turn, Emily was convinced that we'd lost the Uber that Rook got in. But we'd made it to a shipping warehouse just next to Pier 80. It wasn't suspiciously out of the way or anything...

We staked it out, watched a few people go in. Black hoodies and cargo pants. No one was coming out.

"Believe it or not, we also managed to find addresses with paper maps," Tom said. "Any given person used to have about seven of them folded up in that pocket behind the passenger seat."

"That's what that's for?" Emily gasped.

Tom looked at me in the rearview mirror. "You okay back there?"

I nodded, putting on the last of my armor in the back seat

Emily looked back. "You're not usually this quiet."

"We don't usually run jobs like this," Tom said, then he looked back too. "You know what to do?"

Another shady person entered through the same door Rook did, looking just as suspicious.

A lot of time was wasted with Tom and Emily figuring out how I could get into the building without someone spotting me.

"At this rate," I said, "Rook is going to be out of there before I get in."

"The Gentleman might have set up hidden cameras," Emily said.

"Thanks," I grumbled.

"We shouldn't need to worry about those. This meeting place seemed last-minute. The warehouse gets a lot of use, but empty on weekends." Tom bobbed his head. "But you should still expect to make a quick exit, in case he does have eyes on us—"

I swung the back door open and lurched out.

Tom leaned out the window. "Where are you going?"

"I'm not waiting anymore," I said. I'd figure it out as I went. The Gentleman probably knew I was coming anyway.

"What are you doing?" Emily hissed. "We need to—"

"No, no," Tom said. "He's right. If we fuss over unknown unknowns, we'll miss the opportunity."

There was also one of those strange vans parked out back. I kept out of it's line of sight.

The goal was to record as much as I could from the meeting. We'd figure out the rest later. A phone would have been the best option, but the Gentleman made it so that anything with a network connection was a liability. So, a camcorder and Emily's voice recorder it was.

"Is it even safe for us to be using the com like this?" I asked, at the foot of the warehouse, scanning the outside wall for a way up.

"This is over radio frequency," Tom said. "His wheelhouse seems to be internet… Doubt he'd be prepared to intercept low-tech."

He didn't sound convinced.

After scaling a drainpipe, I cracked open a skylight above the main storage room. They'd already started the meeting. For as much as there didn't seem to be anything the Gentleman couldn't do with tech, a council of domestic terrorism seemed a little bit like old-fashioned Hollywood spycraft.

Dead drops would work so much better. Was the Gentleman dramatic? Or did he just not know what he was doing?

The warehouse itself looked older on the inside. Big on concrete and brick. Thick metal crossbeams ran across the rafters below the ceiling and windows. It let me move around above the industrial lights without being seen. Not much light was coming in from above.

Honestly, as risky as this was, this was the most Vigil Ninja shit I'd ever gotten to do.

They had a setup at the back of the warehouse, just before concrete stairs to some offices. There was a collapsible wooden table with a metal briefcase on it, and some paper maps of San Francisco with stickers on them. I set up the camcorder as soon as I saw Rook.

"In position," I whispered into the mic.

"Got it," Tom said.

I kept the camera pointed at the mercenary. It wasn't Hamen, must have been one of the other ones. I tried to keep my hands steady, to see the map with all the stickers. Zooming in so far made the feed jittery.

"I realize this is a bit of a switch up from our regular operations and that this may make some of you uncomfortable," he said.

The mercenary unlatched the suitcase and lifted the lid. "Each volunteer will receive an envelope with instructions. Post-human assets will take the red envelopes. Most of you will be working on different jobs — no, come on up, starting with you—" he pointed to someone, who looked around a little embarrassed, and moved toward the case, "We still have half a dozen more briefings to do, so the faster this goes, the better."

"You listening?" I whispered.

"I can make out enough," said Tom. Could barely hear him through the static.

One by one, they moved forward to get their assignments, counter-clockwise in the arc they formed around the table. A respectful distance between them and the mercenary. Rook would be one of the last people to get an envelope.

And I... I had to do something. I felt like if I let him pick up one of those instruction sets, it would be the end for him. Call it a weird feeling? I got a flash in my mind of Rook getting shipped out of the city in an armored truck.

"I need to do something."

"Do what?"

"I need to..." I struggled. "I need to stop Rook from getting any deeper into this!"

"We'll worry about that later."

And then it was like I blinked, and I was stuck in a white-walled room lit by fluorescent lights. A migraine was on its way. "Great..." I sighed to myself. Because this day wasn't already the worst...

CHAPTER 86
CREEPERS

Saturday, December 2

With my head beginning to throb… I tugged on the elastic gel-cap under my hood.

Tom gave a warning sound. "We can worry about Rook after we're done."

"He's going to pick up a red envelope," I said. Tom didn't really understand the significance of that. But to me, it was life-or-death for some reason.

"If you are caught with these instructions, and the authorities seize them, we will effectively cut you off," Temple continued. "A great deal of planning has gone into this operation. Luckily, the paper that they are printed on will dissolve within seconds of contact with water. That said, avoid getting it wet until you have memorized your role in full. But if you are detained, find a source of water, and drop the paper in. At least that way you will receive support from us—"

The Gentleman slid into the room through a shadowy door. "If you're feeling particularly ambitious, you could also ingest them."

[͡° ͜ʖ ͡°]

He was here.

"I hear they'll *literally* melt in your mouth," The Gentleman said. "Apparently, they don't taste half-bad. I had our very own Mr. Temple sample them—"

"Right, boss." The mercenary said. "Something you need?"

I hissed into the com. "He's here! The Gentleman — he's here!"

"You're sure?" Tom asked.

I huffed. "He's hard to miss…"

Tom seemed a little panicked. "Okay, calm down. Stay discrete and stay hidden."

The Gentleman half-sat on the table, facing the crowd. "I can see it — this is troubling to the lot of you. I really do hate to use you in the way that I have. Many of you have talents — abilities — hopes and dreams."

"Sir," said the mercenary, getting more on-guard, prepping his trigger finger, more alert of the crowd around him, "I don't think this is a good—"

The man in black silently waved him down with his cane-hand. "Some of you could benefit American Culture or the human race as a whole."

[^_^]

"I guarantee you," he continued, "this will be the final time I will call upon you. Thereafter, I will relinquish whatever information I have on you and will even compensate you generously… as a… a bonus! Now—"

"You know, convincing Mr. Lang Jr. to come here was a little cruel," he said… in my earpiece. But he kept talking to the crowd below at the same time. "I'm a man of my word, regardless of whatever other attitude change you may perceive. You people. So cynical, mistrusting. Not that I could blame you. Living in this world."

"Tom?" I hissed.

"I'm here," he said, "I hear him."

"I had agreed to let him go. But… there he is, on the ground looking like his puppy died, while you're up there making sure to document whatever you can. Oh yes, I know you're up in the rafters. Are those rafters? Would they have a different name in a warehouse?" He didn't look up at me.

It was nearly Rook's turn to get an envelope. Since The Gentleman arrived, everyone was so much more agitated. He kept his head trained on someone as they approached. A girl — who took a red envelope.

His face switched.

[^ o ^]

"Yes..." The Gentleman said. "Your com system runs on an antiquated signal. As it's not done through Wi-Fi or data networks, I can't shut it down. But I have to say, I have to commend you for trying to fool me. But none of you are very good at concealing your movements through the city. Or rather... you aren't aware of the multitude of ways I can track you and deduce your actions. You think turning off your phones is enough?"

He kept talking below. I knew he liked to hear himself talk but... That was usually only when he was trying to stall me. Hamen wasn't down there. But he must have been close — If I didn't see him...

I swung my head around.

Open areas. Clear shots.

He was just barely visible near the front of the warehouse.

Shit—

Just as he noticed me spying him, his arm stiffened ever so slightly. I threw myself off the metal beam just as the gunshot echoed, hoping there was something I could grab on the shelves below to stop my fall. Instead, I landed in a pile of styrofoam, cardboard box shredding, and plastic wrap.

Shit-shit-shit-shit—

I pushed myself out of it. When I got to my feet The Gentleman had vanished. Everyone was in a panic. I hoped Rook had enough sense to get out while he could.

A flash of metal out of the corner of my eye.

Hamen.

I threw my weight at him, bashing him against the wall. He sprung back, and started going for blood like he needed to get this over with fast. I took the collapsible staff and flicked it out, smacking him clean across the face and knocking the knife out of his hand.

What I didn't see was the shock gauntlet he wore on his other hand.

This guy and his damn misdirections!

It hit me with a discharge of sparks. Flying through the air, I caught a glimpse of The Gentleman holding open the far door as Hamen slid through without a second look back. He must have told him to make an escape instead of finishing me off.

"I'm fine…" I said, not really able to hear if Tom was asking or not. I pushed myself up — I could have kept up with Hamen if he hadn't cheated like that. God *damnit*. I'd always been so close to owning him, but he always had a trick up his sleeve. He was gonna run out of them eventually.

As I got to my feet, I grabbed his bush knife and followed them through the door.

CHAPTER 87
I DO MY OWN STUNTS

Saturday, December 2

I burst into the parking lot, and the van's engine revved, the back doors slamming shut. "A.K.! Get to the car we need to—"

I took off toward the van just as the tires started to spin out.

"No, no, no — Don't you—" Tom cried out, but I couldn't catch the rest of what he said.

I dug the knife into the side of the sterile white vehicle as it took off like a rocket. With a foothold in the wheel well, I kept my hand fastened to the knife.

"What the honest shit are you—" Tom was having a fit, but he was cutting out.

"…seems we have a stowaway, Mr. Hamen…" I heard The Gentleman say through my earpiece. Immediately, the van lurched to the side to throw me off. I held on, but we were speeding up, passing by intersections.

"A.K…" I heard Tom fizzle in and out. "…off… now… off… call…" Seemed like he was repeating a message but I couldn't quite understand. Okay, that was a lie — I knew Tom wanted me to drop off the van and call it a night.

It wasn't happening if I could help it—

The van swerved one way, then the other, with me hanging off the starboard side. Hamen must have accidentally (or not) side-swiped another car because sparks flew around my face. "Mind the paint job!" I heard The Gentleman cringe a little.

As the van jerked to the right, I pushed up from the wheel well. The spinning tire shredded off chunks of my leg guard, but I managed to throw myself up onto the roof. Not a moment later, sparks erupted from where I'd been.

"What did I *just* say about the paint?"

Hamen cursed. "...pikey git—" Then gunshots ripped through the roof right beside me.

I figured that this was probably my stop...

They always say that you need to roll if you leave a moving vehicle. What they don't tell you is how hard it is to do it right.

I hit the ground hard and did roll... a little. Just in time to see the van make an over-enthusiastic swerve and tip onto its side. Sparks flying as it skid to a stop in the middle of an intersection.

People were shouting, car horns blasting. Sirens were in the distance.

I got to my feet, even though it felt like my bones had been rearranged. I flexed out my arms and legs to make sure nothing was broken or sprained and then figured I should consider myself lucky.

People already had their phones out, recording video. Tom was nowhere to be seen. The earpiece was dead so. Yeah.

Badass.

CHAPTER 88
THIS ASSHOLE, THO

Saturday, December 2

You couldn't really call it a van after that. I saw Hamen crawling out from what was probably the windshield. His left leg wasn't in the best shape. The back doors were crumpled shut. Had The Gentleman been like... wearing a seatbelt? Was he dead? I kept thinking about how I should feel...

Then the two back doors launched off their hinges and flew ten feet away before sliding into some parked cars. A very fancy man stepped out from the back, into the headlights and streetlights, backlit with the glow from strange computers that spat out sparks. His pin-stripe coattails were tattered at the edges, but he stood upright to straighten out his jacket.

[! ! !]

He picked up his bowler hat from the wreckage, placing it daintily over his mask. There was a shatter point at his temple and two long cracks extended halfway across the face — dead pixels running along their length.

He stepped into the middle of the intersection, cane in hand, and looked at me, then Hamen, then back to the van. Then back to me. And with his eyeless gaze trained on me, he pointed back to the van and snapped his gloved fingers. That instant, the inside ignited in a flash of light. The blast didn't blow the vehicle apart, but it incinerated all the equipment inside.

Everyone around the intersection screamed.

Then he turned to Hamen.

[ò_ó˘]

The fancy man strode to the crippled mercenary, who pushed himself back along the ground like a slug away from his soon-to-be-former-employer. The Gentleman grasped him firmly by his neck and pulled him up off the ground, his feet dangling.

Hamen drew his hip-mounted pistol and blasted a few rounds at The Gentleman's chest. Bullets did nothing, but The Gentleman grabbed Hamen's hand and crushed it in his own.

With bones crunching, and blood oozing down to the pavement, Hamen cried out.

[ʊ́~ʊ́]

The Gentleman flicked his cane, tossing away a scabbard, revealing a long, thin blade. "I think that's been more than enough second chances, no?" he said, calmly, and then sent the blade through Hamen's heart. The mercenary went silent at once. Tossed off the blade, he landed in a crumpled, motionless heap on the ground.

There was a loud crackle from all around me, and The Gentleman's voice rang from every phone around the intersection. "I would clear away from the vehicle."

The van erupted in an explosion that scattered the onlookers. I ducked for cover, but The Gentleman just stood there and let his coattails fly in the blast.

Who was this guy?

I could see news helicopters in the distance. Nothing like some carnage for the evening news.

I thought to myself that this was it, I had to keep him talking or distracted long enough for some police to arrive so they could make an arrest.

He cleared his throat.

"Oh, and don't worry about him..." said The Gentleman, reaching down to grab the cane.

[¬_¬]

"Kurt Liam Hamen. His information should be reaching my website shortly. Quite a piece of work, that one. Truly, he had far worse coming to him than..." He waved his hand whimsically at the corpse, "...that."

Clearing his throat, he wiped the blood off the blade against his own sleeve and slid it back into the cane. "He was an animal, for sure. And yes, under my thumb. Better that I kept him on a leash than out in the wild. But all feral things grow restless in a kennel.

"He was beginning to lash out — find places for his old habits. Holly Rolland is in a coma! Without my approval. Was only a matter of time before he resorted to hunting African orphans for sport... multiple accounts of that.

"Well, that's misleading. Most of the time, they weren't orphans before he showed up in their villages. I quickly learned that I could pay him to do anything except show a little restraint. Believe me, I was considering doing away with—"

While he was voguing for his audience, my foot slammed against the back of his head from behind.

He let out a brief wail... but damn, he felt solid. Even compared to his minions with super strength. I figured he used them because he was just the brains with no brawn. But... I'm not that lucky.

He turned around slowly.

[ಠoಠ]

"Really though, Mr. *Knight*?" He said. I was sure he would have been all about exposing me by then. I was in full gear... he could have outed me and there wouldn't be any denying it. But he kept up the charade. "Should I pity your stupidity or admire your tenacity?"

I flicked the collapsable staff out. "Sure, why not?"

[ಠ_ಠೖ]

He swung his cane-scabbard at me. I pulled back, as it whistled through the air. He swung again, but I guarded, feeling the shock from his blow absorbed in my wrists and elbows as his strike buckled my weapon. It was a pressure like I'd never felt before.

I twisted in the air for momentum and kicked him in the chest. Which... it always sucked when I brought out the acrobatic shit and it didn't work. He didn't fall back far, but it gave me a second to get my breath back.

Keeping him busy was the objective, anyway.

I ducked under a swing and then moved around a strike. And again. And again. I was getting worn down, and he was still too fresh. I found myself rolling into a pile on the pavement, and trying to get up again. The crowd booed and gasped like a ref made a bad call against me.

I... was on home ground. This was my home ground. Nobody wanted to see me get scored on.

A news helicopter appeared directly above us. Their spotlight lit up the intersection, drowning out the flickering orange flames.

How was the news on site before the police??? I could hear sirens in the distance, so they couldn't have been far.

I leaned on the hanbo to push myself up from the curb. He came at me, swinging his cane like a golf club. I rolled around it, striking the side of his head as I rose. The hat fell off as he bucked forward.

[Q#@jH]

The gathered crowd cheered. Home team scored.

"Damnable... wasn't built for reflexes..." He muttered, his voice flickered in my ear and around us through devices. But then the news chopper backed away. Spotlight went out.

[? ? ?]

Another spotlight instead. This one was red, tactical. It shone from a silent hovercraft that roared to life as it lit up with micro-lights around its smooth, science-fiction exterior.

This was a Mavericks vehicle! Did this mean that they were back? Or was that one of their reserves?

"You have one opportunity to stand down, mask-freak," said a cool voice over a loudspeaker. I didn't recognize the voice right away, so it was probably the reserve roster.

[...]

Sirens — finally! Never thought I'd be this glad to hear police closing in on me. This was it for him — no getting away! And if everyone was gonna focus on him, maybe I could even slip away.

The Gentleman tilted his head. He reached out with his hand, and his hat zipped to his outstretched fingers. He sat it on his head. "Such interesting... technology you have..."

"You have to the count of—"

The Gentleman's voice took over the loudspeaker. "I say, is the android with you? What does she call herself? C-8, is she? I know it sounded like a legal bill. C-14? Can't recall."

A cannon dropped from the hovercraft's left-wing. It began to power up with yellow electricity.

"Oh no... that won't do at all..." The Gentleman's voice echoed in surround sound.

[☻ ‿ ☻]

He held up his hand — the weapon immediately discharged, almost exploding. It knocked the hovercraft to the side, spinning out in the air, but keeping altitude. Another discharge... The Gentleman stayed in place, but street lights and cell phones flickered. People ran, people screamed.

Time to leave it to the professionals.

I took off through a gardened courtyard between buildings. Other people were running too. Streetlights flickered. Only red and blue lit up the streets.

At this point, I wouldn't even have been mad if I got arrested. But that was more like Plan B. I turned sharp on my heel to the left and bounced my way up the side of a building. Moving anything on the left side of my body hurt. But I made it to the roof faster than I should have for how uncomfortable I was.

"Mr. Myagi?" I heaved into the mic. No answer. "Mr. T?"

I ran down the other side of the building. I was beyond the police blockade, but I needed to re-point myself due north, or northwest or whatever. Jesus, it sounded like a war zone near the intersection. I looked back… the hovercraft was moving southward, which must have been where The Gentleman was headed. It hurt to look at the lights.

The Gentleman must have been on the move and they were chasing him. News copters were keeping a healthy distance from the site… but it would only be a matter of time before they closed in like vultures.

Police would be on crowd control while the superheroes did the real work.

CHAPTER 89
WALK OF SHAME

Saturday, December 2

I kept to the side of an inner-city gravel road where there were no street lights. There was a housing development under construction to my left.

Keeping to the shadows was best... Not just to stay unnoticed, but looking at any light caused... pain. I wasn't in a full-blown migraine, and it was getting better. But I still felt like puking.

And I walked a long time... No police seemed to be after me but my whole body was full of pain and jitters. Whenever I tried to move, I ended up turning a gesture into a full-on arm-flail. My heart was beating from the top of my chest. I felt like my breaths were coming out of the top of my head.

I got the headgear off. Maybe with just the armor, I could pass as a lost dirt-biker or something. What was a dirt biker doing, walking through the inner-city in the late evening?

People didn't normally ask questions to anyone in public for any reason. And most people would probably be inside at a time like this. As risky as it was, I crossed back onto a lit road.

I figured I was close to Holly Rolland's clubhouse. I wondered if the gang was still there. Or what they'd be up to. Maybe I'd come across them. I hoped not, Jesus. I avoided main streets where cops raced past. The Gentleman probably had a bug in their system to slow their dispatch time.

Squinting as I walked, all the street lights seemed a bit dimmer. They flickered. I wondered if The Gentleman was doing something to the power grid. I was starting to buy into Hanna's cyberpath theory.

On Mississippi Street I just... I needed a break. I sat down in the middle of the sidewalk. I couldn't bother looking for cover. Taking a breath, I fished out my phone.

Aaaaaaand — there was a big ol' crack down the screen. "Nice," I sighed. I wondered which narrow escape from death had earned my phone this war stripe...

A few cars passed while my phone started up. Felt like it was taking forever. Missed calls from Tom and texts from Emily. But also I got a text from a new contact I never added to my phone.

Today at 7:58 PM, [(·_·)♡] said:

you do, indeed, pack a nasty hook.

I sighed and ignored it. I texted Tom that I was fine and that I'd meet him at the emergency spot. I was vague because the Gentleman would read it, and Tom and I had never written down our emergency pickup was Potrero Hill playground. We'd never had to use it either.

For safe measure, Tom also made me tell him who his second-favorite Gundam pilot was — just to make sure it was me.

But like. On the other hand? Fuck it. The Gentleman knew who I was. He could come around to my house and blow it up. Or something. But no. I knew if the Gentleman really wanted me out of the way, I'd be long gone.

But I wasn't ready to get rescued yet. So I just leaned back against some chainlink fencing and scrolled through Twitter.

...Filtering out anything to do with The Gentleman.

Slim pickings.

A few pedestrians who passed by must have thought I was homeless or something — so pedestrians who passed just ignored me. But there was one car that stopped in front of me, against the side of the curb.

I didn't look up. I really wouldn't have minded if it was a cop who wanted to ask me some questions before cuffing me. At that point in the night, I was ready to roll up my sleeves and hold my wrists out—

"Hey," Dad said, car window rolled down. "Need a ride, or you waiting on Tom?"

CHAPTER 90
BUSTED

Saturday, December 2

Of course Dad knew. He wasn't stupid. When he was my age, he did the exact same thing. His parents were clueless, but that's because neither of his parents had been vigilante crime fighters.

Inexplicable bruises he noticed on me but never asked about? Letting me off surprisingly easy for missing class? Mysterious absences that he never questioned? I had been acting under the assumption that Dad was too busy to notice — I didn't have the slightest right to be surprised.

Turns out he'd put a tracker in my phone when he started getting suspicious right before The Gentleman's attack on Point Brick. I found that a little surprising... It seemed everything changed after that, though. He was so busy with everything going on, he told us he'd trusted Tom to keep me in line until he could get around to 'dealing with it.'

Dad had no *clue* I was going out without Tom.

But enough exposition.

I had, in fact, ended up taking a bullet to the ribcage. We found that out when we all met up back at Tom's place. I hadn't really said much to Dad, and I wasn't gonna complain about anything hurting. I knew where to find a bottle of painkillers in Dad's car, and that was enough. Not that Dad didn't try talking to me.

"I'm not supposed to say anything without my lawyer present."

"Champ," he said, "right now everything you don't say can, and will, be used against you."

I kept quiet.

But after I had an incredibly difficult time not only climbing the stairs but opening the fridge door, Emily said there might be a problem. My armor had a lot of bulk in the underlay, and it was all black so I hadn't noticed the blood. It didn't seem like anything was wrong until we peeled the bullet out.

The bullet, though a decent size caliber, had already passed through a lightly armored van. So it didn't have the punch it would have needed to cut through the underlay, but it was stuck in there pretty firmly. It had broken my skin a little. Well, more than a little.

The whole of my lower-right ribcage was purple. After making sure there wasn't a serious internal bleed, and that none of my ribs were broken, Tom stood up.

"You know when we were kids?" he said to Dad. "Taking your first bullet's supposed to be cause for a drink."

Dad craned his head upward. Slowly-like.

"But, I suppose we can belay that tradition."

Emily appeared with a bottle of scotch anyway.

Tom cocked his head. "How do you know where I keep that—"

"Don't worry about it," she said.

I sucked in a breath between my teeth. "Also not the first time I've been shot." Tom gave me the same look Dad had given him.

While Tom was patching me up, Dad decided to go off on him. They switched topics too fast.

Dad: "How have you been pulling this off?"

Tom: "Can you be more specific—"

Dad: "If this isn't what you normally get him to do, what is?"

Tom: "Just regular patrols—"

Dad: "Are you always as irresponsible as you were tonight?"

Tom: "Well first off, that's a loaded question—"

Emily and I were just kinda: O_O

When it came to the part about The Gentleman, and how I started going out on my own without supervision, Dad gave me a wicked side-eye, but skipped over it, focusing on how ridiculous Tom was to try and do it behind his back.

He was frustrated, obviously, but he was more smug than enraged. Dad had trusted Tom to take care of me, making sure I'd stay out of too much trouble. Whoops! Tom, though, was quick to point out that it was mostly/all my fault.

"He's not even a legal adult, jackass," Dad shouted. "Don't pussyfoot around because you don't want to take a hit! You're an adult, Tom. Take some goddamn responsibility."

"I wasn't denying responsibility... I was just pointing out that he's going to do what he wants and it is literally not my job to trail him every night and day!" Tom shrugged. "Come on, Andy, neither of us can say that we could have planned for him to go off the rails like this."

"Are you kidding?" Dad cried out, staring at us across the table. "I am his father. I watched him exfiltrate his mother! After being there since day one, how could I not see this coming?" Dad rolled his eyes. "Just hoped that it would have been another few years before I needed to start worrying about this..."

"You know, you were only seven months older than me when—"

Dad pointed at me. He didn't say anything, but he pointed.

"Ah— yep. Got it." It meant 'shut up unless you're a grown-up.'

Tom nodded. "He's got a point. And he's had way more training than you did when you hit the streets."

"No shit, I've seen the news footage." Dad rolled his eyes. "Since he was nine, Tom. Have you been grooming him since he was nine?"

Tom frowned approvingly and shrugged. "You know, I did make sure it was something he was 100% on board for, before going in earnest." Tom quickly went over the training I'd gotten... which was quite a list, when he laid it all out.

"Oh Christ, you sure covered your ass!" Dad interrupted him.

"You want a medal for pied-piper-ing my son and turning him into a fight-machine of the year?"

"But I *am* Fight Machine of the year, though, right?"

I was ignored.

"Andrew, I probed for years to make sure it was something that he wanted—"

"Oh bullshit," Dad called. "It's Luca, you know him — I know him. You dangle something shiny in front of his face and he's after it before the word go. You wanted to take advantage of that for your damn pet-project agenda—"

"Hey!" Tom said. Sternly.

Agenda? I looked between Tom and Dad, but there wasn't anything there I could read.

Dad nodded, backing off on that. I wasn't sure what that meant. "You're not off the hook, Seong."

"I wouldn't expect to be." Tom shook his head. "I'd hoped to keep this going for a bit longer before letting you know. But just doing small stuff. Petty crime only. I've been saying that he's about two years…" He cleared his throat. "Five years off from doing a major investigation like this. This is all on him."

I cleared my throat. "He's not wrong," I said. "Also Emily's fault, she pressured me to do it."

The adults glared at me.

"You know what?" said Emily. "I'll own it."

Tom huffed. "After surviving about ten near-death experiences, including getting shot, your boy hasn't had anything to eat since this afternoon," he said, "I can go out and grab something for us all if you like. Come on," he said to Emily, "let's give 'em a moment."

I frantically darted my eyes between them.

No, no, no, please don't leave me alone with—

CHAPTER 91
LEGAL CONSULTATION

Saturday, December 2

I would gladly go toe-to-toe with The Gentleman again — five times again! Against five Gentlemen at once! Rather than be left alone with someone who had 'I'm disappointed in you, son' in his arsenal of things he had just cause to say.

That said, I was surprised when Dad hugged me for like... five minutes as soon as we were alone. "...Yes?" I said.

"Luca," he pulled away, "are you alright?"

I nodded. "My side's a little sore and it may be a little raw tomorrow—"

"Luca... you watched someone die... and it was brutal. Maybe Tom hasn't seen it yet, but I was watching the whole thing. My contact at CNN isn't sure if they're going to be able to re-air the fight—"

"I made CNN?" I said, eyes wide. "National or Global?"

"I'm just worried about how... well... you're taking this."

I wasn't sure what to say. It sounded like an accusation.

I heard Dad ask if I'd seen anyone else die before. He was really asking if this was the first time I'd seen a murder.

I looked blankly for a second. "No," I said. Dad got really serious. I realized what he said, then what I said. "I meant like, no, I haven't — like, I haven't seen that." Oh crap, I was acting strange. "I'm — yeah it's been kind of, a long night."

Dad nodded. I wasn't sure whether he believed me or not. "You... are re-grounded like you wouldn't believe, though."

"How bad is it?"

"I'm still coming to a verdict. I'll let you know," he said with a sigh, a bit uncomfortable still. "And going forward, I don't want any more of this going out on your own. Even serious Vigils have a support crew who do what Tom does. So I want to keep you on street patrols for now. No more large-scale investigations."

"Yeah. Cool— umm... what?"

"I'm not going to be directly involved because you don't want anyone on support to get emotionally compromised—"

"No, like... you're going to keep letting this happen?"

"Luca, I was your age," Dad said, as if this was all obvious, "I know very well there isn't much that can be done to stop you when you get a taste. Figure you'll have to be like me and just live it out of your system."

"Uh-huh..."

When Tom got back with late-night deli sandwiches, we jointly filled Dad in on The Gentleman thing. It was a lot easier now that he wasn't foaming at the mouth. He was still a little shady towards Tom, but I think that was for going behind his back. They'd get over it. Not their first scuffle.

"You're all in too deep now," Dad said. "We need to keep doing what we can to resolve it. But — I'm going to insist we do this through legitimate channels. How much of The Gentleman's plans did you record?"

Emily cleared her throat. "We got a monologue lifted from Trotsky and a map with marks on it. On a relic of a camcorder."

Dad nodded. "And Rook never grabbed up an envelope?"

"No." I sounded fairly proud of myself.

"Damnit. We could have used something tangible," Dad said. "Well, I'll go over what we do have. I have a bunch of contacts in the police who don't ask questions when I hand them stuff like this."

I crunched on a stray piece of lettuce. "When did you get so sketchy?"

"I'm a lawyer," Dad said. "If I wasn't a little sketchy, I wouldn't be a very good one."

CHAPTER 92
MORNING AFTER

Sunday, December 3

"Yeah, you're fine there," Dad said. On the phone. "Just lay low. You good for food? Need anything from your apartment?" I opened my eyes and saw him scribbling things on a notepad. "Okay, call this number when you need groceries."

I woke up feeling like none of my muscles could work. Dad was on the phone at Tom's kitchen table with a notepad.

It was about... early. Way earlier than I wanted. Sun was barely up. Tom was out... Emily's stuff wasn't by the love seat that she slept on, so I guess Tom brought her home. She must have put up a fight about it. How'd I sleep through *that?*

But from what I could hear in the kitchen, I assumed Dad was on a call with Jonah.

"Now, before I get there, I need you to write down everything you remember hearing from Mavericks command." ... "Yes, even stuff you weren't supposed to hear." ... "I'll deal with Colton when he gets back."... "Yes, I know Oscar Colton isn't 'officially' Riot Rider." ... "Alright, I'll head over. I'll be there before ten for sure. Keep your phone on, and in a closet. Check it every twenty minutes."

Dad kept on his laptop while I rolled over. Making myself move was one of the hardest things I had ever done, but I was getting really sore laying down. I missed my dogs.

A smoothie would have been great, but that had too many steps to make with berries and yogurt and — no, too complicated. I was going to get some cereal but that not only had saturated fats but more steps than I would have liked. I wanted an apple, but I'd have to bend down for that.

I guess I'll starve.

Dad didn't notice me until I was pushing through the dangling beads that separated the living room from the kitchen.

"Jesus!" he said, startled. "You're up!"

I lifted the oversized T-shirt and looked at myself in the mirror. Aside from the big one, I was covered in red marks, blue marks, and purple marks. I wasn't worried about the little ones.

Dad whistled. "I'll get the gel."

"Thanks."

He came over to get a look at me. Poked at me a little to see how I responded. "Well, the internal bleed has let up. Should be downhill from here."

"I thought you said it wasn't bleeding. Internal-like. Not that." I was tired, leave me alone for my sentence-making.

He looked confused. "I said that it wasn't anything serious. But that's what a bruise is, Luca. Broken blood vessels."

"Right, sure."

"Does it hurt?"

"Only when I stretch it. It's just stiff, you know?"

"It'll probably be tender for another few days. If you need to, you can take the day off school tomorrow—"

"You think there's gonna be school?" I asked. "Did another building go down or did I dream that?"

Dad nodded and let out a breath. "Total death toll is up to eight minimum. Including an office dog. Twenty injured, outside of recovery-related injuries. At least another twenty-three unaccounted for or missing." Dad looked to the side. "There's a woman trapped inside a crevice with another three people. She's live-tweeting the whole thing. They're trying to figure out how to clear the rubble without collapsing it."

I didn't know what to say. "That's... something."

"You know... Everything before this point I was on board for. Sure, make my life hard. Break a few eggs. I didn't choose my life because I wanted it to be easy," he said. "Even if he was just in it for the money — which I'd bet you your college fund that he isn't — if the effect is a positive change, then do it. But—"

"I think he found the line."

Dad nodded. "And his opposition is now making very strong statements about how this is the end-scenario of everything from public-option healthcare, to rent control. You know congress is opening an investigation into homeless shelters across the country?"

"That's not going to go anywhere though, right?"

"Just a bunch of politicians trying to make this issue about politics," he said, and then made me sit down while he stirred hot water into a bowl of instant oatmeal and set it in front of me. I poked at it a little before looking over to him on his laptop.

"So," I said. "You're... brutally honest, right?"

"Depends," he said.

"Is this our fault?"

Dad snorted. "What, you think that this wasn't something the Gentleman was capable of the whole time? Don't apologize because you tried to treat him like he wasn't... fucking insane." He looked at his phone and shouted: "Hope you heard that! Son of a bitch..."

CHAPTER 93
CRACKED

Sunday, December 3

Tom came back with breakfast. While we were all at the kitchen table, Dad leaned forward. "So," he said, "what do we do?"

"What's that mean?" Tom asked.

"Look at the bigger picture. People are dying yes... but the Gentleman is sitting on a powder keg," he said.

"Right, the stuff that Rolland was going to hand over to the feds—"

"Tom..." Dad said, shooting a glance.

Tom held up his hands. "I wasn't judging. I don't want to think about what I'd do with that info."

Dad rapped his fingers against the table. "Well, that's exactly what we need to do. Right now." He looked around. "Look, we have very unique access to a possible solution. We're in a position of having multiple access points to different clues and contacts that the Gentleman doesn't know we have. If we don't take him down ourselves... we can choose who does."

"And who gets the Gentleman's cache of intelligence?" Tom asked.

"That's not my focus..." Dad took a breath. "The Gentleman seems to be able to collect information with a greater degree of efficiency than Google itself. He must have introduced new algorithms into the system to help him..."

"So?" I asked.

"He's saying, and I may be mistaken," Tom said, "that The Gentleman may have inadvertently created a very dangerous tool."

Dad nodded. "By now, the CDG basically has an entire 'Gestapo division.' Thanks to our current President, who told them he'd give them something to do if they helped him get elected. Instead of sitting around twiddling their thumbs like they had been for the last few decades...

"That's the problem with a branch of the government without any clear mission statement. Now, instead of organizing post-humans in vigilantism, they're used to root out and hunt down post-human Americans—"

Tom scoffed. "Don't lie to yourself, Andy. You know that's the way it's been since Truman, back under the Progress Act."

Dad ignored him but didn't disagree. "Your friend, Rook. People like that. It's terrible. Right now, they can only target the ones who draw attention to themselves, like Jonah.

"Which means they wait and observe. And because it seems Rook is smart about it, he may have never popped up on their radar. But if the CDG gets what The Gentleman has... Or the NSA. The FBI. It'll be a witch-hunt." Dad paused.

"Everyone throws that term around a lot," I said.

"In the dark ages of Europe," Tom said, "they'd tie a woman up and throw her into a pit filled with water. If she floated to the surface, it meant that she was a witch and had to be burned. If she sank and drowned, it meant that she wasn't, and her soul would ascend to heaven. It's not an exaggeration to call it a witch hunt at this point..." Tom added, getting very dark.

"I've seen it. The results," he continued. "Sometimes... there's nothing you can say or do to prove to them that you aren't post-human. And when they feel they can't take your word for it... they'll crush your bones, they'll puncture your skin, electrocute your muscles, launch sharp things at you down the length of a tube to test your reflexes.

"If you fail their tests, they'll tip their hats and drop you off at the nearest hospital without picking up the tab. But if they can't crush your bones or break your skin… they'll drop you into war zones. No better than getting drowned."

"So what's that mean for us?" I asked.

"The corporate lawyer in me says that this is The Gentleman's last line of defense. Morality." Dad sat back. "He seems to have set himself up quite deliberately that the only way to get close enough to take him down is to know the whole story. And to be dedicated enough to get there. So… he may have very well intended to make it so that whoever has the option of getting close to him has to pass this dilemma.

"Either let a deranged psychopath rip down the city or let the American government have access to one of the most powerful data collection tools that have ever been written." Dad thought for a moment, then shrugged, talking mostly to himself at this point. "He's hoping that his opponents would be looking at this like a typical trolly-cart dilemma. His defense depends on a human pattern to sort ethical solutions into two choices. Do or don't."

His eyes widened, and his voice rose in thrill; he started to talk with his hands. "Ethical dilemmas are great. They're good for hashing out ideas in situations where options are limited, but it's all hypothetical—"

"So you have an idea?" Tom said dryly.

"Shhhh! Getting there — limited-choice dilemmas are less significant for actually developing a functional ethical model, but more for giving someone a character test. Seeing what they would choose, if they had to choose. 'If' — being the important part. But real life doesn't function like a dilemma.

"Real life doesn't have limitations. Trolly cart barreling down on those three people? You don't have to hit the switch to kill the one guy. You can shout at them and tell them to move. Or better yet, you can have the foresight to put up signage to tell people not to stand on the tracks.

"The Gentleman's dilemma. It's a fortress. The easiest way to defend a place is to limit the number of approaches, right? It's mind games. You make your opponent think they can only use those approaches. That's why flight became so pivotal in World War One. Fortresses of old Europe weren't designed for airstrikes."

"Do you have an airstrike?" I asked.

Dad snapped his fingers and pointed. "Yes. Maybe. Thank you for following through with my analogy, though. I can look into it."

"What is it?" Tom asked. "Paint me concerned."

"You won't like it—"

Tom scoffed. "You want to hand this all over to the Mavericks."

Dad bobbed his head. "Yes. I know, I know — evil corporation."

"Can we trust him? Really?"

"No," Dad said, "Colton's a corporate guy. But he's also micro managerial, excessively private, and suspicious of everything. He won't use any of it because he won't want anyone to suspect he might have it."

Tom shrugged. "Probably won't even look at it."

Dad started packing up to get on his day. He had a full day of scanning his contacts while Tom had a full day of putting pressure on his. Tom's underworld contacts might have had some information about where the Gentleman was operating from. Or at least enough evidence to triangulate some truths.

"Can I come with you to check on Jonah?" I asked Dad.

I hadn't mentioned much about my connection with him, but Dad looked me up and down, and I think he got the gist of it. But then he shook his head. "Best if I keep his hideout a secret. For his peace of mind."

"He's not still with the other guys is he? Holly's gang?"

Dad ruffled the back of my head. "Keep safe. I'll be back here as soon as I'm done with Jonah, so don't try and sneak out."

CHAPTER 94
DEAD DROP

Sunday, December 3

I ended up getting a very cryptic text from Rook, telling me to meet him 'at the homework place,' meaning The Mission Bay Library. I rolled my eyes at how dramatic it all was, but I didn't blame him for being vague over the phone.

I snuck out the back, a little bit more limber than when I woke up.

I got to the library before Rook and waved him over to where I was by the benches. I figured it was the best place to spot anyone who may be eavesdropping.

"Are you okay? I know you're hurt but—"

"I'm fine. Your phone's off?"

"It is now." He went into his school bag and handed me a crumpled-up envelope.

"That's not—"

"I grabbed one in the confusion yesterday," he said. "I'm not sure if the red ones would be more helpful. Probably should have went for one of them... But there's plenty in that one."

I didn't know what to say. He looked like he hadn't slept or ate. He was jittery. Had The Gentleman been trying to get in touch with him? Part of me wanted to sit him down and make him tell me everything he knew about The Gentleman's inner circle. But a bigger part really hated putting him back in the line of fire in the first place.

"Does The Gentleman know you helped me?"

Rook sighed. "Of course he does—"

"Is he threatening to expose you?"

"No," Rook said. "It's mostly been a DDoS attack against Dad's website. Also hate-spamming Dad's inbox with flyers and coupons for furry sex toys. I haven't checked mine. He's angry. Kind of passive-aggressive... But he's not turning me over to the CDG, so that's okay I guess?"

"Jesus I'm..." I swallowed. "I don't know how to apologize—"

"Look, this..." His head darted around. "I read it. It's been planned for a long time, and it won't take much effort to set it off."

"Okay. First things first, you need to pretend like you never read it in the first place," I said. "Probably is what my Dad would tell you. Did your dad read it?"

"He doesn't know I have it... So no."

"Okay good."

"Luca look... Don't worry about me right now. You may not have very long to stop it. I don't want to..." He shifted his eyes. "I need to leave."

"Right. Can we talk about this at school then?"

"No..." He huffed. "I need to leave."

It took me a minute. "Like... the city?"

"Maybe. Maybe more. I need to be away from this, Luca. I don't know what's going to happen to me..."

"Come on," I said, more trying to reassure myself, "we'll get this sorted out."

"Maybe. I need to play it safe though."

I nodded. "Alright."

"Yeah. I got to go. I just... I hope this all works." He started to leave.

"Text me when you get home. Tell me the answer to one of those Geo questions we got assigned so I know it's you."

He smiled. "If you want to copy my homework like you always do, just ask."

I tried to smile too. "You know, I didn't want to ask, but that would be great."

I wanted to open the envelope right there. But I didn't know if I could handle what was inside by myself. So I sent a text to Dad and Tom — they'd both want to know about this. And hopefully, between the two of them, they'd figure out how to deal with it.

CHAPTER 95
TRUST ISSUES

Tom's solution was to not open it.

"Are you insane? Just hand it off to whoever and hope they do something about it?" I shouted across the table. Dad gave me a look that told me to settle down.

"There could be something in there," Tom said. "I don't know — anthrax? Do people still do that?"

"So you don't trust Rook?" I said.

Dad cleared his throat. "Rook is under a lot of pressure. We don't know what The Gentleman is telling him to do to keep him off the radar."

"Rook wasn't lying," I said. "He was jittery, couldn't stop looking places."

"He could have been looking to a contact for reassurance," Tom said. "The presence of authority will make people do very strange, out-of-character things."

I crossed my arms. "Maybe if he was looking at one place."

"I wasn't there so I don't trust him," Tom said.

I groaned. "Then what you're saying is you don't trust *me*."

"You take everything so personally."

Dad gave Tom a very sympathetic look.

After a second of looking at the envelope, I made up my mind and grabbed it.

"No, wait—"

"Luca no—"

I shook the envelope out onto the table. Just a few pieces of folded paper, and a torn-off strip of notepad. "See?" I said, sitting back down. "No anthrax."

I didn't even really know what anthrax was.

Dad and Tom didn't take a minute before diving into what was there, so I took that to mean that everything was cool.

"Told you," I scoffed. I reached for the slip of notepad, which seemed to be just a list of names in Rook's handwriting.

Dad snatched it out of my hands. "Hold on... This is the kind of thing that gets you into trouble..." His eyes scanned the sheet. "Oh... oh yeah."

Tom flipped through the other sheets of instructions and sighed. "This is all compartmentalized. Good planning on his part but bad for us."

"Anything useful though?" Dad's eyes darted up from the yellow page.

Tom took a minute more to read. "It's very clear this has been planned for a while. Might be able to match up locations as potential threats. Lots of *Site A's* and *Site A2's*..." He squinted and then flipped back to another page. "Definitely some information about the structure of the organization... Definitely does indicate that everyone who showed up to that meeting was a willing volunteer." He tossed the letters down. "So... He's not blackmailing anymore, he's just exploiting anger. Big win for us."

Dad shot him a glare.

"That was sarcasm..." Tom cleared his throat. "Because it's definitely not going to help the case of everyone involved when the Gentleman gets brought in."

"Then we need to make sure we're very careful with who sees this." Dad turned to me. "Did you read this before you brought it here, Luca?"

I shook my head. "No…"

"Good." He held it up. "This is getting photocopied, and then the original is going in my lockbox." He looked at each of us to make sure we heard. "I'm going to blackout certain parts and send the photocopied versions out."

"To who?" Tom asked.

"Contacts on the force. FBI. Redacting sections about post-human involvement, everything else could help authorities predict targeted locations that weren't on the map."

"Can they handle it?" Tom asked.

"Hopefully. But we sure as hell aren't going to," Dad said. "Which is the point."

"You just said we were in this!" I insisted.

"I said we were going to put this through legitimate channels."

"This isn't 'we' — it's 'you'!"

He waved the list. "This changes a lot. I'll be in touch with Mr. Lang to make sure he's getting Rook the correct legal advice. Suffice to say, this list is *not* going to be given to authorities because it very closely ties the Gentleman to post-human interest groups—"

"Wait, is *Warden* listed?" Tom asked.

Dad paused. "No… but one of her associates' alias is on here."

Tom cursed. In Korean. Which was super rare. "I'll take care of it."

I looked over. "Take care of what?"

Tom sighed. "Luca—"

"One of Tom's informants," Dad cut in. "I need Tom to make sure that the Gentleman wasn't fed specific information."

"A little embarrassing on my part," said Tom.

"It sure is," Dad said.

There was more going on there. But I knew the difference between things they didn't want me to know and things they were keeping away from me because it was deep shit. "So that's it?" I asked. "Hands off?"

Dad snickered. "Luca, you've already done more than most A-list vigils get done in their whole career."

"Rook said that this has been planned for weeks! Are the police going to be able to handle this? And handle it properly—"

"Giving this to my contact isn't giving this to the police," Dad said. "She has access to channels that we don't."

"The Gentleman can take down the city if he gets a hangnail!" I said.

"Luca..." Dad looked at me.

I leaned back on the chair. "Ugh. Alright, fine."

"Glad we're on the same page," said Dad, and then started to pack up. "Tom, mind helping Luca get his stuff together—"

"I can get it *myself*."

Tom nodded. "He can get it himself."

"Whatever you like, just have it all ready to go while I bring the car around out front," Dad said. "Tom you're welcome to come to our place to ride this out."

"I'll swing by later, after I collect some updates from my contacts," Tom said. "I'm guessing that's what you were after."

"That would be great, but I really just need someone to..." Dad nodded at me while he was halfway out the door. "Keep an eye on him."

"Really should get paid for babysitting..." Tom said when Dad was on his way down the stairs.

By the time Tom came around to help me get my stuff in my backpack, I was already packed up. It was mostly about proving a point. "So ...?" I asked.

"I think your father's wrong, but for the right reasons."

"So what are we—"

"I'm going to do what I can," Tom said, "but your father runs the Avalon Knight show now."

"Bullshit." I slumped back. "Dad had his turn!"

Tom looked onward. "You're absolutely right, but for the wrong reasons."

I rolled my eyes. "Please. Get more cryptic. But progressively."

"Awfully big word for a guy like you."

"Shut up. I'm friends with smart people," I snapped.

Tom nodded slowly. "Well, it's probably for the best that you don't have any way to find The Gentleman again, right?" He said it very plainly, not breaking eye contact with me. "You gave the only hard drive you had to Rolland's crew, right?"

"No, remember, I have—"

Tom motioned a zipper across his mouth. "I'm telling you... that as long as you don't have any way to find The Gentleman... there's nothing you can possibly do from here..."

CHAPTER 96
COLLAPSE

Sunday, December 3

Nothing much to do at home. Dad was sticking to his office, Emily was at her place. The whole Gentleman thing was all anyone was talking about so texting friends wasn't gonna help me get it off my mind. And the only thing anyone online was talking about was the Gentleman's new videos, now hosted directly from his website, and being dropped every hour.

"You know, I've been reading comments," he said, his mask blank, "I do quite frequently, actually. And a number of people are expressing concern about the number of people fleeing the city. They say 'people are leaving because they're so scared!' and 'you're killing the living culture of the city.' Well, I'm paraphrasing, of course.

"But that's semantics about what culture is. Living culture... that's whatever is created by people. This living culture becomes embodied in the physical location. I really don't mind people leaving The City. Once, I thought to re-align the current culture of San Francisco with what it was in the seventies. Minus police brutality. I digress.

"I realized... the nature of culture is to change. And there's nothing that can be stopped about that because it's just... so human. I wouldn't take issue with it if I could guarantee that the replacement culture would be just as valuable... but it seems termites burrow through the foundation. They'll turn anything into a rotting log, full of holes.

"This city has been a gem of artistry, the beacon of human rights in America, and a symbol of the human will to endure and rebuild. But with every condominium that is built on the rubble of a cherished... I don't know... independent flower shop... it loses some of that. Why are the structures that survived the great quake of 1908 to be raised on a pedestal, when landmarks from the sixties can..." he waved his hand, "fuck off, apparently. Truly, the only way to ensure this City's value to the rest of America is to remove America from it—"

"Off, please."

I spun around so fast I hurt my ribs... it was only Dad, but he got me in an almost-panic.

"I was just—"

"I don't want you involved with this anymore," he said. "Has he tried to contact you?"

I shook my head. "No. You?"

"Like I said, I don't want you on this anymore. This isn't your fight. Reserve Mavericks are on duty, they can—"

"He's going to target the newest buildings in the city," I blurted out.

Dad looked at me for a second. "How would you know that?"

I shook my head. "You mean it isn't apparent already? When you line up the circle on the map, they're all buildings that are either brand new or still under construction. And it fits with his whole preservation—"

"Enough!" Dad shouted. "This is being handled by people that can handle it."

"I can handle it!"

"Luca — No... you cant," Dad grabbed my shoulders. "You're street level. You don't have superpowers. And you're recovering from an injury. You don't have nearly enough training. You need to keep your head out of this one, now."

"Dad, I can help."

Dad sighed. "It's only a matter of time before they find The Gentleman and end him."

"Have you not noticed that the actual Mavericks aren't here?"

"How do you plan on helping, Luca?"

Dad assumed my lack of answer meant that I didn't have a plan.

— — —

By 1:00 PM, six buildings around the city began to report tremors. On and off. But by the time the police investigated, the buildings weren't shaking. People started to panic and flee the city, even though the police just advised people to stay indoors and take fire alarms seriously.

By 3:00 PM, three different buildings did the same thing. Fifteen minutes of shakes — then nothing. Police didn't find anything. "The machines don't need to be big!" I said, barging into Dad's office.

"I know. I read his plan layout," Dad said, without looking away from his computer.

"Then the police should know that! They should look harder!"

"I know, Luca."

"Does he have someone in the police force on the payroll? blackmail."

"I don't know Luca." Dad looked very irritated. Maybe not at me. "I'm sorry, but I'm a little busy."

By 3:30 PM, cars trying to flee the city had backed up into the suburbs. Our road got a lot more traffic than normal. Rush-hour never really got to Missouri street, but horns were honking nonstop. Everyone was in a panic.

The SFPD was blockading the streets, caging people into the city on all sides. San Francisco vigils on patrol in the gray, overcast daylight. Doing what they could to keep the panic from breaking into a riot.

No, none of the 'real' Mavericks were around. But the other smaller-city-known heroes were filling the gaps. Some of them were 'official' Mavericks, even if they were only on the reserve lists.

The important part was that they were all out making their presence known, and making sure to tell the cameras that the Mavericks had the situation under control. Because helping people out of log-jammed traffic was 'the situation'... Because it was more important to be caught on camera helping people than to fix 'the situation.'

But how they looked handling the crisis would have a major impact on where they landed on the official team roster when all this ended. So who could blame them, right?

CHAPTER 97
CLASSIC MISDIRECTION

Sunday, December 3

"They should be going after The Gentleman! Like you said!"

"Luca, I swear to God, if you don't settle down…"

"This is what he wants!" I said. "He wants everyone running around looking like they don't have a clue what's going on!"

"Our home Vigils—"

"He wants this kind of narcism! That feeds into the chaos!" I threw my head back. "His whole scheme is making you see which eggs are rotten by cracking them all open! They need to be going after him to prove him wrong! And they're taking the bait!"

"Not your call."

"If it was, we may have got him by now! Are your shady police friends doing anything?"

"I'm a little busy to be babysitting."

"No, because The Gentleman has dirt on every sketchy person in the city so the stuff you passed along went into a—"

The front door opened. Dad's hand instinctively went for the pistol he had secured under his desk.

"Just me!" Tom said. The dogs went for him. "Hey guys…" He said to them, taking off his jacket and shoes.

"We're in here!" Dad called. I heard him flick the safety on.

"You know you should only take the safety off when you have the sights lined up. And even then…" I said to him.

He looked at me and bullets came out of his eyes.

Tom cleared his throat. "Didn't feel very safe where I was. Studio window is probably going to get a brick soon. I had to ditch my car in a parking lot off DeHaro. You know, by the church? I didn't see a way to get it through to here. Roads are crazy," he said. "I have some supplies in there. Food. Movies. If we're going to weather this, it may as well be together. Maybe I can take Luca and grab them later."

"Probably not," Dad said.

Tom turned to me. "I need to talk with your Dad," he said, nodding his head as a gesture for me to leave.

"About what?" Dad asked. "I'm busy?"

"Are your friends in the police..." Tom wasn't good at approaching things gently. But he was trying, he waved his hands around instead of looking for words.

"Are they?"

"Doing... anything?" He took a seat across from Dad.

Dad's shoulders tensed. "I honestly don't know, Tom."

"Are you doing anything?"

"I'm trying to pull favors with people who owe me, reasoning with people who don't, and offering favors to people who won't see reason."

Awkward silence.

"So... the goal is to get more Vigils here?" Tom asked. "Because it looks like that's what we need. The Mavs Lite are too swamped to—"

"Yes, Luca has been on about it all day," Dad said. "And no. More Vigils doesn't mean Luca. The favors I'm looking for are all counter-intelligence. The Gentleman is a hacker, we need to out-hack him."

"Do you even know what 'hacking' means?" Tom shot Dad a glance. "Outside of movies?"

Dad blinked. "Honestly, no."

Awkward silence.

"I'm just... trying to figure out who knows... what we can do about any of this."

"… we should do?"

Dad shook his head. "Find him. Root him out… and arrest him. Call in some legal favors to make sure The Gentleman's information ends up in Oscar Colton's hands… in a refrigerated server, locked away twelve stories below ground. Colton's good at… deliberately forgetting things."

Awkward silence.

"Well… If we're gonna give Colton credit for anything, it's his slippery memory."

"Sometimes, what you hate about someone is an asset," Dad said.

Tom nodded. "Not a bad plan. Gotta find The Gentleman before the city goes up in flames."

"Not the whole city. He loves it too much." Dad scoffed. "He was turning into an icon and now he's making everyone who didn't immediately demonize him look like terrorists. You know I've had clients drop me because they accused me of being a 'Gentleman Commie'? And I was representing them for free."

Zero slinked back into Dad's office about then.

"Well, you've been saying for the longest time that all we need to fix the country were some liberals with a spine."

Dad waved his finger at Tom. "This isn't what I meant."

"I know, I'm just… trying to make light."

"And I'm trying to work!" Dad snapped.

Dad had his hand on Zero's head for a short minute as he and Tom sat in continued uncomfortable silence. And then Dad realized how odd it was that Zero would be going to him for affection. Normally, Zero was glued to my knees… unless I wasn't in the house.

He exhaled a shaky breath and looked at Tom. "You're a son of a bitch, you know that?"

Tom shrugged but kept an eye on Dad's shooting hand.

CHAPTER 98
LATE TO THE PARTY

Sunday, December 3

I really hoped I was reading Tom's signals properly...

I knew I wouldn't have long before Dad would ask where I was. So as soon as I got to my room, I hooked up both of the spare SSDs to my laptop and dumped a bunch of memes onto them to try and get them to send off their data packages. I figured that it would go fastest if I used a computer, instead of a toaster that aspired to be a computer.

Also, it didn't take long to get his attention.

```
Director Entry: young wexler. i'm glad to see
               you're alright, but what are you
               doing?
```

I kept working, not responding to his messages. I needed to be fast. I doubted he had the ability to just shut down my computer... but I didn't want to give him the chance to uproot himself. If his headquarters was one of his mobile computer-vans then I was screwed. But this was the only chance I had.

```
Director Entry: how common is it for
               teenagers to have such eclectic
               pornography stashes of this volume?
```

I ignored the messages. He was probably going to expose me for this. I'd get arrested... Get a fine. House arrest... maybe even jail time. (Also a spike in popularity at school.) As far as future prospects went... most employers didn't look at vigilantism charges as a demerit.

But I had to focus on tracking where that information was going.

```
Director Entry: just looking through it and…
            well it's a little educational. but
            — what on earth do you think you're
            going to accomplish?
```

He left himself open. I wasn't sure if that was good or bad. But it was my only lead. I had to take it.

— — —

Running down 19th, I saw what Tom meant about the roads being clogged. So many people were still in cars. A lot of fender-benders. There was a crash in the Arkansas Street intersection where people waited patiently for some kind of authorities to arrive to do... anything about it. People trapped in traffic had given up on honking. Some people weren't even in their cars anymore.

As I ran, I had to dodge people — urban refugees who had spilled out onto the sidewalk. I almost tripped over a kid who lived near us. It was quiet chaos. When Americans were too tired and scared to shout at each other, you knew there was a problem.

— — —

The duffle-bag of Avalon Knight stuff was in Tom's trunk. There was a key hidden in a compartment under the wheel well that maybe I shouldn't have known about?

I'd tracked The Gentleman's signal to the Thirty/Thirty-Two Complex. A business/residential development built on the joint piers of the same name. Some big pharma company from up North bought it all up to build their new San Francisco offices. And then sold what was left to be used for 'middle-income' apartments. Philanthropic kinda thing. Figures the Gentleman would like it.

I called Emily.

"Luca, I—"

"Do you still have my old skateboard?" I asked, out of breath. I wasn't proud of my' skate or die' phase, but this was an emergency.

"What?" Emily said. "Why are you on the phone, aren't you still worried about—"

"Emily! Skateboard!"

"Yeah… um… Sean's learning to use it—"

"I need to borrow it. Or a bike. Or something. Get it to me in the parking lot off of De Haro. Same block as… shit. That… brewery…"

"I know the one."

I expected The Gentleman may have sent one of his remaining mercenaries after me once he'd realized I'd successfully cyber stalked him. Instead, Emily showed up as planned. On her bike, with her board under her arm.

"You can ride this." She got off her bike. "What's going on? There are more—"

"I know where he is!" I said

"What?"

"I think. I need to move fast." I threw my leg over her pink bike. Ugh.

"Luca…" she said. "Like… eight buildings are earth-quaking."

"Since when?"

"Just before I left." She went to her phone and checked it. "They haven't stopped, according to Twitter. We need to go."

"No, I need to—"

"Shut up," she barked, "I'm coming with you."

"No, you need to go get Dad and tell him that The Gentleman is at the Thirty/Thirty-Two. I'd call but my phone's basically a tracking device at this point."

Emily looked disappointed, but she knew I was right. So off she went on her longboard. I was really glad I didn't have to skateboard across the city. I'd rather get decked out in pink than re-live that awkward middle-school phase of my life.

CHAPTER 99

THIRTY-THIRTY-TWO
(PATENT PENDING)

Sunday, December 3

I would have been standing in the shadow of one of the tallest buildings in the city. Forty-five stories. It looked weird. Kinda round, kinda hollow... almost a U-shape. It had this central courtyard that skyways passed over that made it kinda look like DNA.

Smaller buildings around the base, planned gardens, a Starbucks. None of the siding was on, and only some interior walls had been installed.

For all the city was creaming its pants over it, construction had been on hold for the last month. Apparently, the company wasn't fond of how the construction contractors were paying their workers so little. Which made The City's pants even creamier.

I would have been in its shadow, but this late in the day, the sun was behind me. I could feel tremors under my feet. Seemed like The Gentleman wasn't letting up this time. I wouldn't have long...

It was stuck between the waterfront and Ebarcadero road, which was one of the first streets that was shut down, with only the occasional police cruiser or fire truck passing by.

The lock on the gate was cut. The construction site was dark, and getting darker by the minute. Construction materials were neatly piled, left where they were since October, dormant since shortly before this all started.

Hidden behind some thick stairwell column, I saw a white van, doors open, it was completely empty. "You planning to lure me inside and then blow it up?" I said, under my breath.

A sigh came from my phone. "Not my intention. But, meet me up top. If you must."

Not far away, a utility lift sprung to motion. From the penthouse floor, it descended on its exposed cables.

When it took me to the top, there was a clear view over the city. Perfect watching the sun set into the Pacific ocean and for watching half the city come down.

Poking over the hill and the tips of skyscrapers to the east, the dusk horizon lit up the clouds like fiery smoke. We were higher up than many downtown buildings. The wind howled, whistling through half-constructed walls.

The Gentleman had a... parlor... set up close to the western edge of the floor. Persian rug, a sitting area with an antique table and armchairs. A large industrial suitcase laptop lay open on the table. Probably a mobile version of his HQ...

There was a mini-bar, and classical music playing from a Bluetooth speaker on a desk to the side, just off the rug. Next to the industrial laptop, steam rose from a teapot made of the kind of china you'd expect to see in a period piece Oscar movie.

A man, dressed in black coattails faced away from me. His suit was the most formal I had seen him in — his 'Sunday Best.' With his arms folded in front of him, he slouched on one leg, with his cane jutting out to the side.

He turned his head back. "I considered running, you know."

CHAPTER 100

(ノ●ワ●)ノ:・゜✧

Sunday, December 3

"Flee and endure to push back against establishment oppression another day." He sighed. "But I figured I'd best not. Best deal with this... pain in the ass myself. Because nothing else I've tried works. And you'll just keep at it, and I can deal with you anyway so why not just get it over with?" He sighed. "I digress. How's that gunshot wound holding up, Luca?"

There was a sharp pain in my side. "Mostly just stiff. Hurts now. Probably because you reminded me."

"Ah yes." He nodded. "I'm sorry about that. But... there does come a point of protecting my own interests. Some people are simply so persistent that the only way to remove them is to 'remove' them, you know?"

"Going to kill me?"

"I wouldn't want to," he said.

The portable computer on the coffee table had a window open, and a few progress bars displaying information. If I had to guess anything was an earthquake machine...

I went to it, but as soon as I got close, it snapped shut and locked itself.

"I've brushed up on some human anatomy. Figure I could leave you crippled for the police to arrive. Get you taken in. Put into the system. Implicate your father. Destroy his career. All the good people he's helping..." He held up his hand and stretched his fingers out. "Poof. There goes their support. And Mr. Seong? All the work he's doing with his underground emigration network."

He did the gesture again. "Poof. All because some legal minor had something to prove. Because none of you seem to be able to tell good from bad. Because none of you care."

"We lived here before you did, you British bastard! Is killing a city that's *already* been gentrified going to work? You learn about this stuff in literal high school! Places boom. Then they don't boom forever. And then they suck. And then poor people move back," I said. "By not protecting places that *haven't* been gentrified yet, you're just another outsider who's obsessed with establishing shots from *Full House*. You want to make this *your* version of San Francisco, and everyone else can get bent."

The Gentleman's head slouched. "Maybe Barnett should have let you do some of the talking. That really did hurt. Maybe a little true..." He looked up. "Did you come here to debate, Mr. Wexler? To negotiate? Or do you want to skip to violence?"

"I came to apologize," I said. My voice cracked a little.

The Gentleman's head reeled back. "Beg pardon?"

"You wanted the right thing," I said. "But the rules were stacked against you. You had to do things. You had to get attention and you had to break the rules to get it. It wasn't a fair fight, so you had to fight dirty. And everyone assumed that meant... that you were messed up.

"Everyone got mad because we all had a different idea of how doing it 'the right way' was going to look. I don't think anyone really knew what they were doing... But I think everyone was out to prove that they were better than you — because you were the only one who was making any progress.

"But you needed more than buy-a-poster support... and maybe if the rest of us had offered... you wouldn't have felt like you had to do shitty things to get what you wanted," I said. "So... you're kind of a murderer and psycho, and this is all still your fault, but I'm sorry."

The Gentleman looked down. And then he turned around back to the sunset behind the city skyline. "You have no idea how it feels to hear that," he said, across all the speakers, but not coming from him. "It's very kind of you, truly. But kindness accomplishes nothing right now. Like you said… this is all my fault. You're not wrong. I chose this. You're not wrong. And what would 'un-choosing' this look like? Was I supposed to call the whole thing off because you explained my own struggles to me?"

"I mean…" I shrugged. "It was kind of a long shot but like… you're kinda being crazy and it's not a good look for anyone. You 'preserve' San Francisco, but America turns against anyone trying to help. You do realize that there are other issues? Aside from resurrecting some hippies?"

He shook his head. "Tsk, tsk. The emotional stuff is certainly a strong point. Empathize and relate. But the rational stuff is really what you should bring Barnet for—"

I grabbed my collapsible staff, flicked it open, and batted the portable speaker at him. It bounced off his head and he turned around. No sooner, I vaulted over the couch and slammed my knee into his chest, knocking him to the ground.

He slowly pushed himself up, dusting himself off and commanding his hat to return to his hand.

[ᴄ•ɔ_ᴄ•ɔ]

I shrugged. "Can you like… shut up?"

[-sigh-]

"Well… I'm already killing people," he said. "What's a couple of broken legs at this point?"

CHAPTER 101
BALLS OF STEEL

Sunday, December 3

I went at him again. He was solid as a rock and didn't even bother pushing away the blows. He just took them. It felt like I was barely making a dent.

Most of what he threw at me I could bob around. But when he connected, I felt it. And I'd probably be feeling it for a while.

So going on the defensive wasn't going to work. I needed to stay active and on the offensive. I had to wear him down until he would slip up and I could knock him out. Or hold him off until Dad got the Mavericks or the police here.

He surprised me though. Before long, he managed to grab the staff from me. "That's... quite enough." The metal crumpled in his hand. Before I could even let go, he connected his cane with my ribs — the exact spot I'd gotten shot.

I felt for a second like my brain was going to squeeze itself through my eyes. And there I was, at his feet, trying to get my breath back.

"I'm sure it says somewhere in the Art of War... or some similar text — never to go into a battle where your opponent knows your weakness." I heard him swing my weapon at my ribs. I rolled out of the way, but it did clip my shoulder.

He tossed my useless staff aside, onto the fancy table he stood next to. "Come now, Mr. Wexler, what did you expect was going to happen? Just sit down and watch the demolition. It'll be fun."

Fighting to get a breath, I ran at him again, but he stepped forward, grabbed an armchair, and tossed it at me like it was cardboard. Didn't hurt as bad as the cane. More cushioning. But it knocked me back onto my ass. Took me a second to get back to my feet.

He took a moment to think, his mask blank. "Hm. It seems my machines have stopped. Closing the briefcase must have…"

He turned to open it but I ran at him. He was expecting me, swinging around to hit my head. Ducking low, I slid on the ground and tangled my feet in his legs. I spread his feet so wide apart I felt his tendons pull…. though there was something weird about how it felt…

He toppled over as I twisted around on the ground, lurching him to the side and over the couch. He landed face-first onto the ground.

Before he could recover, I grabbed the briefcase and made a limping run for the stairwell. As long as I had it, he couldn't keep up his doomsday routine. "Damnit, Luca!" He called out, but I was already headed down the stairs. I had all the adrenaline in the world but couldn't manage a single breath.

The loudspeakers through the complex crackled to life, playing classical music and carrying his voice. "Please don't, Mr. Wexler. This is getting sad. Are you going to run away with that? Give me a few hours and everything will be back up and running. Ultimately, and I mean that in the lexicological definition of being the final entry in a lengthy catalog, you have accomplished nothing thus far, and you will accomplish nothing as a result."

I tossed the briefcase down and ripped off my chest piece. Breaths heaved out of my lungs. I got the half tube of contusion cream and smeared it up under the underlay, taking heavy breaths. On my hands and knees, I crushed a painkiller between the heels of my palm and licked at it with the bottom of my tongue.

The Gentleman stepped out from behind a pillar. I looked up at his now cracked face and could feel a thin line of blood trickling over my lips from my nose.

[π ⌢ π]

"You don't have to make this harder on yourself than you already have."

The stinging pain was fading to a background ache — a combination of adrenaline and placebo effect. I pushed myself up.

He sighed. "So be it." Cane in both hands, he drew the blade from within, tossing the scabbard aside. "I'll have you know this is very admirable behavior. I'm sure your father and teacher would be very proud. Maybe I'll send them the footage."

I knew how to handle bad guys with knives, but swords were something Tom hadn't exactly prepared me for. So the only thing I had to go on was: 'avoid the sharp part.' Didn't help that I didn't have anything to fight with... but it did help that he had no idea what he was doing either.

I made him swing the blade into metal supports, thrusting it into boxes of building equipment. He wielded it like a rapier — again, something I wasn't familiar with.

"It is quite frustrating that you—" the blade crashed into a stack of sheetrock. "—refuse to accept physical harm. Neither threats nor deterrents. How on earth does your father parent you?"

"He does his best," I said, deflecting a slash off my arm guards, I kicked into his side, pushing him away from me.

I didn't feel it when the blade caught my thigh. I don't know if that was exactly on the upside though. I was only holding him off, but I was wearing myself out. And he was stupidly refreshed.

"I really hate that...." I heaved between breaths.

He dropped his form and swung his arms out. "What that?"

"You killed Hamen... Really wanted to know if I could have kicked his ass in a rematch." I stood up straight. "But you killed him while he was on the ground. Pussy-ass move. So like... I dunno if kicking your ass means I could have taken him." I shrugged. "Now we'll never know."

He rolled his whole head. "I really would have the chance to admire your tenacity, Luca. But you keep putting us in situations where you're standing in my way."" I ducked under a slash, kicking at his knee. With him staggering, I rolled to the side. He caught himself, and turned around, following me as I weaved through support beams.

"This is not a slasher film, Luca. You're either wearing yourself out or running away," he said over the speakers. "Where did you go... don't suppose you'd come swinging down from the ceiling—"

I came at him from behind and bashed him over the head with a plastic plumbing pipe.

"Damnit!" He slashed at me, cutting into my arm a little. I got in close and elbowed him in the face, but his free hand grabbed my arm and tossed me to the side.

Right next to where I'd dropped the briefcase.

He was over me, elbow lurched back to thrust the steel into my chest. My arm jutted out, seizing the briefcase handle, and bringing it between me and the blade. It slid into the metal before it jammed against something hard. He gasped.

I sacked him, not getting nearly as much of a response as I wanted. Instead, I tossed the briefcase away, and his sword with it. I pushed myself up but The Gentleman grabbed me, picked me up by my arms, and slammed me against a concrete beam. His face was blank, but the white screen flickered, dead pixels spreading across it.

"If you didn't have your strength, you'd be nothing." I ground my teeth.

"High and mighty words spoken by every loser in history."

I took a labored breath. "We're not done yet."

He squeezed my arms, I flexed against his grasp. "Oh. Oh yes, we are," he said.

But I kicked off the ground, twisting my left knee around his elbow, and used every core muscle I had to straighten out my body. He cried out in more shock than pain. I suppressed my voice as fire ripped through every nerve in my body. I did whatever I could to dislocate his shoulder. His mask's voice filter went fuzzy and distorted.

I heard a pop from his elbow… not like a dislocation… something was wrong, but I didn't stop. I twisted against the concrete pillar, flipping him to the ground.

I pushed myself, not even taking a moment to breathe, and curb-stomped the back of his neck. He made a swipe for my foot but I pulled out of the way and grabbed a piece of loose rebar.

Dad taught me to golf. Said it was a skill every successful man needed to know if they were going into business, even if he wasn't good at it. It just so happened I was *very* good at it.

The Gentleman looked up just in time to see me drive the rebar into his mask.

The music stopped.

I was frozen for a minute. I saw the white mask flying to the side, one last image on its face.

[o□☉]

I hit him again.

I felt my arm and the side of my chest light up.

I hit him again.

He desperately grabbed the iron bar between his arms. I kicked his gut and pushed him a short distance.

Lifting himself up, I saw that his coat was in tatters, shiny metal showing underneath tears in his suit. Sparks shot from a damaged arm and singed loose threads. No blood. Not anywhere. He squirmed and groaned, turning around. Reaching up to his head, his fingers grasped his hair and yanked off a wig.

His… 'face' was made of transparent carbon fiber plates on top of a metal skeleton. His 'eyes' were four small lights in the middle of his face: a triangle of red, blue, and orange, and a blinking white light in the middle. His face was featureless.

Adrenaline was replaced by awe and shock. "For real? You're a robot?"

"Really?" His voice was mechanical, raw. Like a text-to-speech app. "Really? This is where you draw your suspension of disbelief?"

CHAPTER 102
FUTURE-PROOF

Sunday, December 3

I didn't… really have anything to say.

"I'm surprised you're surprised. I thought you already knew."

"What? No!"

"What? With the hacking everything in real-time, being everywhere at once… and the bizarre computer code—"

"Everyone thought you were just a cyberpath?"

He stopped to think on that for a moment. "Really? I thought I was doing rather shoddy work at simulacrum."

"Why is your body still moving like it's breathing?" My voice cracked mid-shout. It was… I couldn't even.

His hands went to his hips. "Well excuse me for aspiring to pass a Turing Test!" He straightened out his lapels. "As it turns out I didn't do a half-bad job. Suppose that's a compliment?"

I just kept staring. "Really?"

"Yes," he nodded, "really."

"No, no way. There's a nerd in a basement somewhere pushing your buttons."

His voice sounded over the speakers. "I assure you, the only human being pushing my buttons right now is a young man who's kneecaps must be stabbed so I can send him packing to his father," he said. "Now, I'd consider giving you a final opportunity to walk away, but the thing I admire about you is that you wouldn't take it. Youthful pride and—"

I immediately went to my left and took his sword in my hand, kicking the suitcase off of it. Ready to cut this bastard into pieces.

"So you won't kill a human, but it is acceptable to murder an artificial intelligence?" He asked as I got closer. "Where do you act so high and mighty to draw a line about what is or is not a life?"

"Your personality is saved to a hard drive and can be rebooted."

He shrugged. "It was worth a—"

I swung at him, hard. He held up his arm to guard, but I cut through his sleeve, feeling the blade grind against carbon fiber. He tried to come at me, but I was faster. In spite of the waves of agony, I kept moving, circling him.

Swinging the sword like a baseball bat, frayed fabric fell off him as I pushed him to the edge "Luca—"

Closer.

"I'm not going to—"

He was weaker, losing steam, or whatever the crap he ran off of. Sparks flew out of what I'd cut.

"No, stop—"

I sliced across his face. Cutting open the casing, the bottom half of it popped off. I ducked under a last-ditch strike and drove the the blade into his head, grabbing what was left of his jacket.

"That's not going to kill me..." He said, only through the loud-speakers. "A little uncomfortable, but—"

"No." We were on the edge of the floor, hanging over nothing but a long way down. I turned his head to look at the ground.

"Well. Shit." He sighed over the speakers. "Thank you for letting me have the last word, at the least."

"Fuck yourself." I ripped the blade from his head, tossing his body off the edge.

He twisted in the air, frantic, trying to grab for anything.

One of his coattails flew off. So did a sleeve.

He fell so quickly I lost sight of details faster than I could remember what he looked like.

I watched him fall for forty-three stories.

The ground-level construction site lit up, as his body exploded into a shower of sparks in the late dusk shadows.

I tossed the briefcase down after that. It landed not far from The Gentleman's body, hitting a pile of concrete slabs and shattering. Just in time for me to notice the red and blue lights cutting through the darkness.

Waiting around wasn't the plan. I squeezed some of the gash-sealant out of the tube before I bled too much. Exhaustion hit like a train. I wanted to sit down and take a rest, but if I hurried, I knew I could sneak out before the police quarantined the place.

But at the door to the stairwell… I turned back.

I took his mask and his cane with me. I stashed them under a bush about a block away before I met up with Dad and Tom, who took me to the hospital. By then I'd already lost a lot of blood, so couldn't remember much after that.

CHAPTER 103
UNSUNG HERO

Wednesday, December 7

"Gentleman found deceased—"

"Believed to be post-human—"

"No sign of mysterious Vigil who killed—"

"…can confirm that the reserve members of the Mavericks are responsible for ending The Gentleman attack—"

"Talking about post-human witch hunts—"

"Still no word from the Core Mavericks. Bulwark, the most recent full-time recruit, has—"

"The CDG is increasing—"

"Forensics has ruled The Gentleman's death accidental—"

I looked at Dad, who hadn't left the hospital since I was admitted. "Did they not… notice he was a robot?"

Dad squinted at the tablet screen where we watched news anchors deconstruct the event. "I saw the body… er… platform. Robot thing." Dad went quiet. "What's done is done. If Colton thinks that protecting America from a Rogue AI scare is what we need… that's his prerogative."

I sighed.

Dad looked at me with a half-smile. He rubbed my shoulder. "I know it sucks that nobody knew it was you."

"Yeah…"

"But, you live to fight another day. That's what matters."

"I know… but this was pretty big, right?" I said. "Everyone knows it was me fighting The Gentleman in the intersection… but I had my ass handed to me in that fight…"

"You didn't get your—"

"The Tsunami Girl went on CNN and said I, personally, was endangering the lives of everyone there because I was so out of my league, and 'escalating' things." I huffed. It was the opinion of almost every other news personality too. "I 'escalated' things out of control."

Dad frowned.

"I saved the day, and I'm a huge joke." I sighed. "Guess it'll keep me humble."

Dad patted my knee. "Would some jello make you feel better?"

I sighed.

And then I nodded.

CHAPTER 104
GOOD DEEDS

Monday, December 11

"Yeah... not getting the credit is always rough," Holly said from the wheelchair she was in.

We were outside. I was on crutches on a recommended walk around the yard. Tom was pushing her along.

"Some of the best busts you'll ever make are ones before the bad-guy gets any big media attention. Most doomsday threats are put on the shelf before they even get a reporter on the case. I remember there was some guy pushing a drug where a long-term side-effect was aneurysms. But this guy was *convinced* that it would make people psychic."

"Oof." Went Tom. "I remember this."

"The developer was planning to highjack dealers and have them lace it into cocaine. Why?" Holly shrugged. "Best guess is that he wanted to test some theory. Learned later that he got booted out of Brown for sketchy ethics. But the scale he was going for — this was gonna be big. Like. Chicago to Portland. He was held up in Denver. We — your Dad and I — caught up with him two days before he was gonna ship out his product to suppliers. This would have had hundreds of thousands dead. We busted down the door, saved the day. Probably to this day — one of the biggest crises I've put to rest. Nobody knew about it, so we didn't get the hero treatment."

"Where was Tom?" I asked, having a tough time following from the drugs they had me on for pain.

"Me and Jong-Su were with the family at the time," he said.

Holly patted his hand behind her shoulder. "Both of you helped out with the prep work."

"I suppose we did. We didn't know what we were getting into at the time, else we would have stayed."

She looked at me and nodded to Tom. "He just wanted the ego-boost."

"I've got plenty enough ego," Tom said.

I nodded, and a few steps later I started to get dizzy. "Ooo... Okay need a rest."

"Oh? Alright—" Tom abandoned Holly and helped me down to a bench. It was still a little wet from the rain we got in the morning. Sun hadn't been out yet.

"So..." I said. "You... Everything's fine between you two? About... everything?" I knew Dad was pissed at Holly for not telling him about me. But I'd made it clear that wasn't her responsibility to tell him.

"Honestly, I probably wouldn't have been as gentle on you if Holly wasn't involved," Tom said. 'Gentle' he said. "At least there was a grown-up around."

"Give the kid some credit, I didn't need to look out for him that much at all," she said. "Gotta hand it to you, he was a cut above most of the other kids I was wrangling."

"Don't say that, It'll go to his head."

"He threw a robot off a forty-story—"

"Forty-three," I corrected.

"He threw a robot off a forty-three story building and you don't think he's gonna be full of himself for it?" Her smile disappeared. "Honestly I still don't believe that it was a rogue AI the whole time."

"I showed you the picture I took—"

"I know... and in retrospect, it makes a whole lot of sense but... What a world."

"You know I've dug up every contact I have — Andy too — and there is *nobody* speaking a word about this. I don't know how the police are so tight-lipped. They must have the remains... how are there no leaks?"

"I'll tell you," said Holly. "Humans aren't born. We're made. AI's don't just 'develop' on the internet. AIs are made with a very clear intention. And they are stored on servers that someone built and which someone owns. Somebody knew about him. The whole time. And I guarantee you, whoever knew about him was on site before the feds. And the police are just peddling the story they were told."

"I wouldn't know the first thing about it," Tom said.

Holly patted his arm. "I know you don't like to talk about it. And I can assure you... if I'd have known any of this... I would not have let the kids go after him. Would have checked out a... trafficking ring or something. This got... this got out of control."

"Wasn't this the kind of thing a rogue vigil group is for?" I asked.

"This was supposed to be on-the-job training. Learn the ropes of an investigation. It wasn't supposed to be anything apocalyptic." She patted her chest. "I consider myself lucky things turned out the way they did. If things had gone wrong, I wouldn't be hearing from your dad or Tom anymore."

"Things went pretty wrong," Tom said.

Dad was pissed at Holly sure, but mostly for not telling him about me. Even if he already knew I was up to something, he would have liked to know the details. Like Tom, I guess he was glad she was there in the first place.

"Nobody died," she said. "Except an FBI agent who didn't wear concealed body armor for a hand-off. I specifically sold him the data because he was too dumb to know what to do with it..."

"Did you at least get paid for it?" Tom asked.

"Absolutely. My operation is good to go for the foreseeable future," she said.

"So you're still in touch with the misfits?" I asked. "Figure with the FBI contact they would have written you off."

"Silhouette and Afterglow vouched for me. Hanna and the asshole—" (she meant Six-Shot) "—weren't happy about it, but they came around. Certainly helped that I took a bullet for it."

"And Jonah?"

"Did that… dummy… tell you his name?" She sighed. "He's keeping to himself."

"Your Dad's keeping him on the back-burner. Don't worry about him."

"Don't worry about it, you tell him." Holly looked up at Tom. "Have you seen this Jonah? He's not the kind of fellow Luca could keep his eyes off of for very long."

Tom groaned. "Gonna have to work on 'distractions' then?"

I scowled.

Holly shifted uncomfortably. "Can't wait to get out of this thing."

"Not your first time in a wheelchair," Tom remarked.

"No… But I got used to active wheelchairs. These are just uncomfortable."

"You'll bounce back," he said. "Always do."

"Last time I 'bounced back' was fifteen years ago," she said. "I won't bounce back as spry this time. And probably not as quick."

I looked over to her, and then down. "I… I left you on the roof," I said, "and I really wish I hadn't. I'm sorry—"

She scoffed. "You think I'd have wanted you getting arrested for getting dragged into my shit like that? There isn't gonna be a next generation of heroes if we need 'em to clean up our messes."

CHAPTER 105
DEMON'S DUE

Friday, December 15

While I was in the living room on the couch, Dad slowly wandered in. "How you feeling?"

"I am..." I lifted my arms above me and looked at my fingers. They were like birds. Like a flock of birds who moved like one thing. Starlings. Star-lings. They were beings from the stars. Beings made of stars. That's why they moved like that, because they were their own universe and they moved in the shape of it. And they looked like a flock of fingers. "I'm a sea of orchids in the sky..."

Maybe I'd made the switch to home-grown 'painkillers.'

(Dad's idea. Not that I was complaining.)

I looked at him. "How are you?"

Moving Zero aside, he sat on the couch beside me and patted my leg. "I'm good. Great. Glad you are... Just wanted to... check something out. You mind if I...?"

"Yeah sure." I had no idea what he was asking.

"What's going on in the world today..." He brought up the TV Remote app on his phone and flipped it to national news.

An attractive anchor — a woman. She wore a shiny beige blouse. "—New information based on leaked photos from the Gentleman's crime scene at the new Pendragon Group's San Francisco headquarters. These photos, leaked from footage of the construction site that's being withheld by The SFPD, clearly depict a confrontation between the Gentleman and who appears to be the unregistered San Francisco Vigil who is using the Avalon Knight moniker."

"Oh my gosh!" I gasped. "I know this! Yeah, I know this already!"

Dad snickered.

"The same Avalon Knight who was recorded facing off against the Gentleman a few nights earlier, who many accused of instigating violence in a residential area. It now seems as if this unregistered Vigil had been undergoing a private investigation into the Gentleman for a longer duration than anyone thought. And, it seems, was able to bring this terrorist to justice, while other Vigils were berating him for being a nuisance.

"Three months ago, local San Francisco Vigil, The Brass Horn, said this about the new Avalon Knight:

It switched to footage from a local radio show where The Brass Horn said: "Yeah you look at these new guys and you see what they're doing and you're all like: '*What* are you doing?' Right? Like. You hear witnesses talk about it and it's all being done wrong."

The host: "Well yeah it's just irresponsible to make a pony show out of people's literal safety right?"

"Oh yeah!" The Brass said. "Take this new Avalon Knight guy—"

"A new one?"

"Yeah. Small scale stuff. Really just… sloppy work."

"Ahhh seriously?" The host threw his head back. "Is nothing sacred to these kids anymore?"

"Who does he think he is, right?" The Brass asked.

The host went on. "Like, I used to *love* the first Avalon Knight. I had comic books, action figures. I still have a T-Shirt because I refuse to throw it out. I haven't fit into it for years—"

The Brass laughed. Way too hard. It made me laugh because he looked like such an idiot when he did that. "Exactly. Like, this is a literal legacy. It's just arrogant and… no respect. What does he possibly think he can do to live up to it?"

It cut back to the anchor. "When approached, The Brass Horn said he was too involved in relief efforts for the city and was unavailable for comment."

I snorted. "What a dick, right?" I pointed. "Look what he's saying. He doesn't even know I'm you. Like. With the face. The other face, right? It's got like. Blue sharks?" I started laughing.

Dad smirked. "You have no idea what's going on right now?"

"See... 'Sharkeedo' — get it?" I kept giggling.

"I'll give you half an hour, okay?" Dad got up and went back down to his office to do more work.

— — —

Twenty minutes later, I busted into Dad's office. "Holy shit!"

He nodded. "Yeah."

"Everyone knows!"

"Yeah!"

"Everyone knows I did it!"

"They do."

"Holy shit! I need a Twitter!"

"Calm down—"

"And an agent!"

"Back up—"

I shot out of the office. "I'm hungry! Let's go get food!"

CHAPTER 106
THE WEXLERS

Wednesday, December 20

"No, no, honey," Nima said. "No, don't you dare. Andy! Don't you let this boy lift a finger to unset the table. Shame on you." She turned to me. "Sit back down." Back to her son. "Andy, you and Tom, — that's right you too — you clear the table. This boy's been through hell and you want to put him to work? Gettin' mugged, stabbed, and left for dead? Here in San Francisco?"

Dad grumbled and grabbed her plate.

Tom cleared his throat. "Actually, Natty, the city actually has a high crime rate..."

"Really? Even with all the gays here? I don't believe that for a minute. Not a minute." My grandmother shook her head. "Though, I suppose what with rumors of this new cult popping up. What? The one that worships bees because they're disappearing? Have you heard of that one, Tom?"

He shrugged. "I hadn't heard that last bit about bees."

"Ah, well, I heard that from my friend, Geraldine. Her brother works with some guys in the FBI, you see."

Tom nodded, making it clear to me, at least, that he was going to stick to his own information.

"With the nation's superheroes disappearing left and right, I don't think anywhere is safe these days. Not really. No wonder you got stabbed on a day like that. Oh! I can barely think about it. My own grandson! Gettin' stabbed."

"It was like, a month ago. And it wasn't much more than a scrape," I said.

"So says the eighteen stitches you had to get," Dad called over from the counter.

I started to collect some empty water glasses. "I'm fine."

My grandmother grabbed my arm. Her long red nails digging in through my shirt. "Sit. Back down. Dear. I'm not kidding. You never know when you've recovered. Stitches pop open all the time. I read it somewhere. Probably a magazine. Probably. A good one. Not some tabloid. Stitches. You need to let them rest until they're out, I say.

"And you!" She lightly smacked my arm with her knuckles. "What are you doing? You're not eating nearly enough? The last time I was here, you ate half the table. By yourself. It was like hurricane Luca over the kitchen table. But you're never going to get better if you don't load up on the things your body needs to heal itself—"

"Well, I can't exercise so I need to limit—"

She put a finger on my lips. "Don't. You. Dare. Don't you dare give me that Mr. Luca Wexler. You're a growing boy! You need to eat as much as you can. Even if you put on a little bulk, a woman never minds a little extra bulk, no matter what she says. And I'm sure the gay ones are just like the straight ones—"

"They're not, mother," Dad said.

She turned to him. "And what would you know? Is that the reason you never let me meet this girlfriend? The one who's 'from Canada'?"

Dad cleared his throat. "If it's Marianne you're talking about, she's actually my assistant, and married."

"I think she's talking about Vicky." Tom grinned.

Dad scowled.

"Vicky, that's her name!" Nima said. "Why don't I get to meet her?"

"Probably because she's more like what the kids call a friend with benefits," Tom replied.

I snorted.

Dad went red. "Around my son, Tom?"

"Treating women like that," Nima said, shaking her head. "Maybe I'd prefer if you were gay. At least they respect their women, right Luca?"

"Oh! I... Guess?"

"Then again from what I hear, they're not very respectful to other gay men. I dunno. I think men can take a hit. Give women a break for a little bit." She thought for a minute. "Or wait! You're that one that likes both of them. That used to be bisexual, but nowadays, I don't know who goes by what."

"Bisexual is still a thing, mom," Dad said.

"Oh well what's the other one?"

I cleared my throat. "Well there's pansexual, demisexual, omnisexual—"

"And which one are you?"

"Bi... I guess?"

She patted my knee. "Sorry, dear, nobody should be pressuring you to have it all figured out. There's so much information out there! I used to think I was in the know until I started getting tips from my hairdresser. You know they gave me a whole lesson about the animal kingdom of gay men while they put in my highlights? I thought it was just 'bears' but no it's—"

"Mother..."

She rolled her eyes at Dad and looked back to me. "Speaking of boys — what's this that your father is telling me about you and this big, burly boy you've been seeing? Are you two sleeping together yet?"

"Da-aad!" I hissed.

Dad and Tom snickered.

"Oh don't worry, is it on the down-low? Is he not out? Are you not out? I'm not entirely sure where you are on that. I mean out as gay, not the other thing. Which, I don't understand why you need to be out about it. Andy — your father — he's always saying how you need to come out."

"Is he? I've never once heard him say that!" I glared over at Dad at the dishwasher.

"Well yeah, but that's him because he lives in a bubble of information. What's he know?" she asked, taking a sip of wine. "I don't think you need to come out as whatever, because when anyone in the world takes a look at you they're just gonna see a guy! I mean take me. Every time I think back on your childhood, I just see a little boy running around. There. Plain and done. Nothing to think over. Just a little boy."

"Mother..." Dad said.

I looked over and nodded. "It's okay."

"Anyway, dear, I'm just saying that between you, and whoever is obsessing over what should or should not be going on in your pants, they're the freak." She held her wine glass up to her lips before taking a sip. "And that includes your mom..."

Dad spun around. "Sorry, what?"

My grandmother stuck the bulbous glass to her mouth instead of offering an explanation. She kept it to her lips long enough for Dad to sigh and get back to work.

CHAPTER 107
KLEPTO

Wednesday, December, 27

Took forever before there was a day when I had the house to myself long enough to take an Uber downtown. By then, I was worried that someone might have found my stash. Thankfully, everything was still there.

Before I tucked the hat and cane away behind my dresser, I got a closer look at them.

Didn't take long to figure out how to snap the sword out of the cane. Even for the Gentleman, it was a little dramatic. Relatively short blade, but had ripples across the metal like folded steel. Wiping my crusted, flakey blood off, I almost cut an old t-shirt in half. Still sharp even after that thing sliced through industrial piping and stabbed through a computer.

The mask, though... I didn't know what to think of it. Even in spite of what he was, it was something that I could easily wear. Generous space to breathe and a blank view screen. It didn't seem like it was something specifically made for him.

Also didn't know why he went so high-tech with it when a Guy Fawkes mask would have worked just fine. I couldn't even figure out how to turn it on.

I wondered how long it would take before I could tell Dad I stole this instead of letting it rot in an evidence locker. This was absolutely something that needed to go up on the wall.

You know me. I can't turn up a trophy.

THE AVALON KNIGHT

will return in

FOR QUEEN AND COLONY

AVALON KNIGHT
—BOOK TWO—

"Thou hast seen nothing yet."

~Miguel de Cervantes Saavedra,
Don Quixote

ACKNOWLEDGEMENTS

Thank you to James, for all the work that he put into this. His help has been absolutely invaluable, and it would not sparkle the way it does without him. Thank you also to the community that has been built around his YouTube video essays — the folks who have been good company during these plague times.

Thank you to my single mother, who praised imagination as one of the greatest virtues, who transcribed my earlier stories before I knew how to write.

Thank you to Luca, who, for a fictional character, I talk about like he's real. (All of my friends are dead sick of getting regular Luca-lore.)

Thank you to said friends who put up with hearing about the random interests, details, and opinions of my characters. And for letting me make them tea and/or coffee. Thank you also to my thoughtful and patient early readers. I am so grateful for the opportunities to receive constructive criticism, and for the confidence that good feedback gave me.

Thank you to Hector, not only for beautifully bringing Luca to life, but for letting me know that working with an artist doesn't have to be frightening.

And thank you, reader, for reading.

You may never know how much this means to me. :3

POST-CREDITS
SOURCE CODE

Later

This was in Seattle.

A crow-haired woman rode the elevator up with her father's assistant. He was tall, lean. Remarkable in how unremarkable he was. You'd spot him on the street and forget about him after a few sips of coffee. When the doors to the penthouse slid open, she strode out of the elevator, outpacing him.

She was graceful, not tall, though proud in her stance, in her walk. In the way nobody could tell what was behind her green eyes. By contrast, you'd see her once and wouldn't forget her until the day you died. Red heels echoing off the marble walls, and tall, glass windows.

A containment drive dropped onto some papers on the CEO's desk. "It's all here, Dad," she said, warmly, but without a smile.

The CEO of The Pendragon Group was talking with an associate by the bar beside the window. They were celebrating the return of company property — the containment drive that had just been delivered.

"Did the police give you trouble?" he asked. It wasn't a question, because he already knew. "Did Mr. Colton?"

The man from the elevator appeared, but no one had noticed him walk in.

"Colton doesn't know we have it. He'll wonder, but I covered our tracks." The daughter said. She gestured to the containment drive. "The Gentleman. Everything he was. Is."

The CEO looked to the man from the elevator. "Is Mr. Colton at *all* suspicious of us?"

"He suspects foul play, but not you. Not us," he said. Stoic expression and poise, he was closer to furniture than a person — though dangerous nonetheless. Especially for those who knew how to properly deploy him. He had his uses.

"Thank you," the girl with black hair dismissed him with a smile. Not a nice smile.

He bowed his head and shut the door on the way out.

The associate chuckled. "How do you acquire such people?"

The CEO smiled. He was a handsome man. Black hair, with a pointed face. Like father like daughter. Proud, though not too tall. Dark in manner. "Morgan?"

"Dad?"

"Take this to the Lake Vault."

"Not the sub-level?"

"I'd rather keep it tucked away until we need to use it again."

She hesitated.

"Morgan?"

"We should study it." She announced. "It was clearly unstable. Something was wrong. With observation, we can discern whether the KGB remnants didn't know how to iron out all the bugs, or whether they deliberately let loose an unstable AI. Either way, we can take steps to reverse engineer their programming and intelligence methodology—"

"And sell the information to US intelligence agencies," said the business associate.

The CEO nodded. "Yes, Morgan. Let's do that."

"Sub-level eleven, then," she said, and reached for the containment drive on the desk.

"Leave it be," said the father. "I'd like to take it myself."

Morgan nodded without expression and walked right back out the doors with the containment drive.

"Smart girl," said the associate. "Hope she does as good a job as you do when she takes your job."

"If all goes well, we won't need you for that long." The CEO downed the rest of his drink. "Let's talk shop... you follow much about Andrew Wexler these days?"

"We've rubbed shoulders. I've heard he's a pain in the ass."

The CEO smiled and ran his fingers over the containment drive. "You don't know the half of it."

THE AUTHOR...

N.T. HERRGOTT (any pronouns) has been part of too many fandoms, drinks too much coffee, avoids too many phone calls, and writes too many words. The latter inevitably end up in a 'removed sections' folder on his computer, where he promises himself they will work their way into a sequel.

When not writing fiction, he is a video-essay writer, photographer, graphic designer, bad player of video games, tree connoisseur, animal tweeter, and — most importantly — an avid daydreamer.

This is a safe space for reading the last chapter first.

Lightning Source UK Ltd.
Milton Keynes UK
UKHW010642191021
392466UK00002B/236